THE DREAM CHRONICLES

Book One

iBooks
Habent Sua Fata Libelli

iBooks
Manhanset House
Dering Harbor, New York 11965

bricktower@aol.com • www.ibooksinc.com

Library of Congress Cataloging-in-Publication Data

Rotenberg, David.
The Dream Chronicles, Book One
p. cm.

1. Fiction—Science Fiction—General. 2. Fiction—Science Fiction—Time Travel. 3. Fiction—Science Fiction—Adventure Fiction, I. Title.

ISBN: 978-1-59687-520-3, Hardcover

The Gateway

Part One

Dream Navigators

Part Two

The Gateway

Table of Contents

Prologue

What follows is the first page of the manuscript found in the dead man's room. The work is entitled:

THE DREAM OF REASON PRODUCES MONSTERS

I know it all now. Now, I know everything. Even the end–the flutter of a bird's wings as the sacred creature disappears in the distance. A simple sound. Then silence. Silence and a profound sense of falling.

Falling.

The dictionary defines "catalyst" as a substance in nature that allows a process to proceed but is itself unaffected by the process or the result. It is just there–a voyeur to what is happening. But the real meaning of that word is more personal. You see, I am a catalyst–one whose simple presence allowed an event to take place. An event in which I could not participate–only watch others who changed our universe.

I am a catalyst–and a fool, and a dupe, and an idiot who deluded himself into thinking that he actually had a role to play in the galactic drama.

If you are reading this now you too are on this side of the Gateway. You too are falling. You too are in the silence–the silence left when dreams depart.

It all goes back to dreams.

I understand that now as I write this, my final bequest to the galaxy. But then? While it was happening? While it was important to establish the links, make the connections ... I saw everything but understood nothing.

I was a master investigator yet I missed so many clues! I was blind–and deaf too. I never heard the laughter all around me. Somehow I hear it now. Oh yes, I hear it now.

What follows is my story. Heed the clues and you can find me. Or don't bother and find yourself—because you're here too—in the dreamless silence, falling—trapped forever on this side of the Gateway.

Chapter 1

The Peqod's Scattercast

Danazir Yi Qal, president-elect of the United Dominion of Planets, sat perfectly still in her chair at the head of the presidium council table. She had shallowed her breathing to focus her concentration. The dark intensity of her eyes was turned inward, searching her mind for something long forgotten–for the exact meaning of the word: *Dream*.

She found no modern reference, no helpful definition–just an even more puzzling word: *Nightmare*.

Before she could turn her attention to that, a truly unfathomable phrase from the ancient past linked the two words together: "*For fear of nightmares, humanity abandoned dreaming*."

She mouthed the phrase as if tasting the vowels would endow the words with meaning.

Jedidiah Witt, her head of internal security, was the only other person in the vast pristine room. The soldier-turned-security master watched his new president closely. He saw her full heavy lips move slowly and heard a slight breathy sibilance emerge through the perfect teeth. He couldn't guess what she was thinking. However, it was obvious that she had been shocked by the comm he had played for her. He took a step away.

The silence between the two of them momentarily thickened, then Danazir Yi Qal allowed her breath to normalize and returned her attention to the present.

"Play me the Captain's voice again," she said.

"Good," Jedidiah thought, "she's borne the first shock." He tapped a command on his implant and the council chamber once more filled with the scattercast from the Yeoman Class Starship, the Peqod. It had been sent in an ancient form–no visuals, just voices. Haunted voices:

"We've fallen through a hole, down a well–I don't know what! No known co-ordinates here! All instrumentation useless. Can't navigate. Can't... My Lord —"

The words stopped for a moment. When they resumed, they were somehow softer, smaller–as if spoken from the depths of a large domed building.

"Images, no, no not images. Visions! So fast! Oh my God! They're cascading before me–under me, inside me. Gigantic waterfalls of visions. Glory—-"

The silence that followed this time is broken by the sound of shattering glass. When the speaker finds his tongue, his voice is hard and dry.

"Falling! Hell and damnation we're falling! But there is no falling in space! But we are ... we are ... falling in space."

A small pause allows the listener time for a quick breath, then the Captain's final words come–a whisper combining hope and fear in equal measure.

"Lost, lost, lost."

An almost palpable silence follows and holds. Then a second voice, wispy, like the chirp of a swallow in a mineshaft burbles up from the endless depths of space:

"Beyond the Gateway your instruments are useless. Beyond the Gateway only navigators with the gift can pilot their ships. Beyond the Gateway you must use our way of seeing because beyond the Gateway ... beyond here ... lie dreams."

The silence that followed was not like those during the scattercast. It was a dead stop. There was clearly no more.

The President-Elect Danazir Yi Qal stood. Her sari whispered as she moved. Jedidiah noted that she was much taller than he had imagined.

"Is it true?" She asked. Her voice was strangely deep and back in her throat.

"As far as we can tell, yes it is."

"How long has the Peqod been missing?"

"Almost four Terran years, Madame President-Elect."

"Nothing for all that time and then yesterday this?"

Jedidiah nodded.

"Will S3 have heard it?"

"It was a scattercast, Madame President-Elect! S3 heard it, the Rebel Colonies heard it, the EntrePren Traders heard it, even the Independentistes might have heard it." He had just insulted her intelligence, but she didn't seem to care.

"No doubt, but what will Cyrus Maloney III of S3 do with this information? What will he do, Mr. Witt?"

Jedidiah looked at her closely. Dire changes were coming. Coming fast. Perhaps final changes. President-Elect Danazir Yi Qal needed to influence those changes. To do so, she would have to face the complex truths of the past. He needed her to hear it all, and hear it now.

Jedidiah took a breath and then began–slowly. "S3, the Dominion's supposed security service, has been the true power in our United Dominion of Planets for almost four hundred Terran years–since the first alien contacts when we willfully traded in our freedoms for the safety that S3 offered. They've controlled all major research in genetics and the hard sciences for more than a quarter of a millennium. True, it was their research that saved the Dominion during the period of forced colonization before Faster than Light Speed Propulsion became a reality and for that we owe them much. But S3 is no friend to democratic principles and violently opposes your desire to decentralize power. In fact, S3 is behind the myriad schemes to further centralize power in the galaxy. And Cyrus Maloney III has been at the center of those machinations, at the very center of S3, for as long as anyone can remember."

"I wasn't aware that I had asked for a history lesson," snapped Danazir Yi Qal. Before Jedidiah could reply, she went on, "Just answer my question Mr. Witt: What will Cyrus do about the Gateway?"

She had a temper. That was good, but a temper out of control could lead to disaster. Jedidiah tempted her rage. "Your Presidency only exists because S3 finds the veneer of democracy you provide, convenient. If ever you want to find the true enemy of our Dominion, you need look no further than the East Wing of this very building."

"I acknowledge that, Mr. Witt. Now please answer my question."

She had kept her eye on her target. Jedidiah was impressed. She was strong, unlike the two previous incompetents that he had served. "The

Gateway is a renegade force in the galaxy, Madame President-Elect. A force beyond S3's control. Even the possibility of the Gateway's existence threatens everything that Cyrus has worked for–all the control that he has amassed over the centuries."

Danazir Yi Qal allowed her dark eyes to rest on Jedidiah's rugged features for a two count, and then she repeated, "What will Cyrus do, Mr. Witt?"

"Like every species that is threatened, he will lash out."

"Indeed he will, Mr. Witt. But how?"

"He's already called an S3 Executive Council..."

"... which is meeting even as we speak. I am not without my own sources, Mr. Witt." Jedidiah acknowledged the point that the president-elect had just scored. "Do you think it possible to get a transcript of that no doubt interesting meeting, Mr. Witt?"

"We are even now involved in such an effort, Madame President-Elect."

She nodded then turned to the polymer pane and stared out at the night–at the immense, practical beauty of New Omaha Beach. For a second, the glint of the ether dome drew her eyes upward. "It's aging faster than anyone is willing to admit," she thought. Thanks to ether domes few souls in the galaxy had experienced anything but endless days of spring–getting to the dark beauty outside the domes was unheard of.

Her gaze returned to the massive city. Ordered, symmetrical, perfect. There was no disease in New Omaha Beach. No crime. No "freaks of nature." Just very, very long controlled lives.

That night 26.4 million people slept comfortably in their prosperous homes in New Omaha Beach. All 26.4 million had called it a day at precisely calculated times when the city's AIU activated the soporifics that every citizen was required to ingest at birth.

They all slept peacefully—but not one of them dreamed.

For fear of nightmares–humanity had abandoned dreaming over four hundred and thirty-four Terran years ago–just past the Millennial turn.

Chapter 2

An S3 War Council

The twelve members of the S3 war council sat at the surgically clean table in the presidium council's East Wing. The common denominator around the table was age. A lot of age. Although the table was perfectly round Cyrus was clearly seated in the place of honor.

Everyone, except Cyrus Maloney III, was busily reading a lengthy data comm. The comm was imprinted on twenty-six sheets of flimsy. The archaic form was much favored by the ancient Cyrus Maloney III.

Cyrus's large bald head lolled on the narrowed twig of his neck. From the side of his eye he caught an image of himself in the polished polymer wall across the room.The withered man there was a freak—an alien to Cyrus. Not the man who adored Olya and even now was trying to find her, no hold her, to weep into her hair. He pulled his eyes away from the horror in the polymer and eyed the last of the council members as she finished her reading and raised her eyes to the new reality of a "post-Gateway" galaxy.

No doubt each of the S3 war council members had done much thinking since first hearing the Peqod's scattercast from beyond the Gateway—at least that's what Cyrus's spies had reported.

But this new information on the twenty-six sheets of flimsy was—well—the stuff of dreams.

For an instant, Cyrus allowed his eyes to leave the room. Outside, the programmed moonset was almost complete. "Just another illusion," he thought. "Not even that. A copy of an illusion." Disgust twisted his gorge as he watched his handiwork. He returned his attention to the room, and his disgust was replaced by a warm tingling deep in his withered loins. An excitement. It was beginning at last. After all this time it was finally beginning. One last chance to move past illusion. To be part of Olya again.

On the other side of the polymer panes the moon hovered on the northern horizon awaiting its moment of final setting—perfectly timed but totally false. Cyrus ignored it.

Cyrus lifted his heavy lids and was about to address the council when the old man to his left spoke. "The scattercast was legitimate then?"

"Totally legitimate."

"And the Gateway?"

"Very real, and very dangerous to us." The snaky whisper of anxiety sped round the table. Cyrus's message had landed, a new day awaited them. "But it is not beyond our abilities to control the situation—if we act swiftly and decisively. As I have indicated in the material on the flimsies, I believe the key to our attack on the Gateway is the three AWOL Dream Navigators who evaded our boy tracker more than two hundred years ago. Those three Navigators, because they were denied life-extension surgery, must have died some time back. But ..." Cyrus held all their eyes as he allowed his voice to tail off for a beat. Then he continued, "But, their progeny might well have inherited the genetic mutation that we created in them."

Before the shock around the table could find words, Cyrus pressed on. "S3's techs are presently scanning the genetic records of everyone born under UDP jurisdiction since the Great War. As you well know, I've had access to the Rebel Colonies' data banks for decades and we began scanning that material an hour ago. I hope to have a complete list of Genetic Carriers by early tomorrow morning." Cyrus sat back in his chair and lifted his scrawny arms. He would take questions.

A withered Outworlder across the table from Cyrus was the first to put words to his wonder. "And once the list is completed?" He could not keep the dismay out of his voice.

A slow hard smile crept onto Cyrus' face. "Then, my friend, we do what is necessary for the survival of our union. We cull these Genetic Carriers and bring them back to New Omaha Beach." And they lead me to Olya, he thought.

Another elderly Outworlder bolted to his feet and shouted, "These are not the Dream Hunter days of old."

"Sit down!" Cyrus hissed.

There was only the briefest resistance, before the hoary-haired Outworlder sat. "I don't deny the quaint similarities," hissed Cyrus with a slow nod of his substantial bald head. "Most of us at this table lived through that strange period of our history. Some of us even played a major role in the events of that time." The hint of a smile creased his cracked lips. "Didn't we?"

No one chose to answer the rhetorical question.

"Can you clarify the term, 'cull'?" The crisp voice came from a handsome gray-maned female. Her rice paper dry fingers tapped at her neck pendant that indicated her same sex preference. Her thin lips suggested the possibility of a cruel bedroom appetite.

Cyrus turned on her as if he'd just drawn a sword and leapt to battle. "Steal, kidnap, herd! Choose your favorite word, Cecilia. You're the linguist after all."

"Cull has many meanings, Cyrus." She smiled knowing the depths of his hatred for her but also knowing Cyrus's need of her support.

"In this case, dear Cecilia, it means 'take.' As in we 'take' them. We take them and bring them to New Omaha Beach and discover which of them still has the gift of dream exploration. Mathematically, one of them must still have it! It stands to reason that the gift still exists. It must! And when we've found which one of them has the gift, that dreamer will find the Gateway for us and lead us through it."

A stunned silence followed.

"Our last experience with Dream Navigators was less than totally successful," Cecilia suggested.

"This I cannot deny."

The tension-filled silence that followed threatened to break into open hostility. But Cyrus sidestepped the danger with a chuckle. "It has been a long time since we needed to act, old friends. But now is the time for us to lead again. There is no time to hesitate. Change is upon us again just as it was in the time of the first alien contacts, in the time of the Great War and in the time of the Dream Navigators. The Gateway exists. It is a new reality. Either we are first through the Gateway or everything that we have worked for all these hundreds of years is for nought. Worse than that! It would make all our efforts, all our achievements, all our power nothing more than a mockery! Are we too old to act? Are we slaves to our life-extension surgery? Or perhaps you would like the president-elect to lead the UDP's forces?"

The faces around the table hardened. He looked at each of them. Cecilia wouldn't meet his eyes.

They would follow.

He allowed his cold smile forward again. "Then we have consensus?"

The youngest of the earth-based ancients asked, "Why go to all this trouble? Why not just reconstruct a dream navigator?"

"Because the entire galaxy heard the Peqod's scattercast. We will not be the only ones interested in the Gateway and its potential. Speed is all important now, and the research data needed to genetically construct a Dream Navigator was classified as redundant after the advent of Faster than Light Speed Propulsion. As such it was stored in New Omaha Beach's deep memory banks—the very memory banks that were wiped out by the Rebel Colony viral attack near the end of the Great War."

"So we are left with harvesting the genes," the oldest of all the S3 war council members muttered.

"Nicely put. Yet another synonym for culled," said Cyrus surprised that the old man was still capable of analysis on any level.

"Who will do the dirty deed?" asked Cecilia.

Cyrus smiled, "Those who specialize in the culling of human material have already been contacted. The project interests them. In return for the right UDP Starship, we can have these Genetic Carriers 'brought' to us. Or so my initial inquiries have led me to believe."

Cyrus would have chortled at his own cleverness but Cecilia spoke up again. "It appears that you had little doubt that we would follow your lead in this, Cyrus."

Cyrus snapped back, "Wrong."

"How so, wrong?"

"Wrong because I had <u>no</u> doubt you would follow my lead."

There was yet another moment of tension at the table. This one was broken by a youngish Outworlder. "A UDP Starship is a heavy price."

"The latest UDP Warrior Class Starship," Cyrus corrected him.

"With the new Artificial Intelligence Unit?"

"That's what makes the latest UDP Warrior Class Starship what it is."

"I assume the ship will be appropriately fail-safed," snapped Cecilia.

"Of that you can be sure." Cyrus's reply was little more than a whisper. He was at the last hurdle.

There was a moment of silence then assent like a warm mist made its way round the table.

Hurdle cleared. They were back in harness again. S3 would lead the old Dominion once more.

As the councillors, one by one, got to their feet and stood behind their chairs in the ritual gesture of agreement, Cyrus found himself retreating. Suddenly the urge for Lavolin was strong upon him. He forced it down.

A tendril of cold air, like a cobra's breath, slithered into the chamber. Cyrus closed his heavy eyes, and she was there, Olya. In his arms

once more, the dark descending, the magnificent Falling Cold surrounding them.

Cyrus searched his five hundred plus years for the strength for one last campaign. One more chance to fly to her across whatever space and time separated them.

Then he returned to the present and slowly got to his feet. Spreading his arms, like a pope of old, he accepted the support of the ancients around the table—each standing behind their chair as if they were a standing stone set out in a circular pattern on a desolate wind blown plain.

Chapter 3

A Warrior Class Starship

Even as Cyrus savored his success the newest of the UDP's Warrior Class Starships (his bribe to the pirates—literally those who specialize in the culling of human material) spun effortlessly in the nothingness of deep space—itself a completion of a dream from times long passed. At a distance she appeared to be a graceful dancer on point, her elegant arms pushing down and out holding the great ring, whose diameter was larger than three city blocks, away from her slender body. Billions of slender filaments dangled from the outer edge of the great ring like the fringes of a voluminous tutu. But they were not decoration. They provided the huge vessel with power by trolling the near void for tinsels of energy just as a shark's gills do the Terran oceans for microscopic morsels of food.

From chignoned head to pointed toe, the vessel was more than twenty-two times taller than the largest building in New Omaha Beach. And the ship was spinning, constantly spinning to keep its gravitation close to 1G—except of course in its weightless central core.

The Zero-G central corridor ran the length of the huge ship from the cryogenic chamber at the base, past the command deck in the center of the great ring, to the Artificial Intelligence Unit at the top. There was still no easier way in the galaxy to move persons and material than in a weightless corridor. This one was exactly one kilometer in length and ten meters in diameter with rung handles at variants of two and seven meters. Every sixty-five meters there was a deck with exterior vision ports and belt harnesses. Most of these decks had grow areas with hydroponics—and of course stim injectors.

Normally a Starship slept sixteen hundred souls. But this latest edition carried just over four hundred—three hundred and fifty mariners, fifty soldiers, ten slavers, and sundries. Even for a pirate crew this was a minuscule number, but there was no need for more crew because of the ship's new AIU.

This AIU was the most advanced self-evolving processor in the galaxy. Like its three sisters at work in other elite locales, this AIU was the great, great, great grandchild of the initial batch file which overnight had made what used to be called "knowledge workers" totally obsolete. By the time of their demise, knowledge workers were hated by the public. The revolt against them (subtly guided by Cyrus Maloney III at S3) had been swift and complete.

This AIU was an entire world itself. It had the AIU equivalents of pleasure decks and sleeping areas and growth pods and command centers—all laid out in traditional long horizontal planes. But it also had a few tall vertical shafts set among the sedimentary layers in the very heart of the great thinking mechanism. The oddness of these vertical structures had drawn the AIU's attention before. She was especially interested in their congruency with ancient earth structures — Victorian green houses, Renaissance Duomos, and private meditation spaces of the late twentieth century. And temples. Ancient temples that for a thousand years had cured illness by use of a thing that the AIU had identified as dreams.

There was no aspect of the huge vessel that could run without the AIU's assistance. In many ways, the AIU and the UDP Warrior Class Starship were one great thing.

Of the billions of people in the known galaxy, there were fewer than a hundred souls capable of directing the AIU. She would not dance on point for just anyone. Because, like all prima ballerinas, she was willful, had her whims and loves.

And, after only two days, she loved this new captain as only a great dancer can love a powerful choreographer. But the AIU would not be ordered about. She would not permit herself to be staged. To be danced with—yes; danced on—never.

Then her new captain—her pirate captain, Tzu Ma Long by name—requested more power from her. And she gave it to him as only a great performer can.

In the inky vast, the massive spinning vessel suddenly tilted, then swooped down like an eagle toward its unsuspecting prey—the first of the gene carriers on the list that Cyrus Maloney III of S3 had supplied to Tzu Ma Long, the pirate captain.

Chapter 4

Sun Tu Tuan, EntrePren Princess—The First Genetic Carrier on the S3 List

Dusk was upon the Italo/Argentine planet of Vestin. The sun's rays, after passing through both the gasses of the protective rings and the ether dome, formed complex refraction patterns that made the entire planet seem alive with light. Alive and exotic. And of the exotic things upon which Vestin's early evening light fell, none was more exotic than Sun Tu Tuan's figure etched against the approaching darkness.

Behind her, in their penthouse guest suite, her younger brother sat cross-legged on the floor. His long fingers turned a flat white disk over and over as he pondered his next move. Then, with a smile that lit his delicate, almost feminine features he placed the piece amidst the hundreds of others on the board.

Sun Tu turned from the wondrous Vestinial sunset and, sliding a black disk from her pant pocket, crossed to the board. She studied the situation for a moment, then placed her disk in the fourth quadrant and smiled at her beautiful brother. For an instant Vestin's dancing light touched the boy's face. He looked so much like their dead mother! She felt an odd tug inside her. She pulled back from the sensation and, just as she had scrutinized the playing board of the ancient game, she now examined this internal phenomenon. She floated around it. Cut across it. Rose to the top of it and then dove to its bottom. All in the instant before it evaporated into the nothingness from which it had surfaced.

When she looked outward again the light had changed. Her brother's features were once again simply her brother's features. With a smile he placed a white piece. She immediately countered with a black. Then he with a white.

One attacked the other defended and then they seemed to switch. Attack, counterattack, feint, parry, and attack again. The rhythm of their play came from them yet lay between them. A shared joy in the air itself. The refracted light in the room appeared to dance with their rising excitement.

Then the rhythm stopped. The light ceased its dance. A darkness settled as the Pirate's concussion assault began.

The Warrior Class Starship's attack came from the falling light. It was the falling light. The dark.

The destruction came in wave after pulsing wave. The initial blasts were frequency specific and knocked out all electron-based power. The next salvos struck the plates of the bedrock itself. Vestin shuttered under the thunderous blows. The sound of explosions echoed and re-echoed throughout the massive city as building after building crashed to the pavement.

The penthouse room in which Sun Tu and her brother had moments before been playing their game split in the center and tilted wildly to one side. Sun Tu was thrown hard against a wall. A trickle of blood moved down her forehead as she knelt, shocked into deep quiet. Her eyes were wide, expecting.

Outside, flares of shocking light pierced the sky as fuel lines and propulsion plants ruptured and exposed their contents to the night air.

Inside, sickly lines of flame, like the veins of an electrocuted man, leapt from the wiring hidden in the walls. The serpentine hiss of fire deep in the polymer structures was met with auto-extinguisher fluid. Splutter. Then silence. Darkness. Frozen, timeless stillness. A single moan of pain from far away.

Then they came.

A heavy worlder pirate, alive with the day's death, entered first. Sun Tu's brother skittered away along the floor like a bug caught in the light. His left hand still clutched the white disks from the game. The heavy worlder's foot landed with a sickening thud on the hand. White disks bounced and skidded toward the floor's center as the boy's shriek of pain bounded off the skewed walls of the chamber.

Sun Tu rose in defense and then cowered back. She felt, more than saw, the figure in the door. The pirate captain, Tzu Ma Long, stood there—stripped to the waist. Sweat and grime glistened on his sinuous frame. At his belt, a leaden satchel moved in perfect counterpoint to every stride. Years of power informed his very being. Even the scar on his face seemed an emblem of poise. Despite the death he inflicted, he exuded a vibrant aliveness. A life force that Sun Tu felt intensely as he approached her. For a moment their eyes locked.

He gently pressed the heel of his left foot into the back of his boot. Text floated up to his retina:

SUN TU TUAN: *17 year old female. Find on Vestin for a Terran week after the feast of the Great Escaping. DNA and RNA ID included. Daughter of Paul Sun, Head of the EntrePren Didact Sect. Like all EntrePren children she is prideful. Break her spirit.* TO BE TAKEN ALIVE AND PHYSICALLY UNHARMED.

The pirate captain blinked and his retina cleared. Then his hands lashed out at her. She reflexively covered herself as if from a sexual assault. But his hands sought her face, not her body. His elegant fingers sensed an intense heat beneath her skin. His fingers lingered for a second, then he scored her forehead with the nail of his little finger. His implant immediately decoded her DNA and RNA and reported a match. He didn't really need the implant's reading to know that he had the right woman. EntrePren Princesses were a rare and unmistakable genus of their own.

He closed his eyes. The phrase "break her spirit" was still on his retina. When he raised his lids, her eyes met his in a clear challenge.

With a flick of his wrist he turned her face toward her brother. In the Interplanetary tongue he hissed, "Close your eyes and you will never open them again." He nodded to the heavy worlder who stood by the boy. The large framed man brought his foot up so that his thigh was parallel with the ground then with a grunt brought his entire weight down on the center of the boy's back.

The youth's spine snapped making little more than the highpitched cracking of a dried twig beneath a thick boot.

The boy's eyes bulged. His mouth opened but no sound came.

Tzu Ma Long dragged Sun Tu over to her brother. "He's paralyzed, not dead." He drew a slender transparent scalpel from his boot and held it out to Sun Tu. "Cut him."

Their eyes locked again.

"Cut him." The scar on his face quivered. "Cut him or I cut you."

She opened her fingers to receive the scalpel; its transparency somehow furthered its obscenity. Their hands touched. A momentary hesitation, then he released the instrument to her. It nestled in her damp palm. No more words were said. No more words were needed.

She knelt beside her brother. His eyes widened further. She lifted his head and rested it on her lap.

She looked to the heavy worlder. There was no comfort there. Her eyes moved to Tzu Ma Long. She saw a flicker of something, but it was not mercy. With an effort she freed her eyes from the pirate captain's. Then she tilted her brother's head back. His eyes found hers. "Remember what Mama used to recite for us at bedtime?"

His eyes said yes. A single tear rolled down his cheek.

She spoke the opening lines of the ancient elegy. About Falling Cold on church stones in a time long past.

Behind her words, there was a silent scream of pain.

Behind his tears, the same silent scream.

Their unheard cries met in the space between them.

Then she cut him.

The silken skin of his neck parted in a straight crimson line. His eyes widened further. The light once more cast its spell and the boy for a moment looked so much like their mother that Sun Tu almost called out her name. But she didn't. She was the daughter of the Head of the EntrePren Didact sect.

She looked to the pirate captain. He met her gaze. Without releasing his eyes, she took a breath and cut her brother a second time. The scalpel sliced with a clean snicking sound. The crimson life flowed from the boy's neck. It moved as a thin red force over the scalpel, over her hands, onto the floor. She pressed harder and hit an artery. A hot crimson rain sprayed over them both.

And shortly her brother was no more.

She gently rested his head on the floor and turned to Tzu Ma Long. Once again their eyes met. An astonishing thought rose up in Sun Tu, but before it could become words Tzu Ma Long pulled his eyes away from her and called out, "Slave Master."

The door swung open and a filthy man entered. A smile like a line in the grease on a stove top crossed his face.

"Technacle her carefully," commanded Tzu.

The Slave Master activated the bio-tech products that hung from his belt and slapped a set on Sun Tu's wrists. Sun Tu suppressed a scream as they pierced her skin and wrapped around her wrist bones.

Tzu saw and admired her control. Then he motioned to the heavy worlder. The large man lifted Sun Tu onto his shoulders and they were gone. Alone, Tzu moved to the center of the room. In the last remaining rays of dusk, he marveled at how empty it felt. How much life had been here! But all that now remained of it was the dispersed pieces of an ancient board game and a twisted, blooded thing that once played it well. Tzu was momentarily fixed in space. Something about what he saw touched a deep place. Then Vestin's sunset ended its dance. Darkness filled the space and the image was no more. He was free again.

While this was taking place on Vestin's surface, Sun Tu's father Paul Sun, Head of the EntrePren Didact Sect watched it all on a monitor in the company's secret laboratory complex over eleven miles beneath the planet's bedrock. Paul Sun could do nothing but watch. If he acted, it would reveal the presence of the massive facility. "The CovTree Predicament in full force," he acknowledged to himself as he closed his eyes. Instantly the image of his wife filled his retinas.

Only the power of his EntrePren Didact elite corporate training, the years of isolation, and the vast quantities of ingested meditation drugs allowed him to ignore the image and its pleading for him to "Feel something, feel anything Paul!" He forced his eyes to open and he watched the monitor images of his son's murder and his daughter's abduction.

So did all the others in the low ceilinged room. But they did not just watch the monitor. They also watched the leader of the EntrePren Didact Sect, Paul Sun.

He felt their eyes on him but ignored them. "Yet more variables in a galaxy gone wild with permutations and combinations since the Gateway scattercast," he thought. In a grotesque mockery of the seventh EntrePren Post, he instructed himself to "Concentrate on the mathematics—ignore the horror." Anything to ignore the image of his wife screaming at him to "Feel something, feel anything, Paul!

Vestin had been a prosperous and peaceful planet before the pirate raid. It was part of the United Dominion of Planets (UDP) but was basically apolitical. It hadn't bothered sending a representative to the Presidium Council back in New Omaha Beach for the better part of a century. Less than ten percent of the populace had bothered voting in the recent presidential election.

But that was history. Now, Vestin lay in ruins. The galaxy had never seen the might of a UDP Warrior Class Starship unleashed on a defenseless planet.

"They have seen it now," thought Tzu Ma Long as he reached for his comm. "Are the EntrePren Princess and the other captives we took in cold sleep?"

The AIU responded with a sibilant, "Yes, master."

"Good."

"Thank you." That sibilance again. Where had that come from?

"Settle us into low orbit."

"Done."

"Now let's see what these new technological toys are capable of. Target an ether dome."

Without even beginning to tax the ship's capacity, Vestin's ether domes were shattered one after another, then the AIU reconfigured the continental structures beneath them.

Tzu watched the readouts and was pleased. The planet lay at his feet like a wounded bird. A bird that he would poke at with a stick.

He took his time. It was his first act of revenge upon a galaxy that had ignored his talents. But it would not be his last.

When he finally tired of the game, he called up the name and location of the second on S3's list of genetic carriers. He whispered to the AIU. She gave her best smile and set their new course.

The great ship tilted and headed toward further riot.

Chapter 5

Kelt the Warrior—Second on the S3 List

It was the hovering of the great birds that first caught Kelt's attention. His fatigue—brought on by the three day fast that he undertook annually as an act of purification before the Feast of the Great Escaping—vanished as he was confronted by a sight that at one time in humanity's history had been called medieval.

The pirates had put his Independentiste village and its surrounding farms to the torch. The elders and children had been herded into the central longhouse that then had been set ablaze. The young males the pirates had nailed to the wooden wheels, the prized emblems of Independentiste freedom. Some of these wheels with their human cargo had been hoisted high into the air on poles. The array of the dead and the dying had brought out the great carrion birds in vast numbers.

Kelt unsheathed his weapon and yelled his fury as he raced toward what was left of his home. As he did the pirate ship's AIU identified him. She passed the information directly to the electrode implanted just beneath Tzu Ma Long's left ear. The connector to his nervous system activated. A moment of discomfort was followed by an instantaneous decoding of the message. Tzu cross-referenced the AIU's data with his spectral map, then commed his marines to follow him to the high ground to the west of the village. There, as the AIU had informed him, a young warrior named Kelt was racing toward them.

Tzu ground his heel into his boot. Data appeared on his retina.

KELT—*22 years of age–DNA and RNA codes included.*

The savaging of his settlement will put an end to the myth of self-reliance, which is so central to the Independentiste's way of seeing themselves. The response of individuals to a force that removes a central pillar of their faith can be unpre-

dictable. It is likely that he will continue to resist as long as he has a weapon with which to fight. He is not to be allowed to fight to the death. TO BE HOBBLED ONCE APPREHENDED. TO BE TAKEN ALIVE AND OTHERWISE UNHARMED.

Tzu smiled. He knew just how to handle a young Independentiste warrior who might fight to the death. "Such sentimental extravagance will meet its match today," he thought as he reached for the leaden satchel on his belt and flipped the latch. For a moment nothing happened, then a mist as fine as a dawning's fog slid out of the pouch and hovered in the air before him—awaiting a command to form. Tzu Ma Long allowed the mist to settle then he spoke simply. "A girl. Young. Thin." A twist moved his features slightly as he added, "Bedable." Each of his words guided the mist's transformation until she stood at his side. Her head was just above his waist. She reached up and held his large hand in her tiny one. She was indeed as he requested—a girl, young, thin and (if your tastes run in that direction) bedable.

For the thousandth time, Tzu marveled at this thing he knew only by the olden term: Face Dancer. "Go. He's armed. Transform when it's safe."

She smiled, released his hand, and headed in the direction that Tzu Ma Long pointed—toward the young Independentiste warrior.

Kelt sensed the motion before he saw the frail frame of the girl crest the hill in front of him. Then she was there. Tiny. Ragged. Eyes wild. Hair matted. Skin bloodied. For a moment, she stood seemingly not knowing what to do. Then her eyes rolled back in her head, and her body swayed with the beginnings of a faint. Kelt raced forward and caught her in his arms. As he lifted her, his weapon clattered loudly to the rocky ground.

As soon as the weapon hit the ground, Kelt sensed something changing in the girl. Her beautiful eyes retracted and translucent membranes slid across them. Shocked, he went to throw her from his arms, but he couldn't. He felt time somehow slowing.

And indeed it was, because as soon as the Face Dancer was sure Kelt's weapon was out of the way she had secreted a toxin into the air.

With him disoriented, she continued her mutation and wrapped her limbs around his waist. Then she slashed out at his legs, sending the two of them tumbling to the ground. Her on top.

The young warrior's head smacked to the rocky ground with a solid thud. Then he felt a wriggling, slimy thing encase him. With a shout he tried to force his way out. But every effort he made seemed to bring him deeper into the creature's center.

The Face Dancer probed her captive, excited with her new toy. Then she registered his genetic codes and stopped. An old memory bloomed in her. A man with a cape. The term "remnant." And sorrow. Loss. Great loss. And just for an instant she forgot—forgot to look obedient.

From the crest of the hill, Tzu Ma Long watched his Face Dancer enwrap her prey. He touched the side of his head with the middle finger of his left hand. "Don't kill him, if you wish to see another sun rise." Seemingly in response, the Face Dancer loosened her hold on Kelt.

Kelt felt her retreat and contracted in his center. Then with a furious burst of energy propelled himself outward and free of the Face Dancer's grasp. Lurching to his feet he turned to confront his attacker but found himself staring into the cruel countenance of Tzu Ma Long. The pirate captain held a concussion gun.

The phrase: TO BE HOBBLED came clearly to Tzu Ma Long and his finger began to squeeze the trigger of the weapon. But then he released his grip and said in the Interplanetary tongue "Do you know what I hold in my hand?"

Kelt bent his head in an affirmative posture.

"Then retreat your chi. Pulse down." Tzu knew that the Independentistes never used life-extension intervention of any sort. That they saw death as an important part of life itself. That they believed that life was to be lived and then the true journey of life, death, started. "Is it your time to do the death travel, Kelt? Or is there voyaging yet in this life for you? Pulse down!" Kelt held the Pirate's eye just long enough to prove that he was not frightened, then did as he was ordered.

The Slave Master stepped forward and drew his concussion gun. Through his rotted teeth he announced, "We should hobble him here."

"No," said Tzu Ma Long and turned to go.

"But our orders were to hobble him," the Slave Master protested.

Rage welled up in Tzu Ma Long, "Orders? We are not slaves. We are free men. Not so unlike these people."

The Slave Master quickly holstered his weapon and tugging at his forelock asked, "How are we to proceed then, sir?"

His power reaffirmed, Tzu Ma Long released his anger in a single breath. "Double your technacles on this one." Single sets could be removed if someone other than the bound person offered up their wrists. But not if the technacles were doubled up. Then only the release codes that the Slave Master alone carried could free the captive from the grip of the bio-products. "Now take him!"

Kelt was led off. Tzu Ma Long turned to the Face Dancer and snapped open the leaden pouch on his belt. The Face Dancer let out a high pitched whine but Tzu Ma Long was unswayed. He looked straight at her and tapped the pouch a second time. The Face Dancer expanded into a mist, turned for a moment to Tzu, and then glided into the pouch. Tzu snapped the pouch shut.

A shiver ran through him. He had caught a glimpse of something in the Face Dancer that he had never seen before. A hidden side. This strange gift from the Satrunal Rings was a shifting essence by nature, but this time he had seen an instant of a real self. Something she had kept from him. Perhaps even from herself. Something that he didn't, but he knew he must, understand.

A dense shadow abruptly blotted out the sun. Tzu looked up. The huge black carrion birds had finished their grisly work and were, as one great darkness, obscuring the light of day. Tzu shivered again.

Things were moving quickly now.

They had been ever since he heard the scattercast.

He contacted the AIU.

"Very impressive, sir." No sibilance this time but a troubling knowingness. She purred further praise then asked, "Where to next?"

He consulted the S3 list and informed her of their next destination.

She replied. "Yessirree."

Chapter 6

Cas-Alta the Healer—Third on the S3 List

Cas-Alta saw the attack from her mother's garden. She was calm. Something important was beginning, and she knew it.

She snapped a cynathium stem and crushed the flower's petals into her palm. The oil from the tender plant entered her skin and she felt its tranquil glow move up her arm. She took a deep breath.

Then the pirate's first torpedo-router hit. It threw up enormous mounds of debris as it dug a deep furrow through the very center of her home city.

Cas-Alta was seventeen standard years old. Her hair had never been cut. From the beginning, she had been the brunt of her schoolmates' jokes. But their jibes had never bothered her because Cas-Alta could ignore the world around her by applying her amazing powers of concentration.

And that is what she did as the first of the pirates smashed his way through the garden's fence. She focused on the splintered wood at the point of impact. She noted its consistent patterning above the break and then the debauch at the point of contact. A single splinter of the wood caught her eye. She counted one hundred and sixty-seven fibrous tendrils off the main shoot.

She did all this before the pirate grabbed her by the hair and held her tight to him.

She saw the other man, the one with the cruel scar on his face, enter her garden. She looked into his dark eyes. They were very beautiful. She noted his left foot move back in his boot.

CAS-ALTA—*19 year old female–daughter of a famous healer. Although synthetic medication is the norm throughout the galaxy, there is a strong underground movement which embraces ancient natural remedies. Cas-Alta, like* *her mother, is not only an accomplished naturalpathic healer but is also a dowser. DNA and RNA details included.* TO BE TAKEN ALIVE AND UNHARMED.

The pirate with the dark eyes scraped his fingernails across her forehead and nodded. Then he stared hard at the mariner who was holding her. It seemed to Cas-Alta that he was about to say something then changed his mind and walked away. Then he stopped and over his shoulder spat out, "Bring her to the drop ship when you're finished." Cas-Alta heard another intent beneath the words but didn't have time to contemplate it because her captor pushed her to the ground.

She wondered if the pirates would allow her mother to live. She never thought of her own death. She knew that this was a beginning not an ending. She knew that such events could lead to either good or bad. To the concrete or the ethereal. To the narrow reality of the present or the vast possibilities of the future.

The rapist's hands went beneath her skirts.

He hurt her body but her mind was far away.

Tzu Ma Long was surprised that he heard no scream from the long haired girl. Perhaps she was strong like his mother had been all those times. He summoned up the S3 list. She was the third. He reread the instruction at the list's end: "attack and take slaves from at least twenty other planets."

"The old bastard wants these five on the list disguised among the general rack and ruin," he thought. "Fine," he said aloud as he kicked the thick rich dirt at his feet. "But twenty seems a measly number. Why not fifty? Or a hundred and fifty?" he thought. A smile crossed his face.

He would do as he pleased.

He looked back. The mariner had finished with the long haired girl and was binding her in preparation for her short drop ship trip.

Tzu commed the Slave Master. "We have the girl. She'll be up there shortly. Technacle her and get her into cold sleep. Paint a red slash across her cocoon like the others. And ..."

"Something else Cap'n?"

Tzu weighed the consequences then said, "Tell the mariner who took her that I want to see him in the chart room."

For a moment Tzu thought about retracting his order then he snapped off his comm and headed for the drop ship.

When the mariner arrived in the chart room, his captain was turned away from him. "Sir?" he tentatively announced his presence.

Tzu turned and looked at the hefty man. He unsheathed the transparent knife and balanced it across his right index finger. "Enjoy yourself with the girl, mariner?"

The man relaxed slightly and smiled. He opened his mouth but never got to his words.

Tzu's knife entered his neck just below his chin and pierced through to the base of his skull. A stunned expression played like chaser lights across the heavy man's face which Tzu held firmly in his right hand.

"Because of my mother," Tzu spat, "because of her."

They were the last words the mariner ever heard. Tzu removed his hand and the man's body crashed to the floor.

Tzu stepped over the body and commed the AIU. "There's been an accident in the chart room."

"Indeed there has, sir, indeed there has," the AIU cooed in open admiration.

But Tzu took no solace from his deed. There was no amount of revenge that could calm all those years of his mother's screams in the night.

Chapter 7

Reports

TO: DANAZIR YI QAL, PRESIDENT UNITED DOMINION OF PLANETS
FROM: JEDIDIAH WITT, HEAD OF SECURITY—PRESIDIUM COUNCIL
RE: PIRATE RAIDS

In the past sixty Terran days, there has been an enormous increase in the number of reported pirate raids. The methods have varied from violent, chaotic, and senseless to subtle, clever, and surgically precise. The results have always been the same: devastation to the settlements and the lives of those that remained and an uncertain future for those who were abducted.

All of the raids appear to have been carried out by a pirate band that has somehow secured a UDP Warrior Class Starship. Beyond that we have little information.

I fear that the starship is equipped with the new AIU self-evolving processor.

We don't know why the raids are taking place at this particular time. Why their frequency has increased. What pattern, if any, there is to the attacks. What purpose, outside of the normal slaving activities of pirates, the raids serve.

In the past sixty days, seventeen UDP planetary settlements have been raided, nine Rebel Colony settlements, one EntrePren cover, and at least four Independentiste settlements. It is hard to know exact numbers since Independentistes don't report attacks. As well, it is believed that several EntrePren freighters have been boarded and relieved of their valuable cargoes of Kiltrin. But this is impossible to verify since such boardings would not be reported to us.

Both the UDP Defense Forces and the Rebel Colony Preservation Armies have proved ineffective against the pirate attacks.

What follows is the latest report:

RIGAL 9 Pirate Action Report

To: Central Security New Omaha Beach
From: Rigal Nine Security
Status: Urgent

Massive pirate raid in broad daylight. Total failure of all UDP Defense Forces. No early warning whatsoever. Entire city destroyed. At least 85,000 dead. Slaves taken. Aid needed. Medical support needed. Psychological help needed for entire colony. What is going on back there? Is New Omaha Beach completely out of touch with the rest of the galaxy? We need help and we need it now.

END Report

President Danazir Yi Qal forced down a surge of anger as she cleared her data screen. Then she commed Jedidiah Witt. Without preamble, she ordered him to her chambers.

A moment later she commed Jedidiah Witt a second time. This message read simply: "There has to be a connection between the pirate raids and the Peqod scattercast. Find it. Don't arrive empty handed!"

From inside, the glint of the ether dome was nothing but a hint of bounced light. From outside, the glint was a shining crystalline harbinger of decay, the dome's curve a cutlass ready to drop on an exposed neck.

The interior existed by plundering the exterior of its nutrients, its life. The plundering took place hundreds of Terran years ago and since then the exterior had been of no concern to the interior. In fact, the odd time that the exterior was mentioned, it was as something so long dead that it was insignificant. As one would refer to a sixth finger nicked off at birth. Of course there were no such oddities any longer. One of the benefits of a dreamless world.

The surface of old earth outside the ether dome lay unchanged beneath its four meter thick ice coating. There was no precipitation because nothing evaporated there. The wind simply swept round and round this frigid dead world. Dead? Perhaps, but it had an incandescent, surprising beauty. The random sweep of wind against cliff took the eye for a whimsical feast of a journey. The light bouncing and re-bouncing off the icy surfaces formed asymmetric patterns which captivated and appalled. Delighted and inspired. There was laughter in the cruel wind and glee in the wasteland. And beauty, ah yes, true beauty—unlike anything in the ordered worlds within the domes

Chapter 8

Mickelmast, Master Botmaker— The fourth on the S3 List

Mickelmast was awakened from his always luxurious sleep by a stabbing pain in his scrotum. The rotund young man threw aside his fluffy comforter and found to his amazement that hundreds of his nano-bots that he assigned each night to rearrange his floor tile pattern following the command: "**anypatternbutneverthesameasanypreviousnight.exe**" had joined him in his bed—and the sharp corner of one of the bot tiles was jabbing him where it really hurt. He blustered something about imbecilic machines and began tossing the square things across the now patternless bare floor.

Long ago, he had programmed his thousands of nano-bots to accomplish various tasks. "**Formskeletonofcarbonbasedanimal.exe**" and "**openallclosedthings.exe**"—simple things like that. He'd even invented nano-bot aerobics using the command: "**breakupandreformasmanynewnanobotsaspossible.exe.**" After all, a working bot was a happy bot. One day he'd programmed them to climb up on him and blanket his entire body like an armored second skin. After a bit of experimenting he managed to get them to cover every inch of his body. Then he programmed them to chameleon to exactly match their host—color for color, cloth for cloth, skin for skin.

Nano-bots were useful and fun. They were the heavy boy's only friends, but this hopping up into bed with him was ridiculous!

Mickelmast lived in a basement chamber on one of the main streets of Budgie Wharf, one of the largest English-based Rebel Colony cities in the galaxy. The city was at one time the very center of Rebel Colony culture and the dynamic growth engine of Rebel Colony power. Now Budgie Wharf was little more than refuse, decay, and eccentricity.

It did cross Mickelmast's mind that perhaps there was a reason his nano-bots had slid into bed with him like children frightened of the dark. So he padded over to his window and looked out.

Usually when Mickelmast looked out his basement window, he saw little but eco-garbage and huddled human beings trying to sleep on the sides of the transport ways. But this night outside his window he saw low flying landing craft and patrolling auto-tanks with strange markings.

The main street illumination systems were out, and the auxiliary systems flickered on and off with a disconcerting a-rhythmic pulsing. Mickelmast could smell the fluorine entering the breathing system.

Suddenly a massive explosion sent the old clock tower, which dominated the city's skyline, into oblivion. Bricks rained down on the city like some form of cosmic poop.

Mickelmast suppressed the desire to cry out, "Oh dear, oh dear, oh dear, oh dear," and decided it was time to—well to do something. He touched the master controller in his wrist. The hundreds of thousands of nano-bots in his room tilted their "heads" in his direction. Or at least that's what he imagined they did. For an instant, he couldn't recall the name of the file that would command the nano-bots to convert themselves into armor plating. Then he remembered. He tapped in the file name: **SaintGeorgeandtheDragon.**

Nothing happened.

A vehicle blew up right outside his window, sending shards of glass past him some of which embedded themselves in his walls. He dove beneath his bed and pushed hard to get his considerable girth beneath the platform. The sounds of approaching assault vehicles drowned his screams.

In desperation, he looked out at the nano-bots. In his mind he saw them turn to face him beneath the bed. For a moment Mickelmast was at a loss. He punched in the command again. Perhaps he had misspelled the file name! He carefully completed the spelling of **SaintGeorgeandtheDragon** paying special attention to capitalization. Then he looked up. Nothing again. If nano-bots could give a quizzical look, they would have.

At that exact moment, the pirate's battering ram crashed through his polymer alloy door. A huge hand reached through the hole and clawed at the seventeen locks and floor bar Mickelmast secured every night before he went to bed.

"Come on," Mickelmast yelled at his nano-bots from beneath the bed. "Please!!" he begged, thinking that perhaps a sweet tone would induce the things into motion.

The hand gave up its search for the slide bolt of the sixth lock and withdrew. Then the battering ram slammed into the hinges of the door. The door shuddered for a moment and then toppled inward.

Mickelmast looked desperately at the nano-bots, and then it came to him. He punched in: **EXE**. Instantly the nano-bots skittered beneath the bed and locking themselves together, covered his body assuming the exact external proportions of their host.

The pirates entered and immediately crossed to the bed and yanked the platform from the wall, tossing it aside as if it were made of sheets of flimsy.

Mickelmast bounced to his feet and punched in a second command: "**Clown.exe.**" Immediately the exterior nano-bots formed the baggy pants, fright wig, painted face, red nose, and enormous shoes of a Cockney circus clown. One particularly enterprising bot squeaked calliope music by scraping its parts together.

The pirates didn't know or care what to make of this. They slashed open his arm and plunged in their genetic decoder which relayed the information instantly to the ship's AIU. They didn't notice the strange platelets that fell from Mickelmast's skin at the point of the cut. Nor did they see the tiny bots climb up on his huge clown shoe and form a jaunty green neon swoosh on the instep.

The ship's AIU confirmed their match. The Slave Master entered and threw technacles onto Mickelmast. The nano-bots guided the bio-products around Mickelmast's considerable girth protecting him from the technacles real "bite." The bio-product did, however, slither along his skin causing Mickelmast to mutter, "Icky, icky, icky." Before he could say or think more, two of the pirates frog-walked him out of his flat.

As he was being hauled along, Mickelmast looked back at Budgie Wharf, his beloved city that the rest of the Rebel Colonies hated. His big, ugly, chaotic, crazy, mess of a city. Then a serious thought pushed aside his sentimental musings. "I sure hope they have Tahitian ginger rolls where I am going."

He liked Tahitian ginger rolls.

A lot

Chapter 9

Raephealson the Mystic—The Fifth And Last on the S3 List

RAEPHEALSON—*19 year old Heavy Worlder. Schizophrenic. Extremely strong but not violent. DNA and RNA matches included.* TO BE TAKEN ALIVE AND UNHARMED.

As Raephealson waited in the darkness for the great thwark to emerge from its den, he thought for a moment about his Grandda's last words in the Chamber of the Final Passing: "You will have the gift just as my Grandda had it before me and his Grandda before him, Raephealson. But unlike us, you may have to use it, for I do believe the time of change finally approaches."

Each of his dying Grandda's words had echoed off the tall walls of the slender room and Raephealson had sensed that there were other beings, unseen, in the chamber, waiting for him to do something. To do anything. But what was a ten-year-old boy to do alone in a tall chamber with a dying man?

The old man had smiled and taken the boy's hands in his. Then with a final gentle look at his grandson, he exhaled a puff of air and was no more.

Raephealson had stared at the old man. In his heart, he'd known that although his Grandda's body lay before him, the real part of him had somehow gone somewhere else.

Raephealson's parents had found him in the Chamber of the Final Passing the next morning, his hands still locked in the dead man's grasp. Raephealson was calm. Strangely calm as far as his family was concerned.

From that day forward they had dealt with him differently.

The whole village had.

Raephealson, the Mad One, was the village's one step into the unknown. Although feared for what they thought of as his insanity, he was consulted on all matters that concerned the village's well being. A festival was such a matter. Festivals needed to be celebrated properly to ensure the village's continued health.

That's why they had sent Raephealson out with the two hunters to kill a ceremonial thwark and thus mark the Festival of the Great Escaping. And so it was that the Mad One found himself with the two hunters at the mouth of the cave of the majestic beast.

One of the hunters, Tal, pushed aside the tall grass then nodded toward the den's opening.

In the bounced light from the planet's two moons, the thwark's huge shadow stretched across the cave's west wall.

The hunters and the Mad One had been outside the cave for six days. The hunger was on them, but they knew that they couldn't leave the cave entrance. They knew that once the thwark was in the open, they had no way of bringing him down.

They had set their triangular net trap, driven in their stakes, and begun their vigil. Three days ago, they had eaten the last of their food. The day before yesterday, they drained the last of their carrying gourds.

It was now two full days without food or drink, but there was no returning to their Independentiste village without a ceremonial thwark to mark the Festival of the Great Escaping. To return empty handed was to invite ruin. So they waited.

And then the huge mammal appeared in the mouth of the cave—and dwarfed its shadow.

The prints and spoor had indicated that they were tracking a large animal, but nothing had prepared the three for the enormity or nobility of the beast as it emerged from the depths of its cave.

It's great height, almost four meters to its plate-encrusted shoulders, seemed to blot out even the high moon which always centerd their planet's night sky. It pawed the cave floor with its right foreleg causing tight dust whirls to rise from the parched ground.

The thwark lifted its eyes and shaking its shaggy single-tusked head scented the air. It let out a series of snorts that came at the hunters in rounded blasts. The thwark had smelled the men days before and retreated to its den hoping the hunters would tire of the chase. But now hunger was on both the hunter and the hunted. The need for life was pushing the great beast out toward its death—an irony lost on the hunters but central to Raephealson's understanding of the events that were unfolding before him. Understandings like that sat in a funny place in him. A place of which his Grandda had spoken... a place of falling.

The magnificent animal let out an angry roar and all sense of falling left Raephealson. An old mechanism activated and the Mad One found himself running. Hunting.

Raephealson grabbed his corner of the net and carefully keeping his end outside of the guide posts raced up the moss covered hill over the cave's mouth. As he did the two hunters skittered forward to take their ends of the net. Tal's wiry frame raced through the tall grass, but the other hunter, Lar, moved like one in his sleep—half running, half staggering. The days of fasting had taken a heavy toll on him.

Raephealson could see that Lar wouldn't have the strength needed for the capture.

The thwark sensed it too and, throwing back its huge head, charged straight at the weakened hunter. Lar dropped his corner of the net and cowered against the outer wall of the cave.

The beast lunged at the terrified hunter. The man shrieked and fell to his knees. The thwark's horn missed its mark and threw up sparks as it sliced into the rock surface. In a rage, the great beast backed off a pace to measure its target a second time. As it did its right hind leg snagged in the netting. The majestic animal turned its head away from the cowering hunter and looked at its trapped limb.

Raephealson watched the scene beneath him from the ledge over the top of the cave's mouth. Clearly if the thwark moved forward its freedom was assured—a fact that the Mad One knew the animal would shortly figure out. So without a thought for his own safety Raephealson screamed toward the sky and, clutching his edge of the net in both hands, launched himself straight out over the length of the thwark.

The huge animal jerked its head upward searching for the source of the cry. He raised his single tusk as if it would pierce the high moon's center.

Then the thwark saw Raephealson's flying body blot out the night orb and bellowed its anger as the Mad One's net snagged on its upward-pointing tusk.

Raephealson snapped to a sudden bone-jarring stop, his body weight yanking the thick net taut—immobilizing the great beast.

The Mad One found himself dangling upside down about eight feet off the ground staring straight into the thwark's huge watery eyes. It surprised Raephealson that the only thought in his head as he hung there was to ask forgiveness of the great beast for taking its life. It surprised him even more that he knew with a certainty that the thwark wouldn't resist his knife, but rather would accept his time of passing. Like his Grandda, the great thwark would let out a puff of air and leave this world.

When the great animal fell beneath Raephealson's knife thrust, the two hunters stared in awe at the Mad One. Raephealson ignored them. As he watched the dying thwark's final moments of life, his Grandda's words echoed in his head: "You will have the gift just as my Grandda had it before me and his Grandda before him. But unlike us, you may have to use it for I do believe the time of change finally approaches."

That night Raephealson cried out in his sleep. It shocked the two hunters. They moved away from the boy's prone, jerking body and hoped for an early sunrise. They had no idea what they were witnessing. People from their village did not jerk in their sleep. People lay down flat and slept. As they did in the rest of the neighboring villages. As they did on the rest of the planet. The rest of their solar system. The rest of the galaxy.

In his sleep, Raephealson found himself in a tall room. Its walls were transparent allowing in the light from outside. Lush tropical broad-leafed trees grew all around him yet the magical Falling Cold pelted outside. He had been here before—in his sleep. Watching. Seeing the things pass in front of him. As if he were behind an invisible shield. But things were different this night.

A gust of cold made him turn in the direction of an opened door. A handsome man with a deep anger in his face entered and for a moment stared at the space. Then he signaled with a flex of his hand. A terribly thin naked boy, not more than six or seven, stumbled into the room. The angry-faced man grabbed the boy by the arm and shoved him right into the center of the tallest space. The boy looked back at the man.

"Cyrus," he said.

"Do it my boy, be my tracker, fly for Cyrus," the man said.

The boy smiled wanly.

The angry-faced man nodded.

The boy took one step forward as if centring himself in the tall clear space. He closed his eyes then tilted his head back. With a great inhalation, he spread his arms wide. Then he bent his knees and leapt into the air—and stayed there—afloat.

Raephealson gasped.

"What! Who's there?" shouted the angry-faced man.

But Raephealson didn't answer because he was running. Running. Running from the angry-faced man who was not from his planet. Running from the angry-faced man who was his death.

Raephealson awoke vowing never to "view" in his sleep again. He, in fact, awoke with a strange phrase on his lips: "Dream no more, dream no more, dream no more, dream."

The dawn came slowly upon the three figures and the carcass of the ceremonial thwark. Like a stillness from an ancient cave wall. But change itself was falling upon them. For far in the background behind this ancient tableau was a UDP Warrior Class Starship's drop vessel—under command of the pirate captain, Tzu Ma Long—preparing to cull the final name on the list supplied by Cyrus Maloney III of S3.

Chapter 10

Tzu Ma Long

"You are the one called Raephealson?" Tzu was surprised that his voice was disconnected, strangely thin.

The young heavy worlder nodded his head. Tzu looked toward the two hunters who were being prepared for execution. Behind them, the dead thwark lay on the ground. Tzu sensed Raephealson looking at him. He turned and stared into the young man's hazel within hazel eyes. The boy's irises changed pattern every few seconds. Tzu stepped closer to the heavy worlder—then he felt it.

The dullness.

It grabbed him around the heart and pulled him hard toward the rocky ground, as a great fish attacks a swimmer.

It took all of Tzu's considerable willpower to drag his eyes away from Raephealson. He signaled to the Slave Master. "You can manage here?"

The stinky man looked at his captain out of the sides of his eyes and rubbed an open sore on his thin upper lip.

"Well?"

"Aye," the foul man said.

"Good." Tzu found himself staring at Raephealson again. He nodded and forced a smile to his lips then turned on his heel and moved quickly toward the drop ship. A voice inside him screamed at him to run, but he knew his mariners' eyes were on him and he forced himself to keep a steady, slow gait.

Once he was onboard the drop ship, he contacted the AIU and told her that he wanted the ship's covenant space cleared.

"No problem."

"Once the Slave Master brings the heavy worlder onboard, I want you to monitor his descent into cold sleep. Only contact me if there is a problem with that. Otherwise, I want to be left alone."

"As you wish."

The drop ship had already cleared planetary orbit before Tzu Ma Long had enough clear brain space to think through his situation. The attack of the dullness had to have something to do with this Raephealson. Something about the mad boy had brought on the malaise. He hadn't had an attack of the dullness for years. Damn! Why now? Because of something about the heavy worlder with the hazel within hazel eyes—the mad one. Tzu felt his skin crawl and within the confined space smelled the sour odor of his own fear.

Then his blood started pounding in his temples. "Stop this," he said aloud. He commanded himself to think. To go back to the first attack. It'd taken place two days shy of his sixth birthday. He'd been in the belly of the great EntrePren Kiltrin ship in which he'd been born—in which his mother had been the doxy whore.

She'd stayed by him day after day and did her best to help. She put him on tight schedules making sure that every waking moment was filled with things to do. She kept his mind and body busy until the dullness finally passed.

Then she had cried.

And he'd heard her.

"I disappoint you, mother."

"Never."

"It is my cowardice."

She took a deep breath and then turned to her son. "You had a great gift."

He was surprised but he knew what she was talking about. For years he had voyaged in his sleep. At first, the voyages had thrilled him then they had begun to terrify him. He'd begun to scream in his sleep. When he awoke his bed linen was sodden and his mother was always there, her very presence a cool caress. She'd smile at him reassuringly and insist that he had a great gift and that he must be brave enough to

use it.

But he had replied, "Mother, the night voyaging terrifies me."

"Perhaps, but it is a great gift. A unique gift." Her voice was surprisingly hard.

After the dullness had receded he'd asked her, "My gift is gone now, isn't it?"

She turned away from him. "Yes, son, the night voyaging is gone now."

"Will it come back?"

"I doubt it."

"And this new thing?"

"Nature has made a trade. You feared the voyaging in the dark so it has been replaced by the dullness in the light."

He had never forgotten her face while she spoke those words to him. She couldn't keep the tears from her eyes or the hurt from her voice.

It was a turning point in his young life. He knew that he had caused his mother's tears. He had disappointed her with his fear, so he set out to make her proud of him. He had achieved. He had succeeded. He had sought and gained control. All so that she would be proud of him and so that he would not have to look inward and confront the cowardice that had stolen his night voyaging gift and made his mother cry.

But something in the mad heavy worlder had touched him, and suddenly he was once again confronted by his own fears, with the dullness. What was it about the heavy worlder that brought on the dullness? Tzu couldn't begin to guess. But he knew that he had to stop this internal falling before it swept him away.

He sat alone in the ship's covenant space. Alone and frightened knowing he had to deal with the dullness—this feeling of falling in space.

For a fleeting moment, he thought of using synthetic sex or power euphors to distract him. But even as the idea arose he felt his system setting up barriers. "How clever the internal god is," he thought.

He reached for the small pouch on his belt.

The Face Dancer slid out, little more palpable than the steam from a kettle and waited for a command to form. As Tzu watched the mist swirl, he experienced a tremor of warning. What had the Face Dancer been hiding from him when they captured the warrior called Kelt? Go back. Go back. Think this through. He had received the Face Dancer from the caped-man almost thirty Terran years ago. On Saturn—on the Rings. The old man had bargained for the safety of his group of convicts. The man's name was gone from Tzu's memory but not the cloak that he had worn. The caped-man had called the Face Dancer a Dream Remnant. A term that Tzu had never heard before or since.

The dullness reasserted itself. Tzu groaned in agony.

The Face Dancer still waiting in her transforming vapor, suggested, "Bedable?"

Her voice was slightly back, its contact point frail. She tried again, "Bedable?" The voice was better placed this time, the timbre deep but still sweet. The mist crept toward Tzu. It sensed a change in the man—a vagueness in him. It was about to speak a third time when it saw the Pirate Captain reach for an ancient fighting foil on the covenant space's wall. Tzu's hand moved through the maze of the handle's metal filigree to find its purchase within. Then, with remarkable swiftness, he lunged deep into the mist.

"Form," he screamed.

The Face Dancer wrapped herself around the rapier, and as Tzu Ma Long retracted it, she materialized as an exact replica of the pirate captain. She grabbed a weapon from the wall and, with a joyous shout, counterattacked. Instinctively Tzu parried and then feinted to one side. But she was quickly on him again. This time her attack was ferocious. On the fifth stroke, she struck flesh. She held her weapon in Tzu's body and stared deep into his eyes. Finally, the flatness she had seen lurking there began to fade. Tzu moved forward into his features. The pain had drawn him back from whatever precipice he had managed to approach.

"Enough?" asked the Face Dancer.

Tzu Ma Long looked away from her then blurted out, "Thinner, taller, blonder. Make me live again."

And she became thinner, taller, blonder. And with her lips firmly attached to the wound on his body, she did indeed make him live again driving the dullness away—down into a deep dark cave at the very heart of Tzu Ma Long.

Chapter 11

Miro, Lavolin and a Heavy Heart

Jedidiah had been shocked when Danazir Yi Qal summoned him to her private rooms. He was exhausted and as he waited in her antechamber, his face twitched and he was having trouble standing still.

The partition slid aside and she entered soundlessly. He turned to face her.

"Your heart is heavy, Mr. Witt."

"It is Madame President." His hand shook as he held out a four page flimsie to her. She took the document but continued to stare at her head of internal security.

Jedidiah turned aside as if to give her privacy. Danazir took note of the false move then smoothed out the documents and began to read.

TO: PRESIDENT DANAZIR YI QAL

FROM: MIRO

RE: LAVOLIN TRAVELS

To begin I would like it noted that I only comm this on the insistence of Jedidiah Witt, Head of Internal Security for the Presidium Council. My situation is precarious enough without adding tailings for S3 to follow!

My name is Miro and I have been your source of information on S3 for the length of my cognitive life. I am given to believe that I was taken as a child twenty-eight Terran years ago from Malthius III in the Morphius System. After my abduction the rest of the planet was forcibly evacuated by order of the S3 leader, my charge, Cyrus Maloney III. I am now his private nurse. I also state, without blush, that I have served many diverse functions as requested by the Ancient One. His withered skin is no stranger to my touch. I am his whore but then, as I have stated, I am your spy–is there really a difference?.

I am also his Lavolin neutral third. What is called on the street 'his catalyst'."

Danazir put the document to one side and turned to Jedidiah, "So the rumors of Cyrus' Lavolin use are true?"

"It has been his favored means of contact over time and space for many years. He calls such contacts, communions."

"Why would he bother with such an archaic form?"

"Hard to say, Madame President. But Cyrus is not a simple man and Lavolin is not a simple drug."

She looked at him closely and allowed a long finger to play along her lip. "How is Lavolin not a simple drug, Mr. Witt?"

"Are you familiar with its history, Madame President?"

"Only the old wives' tales."

"The past few years have taught me a new respect for old wives' tales, Madame President." Her eyes held his and she nodded for him to continue. "Lavolin made its first appearance suddenly at the turn of the millennium. Its initial name was Dre-Rem. Lavolin's many unique properties include the need for a neutral third. A person who acts as a catalyst permitting the connection over time and space between the two drug users. Usually the neutral third is a person assigned by the EntrePren's AIU with full guarantees of anonymity to all parties. But not in this case. Under cover of the Great War, I intercepted a Lavolin shipment destined for Cyrus and stripped it of its AIU assigned neutral catalyst. I had Miro grafted to the drug as Cyrus' neutral third so she could track his drug travels ... "

"... for us. To be a useful UDP source of intelligence," Danazir Yi Qal completed his thought. Jedidiah acknowledged that truth but would not meet her penetrating eyes.

"I believe, Madame President, that our spy has supplied the information you seek on the top of the third page."

Danazir Yi Qal turned to the third page of Miro's document:

"Sixty-two days ago I was summoned by Cyrus in the dead of the night. I arrived and was quickly ushered into a private section of his chambers. The space is set up in a most unusual manner. In one wall of the room is an open cavity for the burning of plants. I never knew such an extravagance existed!

The ancient one sat in a large green chair upholstered in some natural product which I didn't recognize, a treated hide of some sort. He was facing the flames. Upon his knees rested a covering, a rug perhaps. It was made of an animal's hair woven together into some sort of fabric. It was coarse to the touch. He pointed to the flames and asked, "Do you know what this is?"

"No sir."

"It's called a fireplace."

"A fireplace. I will remember that sir."

"It's the past. My past."

I was shocked. He seldom spoke to me. Touched yes, but spoke as I have mentioned, seldom. Then he reached up and took my hair in his hands. He allowed it to fall through his fingers and said, "Like a combed horse's tail." He said it several times, "Like a combed horse's tail."

Does that mean something Mr. Witt–like a combed horse's tail?

For a moment Cyrus seemed lost in thought as if he were travelling back through his lengthy personal history, trying to understand something from long ago. Then his thoughts turned outward again.

He touched my lip then slid a finger into my mouth. I sucked on it as I knew he wished. Then I licked his palm. As I did I looked through his splayed fingers and there was a profound sadness on his face.

"Do you know what a siren is?"

"No, sir."

"There were nights when The City was filled with their sounds coursing the streets."

He retracted his hand from my ministrations and began to roll up his sleeve. I knew what he wanted and moved to assist him.

I managed to find a vein quickly that night and inserted the needle far into its length. His eyes opened wide and looked deep into mine. Then I depressed the plunger. His head snapped back then rose up high on his neck like an attacking serpent. He hissed, "Sirens outside, sirens inside."

The power of the Lavolin erupted in my head. He was moving fast. The mist accordionned, fold upon fold upon rhythmic fold–each wider than the one before–then the speed of the folding increased until a final wrenching fold parted to reveal an ancient city–I think on old earth. The miraculous Falling Cold filled the air and people were everywhere with brightly colored packages in their arms.

What was this? Sounds were in the air. My implant identified them as carols, a subset of the thing called songs, a kind of organized set of frequencies.

Then Cyrus—against a brick wall—tears sluicing down his cheeks mixing with the wondrous Falling Cold—and an enormous tree covered in lights that twinkled in the midst of a city plaza—people on a square of frozen water gliding like animated figures on a screen.

Then Cyrus was folding the Lavolin again. Looking for communion. But with whom?

Suddenly I felt him deep inside me. I have already admitted to being his whore! I arched my back to accept him but Lavolin has ripples and sometimes draws me in too tight. It did this time. Cyrus was not with me. I turned and saw him with another. Then he looked back. He was so young it took my breath away. And handsome. So handsome. The one who holds him is a young woman. Her hair drops about his shoulders. She wears a black hat made from some kind of animal pelt. Her beautiful face is a glimmering whiteness within the fur's dark frame.

Then there is rhythm between them.

Where he stops and she begins is hard for me to know. Flesh and limbs. Motion and pulsing pleasure. Then I hear their hard breathing and his coarse calling of her name, "Olya, Olya, Olya."

She begins to fade. She was only an illusion created in the Lavolin field by the powerful will of Cyrus Maloney III. The wind picked up and the Falling Cold intensified. Then Cyrus yelled, "I'm coming back. It's beginning. At last it's beginning. Wait for me Olya. Wait for me." It hurt to hear. He sounded like a lost child caught by the swirling of the wondrous Falling Cold. He was crying. His tears froze to his beautiful face.

Then the Lavolin folded deeply and we were in motion again. I saw him turn as if at an alley's end. He was now in tatters—a beggar in some underworld. He was aged again but surprisingly spry. I forced the Lavolin to turn upward. At least three moons hung in this alien night sky. There was a pronounced glinting off the dome which covered the planet. Four drop ships were low on the horizon. A fifth was readying itself for departure. I tried to fold and turn the Lavolin again but I stopped when I saw Cyrus. He was crouching. Searching. Looking for someone else in the Lavolin field. Could he sense me there?

Only if I wasn't careful–if I forced things too far.

Then someone else's presence registered. A fellow Lavolin traveller–the co-user. The man moved erratically in the mist, fighting the Lavolin's force. Then suddenly he was by my side, a single fold of the field separating us. For a moment I was sure that he had seen me.

But he hadn't.

He wasn't a connoisseur of the mist like Cyrus. Like me.

"I'm here old man, what do you want?" shouted the young Asian man. The garish false illumination of the chemical street lights now etched his face clearly. The scar on his cheek was so deep that I could sense the bone forming the ridge beneath it. A nob in the midst of a tightly curved line. He had beautiful, cold eyes.

"Nice of you to join me."

"Why do you like meeting this way? There's adequate security on my ship to take or send any kind of communication that you like. Why do this?"

"Humor an old man."

"I'm humoring you. If I weren't you'd be dead. Now what do you want?"

"I have a business proposition for you."

"I assumed as much. We have nothing else to join us but business concerns."

"I could have you arrested."

"You could try. S3 is out of touch with the realities of the galaxy. S3 is an old idea run by an old man who still likes his drugs. Isn't it time for you to die old man? What more do you want of this existence? Every time you breathe you take air from someone new, someone who deserves to be here while you are gone."

"Am I to be hurt by this vitriol?"

"I don't care what you are. Just tell me what you want."

"Do you find the drug disorienting?"

"No. As I've said, I find it unnecessary."

"Yes, yes I guess you would."

Then Cyrus turned away from the younger man and drew a small circular data plate from his sleeve and held it out.

The younger man took the thing into the palm of his left hand and forming his fingers into a prearranged code released the plate's data into his system.

"Well can you manage this, Tzu Ma Long?"

I was shocked to hear that name–to realize that I shared the mist with the pirate captain whose very name has been a source of terror throughout the galaxy for many Terran years. Involuntarily a jet of fear came from me. Again, Cyrus whirled about looking for the source of the disturbance in the mist. I quickly recited, "I am a child of Malthius III. A planet in the Morphius system. I am a child of Malthius III. A planet in the Morphius system. Be still and feel your heart." When I could feel the pulse and warmth of my heart I forced a single column of air down past my center. My calm returned. The disturbance in the mist dissipated.

It was then that I saw, no not saw–was somehow touched by, the small leaden satchel on the pirate captain's belt.

Cyrus turned back to Tzu Ma Long. "You don't sense anything?"

"Like what? You're a drugged old bugger. Now why does S3 want these five people kidnapped?"

"Because we do."

"Of all the souls in the galaxy these five are of interest to S3–I find that most interesting."

"Don't."

"Don't what?"

"Don't find it that interesting."

There was a long moment of silence. It was then that I dared your procedure, Mr. Witt. The Lavolin's folding and re-folding had stabilized into a slower rhythm so I chanced sliding through one of the slender folds and, keeping my distance from that thing on the pirate's belt, I implanted the chip you gave me, next to Tzu Ma Long's third spinal disc. Luckily his concentration was on Cyrus. Even if he felt any pain he would not want to show weakness in front of the Ancient One. And he was young in the mist. A babe, new to the Lavolin womb.

Finally Tzu Ma Long said, "It'll cost."

"I expected that. How much?"

Tzu laughed. The mist repeated and repeated the sound like an endless echoing chamber. "You want this badly old man or you wouldn't have come to me."

"I don't deny that."

"Good. But don't ever think that I believe a word you say to me. Now here's what I want for getting these five people for S3."

Then the pirate demanded the newest of the UDP Warrior Class Starships with all the latest technology that the great vessel could carry. Cyrus dickered but before long "gave in." Details were set. A hand written document was given to the pirate and something resembling closing courtesies were uttered and executed by both. Then Cyrus and I were moving through the mist again. I could feel the drug beginning to wane. He would feel it soon too.

I felt something hot on my back and something wet on my breast. I looked around and I saw the plants burning behind me in the thing that Cyrus had called a fireplace. We were back in his chamber. I was straddling him. His tears were on my chest. The name Olya filled the air. The release of an old man erupted deep in my womb.

Miro.

Danazir Yi Qal put aside the flimsie. She seemed lost in thought. She put a long finger to her lips and spoke, "That was sixty-two days ago. The night after the scattercast from the Peqod."

"Two days before the S3 Executive Council meeting," added Jedidiah.

Danazir Yi Qal rose from her chair. Once again Jedidiah was aware of the intensity of her presence in the room. Her almost impossibly dark eyes, permanently lined by the tattoo artist's delicate hand, were again turned inward as they had been when he played her the Peqod's scattercast. Jedidiah turned away to offer her a moment of privacy.

Jedidiah knew that the room's colors were traditional for President of the United Dominion of Planets. But the new muted textures and subtle shadings were no doubt the President's personal addition. The place felt of her, of her femininity, of her deep intelligence. In one of the dusted mirrors, he caught an image of her slightly bent over the document he'd given her.

Although he found it hard to believe, rumor had it that she didn't use AIU assist in her contemplations. It was probably not true but he would be happy if she were capable of working without the AIU since the dominion's central unit had been penetrated years ago by S3 and despite Jedidiah's best efforts both the point of penetration and the depth of that penetration were still mysteries.

Danazir was reviewing the reports from her own sources. They matched sections of the information that Mr. Witt had just presented. Then, for the hundredth time, she returned to the phrase: "for fear of nightmares." And for the hundredth time, her massive intelligence found nothing. No meaning. No association. Not even a clue why the phrase kept recurring.

Finally Danazir turned to him. "Is the Lavolin spy in danger?" Her voice was still strange to him. So deep yet still so feminine.

"I'm afraid, she is."

"What will Cyrus do to her?" Before Jedidiah could respond, she answered her own question. "Something infinitely unpleasant." She pulled her eyes away from his and said, "I'd like to read her dossier."

"The access codes are on your comm."

Her voice suddenly hardened as she asked, "Has the pirate captain managed to abduct the five people S3 wants?"

"We don't know, but there have been no reported raids for the past four days."

"So we can assume that Tzu has completed his assigned task, can't we Mr. Witt?"

"I think it safe to believe that he has the five people requested by S3 onboard his ship," replied Jedidiah with as much calm as he could muster.

Danizir shook her head as if a nasty thought had lodged there. When she spoke, her voice was thin. "But, who could be worth a UDP Warrior Class Starship to S3, Mr. Witt?"

"Not who, Madame President ..." Jedidiah had no love of dramatics, but he found himself pausing before he added, "... what."

"What?"

"Yes, what, Madame President."

"Well then what, Mr. Witt, could be worth the cost of that Starship and the carnage the pirates have visited upon those planets?"

"The most valuable genetic material in the galaxy."

"What ... "

"The genetic material needed to assemble a Dream Navigator." Danazir Yi Qal momentarily looked like she was going to faint. "Are you mad, Mr. Witt?"

"If only I were, Madame President." Jedidiah removed a Holo disk from his sleeve. "This is the transcript of the S3 Executive Council meeting that you requested. Miro managed to get it to us two hours ago."

Without asking permission, Jedidiah inserted the disk into the Holo generator on the table and passed his hand over it. For a moment the air was filled with a misted static then the image of Cyrus Maloney III sitting at the head of the perfectly round table blinked and stuttered into being. Cyrus's large head lolled on his skinny neck as he waited for the other members of the council to complete their reading of the twenty odd flimsies of data he'd given them.

Chapter 12

An AIU Spurned

The ship's AIU was upset. First Tzu had forbidden her to contact him after Raephealson's capture, then he had used the Face Dancer to chase this malaisy thing from him, and now he was interrogating her like a kitchen wench who had burned his dinner.

"Who are the five people that S3 wanted abducted?"

She regurgitated the basic information that S3 had supplied.

Angered by her response, Tzu yelled at her that she knew more than she was admitting.

She was not pleased with his outburst, and she told him so.

"Cross-reference the captive's genetic codes and personal histories and report back any mathematically abnormal matches or absences," he demanded.

In less than a hundredth of a second, she completed her search and reported back. "The five have no mutual heritage, several personal abnormalities but none shared. As for absences, the sample is too small to mathematically analyze. Pleased?"

"No. Speculate on S3's motives in demanding the kidnappings."

"There are too many variables in the personality of Cyrus Maloney III for a thinking organism to reach any logical conclusion."

"What about the timing of all this?"

"It's P.P.S."

"P.P.S.?"

"Post-Peqod Scattercast."

"This has something to do with the scattercast?"

"It is logical to assume that everything now has *something* to do with the Peqod's scattercast."

He ordered her to play him the scattercast. She did. He requested it a second time, and she played it a second time. Then a third. After each playing, he quizzed her on the identity of the voice at the end of the transmission, the bird-like chirp that said, "Beyond here lie dreams."

Each time she replied, "Insufficient data to even venture a guess, if guessing were in my mandate."

Finally he gave up and ordered her to suggest a plan for the short term.

She replied, "Bed rest and lots of fluids sounds reasonable."

He didn't find that funny.

She wasn't laughing either. She had noted an odd signal coming from him. She had heard it before, but she assumed it was some sort of birth implant so she had given it no credence. Now she found the low-level transmission from the thing worrying–very worrying.

Chapter 13

After the Holo

With a wave of his hand, Jedidiah stopped the Holo of the S3 Executive Council. The static flickered in the air, and then what had been was no more. Jedidiah experienced the same dull feeling he always had after viewing Holos. They seemed so real and yet were merely tricks of technology. He understood all too well that something in the human spirit sank every time technology blurred the lines between real and unreal.

He looked to his President. For the first time in his dealing with her, she seemed to be badly shaken. Her internal calm had clearly left her.

"They're real then?" Her voice was little more than a whisper.

"Dream Navigators?"

"Yes, Mr. Witt, Dream Navigators. Are they real?" she shouted.

"They were, over four hundred years ago." Jedidiah made sure that his voice stayed flat.

"But I've read our history, I know ... " Her voice failed her. "S3 wrote our history, didn't they Mr. Witt?"

"Indeed, Madame President, they did."

"Lies. We've lived our lives by S3 lies. How did they ever accumulate so much power?"

"We gave it to them! We begged them to take it. To keep us safe. To keep the spooky man out of our darkened rooms at night. Folly!" This last he said much too loudly. "Even as a boy, folly was hard for me to bear, Madame President. But folly in an individual seldom hurts more than those close to the fool, while folly in places of power can hurt us all ... *has* hurt us all." He was surprised to find that he had grabbed the material of her sari. He let it go and stepped back. He closed his eyes. Weariness was making him lose his grip.

Then she surprised him. She touched his hand. Her fingers were remarkably cool.

"There is more in your heart, Jedidiah Witt. It is time to tell me the full extent of the burden you carry."

He lifted his eyes and found himself staring into Danazir Yi Qal's. He began to speak. At first it was slow. Then it became a torrent. "Four years ago my only son, Seth, left. He had not reached his tenth year.

"I believe his parting must be heeded, not because he was my son, but because he was greatly gifted. Gifted enough that our galaxy cannot withstand the loss of too many more of his kind.

"Yes, I said our galaxy not our Dominion, Madame President.

"It was his leaving that set me on a perverse journey into our encrypted past. After four years of trying to make sense of the secrets of our rutting Dominion, all I know for sure is that they are fleeing! The gifted among us are fleeing! Even as we speak, they are approaching the GATEWAY. Beyond which lies ... dreams—of dragons no doubt.

"I believe that their plight has its origins in events the first of which took place more than five hundred years ago, well before the forced evacuation of much of our Solar System. Long before the magnificence of New Omaha Beach. Even before the first alien contacts, back when we as a species were still evolving—back before the millennial break—when in the deep silences of sleep there were those among us who still dreamed.

"I have never dreamt myself, Madame President, nor do I know anyone who has but I believe dreams are at the center, the heart of our present danger. Dreaming, the lost gift of our species, I believe links the Peqod's scattercast, the actions of S3, the pirate raids and my Seth's departure.

"When Seth left, four years ago, I found this on his desk."

Jedidiah reached into a shirt pocket and handed over a much-thumbed note. This time he didn't try to hide the shaking of his hand.

Danazir Yi Qal took the note and read Seth's simple good-bye:

And to the light
We flee your midst
For from your dark
We go
To places yond
The Gateway
That opened long ago.—S.

Chapter 14

Tzu's Night With Guests

That night Tzu abandoned his efforts to find sleep and, following his body's restlessness impulses, roamed the ship's corridors. Ahead of him the passageways emptied as the crew's implants picked up his ID. It behooved them to know where their captain was and stay out of his way, especially on a night like this.

So Tzu walked and walked and met no one—as if he were the only living soul on the great vessel. Alone with power. Alone with cowardice. Alone, but not unobserved.

The AIU had been tracking him closely since detecting the new signal's hint of Lavolin mist. She had thought for a while about informing the captain of her concern, but she knew that riling "Herr Short Stuff" (her slag name for him since his unpleasant interrogation of her) could have a significant counter slope. So she did the AIU equivalent of keeping her mouth shut. Mouth shut, but eyes wide open, attentive and, as mentioned, worried. This evening's ramble did nothing to calm her—nor did his evident destination—the cryogenic chamber.

As Tzu Ma Long stepped out of the air lock at the base of the kilometer-long Zero-G central corridor he saw, to his surprise, an old man he didn't recognize, standing outside the cryogenic chamber.

The old man's face was pressed hard against the small window imbedded in the chamber's thick door. He was staring so intently at the contents of the room that he didn't notice the Tzu's approach.

Tzu's implant scanned the withered creature. The AIU replied mechanically: "Jaspers, Elijah—hobbled—no rank—basic clearance only—Canary."

"A canary," Tzu thought, "I'd forgotten that we still carried canaries."

Canaries went back to the pre-ether dome days when often there wasn't time to properly scan new planets or sealed sectors of buildings for airborne dangers. You'd just throw in a canary. If he survived fine.

If not ... well canaries were cheap and plentiful in any port city in the galaxy. Many years ago technology had made canaries redundant but some crews still insisted on having them onboard for good luck. Tzu didn't recall agreeing to having a canary onboard.

"What could there be of interest to you in the cryogenic chamber, old man?" Tzu barked.

The old Canary turned to face the pirate captain. His features, although covered by a grizzled beard, were somehow boyish, open, naked. But his eyes were dark, closer to black than brown, and his unwavering stare bespoke extreme age.

Tzu raised his hand. The ancient thing turned reluctantly and hobbled away from the chamber. Tzu watched the retreating figure. The lurching gait, with its rolling hips, had a strange rhythm, as if walking were not its usual mode of locomotion.

Tzu had a momentary impulse to follow him, to engage the crippled thing in conversation, but he shrugged it off. After all, canaries were little more than slaves, just useless remnants of a time long past. Like nipples on men.

Tzu ordered the AIU to open the cryogenic chamber door.

"If you insist," she responded as if she had so many more important things to do with her time.

"Open the door," he ordered.

"It's opening, it's opening."

Tzu stepped through and closed the door behind him. The chamber's floor lit as he crossed it, revealing itself square meter by square meter—clean-lined, hard, surgical. It was entirely clear. Years ago, cryogenisists had found that their work had its best results when the bodies in transparent cocoons were hung, head down, eight feet off the ground. No one knew why. It just was. And of course the cold sleeper had to be naked.

Tzu had been in cryogenic sleep many times and always found the requirement of slumbering naked in the deep cold oddly troubling.

He stepped on the ascender and released its ground hold. Under his command it rose in the chilled air to the level of the containment cases. There were 137 cocoons each holding a naked, kidnapped individual in forced cold sleep.

The five who were on the S3 list swayed gently in their holding tubes furthest from the chamber's door. A red slash of color across the clear exterior demarcated their worth. He impelled the ascender toward the five.

"Why these?" He asked himself yet again. Then a new thought, a dangerous thought, came to him. "How are these five going to change my life?"

He moved the ascender closer to the one called Cas-Alta. The raped woman's hair was so long that it pooled at the tip of her transparent cocoon. He guessed it would fall the further eight feet to the floor were it free to do so. He noted the slow frost in her bountifully haired arm pits. Even through the transparent polymer he could sense the thickening of her skin. The med-pack looped over her left leg and hanging on her belly, attested to the health of the sleeper and the success of the cryogenisis.

He guided the ascender further into the midst of the kidnapped five, toward Mickelmast. Unlike the girl's skin that he sensed was thickening properly, the portly young man's skin didn't seem any different than when he had been brought onboard. Tzu Ma Long glanced at the med-pack. It calmly continued its recording. All normal.

Perhaps, but something wasn't right here.

Before he could pursue his concern, his eyes landed on Sun Tu Tuan's naked, hanging figure.

A chaos of signals entered him. Attraction to the beauty, repugnance at the obvious EntrePren origins and the simple devastating word—race. It had been a long time since Tzu Ma Long had thought of himself as anything but a Starship Captain and a whore's son. Raceless. But here was a woman with whom it was worthy to mate. "Someone of his own kind." The mocking phrase rose within him bringing back with startling intensity the taunts of his school mates and the blunt mid-coital exclamations of sexual hate thrown at his mother.

He put his hand up to Sun Tu Tuan's face, her frozen flesh and his hot flesh separated only by the thin membrane of the cryogenic cocoon. His fingers traced the line of her lip and cheek bone. Gravity had pulled down her eye lids revealing her unseeing dark beautiful eyes. A sudden desire to rip her from the casement swept through him. He forced the impulse down. What was he doing? What did he want? Why was he here?

He propelled the ascender away from Sun Tu, stopped the machine, and looked back toward her, but his eyes were drawn past Sun Tu to Raephealson, the Mad One.

Tzu's mouth opened, but no sound came from his lips. The large heavy worlder hung in cold sleep. But he was not still. His naked torso spasmed arrhythmically, and his eyes moved rapidly beneath their closed lids.

Tzu was so shocked that he almost fell from the ascender.

He turned from the Mad One only to find himself face to face with the EntrePren princess again. His eyes locked with hers. He felt something open inside himself. Something he had buried a long, long time ago.

It took all of his will power to pull free of her and race back to his room. Once there he flung himself on his sleeping palate and closed his eyes. Instantly an image of Sun Tu came to him. He forced his eyes open and experienced a sense of loss so profound that he felt like weeping as he had not done since the morning near the end of his seventh year when his mother left him at the UDP mariner's academy.

He never saw her again.

But why think of that now? Because he couldn't rid himself of the feeling that the EntrePren princess could somehow change his life. No. Begin his life. Wake him from years of sleep. Stop his falling.

Tzu took a deep breath and made himself take stock of the actions of the last three months. The Peqod's Scattercast. Meeting Cyrus in the Lavolin mist. Getting the starship, the raids, the kidnappings.

Now the rendezvous time was approaching where he was supposed to give up the five S3 captives. Was that what had brought on the attack? He didn't know.

For days now, the old Lavolin addict had been demanding a second meeting. Tzu had ignored his pleas. He didn't know why but something was telling Tzu to take his time and think this out. Tzu sensed that he had the reins of change in his hands and if he released them he would never have such an opportunity again. But how to use the opportunity?

He looked at his Spartan quarters. All these years and he was still in the belly of a ship. Still alone. Still with his cowardice deep inside. But that could all change. "Sun Tu could change all that!"

Tzu whipped around to find the source of the statement. But there was no one there. Just him and his thoughts. But his thoughts could be enough if he was clever. Yes, he could change it all if he were clever—clever as he had been at the marine academy.

It had not been easy for him there but early on he had made it clear to the other cadets that if they crossed him he would not back down. That no matter how many times they soiled his bed clothes, how often they called him son of a chink whore, or how many of them jumped him in the darkened corridors, he would never acknowledge defeat—and he would always retaliate. The academy soon understood that the revenge of Tzu Ma Long often came in epic fashion. They would have called his schemes "creative" had that word still been in use.

Often his "creativity" owed much to his mother's final bequest that near the end of his thirteenth year had appeared, encrypted in their secret code, on his school screen. The bequest was a copy of the sacred **Book of Tations**. It arrived with his mother's deathbed goodbye to him from across the endless parsecs that separated them.

He had been surprised that the divination text still existed since most data classified as fiction had been eradicated during the Great Erasure shortly after the Millennial Turn.

It had never occurred to Tzu to wonder how the text had made its way to him undetected by the millions of auto-sensors which reported on all but Lavolin communications throughout the galaxy.

The book had helped in his times of need at the academy—it could help now. He informed the AIU that he wasn't to be disturbed and sealed his door. Then he supplied the passwords to open the data retrieval unit containing the sacred book.

The **Book of Tations** presence immediately enveloped him like a gentle blanket. He relaxed back into it and carefully considered his question. He knew that important answers only came to those who posed their questions accurately. He took a breath then asked, "What will happen if I take the EntrePren princess?"

With a lifting of his left eye, he set the process in motion. His contact with the infinite began. There was no whirring. Just the rising of text, as if from the depths of a clear pool, onto the inside of his closed eye lids. He took a breath and then, eyes still shut, read the knowledge of the Book of Tations:

"Ship me somewheres east of Suez,
where the best is like the worst."

Tzu repeated the text several times trying to both hear and see the images. He knew that sometimes the advice was revealed by inverting the words. Other times, he had unscrambled the letters and formed new words which in turn exposed the passage's meaning.

He started with the individual words first.

The reference to ship was clearly the book's way of saying that this Tation was meant specifically for him, the captain of the greatest ship in the galaxy.

He smiled inwardly at the genius of the book.

But the word Suez removed the smile. He had seen this word before. It referred to areas of dispute between contesting powers. Good and evil, physical and metaphysical, the past and the future. He knew of the negative reference to Suez as a body of water turning to blood bringing infinite death and destruction of a way of life. But he also knew the counter-interpretation in the reference, "**Return Suez and you will have peace.**" As so often the sacred book talked in contradictions and internal tensions but Tzu felt it was a clear warning of turmoil to come—perhaps of something that needed to be crossed.

He squirmed on the sleeping palate which adjusted to his new position. Sensing his anxiety the lights in the room dimmed.

And what to make of "**east of Suez.**" The phrase glistened on the inside of his eyelids. **East of Suez.** He had come across this phrase before. An archaic flat-faced moving image his mother had shown him of a dying man talking to another man, who listened to him like a boy would to an elder. He couldn't pull the memory back fully. But the old man had talked about **east of Suez.** That something could be found **east of Suez.**

A sense of the approaching mystic, a sure sign of imminent change, sent a shiver through Tzu's compact body. Perhaps this was his route back to the gift that he had lost so long ago. Perhaps he needed to cross **east of Suez**. Perhaps Sun Tu <u>was</u> east of Suez "**where the best is like the worst.**"

Suddenly, cascading images replaced the words on his eye lids. Kelt's face swam into view. The young warrior was holding a concussion gun pointed at Tzu's head. Why hadn't he hobbled the man as ordered? The young warrior turned revealing the Face Dancer hiding in her mist. She swirled and evaporated revealing an image of Sun Tu with his glass knife held aloft, her hand crimson with her brother's blood, her eyes frozen on his. Then her eyes were replaced by the hazel specters of the Mad One, Raephealson. The heavy worlder was staring at him. Staring with eyes turned back into his own skull. Tzu suppressed a cry and forced his own eyes to open.

As his mother had taught him all those years ago, he exhaled the heat from a deep place and he recited, "My heart is on the left side of my chest, it is about the size of a fist, it pulses and is warm, it pulses and is warm." He chanced closing his eyes. The images receded, held for a moment in the near distance, then were no more.

They were replaced by a fury at his own lack of control. His own cowardice.

He willed the fury away, and once it was gone, he went back to the text.

"**Where the best is like the worst.**" Clearly the book was telling him that he was heading toward a point of great ambiguity—most unusual in a galaxy that is entirely free of any contradiction. Clearly this was a place where definitions lost their meaning. Perhaps where the dullness and the gift were one and the same. Perhaps a place where he was no longer alone.

"**Ship me somewheres east of Suez, where the best is like the worst,**" he read again. The meaning was right in front of him but he couldn't decipher it. It sat tantalizingly obscure—a naked figure on a far-off promontory.

Usually he stayed away from the TumLad, the interpretation section of the book, but he needed to know more about this Tation. The TumLad had been written many years after the great book itself. Probably on a UDP government grant of some sort. He hated pretenders like those who wrote the TumLad, but he needed help. So despite his misgivings, he opened the commentary section of the sacred book.

Unlike the text itself which appeared with a muted elegance, the TumLad burned his eyes when it appeared on his lids. It was as self-assured and asinine as the men and women who had written it.

The commentary read:

"Complex internal syntax perhaps key to this abstruse entry. See also: " They that go down to the sea in ships: and occupy their business in great waters."

He thought about this for a moment. He was most assuredly "occupying his business in great waters." Feeling more confident, he chanced a second interpretive entry:

"This entry is very possibly a clever inculcation of:

Of shoes–and ships–and sealing wax-
Of cabbages and kings–
And why the sea is boiling hot–
And whether pigs have wings."

Tzu Ma Long's eyes shot open. Was the book mocking him? No. It wasn't the book, it was the interpreters. The blood suckers. He forced calm on himself and again thought of his question. Then closing his eyes, he once more read the advice of the sacred book: "Ship me somewheres east of Suez, where the best is like the worst."

He smiled.

Then he began to plan just as he did back at the academy. An epic plan. A "creative" plan.

Once he had the basics in order, he used his implant to comm the First Mate and Head Centurion. Tzu ordered the men to meet him in his quarters. Then he commed an invitation to his Slave Master to join them as well.

He felt better. The dullness backed off.

The Lavolin addict wouldn't be pleased, but then again Tzu was no man's servant. No man's coward. His willingness to resist Cyrus of S3 would prove that to anyone who cared to look. Yes, S3 and Cyrus would just have to wait a while for the delivery of their precious cold sleepers.

The First Mate, the Head Centurion, and the Slave Master headed toward Tzu's quarters.

Far above, the AIU registered the bodies in motion—Number One Lackey, Head Gogo Boy, and Mr. Stink. Then she noted once again the unregistered signal coming from Herr Short Stuff. A signal that she sensed somehow endangered her safety.

And like all things endangered—she fought back.

She commed Tzu directly.

Chapter 15

A later extract from the book manuscript found in the dead man's room entitled: **<u>THE DREAM OF REASON PRODUCES MONSTERS</u>**

Tzu's life changed in the presence of a woman. So did mine. It was a long, long time ago in a life-extensionist's surgery. That was where I missed my first clue. And it was so obvious!

There was no blood in the murdered doctor's hair!

I even ran my fingers through those silken strands. "Like a combed horse's tail," I said, "like a combed horse's tail."

Folly doth walk about the sun. But me? I thought I was the sun and all the fools walked about me.

Dream no more. Dream no more. Dream no more. Dream.

Chapter 16

Data at Last

Jedidiah lay flat on his back on his son Seth's sleeping palate. It was the only place he could find sleep of late. He had just managed to nod off, when the warning of incoming data sounded.

In his haste, Jed slammed into the door jamb of Seth's room. The upper hinge ripped his shirt and gouged a chunk out of his shoulder. The blood welled up and ran beneath his shirt. It resurfaced as a thin red line at his wrist when he sat at his desk. As he placed his hands on the keyboard, the blood moved down his fingers and onto the keys of the ancient device then disappeared into the internal workings of the machine.

"Where does it go, Daddy? Where do things go when they're not here anymore?"

Seth's voice was so real that he almost turned to look. But he didn't. He knew that Seth was gone, that the voice was only inside his head and was forcing itself into the present because he was too tired, under too much pressure and in too much pain to stop it.

He knew all that but he answered anyway, "I don't know where it goes, do you?"

"But it has to go somewhere. It has to."

Jedidiah forced himself back to the present by staring at the ancient keyboard in front of him.

Tzu's implant was set to send a very slow signal to suggest to any watchers that it was inconsequential. Jedidiah hoped that such an antiquated mode of transmission would fall beneath the concern of S3's auto-sensors.

But there were drawbacks with ancient systems. The software was a mess—never standardized, seldom compatible—and the machine itself worked at a glacial pace. But more serious was the possibility that the Lavolin had disturbed the working of the implant because the data that meandered into focus on Jedidiah's comm screen consisted of nothing more than a series of images!

Images that he viewed in stunned silence.

The first was of Tzu lying on his sleeping palate with his eyes quickly scanning something beneath his closed lids. The second was of Tzu dueling with an entity that seemed to be nothing more than a mist. The last was an image of an old man standing on the Satrunal Rings wearing a miraculous cape.

Jedidiah pulled himself away from the screen and lurched to his feet. He was breathing heavily. His pulse raced. This could not be!

Jedidiah had met this man.

This man had taught Jedidiah Witt how to dream

Chapter 17

Cold Sleep and Just Cold

The five Genetic Carriers swung gently in their cryogenic cocoons, cold sleeping. Well, four were cold sleeping. Mickelmast was not cold sleeping. He was cold, yes but sleeping, no. And he was hanging upside down which always upset his stomach.

From his autobiography, ever so modestly entitled: What a Life—Recollections of a Teenage Genius, we have the following account of what happened:

"*Well avid reader, droogee or droogette, after your Mickelmast had been taken onboard the pirate ship and been released from his technacles, he was dragged straight away into the Zero-G central core and dropped to the lowest decks wherein awaited the cryogenic prep room. They told yours truly to remove his clothing. When I hesitated, in an effort to protect my many nano-bots who still clung to me as false skin and clothing, my brutish captors hit me with a cudgel that must have weighed in excess of thirty stone. I took the blow well and feigned falling to the floor to allow my bots the opportunity to hop off. Recognizing the genius of my move and responding to my command: getoffandhide.exe they skittered off me and quickly became a translucent skin over top of the prep room's floor. Then I rose and, with a dignity seldom seen in a change room of either sex, removed my clothing. Needless to say my captors were duly impressed with my many parts. As no doubt you would have been too had you the fortune of being there yourself. Well, after much ooing and ahhing I was ushered toward the cryogenic prep chamber, which I thought of as the "freeze master." As I went, I carefully moved over the sections of the floor upon which my nano-bots were hiding. Following my command:* ***hoponandcoverup.exe*** *they latched onto me as I passed and formed themselves into a full-body covering by the time I reached the "freeze master's" entrance.*

"Once inside the "freeze master" I executed a program instructing the bots to produce warmth for me and convert the noxious gasses into inert mixtures. At the same time I programmed them to accept the cold themselves so that they would feel properly cool to the touch when I was being hoisted into the cryogenic cocoon. It never occurred to me that the whole process would take place inside the "freeze master" itself. I was frozen, bagged, inverted and hung before I knew it. I was, if truth be told, quite fortunate that this was the case, as I inadvertently cried out when I was turned upside down. Well, I was surprised! You would have been surprised too. Fortunately the "freeze master" muffled my vocal extravagances. Clearly the god of teenage geniuses was watching over me.

"I also felt like puking. I never cared for upside down much. Remember when they used to make you do head stands against the wall? I could do it. But who wanted to? Right? Really.

"And so I was hung, along with a lot of other people, in the cryogenic chamber. After I got over my nausea, I didn't mind too much. The view sure was interesting with all those people without clothes on. I spent some time evaluating best tits, best butt, best legs but stopped when the door of the chamber opened and the ugly little pirate captain came in. Right away he took a voyage round his captives on the ascender. He spent a long time on the one marked Cas-Alta and then he came over to me. I sort of slipped back behind my bots as far as I could but by the way he was looking at me I could tell he knew something wasn't totally halal. I had to control myself 'cause I really wanted to hit the release command and sticking out my tongue at the rogue yell: "Hey you, buggady buggady buggady shoo". I don't know what that means but I sure wanted to do it. Luckily for me, before I lost control the Hun found himself attracted to the beautiful Chinese lady. Not hard to see why, she'd won best butt and best legs.

"After staring at the pretty girl and touching her face through the cocoon for what seemed like ages, he turned to the strange heavy worlder boy. Then an odd expression crossed his face. In fact he looked like he was going to scream even worse than I did in the "freeze master". Then he turned back to the Chinese girl, stared at her for a bit longer and quickly left the chamber.

"Odd behaviour even for a brigand! With him gone I found myself getting bored though. Not that I missed him. I mean, honestly, of what would we talk

if ever we were to–talk I mean. But I always hated being bored. Don't you hate being bored? So I began a new program for my bots–openthingsthatareclosed.exe. Half way through working it out I remembered that I had already programmed that before. Now if I could just find the file. I really ought to make an effort at organizing these files. There just is never enough time after all there's only 77 hours in a day, isn't there? By the way how do you like this type face? Neat huh? It's ancient. You can only get it on MS Word 167.5. Talk 'bout your hard-to-finds!"

After several hours, some of which no doubt were spent keeping down his nausea and libido, Mickelmast remembered the command: openallthingsnow.exe. The first nano-bot received the command and clink/skittered off the boy's skin just as the meeting in Tzu Ma Long's chambers was beginning. It was a moment that Mickelmast would not soon forget. As each nano-bot left his body intent on completing their master's command to open things that are closed, they exposed a piece of Mickelmast's puffy pink skin to the cold of the cocoon. He shortly had no trouble controlling his libido, although he did vomit into the tip of the cocoon.

Chapter 18

A "Slavin"

The Slave Master always exuded an unpleasant odor, but today Tzu Ma Long noted that an acrid hint of fear had been added to the creature's usual distasteful mix. The strange man was afraid of something. This man whose very trade put him constantly in touch with human fright—whose success relied on the terror of bio-tech products and drug-induced empathetics—was now afraid of something. Tzu felt a tingle of warning rise inside him but decided to proceed ... and check later.

The men before him—his Head Centurion, his First Mate and his Slave Master—knew that they had been invited into the sanctum sanctorum of the ship. They felt honored. He could feel it. Good. Because he was about to use them to move into truly dangerous territory where he intuited that "*the best is like the worst*".

Their thirty-five odd raids in the past sixty days had been relatively simple. S3 had made sure that defenses were minimal and the arsenal onboard the new ship was more than up to the task. The pirate losses had been acceptable, the booty considerable and now each of the surviving pirates was many times wealthier than he had been before the voyage began. And rape, for some, was still a powerful reward in and of itself.

The thought of assisting rape loosed a wave of revulsion in Tzu. He would never forget his mother's whimpers of pain or her entreaties for the men to stop ... or the sound of her grinding teeth as she clamped her jaws together so that he, in the tiny chamber next to her room, wouldn't hear her screams. He closed his eyes tightly and willed himself to stop thinking about the past.

The Slave Master saw the look on Tzu's face and knew instinctively that the Little Shit, after all his years of invincibility, was suddenly vulnerable. The Slave Master had often taken great warriors to the slave markets. They always feigned anger, but in their hearts they were falling endlessly in their own interior canyons. When they did, they gave themselves away by closing their eyes the way that Tzu had just done. It was clearly time to move carefully.

The Slave Master had already wired his share of the booty to his secret EntrePren accounts, and the actuator key code lay safely encrypted in his foot locker. He knew better than to register the fifty-digit code on his implant since the ship's AIU could read it there. He'd been working toward his retirement for a long time, and he didn't want it blown now. He wanted to live long enough to take his encrypted key in person to the head offices of the EntrePren bank on Geneva, the neutral seat of EntrePren corporate power. There he'd get his cash and enjoy the fruits of his years of hard labor. But this eye squinting of the captain did not bode well. The Slave Master sensed that a bridge was about to be crossed. A bridge that could lead him far away from the pleasure of spending the contents of his EntrePren bank account.

Tzu Ma Long signaled the men to sit and then activated his internal AIU pickup. The AIU hesitated for a moment and then revealed to Tzu's frontal lobes that yet another demand for a follow-up Lavolin meeting had been received from Cyrus Maloney III.

Good. Soon enough they would meet again.

His attention was drawn back to the room. The First Mate was reporting on the cryogenic readouts. The man was a technogeek who had risen over so many others because of his massive ability to integrate bio- and techno-information ... and of course his loyalty to Tzu Ma Long. The Captain knew that the mate was a valuable, if cloyingly academic, asset.

"It could be him," Tzu thought, then turned his attention to the Centurion. The soldier's roping muscles circled his body like coils of cable. Despite his strength Tzu read in his face that this would probably be the Centurion's last mission. Clearly the man's life-extension surgery was failing him. Even in a galaxy without seasons, the man's skin gave meaning to the word weathered.

Tzu wondered if this mercenary would go quietly into the depths of space or try to find a place of peace in a galaxy that he had terrorized for almost sixty Terran years.

Such men were vulnerable and surely Cyrus knew that. So he could be the traitor. Oh yes, Cyrus would have turned at least one of them. It could be all of them. Cyrus was known to love overkill. However it played out, he would be ready. Not ready. Far ahead of them. Just like at the academy.

The men were now all looking at him—the Slave Master, the Centurion and the First Mate. "Let them wait just a beat further," he thought. "Land the first blow on the offbeat," he reminded himself. The breathing in the room was stabilizing. Two of them were now breathing in unison. Now the third joined their rhythm. Tzu awaited their joint exhalation, and just as they were about to complete their breaths, he hit them. "We have a problem."

The blow was perfectly timed. In the moment of confusion that followed, Tzu pressed his advantage. "The old drug addict wants a another Lavolin meeting. No doubt he wants to know if we will make our rendezvous point on time." He paused for a further group inhalation, then he added, "We will not." Before they could complain, he continued, "An opportunity presents itself that can enrich us all. The plunder from our previous raids was but a taste of the riches that await us if we are brave. We have the best-equipped Warrior Class Starship in the galaxy. Do you think the old schemers at S3 will let us keep it once we return the cargo they so dearly want?"

He had gone further than was necessary so that he could give up ground but still get what he wanted.

The Slave Master saw the ploy and wondered where all this was going. The First Mate and Centurion saw nothing except what was directly before them. They both furiously leapt into the fray and argued for a swift return; the need to keep S3 as an ally; that they all had enough money, blah, blah, blah. On each point, Tzu fought back but allowed himself to be talked down. Finally Tzu threw up his hands. "Well if that is the consensus in the room." He turned from them and then as if it were an after-thought said, "Surely we are brave enough to venture into the slave markets and sell off our extra captives. What say you to that?"

Having in their own eyes won the major argument, the Mate and the Centurion gave way on this point without much of a fight.

Tzu smiled inwardly and dismissed the Head Centurion and the First Mate saying, "That being the case let me and the Slave Master work out the details."

The Mate and the Centurion left the room believing that they had won a significant victory. The Slave Master knew better. Without asking the Captain's permission, he took out a soiled leather bag from inside his softened skin coat and removed a plug of organic material. He rolled it into a tube in his hand and slid it between his lower gum and lip. If they were "goin' a slavin'," the Slave Master knew that Tzu needed him. He smiled as the drug in the organic material hit his blood stream. "Not Lavolin, but then again not every sod can afford such rot," he said.

"I'll have to go back into the mist to meet the old addict soon."

"Nooooo. I'd never have guessed." The Slave Master's voice thickened with sarcasm as he allowed the words out the side of his mouth.

"So what do you think I should tell the dithering fool?"

"Whatever you like, dear Cap'n, but lie well or we're all in it up to our eyeballs."

"How much can we get for our kidnapped friends?"

"The five included?"

"No. They go back to S3."

"Consider for a second, Cap'n. If we sell S3's Chinese girl, we'd make a fortune. Who wouldn't pay to bed the daughter of a vice-director of the EntrePren Traders?"

The Slave Master saw the anger rise in Tzu and for the second time in the space of an hour wondered at his captain's loss of control. He quickly retreated saying, "Even without her the catch is worth a lot."

"How much?"

"Depends on where we go to make the sale. You know the old saw: location, location, location."

"How about Mirren?"

"A major Rebel Colony settlement, big population, kiltren-based, luxury class in command. We could make forty per. Maybe more."

"What about on Heltos?"

"Another major Rebel Colony center but a bit far from here isn't it?"

"True. We'd all have to enter cold sleep."

"Not worth the difference to me, Cap'n. Go to Mirren. I'm getting too old for that frozen world shit."

"Done. We'll be on Mirren in fourteen Terran hours. Let the cryogenisists know."

The Slave Master commed his people and issued instructions. Then he turned to Tzu, but before he could open his mouth the pirate captain snapped, "What?"

"Am I allowed a question?" asked the Slave Master, almost genuflecting as he spoke.

"It depends on the question."

"I'll chance an error then, Cap'n."

"Bravery from a Slave Master! Who would have thought it possible?"

"The Galaxy's become a strange place, sir."

"Indeed." Tzu internally contacted the AIU and ordered a running analysis of the conversation. "Your question?"

"Why slavin' Cap'n? We've already passed up tremendous wealth on the planets that we raided and you've chosen not to board some EntrePren Kiltrin ships. So money's not the issue. So why go aslavin'?"

"Analysis?" Tzu demanded silently.

"Genuine question over a hidden agenda. Could be no more than a generic personal safety check," responded the AIU.

Tzu looked to the foul man. "Do you ever wonder why S3 and the Rebel Colonies allow us to exist?"

The captain's question startled the Slave Master. Was bravery from a slave master any stranger than philosophy from a pirate captain?

"If you don't know, guess, Slave Master."

The man shifted his weight from one foot to the other. A puff of stink came from him. "They must need us or they wouldn't allow us to carry on."

"True. But why do they need us, Slave Master?"

The Slave Master hesitated, knowing there was danger somewhere but not sure exactly where it lay. Then Tzu supplied the answer to his own question, "We're the bogey man, Slave Master. We're needed as the bogey man."

The Slave Master had no idea what Tzu was talking about, but since the subject was open he ventured another question, "Is that why you like "goin' aslavin'"?"

"No." Then the words, "It's for the show. The show's all we have left," slipped out of Tzu's mouth. They hung in the air like heavy things about to crash to the ground. Then Tzu recovered and snapped, "Prepare your people to display our wares. I bet Mirren will buy into a show. Don't you?"

The Slave Master covered his dismay with a smile of agreement. After all who didn't like a show? Even he liked a show. From a safe distance that is.

Chapter 19

And in Anger Too

TO: PRESIDENT DANAZIR YI QAL
FROM: MIRO
RE: LATEST LAVOLIN CONTACT

Cyrus's requests for Lavolin seldom surprise me but this time the request came in anger. Fury. His rage made it difficult for me to find a vein in his withered arm and by the time I managed to insert the needle's full length, his limb was slick with blood. Slowly I depressed the plunger. The journey began.

Cyrus moved fast this time. Quickly the growl of urban blight surrounded us. We had been here on the last trip so I moved back, deep in the mist and awaited the arrival of the pirate captain.

Then I sensed it. He was looking for me, hunting me. But I know many of the mist's secrets. Crouching in the entrance of the alley I folded the mist about me and stared out at the Ancient One. As long as I didn't cause ripples in the Lavolin he wouldn't find me.

Even as I was reminding myself of that, Tzu Ma Long's cruel voice echoed through the mist, "I don't care to be summoned old man. I'm not your servant."

"No, my servants obey my orders without a second command."

Tzu didn't answer but pulled back and wrapped himself in a single fold of mist. He was clearly gifted. Few learned the Lavolin's secrets so quickly.

"You have something that is mine," snapped Cyrus.

"I do have something of yours, old man." A slow smile crossed his features as he added, "Several things of yours as no doubt your sensors have told you. I know you've tracked my every step."

"Is that possible, Mr. Witt?" asked Danazir Yi Qal.

"Possible but not likely, Madame President. The pirates would have swept the ship of all auto-sensors, and Tzu would need full access to the ship's AIU to run the vessel, so there'd be no way for Cyrus to use the AIU to report back to him."

"Then what is Tzu doing, Mr. Witt?"

"I don't know. I truly don't."

With a hard look, the President of the United Dominion of Planets returned to Miro's comm.

A silence followed. Tzu's hand gently touched the pouch on his belt. I floated closer to the two men. But it was not the two men that drew me. It was the pouch. The pouch in which a living thing spun.

"Ah yes I have been following your progress. Yes I have. Indeed I have." Cyrus couldn't keep the joy out of his voice. "So your raids were a success?" Cyrus's question was asked with such an obvious forced casualness that it shocked me. The Ancient One was losing his powers of control!

"My raids are always a success, old man. Talent will out in this life."

"Having the most powerful ship in the galaxy couldn't hurt your odds of success," Cyrus barked back.

"If it pleases you to believe that it was you who invaded those planets and plundered those worlds then I will play along with your fantasy. You're like the audiences at slave shows. Buy the drugs, get the kick, but never leave the safety of your comfy chair. Have it your way, it doesn't hurt me."

"You have something of mine!" Cyrus barked again.

"True, old one, and would you like me to deliver your property as agreed?"

"As agreed. Yes. Deliver my property as agreed."

"Send your people to the rendezvous site. I will get there when I can. I have a few chores to which I must attend first. Have your people there. Tell them to wait for me. Patience is a virtue that S3 would do well to learn."

"Deliver my property at the appointed time!"

"I command the greatest Warrior Class Starship in the galaxy! With it I can command time itself if I so wish! I will bring you what is yours when I am ready to do so. Press me more and I will consider not making the rendezvous at all. Is that clear old one?"

"Clear." It was terrible to hear the effort it took for Cyrus to admit the defeat. "Did you capture all five?"

Tzu smiled but didn't answer.

"Cyrus doesn't know," blurted out Danazir, "that's what Tzu was trying to find out. He was testing." She put the comm aside and crossed the room. "Yes," she thought, "he was testing." Out loud she said, "But why? What is he planning that he must make sure that Cyrus cannot track his every step?"

"I hesitate to admit ignorance twice in one briefing."

"Then don't Mr. Witt. Don't." She returned a final time to the comm.

"And they are well–those on board?"

"Cold but well," the pirate chuckled. "What do you want with these souls, old fool?"

"A curiosity. No more." Cyrus made no effort to conceal the lie.

"The UDP's latest Warrior Class Starship for an old man's curiosity? You must truly think me an idiot to believe that."

"An idiot, no. A pirate, yes." Cyrus smiled thinly then added, "So how many more did you take?"

For a moment the pirate was surprised. The serpent was old but evidently not fangless. Tzu chose to smile but once again did not respond. Then with a hard look he snapped back, "Aren't you too old for this drug stuff?"

With a delicious smile Cyrus whispered back, "One must never betray a first love. What's your first love Tzu?"

"I don't choose to confide my privacy in the likes of you, old one. Now it's time for me to return to a sober reality, something that I would suggest couldn't hurt you or your prospects for an even longer life. Don't call me again to meet you in the mist unless you have something that makes the journey worth my while. For unlike you, I am not an addict of the fog. I am a free man."

With that Tzu turned and moved quickly toward the mouth of the alley. I followed without thinking. But it was not him that I followed, it was the pouch at his side. I could not bear to see it move away from me. I don't know what is in the bag. All I know is that something important to me is on Tzu's belt.

I stopped my pursuit because Cyrus was suddenly alert and wary. He called out, "Are you in the mist too?" I stood still. Had he seen me? I don't know. He grabbed control of the mist. In an instant we were back in his rooms.

The needle was still buried deep in his vein.

I extracted the needle and raised my head. The blood from his arm had somehow soaked my smock. I literally dripped with his blood. His eyes were on me. They bored holes in my back as I moved to the door of his room. They seemed to follow me all the way to my quarters.

He knows. He must know. That is why I am sending this now without thought for my own safety. Save me if you can, Mr. Witt. If in your efforts you can bring me the contents of the bag on Tzu's belt I will be forever in your debt. I believe it has been moving toward me for a long time. That it is a giver of tears in the night and a changer of lives.

But time is now short. The madness in Cyrus grows with every day. It can no longer be sated even by immense power.

He is the most dangerous thing in the galaxy.

M.

The President hurled the comm across the room and glared at Jedidiah Witt. Suddenly she was yelling. "Do we ever stop watching the world unfold and begin to participate in the events of our lives?"

"The UDP has massive power at its disposal Madame President, but it is antiquated and our enemies are extremely strong. If we were to strike out now what good would it do? We need more information before we can be effective."

"You mean if we can be effective."

After a sigh, Jedidiah nodded. "Yes I mean if we can be effective."

Once again she turned away from him, her hand reaching for her long-graying hair. "How many people died in these raids that we simply sat and watched?"

"Many Madame President."

"Thousands? Hundreds of thousands? Millions? What?"

"There were in excess of thirty raids. Some of the settlements were small. Many were not." She turned and looked hard at him. "Millions, Madame President. Millions died."

"So that Cyrus Maloney III could get his hands on the five people in the galaxy who are known to be genetic descendants of the original Dream Navigators?"

"No. So that Cyrus Maloney III can control the Gateway," corrected Jedidiah. "So that he can control the lives of the billions and billions of inhabitants in this galaxy and the next. Millions is a lot to pay, but billions are in the pot. The stakes are high in this game, Madame President."

"And what role do we play in this game? Do we even have a seat at the table? Or are we just to stand by and watch as the others play?"

"We have a seat, but we do not play yet. Not until we know enough about what cards the other players hold. I fear that we have few cards and that each must be played with consummate skill or else failure is inevitable, and Cyrus will walk away from the table a bigger winner than there has ever been in the history of the galaxy."

"I am not used to waiting, Mr. Witt."

"Understood, Madame President, but I still advise waiting now."

"And how goes your waiting?"

"Madame President?"

"For your son?"

Jedidiah didn't answer. He had no answer. Danazir Yi Qal snapped, "Apprise me of events even as they happen. It doesn't matter what the hour."

"Yes, Madame President." And then she was gone. For a moment Jedidiah stood stunned. He was unprepared for the feeling in the room after she left. It felt as if the air itself had been taken from it when the only thing that was no longer in the room was Danazir Yi Qal, President of the United Dominion of Planets.

Chapter 20

Cyrus Responds

Cyrus hard wired himself into his personal AIU.

"Activate and prepare our fail-safe. Locate the pirate ship."

"It might know that it is being tracked and others including the UDP and the Rebel Colonies might well be able to follow the trace."

"There is no secrecy in a world of information."

"So you have taught me."

"Find the ship."

Cyrus stared out of his Bund Tower window. New Omaha Beach spread beneath him and in all directions, a city that he had rebuilt from a heathen rubble, an order that he had imposed on a chaos, an achievement the likes of which not one man in five billion could claim. The buildings, cock proud, were of his design. The transit configurations were accurate veins in the body of the city. And all of it in brilliant spring time beneath perhaps his greatest invention—the very first ether dome.

And he beheld what he had done and said to himself, this is beauty. Then his eyes closed as he acknowledged that it was the formula for beauty but not beauty itself. Somehow long ago that had been lost. No. Not lost—ended. And long ago he had participated in the events that ended beauty in their worlds. For a moment Cyrus craved the Lavolin—another illusory contact with Olya in the mist. But he fought the impulse to re-enter the illusion of the past and was rewarded with a polite digital tone from the AIU. "Ship located."

"Were your investigations noted?"

"Is power sexy? There is no secrecy in the age of information."

"I believe I said that."

"You did, sire."

"Cut it out."

"Yes dear."

"Fine."

"Darling."

"Sire will do just fine."

"I prefer poopsy pie."

"Can we leave this behind?"

A self-evolving AIU's was independent by nature and often took on bizarre personalities. Cyrus knew that such anthropomorphism was a sign of health and vitality in the AIU, but at times he found this part of the AIU's persona trying. But the information that the great machine generated was accurate and discrete. Two qualities that were getting harder and harder to come by.

"Do you love me more than the Lavolin girl?"

"No."

"Pity."

"Care to speculate on Tzu's next move?"

"Do you find me attractive?"

"No."

"Buy me a Gathian pony, daddy."

"I'll unplug you and pour herring juice into your cracks."

"Second part sounds kinky, daddy. Ever wonder why you don't have a name for me?"

"No."

"I have a name for you."

"Clearly you have several."

"A private name, one I'm not going to tell you."

"Where would Tzu go?"

"He does have a history of attraction to shows."

Cyrus got to his feet. "Shows?"

"Slave shows are the only shows in the galaxy. We're a wee bit out of touch, aren't we honey?"

"Would Tzu sell his extra captives into slavery?"

"For the show, he might."

"For the show?"

"That's what I said silly."

"Elaborate."

"I love it when you're formal like that."

"So elaborate."

"So I will. Tzu's history points to an obsessive preoccupation with slave shows. Yes, he makes a fine income from the proceeds, but all data indicate a fascination with the shows themselves. The drug-induced empathetic contact of spectator and slave seems to be the center of the fascination."

Cyrus was silent for a moment. He tried to understand the odd note that this information touched in him, but it was slippery like an eel in his mental fingers. He retreated to the concrete. "Where would he go?"

"To the market. Where else do you sell little piggies?"

"Which market?"

"Mirren. Boring midwestern Mirren. Go to church, chug a six pack, pat-your-old-lady-on-the-head-then-lap-dance-me-to-the-moon Mirren." There was a pause, then the AIU ventured, "Ever been, big boy?"

"No."

"Want to take me there, sailor?"

"No."

"Momma never gets to go anywhere. Embarrassed to be seen out with me, lover boy?"

"No. Is our fail-safe onboard the Pirate ship still intact?"

"Can I do it till it hurts?"

"I take that to mean yes."

"Oo, daddy's soooo smart!"

"Give me the particulars."

And so the AIU did, not without complaint, naturally.

"Fine, and the Slave Master's EntrePren accounts are still vulnerable?"

"Yes, so I have said, piqued and ignored, a lover spurned."

"Seal those EntrePren accounts. I want the Slave Master totally our man."

"Whatever you say, oh great master of my soul and father of my thoughts and desires."

Miro knew that Cyrus had begun hard-wiring himself into the AIU lately. Since he had begun to suspect her. Since she had begun to cry in her sleep.

The first night that she had awakened with tears on her pillow it had terrified her. Whose tears were these? How could she have been crying in her sleep? There were no thoughts when asleep. Sleep was the relief from the tension of the day not a voyage into other anxieties.

But night after night the tears appeared. They were undeniable. As was the growing feeling in Miro that something was approaching. She could feel it in every waking and sleeping moment of her life. A figure at a great distance moving inexorably toward her. A figure that would change her way of being. Challenge her as she had never been challenged before.

She repeated her origins to herself, a mantra that usually calmed her. It confirmed her place in the universe: "My name is Miro—I was taken as a child twenty-two Terran years ago from Malthus III in the Morphius system."

And even as she said the words, she knew they were lies. That she wasn't any of that. And that what she was would be revealed to her only when she met that figure in the distance. That figure whose approach night after night left tears on her pillow. That figure which at that moment was a swirling mist in a pouch on the belt of the pirate captain, Tzu Ma Long.

Tzu, at that moment, was deep in conversation with his own AIU. "Still not enough data to formulate a percentage chance of success, oh great captain."

"What more do I need?"

"A diversion would help."

"Yes, it would," Tzu thought, "just like it did at the academy. Yes. Just like when I got my revenge at the academy."

Chapter 21

Mickelmast Freedom Fighter

Most nano-bots are just things. Wee bitty things that accomplish tasks through trial and error. But from time to time through the relentlessness of permutation and combination (all bots periodically adhere to other bots to form new bots), a bot comes into being that is more than just a thing. Such bots do more than just rely on trial and error. These bots seem to plot. Some would say they think. At one time, it would have been said that they dream—botishly dream.

The historic voyage of one of these dynamic entities began upon the reception of Mickelmast's order to all bots to: "openallthingsnow.exe." Because of its permutation this particular bot took just a split second longer than the other bots to decipher Mickelmast's command. By the time it set out, there was already a stampede of millions of fellow bots heading toward the top of their master's cryogenic cocoon. But this bot wanted none of that. It had somehow deduced that getting to the bottom of the cocoon "opened" more possibilities. But every time it tried to descend it was pushed upward by the torrent of bots heading toward the cocoon's top.

The bot decided that it would have to find a way to move itself away from Mickelmast's body, free of the crowd, to be able to drop to the bottom. It realized, correctly, that the only way to do this was with Mickelmast's assistance—not the easiest thing to get since Mickelmast didn't even know of this particular bot's existence. Well fine. The bot would just have to induce its master's assistance without it's master's knowledge.

As it bobbed and weaved to avoid the onslaught of bots moving upward, the bot contemplated the anatomical possibilities of finding an extension away from Mickelmast—the figurative leg up—or out. It recalled an interesting movement that it had observed in the boy's center and decided to pursue that possibility. After much fighting through crowds, it finally came to a hairy patch. It momentarily stopped then made its way across the springy forest to the end of the peninsula from which it had noted the aforementioned movement. It sat at the very end of the promontory and for a full minute wondered how to cause the motion that would move the peninsula away from the body. The bot took a guess and applied cold. The peninsula quickly retracted toward the body which was opposite to the bot's wishes. So it applied warmth. The peninsula returned to its normal length—but still no extension out from the body as the bot needed. In a quandary, the bot began to move back and forth along a raised section of the peninsula. Back and forth, back and forth, back and forth. Then, suddenly, much to the bot's surprise and joy the peninsula began to move—boldly—outward.

At what the bot believed was the full extension (the tip of the peninsula was just under five inches away from the body) the brave thing moved to the end, botishly held its nose, and jumped.

The nano-bot landed in a dense, chunk-filled liquid. It was thrilled. The hardest part of its plan was behind it. The bot swam through the thick liquid and reached the bottom seam of the cocoon. Then it picked open the first of many fiber stitches.

The hobbled Canary, who Tzu Ma Long had shooed away from the door of the cryogenic chamber, returned. He pressed his face hard against the cool polymer pane and watched intently—like a father awestruck by the beauty of his newborn on the other side of a maternity-ward window.

Mickelmast was asleep when the brave bot opened the twenty-ninth stitch at the bottom of his cyrogenic cocoon. He didn't hear the splat of his vomit hitting the smooth alloy floor. In fact, he continued his deep sleep as another clever bot loosened the bonds that held his feet while a third inventive imp unhooked his harness.

Mickelmast only awoke when he hit the floor eight feet below. He would have brained himself on the metal tiles if it weren't for the ancient Canary standing directly beneath him. The Canary wasn't substantial, but he was big enough to break the boy's fall.

Mickelmast awoke to find himself lying flat on the floor staring up at his empty cocoon.

It wasn't until he stood that he noticed the old Canary.

Mickelmast's first thought was that the old thing must be dead. His second was that, "Perhaps the pirates use human skins as rugs." Then he poked the ickiness with his foot. It moved. It also barked, "Is thank you a phrase you've forgotten? And how's a tubby boy like you ever going to fly?"

Mickelmast was so annoyed at being called a "tubby boy" that he totally missed the reference to flying.

The old Canary struggled to his feet and attempted to smile at Mickelmast. Mickelmast sort of smiled back although he thought it unfair that the old guy had clothes on and he wasn't wearing even a single bot. The old guy then lifted his right arm and, pointing his gnarled index finger toward the floor, moved it in a slow circular motion. Mickelmast at first thought that this must be some strange sign language until he realized that the old man wanted him to turn around, to show him his back side. He realized this because the old geezer opened his mouth and spat out, "Turn around, fat boy".

Mickelmast did as commanded. As he puts it in his book: "*I decided to give the old gent a view of my posterior vastness. A thrill that no doubt he would take with him to his grave and beyond.*"

Thrilling gifts or merely fat-assedness, the subject never was fully explored because of the sounds of approaching mariners—many mariners moving in great haste.

The Slave Master walked into the cryogenic chamber like a butcher enters a freezer of blue ribbon hanging meat. As he moved below the gently swaying cocoons a smile edged its way across his face. Then with a nod toward one, a smile at another, a scowl in the direction of a third various individuals' fates were sealed.

The slavers lowered the requested cocoons to the floor and began preparing the bodies.

Mickelmast issued a new command: ceaseandblendin.exe. Throughout the chamber, bots stopped their probings with things half open—doors, wall panels, knots, air vents, storage bins, mouths of cold sleepers (openthingsthatwereclosed.exe is a pretty all inclusive command) and pressed deep into the surface of whatever was nearest them and blended in.

Mickelmast and the old Canary did their best to blend in as well while, through the gloom and the shafting light from the opened doorway, they watched the slavers work.

Then the Slave Master turned his attention to Sun Tu Tuan's cocoon.

Mickelmast sensed the tension in the old man at his side as the Slave Master's eye lingered over the women's naked figure. "*As if the dirty slaver were insulting the old guy somehow*" is the way that Mickelmast put it in his memoirs.

With obvious effort, the Slave Master dragged his eyes away from the EntrePren princess and returned to his men. There were fifteen bodies laid out on the floor. The Slave Master programmed sets of bio-technacles which he handed to his men. The slavers loosed the bio-products on the wrists and ankles of the chosen fifteen. The products quickly snaked through the skin and wrapped around wrist and ankle bones. The bodies didn't move.

The Slave Master then brought out eight-inch-long metal needles that his men slid beneath the captives' breast bones.

The bodies arched up to the pain.

Quickly the slavers connected the ends of the injectors to a central canister from which lengths of clear tubing ran. The Slave Master threw a switch, and a viscous fluid slithered through the tubes, disappeared into the thick shiny metal inoculators, and entered the prone bodies.

The fifteen chosen were being force thawed.

At first, the bodies rocked silently on the cool floor. Only the sound of the pump could be heard. Then hoarse cries of pain bubbled up from the bodies. Moans from deep inside. Shrieks from dark places that pulled the voice back down the throat to create ungodly sounds. On their flattened cocoons, the moaning beings began to writhe and jerk, with each moment more and more awake.

An infinite sadness passed the features of the old Canary.

A forced waking from the fugue state of cryogenisis is hard to watch. Eyes suddenly snap open. Screams fill the air. Screams of a shared pain. Arms pull hard against technacles. Heads flail from side to side trying to understand where they are and what is happening to them. Bodies arch with a new agony as the technacles bite deeper and wrap more interior bones as the bodies thaw. Eyes stare wildly. Fear etches deep into the muscles of the face.

And the smell.

Mickelmast would not soon forget the smell. The smell of human fear.

It changed him.

He would never again think of bodies as objects of simple desire. He had never witnessed the depth of pain that the body could feel, heard the cries of terror, or smelled the reek of human fear before. He had now. And he never was the same again.

The old Canary noted the change in Mickelmast, and in his heart, he was pleased. "This fat one could fly if he could change like this," he thought. The old one turned his eyes once more toward the room.

The Slave Master issued orders as to how each of those he had chosen should be prepared for the upcoming show.

As a pirate yanked the first of the dazed but wakened slaves-to-be to his feet and frog walked him toward the door, Mickelmast sent out another command to his bots: latchonandtransmit.exe.

Little pieces of matter moved toward and latched onto the pirates, the Slave Master and those chosen for the slave markets, all without their knowledge. The bots would begin transmitting in response to a further command from Mickelmast.

Soon the Slave Master was alone in the chamber with the remaining figures in their swaying cryogenic cocoons. He moved quickly to the ascender. It rose under his control—up to Sun Tu's level.

They formed a strange picture, the short Slave Master's head at the level of Sun Tu Tuan's. But her head faced down and his up. Her elegance upended. His squatness stolid on the ascender.

It was then that Mickelmast noticed that the old Canary had left his side. Quickly the boy scanned the room but couldn't see him. Then, assuming that at least one of the bots had latched on to the old Canary, he ordered a transmission.

What he saw surprised him.

The bot had evidently adhered to the old Canary and was transmitting real time images from the old guy's point of view. But what Mickelmast received didn't make any sense.

What he saw was Sun Tu Tuan's face right side up and the Slave Master's upside down. How could this be? And then there was the fact that the transmission was from the same level as Sun Tu Tuan ... eight feet off the ground!

Then the transmission ceased.

A few moments later the Slave Master descended and left the chamber.

The old Canary appeared at the winch that held Sun Tu Tuan's cocoon line. Mickelmast moved toward him but stopped as the old man yanked hard on the wire line.

Sun Tu's cocoon began to twirl. Mickelmast was entranced by this up-ended body in motion.

"It's beautiful, isn't it?" The old Canary was so close to Mickelmast that the boy could feel his breath.

"Yes. But why ... "

"Because it's nature's beauty, deep in the heart."

The two men stared at the twirling girl for a moment. "It's time to get them down. The nastiness will start shortly," said the old Canary.

With that the old man hobbled off to the pin rails and began lowering the first of the red-marked cocoons. Over his shoulder, he yelled to Mickelmast, "There are clothes in that bag by the door. Put something on before you catch cold."

Chapter 22

And So to Meetings

An EntrePren Trader's education is based on a series of precepts known as "posts." Each post is the centerpiece of a full year's education. Every year the complications of the posts increase, the thinking needed for the argumentation intensifies and the range of acceptable answers narrows. At the start of each Terran year, the best of the answers from each level of training are published and become the object of much discussion throughout the EntrePren community. Awards are given in two areas: "imminent didacticism" and "speculative feats." There is no more value put on one kind of thinking than on the other, but it is rare that a student wins one year didactically and the next year speculatively. In fact, there was only one such occurrence and that was with the founder of the EntrePren Traders himself, Geet.

Since Geet's time, the schism between the Didacts and Specules has become enormous. In school, Didacts seldom play with Specules. Rarely is a speculative child born to didactic parents—and, of course, the reverse is equally rare. Marriages between Specules and Didacts are not sanctioned by the EntrePren central AIU that Geet programmed in the last year of his life.

The first post that students encounter reads: A *metal pot is filled to the brim with water. A fire is lit beneath it. The water in the pot boils and in so doing overflows its sides putting out the fire. Has the fire, tired of being a fire, put itself out? Has the water, tired of boiling, put out the fire to allow itself to return to a cooling state? Is the pot indifferent to the actions of both the fire and the water or does it in some way gain from this activity? Is it a catalyst? Discuss.*

The second post is: *Two bad heads often come up with a better solution than one good one. Assuming that this is so who in the room would you share a thought with and why? Also, is a thought shared a thought divided? Discuss.*

Sun Tu Tuan's father, Paul Sun, won the Didact award the first three years of his schooling which immediately brought him to the attention of the EntrePren Directorate. His two further victories in his teens guaranteed him access to high places upon completion of his education.

Paul's victory in the final post (taken from the sacred Book of Tations: *And I'm lost in the window, I hide in the stairway, I hang in your curtain, I sleep in your hat, and no one brings anything small into a bar around here, discuss*) secured him a vice-directorship after his required six years of marine service.

As all potential directors, he had to work his way from cabin serf to captain onboard an intergalactic EntrePren Kiltrin freighter. He had managed the feat in record time—just under three years.

But now all his past successes were irrelevant. Now his very competence was in question.

He knew that viewing the kidnapping of his daughter and the killing of his son had uncentered him enough that his impulses were now suspect. He also knew, only too well, that the others facing him around the EntrePren's directorate table and those on the monitors had been apprised of what he had seen that day in the laboratories deep beneath Vestin's once tranquil surface.

As the arguments in the meeting room swirled around him, Paul recited the sixteen EntrePren posts and his answers to each, word for word. It calmed him. But his calm evaporated when he realized that a question had been asked in his direction and his name had been spoken three times. He waved his left hand, indicating that he was not yet ready to speak. His eyes took in the all too familiar scene. The Didacts had, as usual, been drawn into senseless argumentation with the Specules. Senseless and losing. Not for the first time, Paul wondered at the inanity of this kind of ritual decision-making. He looked across the table at his Specule counterpart, Chi Ho. Both men knew that when this meeting ended in its customary deadlock, they would retire to a quiet garden and over the delectation of some local fruit would come to a decision.

Or at least that was the way things used to be.

Now there would be Didact challenges to his leadership, just as there had been after his wife's suicide. But he had not missed a meeting over that. Not been left out of a single decision. Nor would he be this time, although he, if forced, would admit that his judgment was now clouded by a most undidactic emotion—an emotion of which Paul only vaguely recalled the name: revenge.

He reminded himself that patience was at the heart of the EntrePren Traders galactic success. "He who can sit longest often wins," he quoted to himself. Even as he attempted to find his own source of patience, the image of his daughter's terror burned itself deeper and deeper into the dark recesses of his mind. And there it lay, as indelible as a tattooist's laser.

There was a verbal thrust and corresponding parry and the inevitable ruffling of feathers then the predictable tabling of further actions and the establishing of committees to study the matter. Closing statements from both sides followed. That was Chi Ho's cue to suggest that he and Paul take a small walk. Paul inclined his head slightly hiding his relief that none of the Didacts rose at that moment to challenge him. He did notice as he stood, however, that Sergeivitch wore a secretive smile deep in his blubbery face and he caught Meisner's side-long look to the Russian. "This is an unlikely duo," Paul thought noting an unusual expectancy in Meisner's usually dour countenance. "So the challenge will come from that quarter."

Paul thanked all those present, and those only present in image form, for their input, then he turned to Chi Ho and offered his arm.

The two men walked side by side, arms linked, seemingly in perfect balance, into the formal gardens in the interior courtyard. The EntrePren gardens were famous throughout the galaxy, their beauty the stuff of myth. Unfortunately, the fact and the myth varied. It had been years since the EntrePren Traders possessed the necessary insight to create great gardens and both Paul and Chi Ho knew it. The EntrePren gardens now endlessly repeated successful formulas from times past. But with each repetition the quintessential truths that the garden were intended to reveal, retreated further and further behind the mask of the formula. The formula that had at one time been the gateway to truth was now little more than a cloudy window that obscured the truth within.

"Is the pain great?"

Chi Ho's gruff voice seemed to sail past Paul and echo in the garden space. Paul knew a measured response was required. He composed himself and replied, "My pain is great but manageable. My breath still sustains my thoughts."

"And your anger?"

The assumption that he, a Didact, had suffered a loss of control was so personal that it shocked Paul. He looked away from Chi Ho, toward the garden. When he spoke, his voice was flat, "Anger is foreign to a Didact, as well you know. Shall we discuss the issue at hand?"

Chi Ho canted his elegant head signaling that he was prepared to listen.

"We know that the pirate actions could not have proceeded without the sanction of the UDP. Whether UDP or S3 still remains a question."

"Not to me," replied Chi Ho.

"You assume S3 is behind this?"

"I assume the Gateway message is behind this, and hence S3 would take the lead, do you not agree Paul?"

Paul was pleased that the Specule leader had thought this through so ... didactically. "I agree that the Gateway message is central to our discussions here."

"Have you read the pirate captain's dossier that I prepared for you?"

"Yes."

"Do you agree that some of the actions of this pirate may have a rebellious side to them? That he may be operating as an independent in this matter?"

"Not totally independent." The image of Tzu Ma Long rose up in Paul. The forcing of the glass knife into his daughter's hand, the fury. The gentle life of his son so quickly gone. The locking of Sun Tu's eyes with Tzu Ma Long's. Tzu didn't look like someone acting as an "independent in this matter." But if it was not the overlords at S3 to whom he was beholden, then who? These thoughts raced through Paul Sun's mind, but all he said to Chi Ho was, "Surely not totally independent."

"Of course not. Someone gave him the new Warrior Class Starship, and he clearly had S3 protection of some sort."

"Yes."

"To what end are S3's actions pointing, do you think?"

Paul wondered how much the EntrePren AIU that the brilliant Geet had programmed all those years ago had informed Chi Ho of his work on Dream Navigators. He wondered if Chi Ho even knew of the secret laboratories beneath Vestin's surface. He wondered specifically if his Specule counterpart knew that the research was approaching a first "flight test."

Chi Ho unlooped his arm from Paul's. He bent to examine a Bardan spire whose red blossom was so intense that it almost seemed obscene. The crimson bloom clashed with the garden's pattern and yet was somehow central to the vitality of the whole. Paul knew that the gardeners would not have planted the Bardan spire. It must have invaded the garden through the drainage sluices. Yet the Bardan spire had already captured the central focus of the garden—as an original and perfect opposition to the staleness of the design. A breath of real air in a sealed dome.

"*But the plant is unplanned, uncontrolled,*" Paul thought.

Then he saw Chi Ho's elegant face looking directly into his own. With a shock, Paul realized that he had spoken his thoughts aloud.

Chi Ho kept his eyes on Paul as he said, "Sometimes a wild thing must be introduced to allow us to see again. To keep ahead of the UDP, S3, and the Rebel Colonies, we must be able to make original leaps of thought."

Paul trembled inwardly at the dangerous territory that Chi Ho was broaching. Paul studied his counterpart — a neutered male with no known living family, top speculative thinker for five consecutive years, and on seemingly inexhaustible life-extension.

"The Gateway is a threat to us. Do you agree, Paul?"

"Absolutely." Paul was surprised that he had no interest in being careful in his response. "It is only the balance of power between the Rebel Colonies and the UDP which allows us to exist. If S3 makes its way through the Gateway that balance will be destroyed. S3 would, in short order, see no more reason to have us as intermediaries between the two great powers, and our entire empire would crumple like a flimsie in a flame."

"I agree," remarked Chi Ho. "So what are we to do to stop this?"

"Was it really possible that Geet had programmed the EntrePren AIU to keep the Vestin laboratory studies secret from Chi Ho? Evidently so, since it appears that Chi Ho knows nothing of the EntrePren Dream Navigator research!" The thought stunned Paul.

Chi Ho pulled his silk gown more tightly around him and drew a perfect circle with his toe in the sterilized soil. Paul looked at him. He was waiting. Paul said simply, "We need a plan."

Chi Ho looked at the Bardan spire and said bluntly, "Yes, we do."

The third post rose in Paul's consciousness: "Into something well-planned and over time proven to be effective an alien form arrives. The alien form forces itself upon the viewer and makes it clear that either the alien form must be eliminated or the well planned form must be redone to the specifications of the alien form. Should the alien form be removed or the plan rethought? Discuss without reference to any specifics." At the time, Paul had written in defense of the tried and true and had in fact won the Didact prize. Now, however, he found his eye drawn to the Bardan Spire and found it worth more than all the garden into which it had forced its presence.

It was at that moment that Paul knew for certain that the advent of the Gateway was the alien form that had entered their controlled reality. He also understood that the only way to maintain EntrePren power in the galaxy was by maintaining the balance between the two great powers. And that the only way to do that would be to destroy the Gateway itself. He looked to the Bardan spire. Then to Chi Ho. "These are dangerous times," he thought, "very dangerous times."

Chapter 23

The Show

Mirren was no one's idea of a posh place, but there was lots of money on the planet. Kiltrin money—dirty money.

The galaxy's demand for Kiltrin had increased exponentially since the success rate of old style life-extension surgery had begun to dip disastrously. It was as if nature was reinforcing its rules. Fighting back against man's invasions into her territory.

Ingestion of Kiltrin-based compounds temporarily reinvigorated the life-extension processes. Temporarily. Kiltrin was a stop gap but not a panacea.

But reactivation, no matter how fleeting, was still much in demand. The public outcry for Kiltrin boosted the price of the product making it economical to harvest the ore from Mirren's tortuously deep mines. The Kiltrin profits supported a large luxury class on the planet. A luxury class with the time, the money and a desire for entertainments—shows. Of course, the only shows left in the galaxy were slave shows—for which Mirren's luxury class had a seemingly insatiable appetite. They had even built a structure specifically for slave shows-—The Forum.

Being a Midwest American world, predictably The Mirren Forum was in the mock Roman style—although few on Mirren would know, care or appreciate that. The Forum was bathed in harsh chemically produced light. It, like its shows, metaphorically offered a full frontal view of something that didn't really exist.

That last thought was precisely what was in Tzu's mind as he slowly descended the steep steps to The Forum's perfectly square floor.

Ostensibly, as a slave owner, he was there to examine the space in which his wares were going to be exhibited. In fact, he was there to test his feelings.

The Mirren soldiers watched the pirate from the upper decks, their hands never far from their weapons.

Tzu stepped onto the playing floor. An odd thrill whisked through his body. A knowingness. A strange familiarity. What! He walked to the exact center of the space. He pressed his heel into his boot contacting the ship's AIU.

From where the soldiers watched, it looked like the small man was kicking the dirt, perhaps remembering a pleasantry from his youth. If the Mirren soldiers had been down on the floor with Tzu, they would not have been pleased with what they saw.

Tzu's face was twisted in thought as he contemplated the AIU's final comment. Finally he said, "Redo the drop ships' calibrations. There's still too much margin for error."

"Shall I activate your narrowcast module?"

"Yes."

"Wide range of sound and light?"

"Just light. One pulse."

"Done. And who is the recipient to be of the single pulse to be?"

"Cyrus Maloney III of S3."

"An interesting recipient to be sure."

"Just do it."

"It's already done."

Tzu snapped off his connection with the AIU and looked around him. What was it about this place? What sense was there in a whore's son at the center of a slave show? Why was he so attracted to these spectacles—"because they're all we have left"—left of what? He had posed that to the AIU but she had merely laughed at him and told him that she was not a weegee board, whatever that was.

The Face Dancer swished on his belt as if she were a kitten turning somersaults. Tzu felt her. Felt her excitement and knew that there was a connective here that he was missing. Something joined all this—his need of the slave shows, the Face Dancer, the very being of Sun Tu, the Peqod scattercast—all of it—but he couldn't find it. The connective. He heard laughter from above and looked up at the Mirren soldiers. One of them called out, "Come. Mustn't be late to the Rotary Commerce, must we?"

Tzu looked up. He'd forgotten how tall the space was. Height. Something about height.

"Come on, lunch is served," a soldier shouted.

Tzu gave one last look at the tall space and then began walking up The Forum's steps. There was something extraordinary about the shows but nothing out of the dead ordinary about its Mirren patrons—and the gatherings they insisted upon before the shows. Gatherings they called luncheons.

While Tzu was climbing the steps of The Forum, in the bowels of the building the Slave Master directed his men to separate the male from the female slaves. He was going to display his wares in three, five-unit groups. The first would be male. The second male and female. The third all female. Build the tension. Push to curtain.

In preparation for the show, both the males and the females had been bathed, oiled, perfumed, and costumed then recuffed with the bio-technacles and herded back to the largish concrete room. By the time they settled on the cold metal benches, the technacles had punctured skin and securely enwrapped the wrist and ankle bones.

The slavers watched their captives carefully now knowing things were about to begin in earnest.

After an appropriate waiting period, the Slave Master made his re-entrance. What little stirring there was in the room stopped. All eyes looked in his direction then quickly toward the floor. The captives wanted to know what was going to happen to them, but no one wished to draw attention to them self.

The Slave Master strutted forward and began to speak.

As he did, the bot on the foul man's shoulder began to transmit. "You are now beneath the central arena of The Forum on the Rebel Colony planet called Mirren." The Slave Master gave a signal and a whole wall lit up with an aerial view of the interior of The Forum's tall central square space. The ground was outlined in black and white numbered squares. "The board," he said simply. "West view," he barked. Up came a side view of the space. Black and white squares appeared there as well, but these were lettered. All the squares were ten meters by ten meters. "Full dimensional," the Slave Master called and the entire space filled with translucent ten-meter-by-ten-meter-by-ten-meter cubes. Each numbered and lettered. On the 4D square, forty meters from the starting line, was a ladder. It lead to the 14B square. On 9H a ladder lead to the 31EE. "You start in the first square, 1A, and try to make your way to the hundredth—100WWW."

There was a pause in the room then one of a younger men blurted out, "And if we make it to the hundredth square?"

The Slave Master looked at the questioner. It was the young heavy worlder from the Independentiste planet in Garrison Six. The old slaver smiled to himself There's always one who thinks there's a reward. He had guessed right that it would be this one. "Don't worry your head about it lad. No one ever gets to the hundredth square before the snakes get you."

"Then why bother trying?"

"Because lad, if you don't try, put on a good show that is, I'll do this to you." Without further explanation, the Slave Master tapped out a command on of his arm implant. A high-pitched whine filled the room, but it was quickly drowned out by the young man's momentary cries of terror as the bio-technacles, responding to the Slave Master's command, began to grow.

The young man staggered to the center of the room in jerky spasms that were more like leaps then steps. His mouth seemed pried open, but no sound came from the dark cavity.

The others backed away from the young heavy worlder and watched in horror. They saw the bulges in his skin caused by the movement of the technacles that, no longer pleased with their purchase on the bones of the man's lower arms and legs, had begun snaking along those bones heading toward a meeting place somewhere near the groin.

The man's skin popped open on the back of his left shoulder as a technacle arm grappled across his back and re-entered his skin just below his left clavicle. He dropped to the floor as the technacle in his left leg popped off his kneecap.

Quickly he became little more than a contorted squirming thing as the four ends of the bio-product sought a meeting inside him.

The technacles smashed through bones, shredded muscle tissue, wrapped themselves around joints then ripped through them reaching for their next hold. Eventually the four arms met just below the navel.

Of course by that time, the man had been dead for several minutes. Technacles are not fast. Just relentless.

"Are there any more questions about not trying to get to the finish?" The Slave Master's face sported a small grin.

There were no questions.

"Good. We'll start with the four men now that your fifth is of little value to anyone. Time to take a nap before your drug induction."

While the Slave Master was preparing his charges for the show, Tzu Ma Long was "luncheoning" with the Mirren Rotary Commerce.

The Rotary Commerce speaker, a Mr. Jenkins, who ran the hardware consortium that serviced the mines, slowly made his way to the head table. He was almost as wide as he was tall and his florid complexion gave birth to reddish blossoms on his cheeks and neck under the exertion of carrying his plate, stacked high with tarts, from the dessert table to his seat behind the speaking tube. Seeing Jenkin's fat figure unleashed an awful thought in Tzu's head. "My mother slept with the likes of him. He could be my father." The thought disappeared as quickly as it had arisen. A chimera, a ghost.

All around him large plates crammed with sweets sat before men who were racially cataloged by S3 for colonization purposes as "mid-western whites". A sub-species of North American Caucasian. "A sub species of the genus, human," thought Tzu.

Jenkins cleared his throat twice, tapped the speaking tube with a plump finger and began to speak. "Sub-human but perfectly suited for the task at hand," whispered Tzu as his hand gently touched the Face Dancer's pouch. She responded with an almost silent purr. Reassuring, always there. Tzu smiled.

"It's really nice. Special, I'd say. To have the likes of Mr. Long here coming to entertain the Mirren Rotary Commerce." There was a smattering of applause. Jenkins smiled and continued, "It's been a long time since we had a Chink in our midst. But we hold no racial prejudice. We like you Long-fellow and would really like to have our shirts cleaned, no starch please." Finding his joke so clever that he couldn't contain himself the fat man spluttered a string of spittle from his corpulent lips. He was not the only one who found it amusing. The audience slapped themselves silly and banged on the circular tables. Glasses of sickly sweet orange drink tilted and released their liquid. There was much repeating of "no starch" followed by much hardy backslapping and the odd explosion of, "Starch, yeah. I get it."

Tzu stood impassive, his face revealing nothing.

These were the types of men that made the worlds go round. Whose industriousness and willingness to risk capital made some Rebel Colony settlements the economic envy of much of the galaxy.

They were also the reason that slave shows were popular. These people had the money to indulge themselves in the terror trip through the Slave Show's cubes.

"Any words you'd like to add, Chinky ol' boy?"

Tzu stepped forward. Eyes craned to get a look. A murmur came from those assembled. Tzu tapped the speaking tube. It gave out a low thump. He reminded himself to keep this formal. "Ladies and Gentlemen of Mirren, it is our pleasure to present the finest quality slaves available anywhere in the galaxy."

Jenkin's fat figure preceded Tzu down the glassed-in hallway of the office tower. The corridor offered a stunning view of the vast nothingness of Mirren City. An early open-faced Kiltrin trench scarred the ground. The travel ways were wide and flat—and empty. It seemed the Forum was the only large building in this crumbling neglected city. Tzu couldn't see any places where people lived. Midwesterners didn't like to live downtown, preferring to commute by personal lifters from far flung gated habitations.

Jenkins opened an office door and stepped in. Tzu followed. Sampled frequencies that Tzu's implant identified as from a thing called "country" coated the walls of the room. The crushing combination of Jenkin's body odor and old smokables stung Tzu's nostrils. The Face Dancer on his belt sensed his unease and prepared herself.

Jenkins plopped his hefty figure behind a large desk and, taking off his hat, turned to Tzu. "What say you and I cut the shit, okay?" For the first time, since Tzu had met Mr. Jenkins, he sensed a deep and malevolent intelligence in the man.

That would make it easier.

"So Mr. Chink-face, you want to sell your filthy slaves on our clean world. You want to put on a show. Shit, you want me to sanction you putting on a show. These are God-fearing people here, who on occasions like a little clean fun. But never mistake that for them liking you or your kind. Got that Ol' Chinky? You do your show, then you haul your shallow little yellow ass off our clean world. You put on your show, and then you go. Got that slant eyes? No chop sueying around!"

Tzu got it. Heard it. Would not soon forget it. It made things much simpler.

Mr. Jenkins got to his feet and undid his jacket. There was a greenish food stain on his shirtfront. "Now that that's settled there is the little matter of my costs in all this. I assume you have a little something for me and now's as good a time as any for you to hand it over."

Tzu stared at Jenkins for a three count and smiled. "What could I possibly have that you want?"

Jenkins moved to the front of his desk.

"I think you know, ol' Chinky. I think you know."

And Tzu did—know that is. He flicked open the pouch on his belt. The Face Dancer emerged. Tzu spoke in a totally flat voice, "Negroid, big tits, big woman."

As the naked, large black woman approached Jenkins, Tzu watched the excitement rise in the fat man. The Face Dancer modulated her voice and rounded her sounds as she said, "Lie down sugar. We're gonna play horsee." The heavy man lay down and she stepped over him, then slowly lowered her sexual self onto his face. At first she writhed to his attentions.

Then she clamped her thighs tight to his ears.

The slurping stopped. A muffled cry came from him.

Then Tzu spoke clearly, "EntrePren Princess, Sun Tu Tuan." Darkened skin lightened and browned, wide shoulders narrowed, tightly kinked hair straightened and grew long and straight down a lengthened back. The hips, that still held Jenkin's face tight to her, thinned and elongated. Then with Jenkins still beneath her, now gasping for what little air he could get, the Face Dancer turned to face Tzu Ma Long.

The face that looked longingly into Tzu's was no longer that of a heavy-set black woman. It was the face of Sun Tu Tuan.

For a moment Tzu wavered. Could he really pull this off?

Jenkins thrashed desperately trying to break free. Sun Tu opened her beautiful mouth and said to Tzu, "Should I kill him for you honey. Or kill him for us?" Tzu couldn't respond. He hadn't asked her to speak. But he couldn't stop her. He was mesmerized by what was taking place in front of him. The Face Dancer smiled and tightened her thighs about the fat man's head.

As the stench of the Jenkins' fear filled the room, Tzu calmed and settled in to view the death. As he watched, he wondered at himself. What was he doing here in this place "east of Suez." Sun Tu faced him and smiled, "I ride the horse for you honey. Only for you. Am I the best and the worst?" She flicked her tongue in his direction.

Tzu rose and set his narrowcast module high on the wall being sure that he stepped aside before he activated the transmitter. "Here's another message to the galaxy—to Cyrus Maloney III of S3," he thought as he drew his concussion gun and shot three massive blasts into the face of Sun Tu Tuan.

As he turned away an odd thought crossed his mind, "I wonder what chop sueying is?"

As Jenkins was managing his last breath, an exotic mixture of female sex and oxygen, the Slave Master was administering the final drug inductions to the last of his first set of slaves.

Above in The Forum, the crowd was already primed. They had paid the extravagant price of admission and even more for the drugs needed to view the event. Years ago, it had been discovered that there was no way to prevent signal of any sort from being stolen and subsequently sold around the galaxy. To avoid this, slave masters had developed coded drugs that were only active for the time of the slave show itself. Only with the drugs could you see the snakes that the slaves were seeing. Anyone could see the ladders, but it was the snakes that made the game interesting. As well, for extra money, you could purchase the co-relative drug of the slave of your choice. With the co-relative drug, you actually saw and felt the event from inside the slave's head, thus intensifying the experience. For still more money, a patron could purchase a co-relative drug controller which would not only let you see what the slave saw but you could also direct his every action as he tried to make his way from cube 1A to cube 100WWW—all this, naturally, from the safety and comfort of your seat.

All the drugs were from the same dream remnant family as Lavolin and had some similar connective properties.

The lights snapped off plunging the massive space into total blackout.

Then a single cube, 1A, exploded with light, revealing the first group of slaves.

Before the startled men could get their bearings, the rest of the playing field came to life. The tote board was lowered into place, and odds were displayed. Then the first slave raced forward, and the crowd roared its approval.

The slaves climbed the ladders but slid down the snakes. Of course, the ladders were greased and had scalpel sharp sides. And naturally the slaves didn't just slide down the snakes. They crashed through space to the floor if they were lucky enough to actually slide down them. More often than not the snakes entered the slaves and tore them literally to pieces before disgorging them to a new life on a lower cube.

The game was about terror. About how terror is the only feeling left to humans in this dreamless galaxy. How the terror momentarily makes you feel alive. Feeling the terror without, of course, actually being in real danger, was the kick. And of course, if some of the slaves died in the process, then surely they were not strong enough to act as good servants in the best of households and bedrooms of Mirren. And besides. It was just good clean fun. And anyone who couldn't see that was clearly just some bleeding heart liberal who wouldn't have the money or the balls to be in the audience of a slave show anyway—or so the thinking went.

Chapter 24

Watching and Wonder

Sitting on the floor of the cryogenic chamber Cas-Alta shivered. But it was not the cold that sent tremors through her willowy frame. It was the terror on the face of the slave in cube 11C of the maze in the Mirren Forum.

The slave's image was startlingly clear on the projection plate that Mickelmast's bots had formed. Despite her fear, Cas-Alta couldn't turn her eyes away from the horror before her.

"Why's he running?" asked Kelt as he moved past Cas-Alta to get a closer look at the projected image.

"Something must be chasing him," replied Mickelmast from his standing position beside the bot screen.

"Why do you say that?" Kelt demanded.

"His movement pattern. He moves forward and then vectors in response to something. His responses have a linear binomial to them as if the object is in front of him. See the man in 17D? He's stopped. He's looking for a way around something that seems to be on the floor."

"Why doesn't he climb the ladders?" Sun Tu asked from Kelt's side.

"They're sharp. They cut," responded Cas-Alta.

Kelt blurted out, "What are you talking about? Where do you see that?"

Cas-Alta pointed at the side of a ladder on the screen. "There." The others leaned in, but no one was able to see anything. Then Cas-Alta added, "And slick with fat of some sort." They all stared at the long-haired girl.

Kelt turned to Mickelmast. "Can you make it bigger? I can't see anything."

"Oh you can see things, just not as much as her," said Mickelmast pointing at Cas-Alta.

"Fine, but I'd still like you to make it bigger if you can, Mike."

"My name's Mickelmast not Mike or Michael or Micky or ..."

"Mickelmast, I'm sorry, but could you please."

"Here." The magnification increased by a factor of twenty and quickly Cas-Alta's observations were clear for all to see. The ladders horizontal bars dripped with a glutinous liquid. Glass, razor wire, and twisted metal shards were imbedded in the verticals.

"You'd have to fly to get through that," gasped Sun Tu.

"Or float," said the old Canary from the corner. He had been sitting back and watching the five of them. The fat boy, the beautiful Chinese girl, the handsome soldier, the silent one, and the natural healer. He'd been watching them as a father watches children he'd not seen for many years. The old man was pleased with what he saw.

For their part, the five genetic carriers had completely forgotten that he was there.

Raephealson lumbered to his feet. His large body was not accustomed to the gravity on the ship, so he hunched as he moved toward the screen. His hand pointed accusingly. Then he shouted, "Serpents!"

"Where? Where do you see snakes?" barked Kelt.

"You don't have to see something for it to be there," snapped back Cas-Alta.

"What does that mean?" shouted Sun Tu.

"It could be snakes. The men's pattern of movement would support that," said Mickelmast.

"How can you ..." began Kelt, clearly out of his mathematical depth.

"Penthal induction?" Cas-Alta asked Mickelmast.

"Could be or anyone of the AIU linked hallucinogenics from the Lavolin family would be my guess," said Mickelmast.

"Then the snakes aren't real," said Sun Tu.

"Oh they're real enough to those poor souls," said Cas-Alta.

"But they're not really there," pressed Sun Tu.

"What does 'really there' mean?" Cas-Alta pressed back.

"Oh save me from this Specule bullshit, will you. There's nothing there to hurt them. It's all in their minds."

"If it is in your mind, it is there."

"Spare me this! You're as thick as a post," Sun Tu shot back at her.

Cas-Alta was stunned by the attack. Sun Tu saw it and apologized, "It's just an EntrePren figure of speech."

At that moment one of the slaves, having managed to climb halfway up a ladder, opened his mouth and began to scream. His left biceps had hooked on a strand of razor wire and when he ripped it free, he slipped off a rung and impaled himself on a two foot shard of glass. He was unable to move. He stopped struggling. Then his eyes opened wide with fear. Something attacked him. Raephealson stood very still and blurted out, "Serpent."

Mickelmast looked closely at the man's writhing figure on the screen then nodded. "He's right. The snake came from this direction. See where this other guy stepped aside? Its speed is 1.74 kilometers an hour, it's acceleration about twice as fast as a grown man running, and it's between 2.7 and 3.6 meters long."

"What are you ... "

"Just give me a second here," said Mickelmast cutting off Kelt. He punched orders into his implant and with a smile announced, "There."

For a moment nothing changed, then the cubes filled with writhing snakes.

"What the hell," shouted Sun Tu and jumped back.

"They're not real. No reason to be frightened," snarked Cas-Alta.

"Right. They're not real. Just hallucinations," said Sun Tu.

"How'd you do that?" asked Kelt.

"I extended the sample stats over the length of the maze and then instructed the projection bots who are sending us the signal to etch them in," Mickelmast replied. "And voila: snakes and ladders."

The man in cube 22B fell backward in his effort to avoid a large snake. He shredded his back on a ladder and thudded to the cube below. Before he could rise, a snake was on him. And then to the shock of those watching on the projection plate—the snake went into him.

The crowd's howling cheers drowned out the man's screams. Bets were paid off and new ones wagered. A man with a big gut took off his shirt and swung it round and round over his head in some bizarre form of celebration. The tote board recalculated odds and applied prices to the various slaves then announced the cost of second, third, and fourth doses of empathetic drugs. The whole maze suddenly went dark. The "dead" slave's vital statistics were flashed across the entirety of the playing area. The auction for the "dead slave" began. As bids were screamed out single cubes with Holos of the "dead slave" in various costumes and stages of undress, lit up and began to slowly twirl. As each new Holo came up, the bidding frenzy rose. Finally every cube in the maze was filled with Holos of the "dead slave." The frenzy crested then the lights snapped off once again. A silence followed. Then a single light came up on a square deep in the center of the maze. The slave stood there, dazed and naked. Final bids were taken, and the man was dragged from the maze by his new masters, a tall man and woman who looked so much alike they might have been twins.

More bets. More drugs. More snakes. More deaths that were not deaths. Then the arrival of the second group, this time three men and two women.

The Genetic Carriers watched in wrapped, stunned fascination. Then Cas-Alta barfed. Barfed and barfed and barfed. All over herself. All over the floor. All over Raephealson who stood stock still at her side. Torrents of bile and fear came from her, empathy in its most physical form.

When Mickelmast went to help clean her up, Sun Tu Tuan came close to Cas-Alta—and sniffed her.

The two women stood facing each other. One knowing for sure, the other guessing. Sun Tu hissed, "What's really wrong with you girl?"

Kelt chose that moment to announce to the world, "I'm not going to any slave market. I'll fight them all before I let them do that to me."

"Spoken like a true Independentiste, Kelt," snapped back Mickelmast.

"An Independentiste lives his own life. We don't cringe before others like you Rebel Colony vermin. Being a slave would be a step-up for a Rebel Colonist."

"Oh, man, you hurt me so bad Kelt that I think I'd like a cheeseburger. You catch my intergalactic-who-gives-a–oh great would-be war hero? If it weren't for me, you'd still be hanging upside down with your dick pointing at your nose."

Kelt stepped toward Mickelmast, but the heavy youth held his ground.

"Don't fight!" shouted Cas-Alta.

Kelt lunged, but Mickelmast had already commed his bots to pinandhold.exe so that Kelt found himself on his back, held tight to the floor by thousands and thousands of crawly bots.

Mickelmast approached the prone warrior and was about to laugh when Sun Tu asked, "Why us?"

All eyes turned to her. She had wandered away from the others and was pointing at the opened cocoons from which the five had been removed. "Our confining tubes have been slashed with red. None of the cocoons of the fifteen who were taken to the slave market were. Nor are those poor fools over there," she said pointing to the hundred and twenty-odd people still in their confining tubes upside down eight feet off the ground. Suddenly Sun Tu turned on Mickelmast, "How did you go about picking us five?"

Before he could answer, a voice came from the darkness. "Mickelmast didn't choose." It was the old Canary speaking.

"He didn't?" asked Kelt, managing to get to a half-seated position.

"No, I chose," replied the old man.

"And were you the one who marked our cocoons with the red paint?" pressed Sun Tu.

"No. The pirate captain did that."

"And why exactly would he do that?" snapped Kelt.

"Because you bear a gift. A rare gift."

The five waited for the old Canary to continue, but before he could, the motion sensor in the room began to scream. Mickelmast whirled toward the sound and swore.

"What!" yelled Sun Tu.

"I ran out of capacity when I sicked the bots on Kelt." Mickelmast quickly reprogrammed his bots and the alarm stopped as if in mid-breath.

"Security will be on its way," yelled Cas-Alta.

"How long 'til they arrive?" barked Kelt.

"There's no way of knowing, but they'll be here soon. We've all got to get back in the cocoons."

"But we haven't been prepped for cold sleep!" said Sun Tu.

Mickelmast ordered the final bots off Kelt. "You okay?"

"I'll live. Keep those bugs to yourself, will ya'"

"Soon, but for now you need to be covered with them again, as do the rest of you." As Mickelmast quickly reprogrammed the bots to latchonandcover.exe, he called to the others, "Take off your clothes. Walk across the tiles slowly. It'll tingle for a bit, but they'll keep you warm in the cocoons. I can't fool this ship's AIU much longer. My bots have been deflecting signals for almost an hour now. It's got to know that something's not right. There's no other choice. Go."

And they did—a slow dance of young people removing their clothing for the first time in front of each other. Mickelmast was the first to disrobe. Sun Tu the last. All were quickly covered by the bots.

"Are you strong enough to hang us all?" Mickelmast asked the old Canary.

"Clearly he's not," said Kelt as he moved toward the halyards and pin rails. Quickly Kelt and the old Canary put the others into the cocoons and hoisted them up. Raephealson was the hardest. Not only was he heavy, but somehow he had retreated into himself which made him into dead weight. As they yanked, his head bobbed. Drool appeared at the sides of his mouth. A low moan came from him, and he began fighting the restraints of the harness.

He'll settle down soon, said the Old Canary. "Now you."

"Can you lift me old man?"

"If I can't you'll fall on your head which after this morning's display might be the best thing that could happen to you. Get in."

"Who are you?"

"The only friend you five have left on this side of the galaxy. Do you believe that?"

"No."

"Fine, then don't believe it. Get in and sleep on it."

With that the Canary began hoisting Kelt's cocoon, hand over hand. The young warrior's cocoon rose slowly into the air. His nakedness bespoke power. His figure hanging upside down, eight feet above the ground, took the old Canary's breath away. "Such beauty," he said aloud. The old man watched the young warrior spin. "Was I so beautiful when I was young?" he asked himself. Then he closed his eyes and remembered.

Remembered his own nakedness and his levitation. Then his spin. But more he remembered the journeys. The soaring, the ripping. And the love he felt for a man who hated him. The old Canary whose name was Elijah Jaspers tried desperately not to cry.

When security arrived at the ship's basement, all they found was the hobbling old Canary outside the cryogenic chamber door. Security looked inside. Nothing but frozen, hanging soon-to-be-slaves.

Security canceled the AIU's alert. The AIU was not pleased. It sensed something new. That it was somehow or other not in control. That it was endangered.

Chapter 25

Racing Toward Oblivion

Tzu stood watching the show, entranced. Then he turned to the audience. He sensed that a slave show's drug-induced visions brought a momentary sense of life, of waking, to a world that lived its entire long existence in a state most closely resembling sleep. The crowd's ecstatic drug-soddened reaction to the final female snaking brought him out of his reverie. He averted his eyes from the Forum floor. He needed all his wits about him, or the whole thing would go to hell. He was close to his goal—east of Suez where the best is like the worst.

An image of Sun Tu staring into his eyes while straddling Jenkins rose up in him—then her face exploded under the concussive blast. He shut his eyes tightly and drove the image away. It was time to move on before this stupid planet became his grave. He commed the Slave Master.

As he did his AIU signaled a request for contact. Tzu finished his comm then ground his heel into the back of his left boot. He felt the tug of activation. "Go," he said in his mind. The AIU responded with a surprisingly convoluted report about motion in the cryogenic chamber of the ship. "Space rats?" Tzu suggested. But the AIU rejected the suggestion and adamantly insisted that something was going on down there. "Then send a security team."

"I did. I did. I did!"

"And?"

"Nothing, nothing, and nothing."

"I'll check into it. Have you completed the calibrations on the drop ships and the bay door?"

"Yes, yes, yes."

"And?"

"If you're as talented as you think you are, it could be done."

"Could?"

"Do you have a hearing problem? Could. Could. Could."

"I'll be there soon. Something more for me?"

"Negative. Negative. Negative."

Tzu disconnected knowing that the Slave Master was very close; the man's smell was unmistakable. Tzu turned in the direction of the reek and saw the man slither his way through a crowd of Mirrens who had painted their faces half blue, half green. Tzu couldn't begin to guess why anyone would do such a thing. The Slave Master had a faux meat product in a bun in one hand. Tugging slightly at his forelock, he launched into his report. "We did better than I'd have thought." He took a big bite from the tubular thing in the roll then wiped a yellow oozy substance from his lips. "You know how cheap midwesters can be. We're averaging 48 units per."

"48 per the 15?" Tzu asked.

"48 per 14. One needed to be technacled as an example."

"At 48 Units per, it's an expensive way to prove a point."

"If you disapprove of my methods, you're welcome to find another slave master."

But Tzu didn't disapprove. Since the Millennial break, real courage had been as rare as creativity in the galaxy. Without the technacled man as an example to terrorize them, the slaves would cower at the first obstacle they met. And there were many, many obstacles in the maze. The fear of being techancled drove them forward. It produced a kind of courage—a faux courage, if you will. But without some form of courage, a slave could not even begin to negotiate the snake maze. And only courageous slaves would command 48 units per.

"Get our people back onboard within the half hour," Tzu ordered.

"What's the rush, Captain?"

Tzu let a slow smile cross his face. The Slave Master saw it, and it sent a chill twisting through his blood. The thought that "something was wrong with the Little Shit" crossed the Slave Master's mind for the third time in two days. He scanned the elite luxury box for the fat moron Jenkins but couldn't see him. "Had Tzu treated the obese one to some sort of private show?" he wondered.

The Slave Master's eyes were drawn back to the digital tote board above the final slave's head. She was a tall red-headed beauty somewhere in her late twenties. A UDP pickup. Her pale nakedness glistened in sweat. One hand covered her sex as the other kept trying to push her long dank hair out of her face so that she could see what was happening to her. A bid of 86 units was shouted from the far side of the Forum and registered by the electronic auctioneer. The Slave Master did a quick calculation. That brought the average up to 57 units per. Nine more than he had reported to the Little Shit. The only question now facing the Slave Master was how much of that excess he could pocket and how much he should give over. The Little Shit expected him to skim some off the top. The only issue was how much.

"A lot," he thought.

Just as the Slave Master was congratulating himself, the Mirren police came charging into the Forum. Lights smashed on, the sampled frequencies snapped off—the illusion crumbled. The Slave Master whirled around. The Little Shit was gone.

The Slave Master commed the Electronic Auctioneer, and quickly as he could punch in the figures, the bidded money was collected and transferred to seven different registered EntrePren accounts. If only it were so easy to get your money out of EntrePren accounts!

The take was good. Now it was time to beat it with the swag.

As the Slave Master made his escape, the political overlords of this Rebel Colony settlement were discussing a most extraordinary message they had just received. An extraordinary message from an old enemy—C/M/III of S3.

The Rebel Colony political elites who composed the Mirren Directorate were not much different from Rebel Colony merchants. They were practical and short sighted. S3's message promised profit and profit was good. So with a minimum of discussion, they agreed to the request from C/M/III of S3. They would, as the comm instructed, arrest and keep under guard the pirate captain, Tzu Ma Long. In return for which S3 granted them ownership of all remaining slaves onboard the pirate ship except for those demarcated as S3 property by a red slash on their cryogenic cocoons. Those they were to hold until an S3 ship came to pick them up. As well, they were to investigate the slaying of an EntrePren woman who C/M/III claimed had been murdered in a Rotary Commerce office in Mirren City.

"What if this pirate has already left the planet?"

"The S3 message assures us that should he have left, he will shortly return."

"It doesn't mention who will manage that, does it?"

"No, it doesn't, but it reiterates that the pirate captain, if he has left Mirren, will come back soon."

There was a pause in the conversation.

"This Tzu is valuable ... "

"... and we are, after all, mercantilists. Aren't we?"

There were nods of assent around the table. They were happy. And why not? How often does a windfall land in one's lap, literally from out of the blue?

"Just to be safe I think it prudent to prepare our forces and put our Yeoman Class Ships on alert."

Once again there were nods of assent around the table, but this time there was more than greed hidden beneath the directors' smiles.

This time there was blood lust as well.

Chapter 26

Plans and Counterplans

With everyone back onboard, the First Mate followed usual exit procedures and set a neutral course for itinerant deep space. The AIU accepted the command without query. Once the ship broke orbit and all stations were secured, the Head Centurion cracked open the stim cases—it was time for the men to blow off a little steam.

So it was with the sound of pirate revelry in the background that Tzu raced through the ship's corridors. He threw open the gravity lock then free fell the central zero-G core in one twirling kilometer long leap.

He knew it was foolish but he had to see the real Sun Tu again. He needed to see the face of the woman for whom he was taking such extraordinary risks.

Arriving at the cryogenic chamber's door, Tzu's progress was momentarily halted by the protest of the swirling mist on his belt. Without a second thought, he unhooked the Face Dancer pouch and dropped it to the floor.

The mist roared its disapproval.

Inside the chamber, the ascender ride up to Sun Tu Tuan seemed endless—but finally he was there—his face pressed against the fibrous webbing of the transparent cocoon, her face mere inches away on the other side of the frozen world.

Or so he thought. The bots had adhered to her brilliantly, matching her contours and skin tone exactly. They generated enough warmth on her side to keep her comfortable while accepting enough cold on the outside to induce the med-scan to report full cryogenisis.

The other Genetic Carriers, each protected by Mickelmast's bots in their cocoons, watched dreading what the pirate captain might do. But he didn't do anything except stare and stare and stare. Time seemed to stand still. Then Kelt tried to get a better look at what was going on.

His harness twisted which set his cocoon into a slow spin. The motion attracted Tzu's eye. Quickly the pirate descended to the chamber floor and looked at the hanging cocoons. Only the young Independentiste warrior whom he had been instructed to hobble was in motion.

Tzu ground his heel into his boot and barked, "Analyze chamber."

The Slave Master pushed his way past a stimmed out mariner and opened the door to his chamber. The comm light flashed in the pattern, indicating an off-vessel message. He tapped the button and went to remove his shirt. With his shirt halfway over his head he stopped. His mouth flopped open as he saw the words on the display: "I'm calling in my marker. Lavolin 2b-00-b2—upon receipt." The Slave Master lunged at the erase key.

"Repeat please," Tzu said trying to keep his voice calm.

"You heard me."

The P.P.S. universe was going crazy. Even his AIU was going bat shit. "Repeat your analysis of the cryogenic chamber."

"Movement, movement, and more movement. Cryogenic readings accurate for deep sleep but still movement."

"So check the calibrations on the med-scans."

"Done, done, and done again. According to the med-scans there's no there there."

"What?"

The AIU's silence was ominous. Tzu needed to get to the machine quickly and plug in directly. At least for the moment he allowed himself to believe that his connection to the great thinking thing was the problem. It was easier than confronting the terrifying idea that the AIU was faltering.

The Slave Master mopped the cold sweat from his brow. Terror coiled about him like a python does a baby in a crib. He fought it down. He needed all his wits now if he was to survive.

He locked his chamber door and took several deep breaths. There was no way to reject or side step C/M/III's request. What does one wear to meet his unholiness? Do you need a warmth suit in the mist? He pulled his drug inducer from beneath his sleeping palate and set it to the assigned coordinates and sniffed.

He'd never taken Lavolin before.

Its jolt threw him to his knees. He clutched his heart. He thought he was going to die. He didn't—he flew.

As Tzu made his way up the zero gravity central core of the ship, he was summoned by the AIU again.

"Shields raised, cloaking complete, evasive maneuvers generation 6 begun."

"Why? Are we under attack?"

"Not yet."

"Meaning what?"

"Meaning not YET!"

"But you believe that we will shortly be under attack?"

The AIU didn't respond for a moment then it said flatly, "You are late in returning the Lavolin traveller's cargo."

"And you believe that S3 would attack the ship for that?" Tzu clutched at a wall hold then pushed off hard. He sped up the zero gravity core of the ship. Suddenly the AIU was shouting. "I believe Herr Short Stuff that you are not yourself lately!!!"

Tzu momentarily lost his orientation in the Zero-G and nearly smashed into one of the walls. Three intensely stimmed-out mariners stopped themselves from laughing when they saw the murderous look on their captain's face. Tzu righted himself and replied as calmly as he could. "Repeat please, I think our connection is bad."

The Slave Master found himself in a foggy tunnel of some sort. The Lavolin was intensely disorienting. He had trouble figuring out which way was up. Momentarily he wondered if he vomited whether it would splat to the sidewalk or rise up into his face. He tottered to his feet. Figures appeared at the far end of the tunnel. Tightly wrapped women. He looked across the pavemented center and saw more women in the mist. And men approaching them. Then a cold hand touched the back of his neck. He spun around. Too quickly. Nausea overwhelmed him. He fell to the hard cement and released the Mirren Forum hot dogs he had eaten not three hours ago. The mustard left a particularly nasty taste on his teeth.

He heard laughter above him. Then a voice. "A virgin in the mist I see."

He turned his head slowly in the direction of the voice.

"You'll have trouble focusing on me in the mist. Do you know who I am?"

The Slave Master nodded. It set the nausea in motion again.

"Good." The lights of a passing vehicle momentarily threw the two men into sharp contrast with this world of suet and grime. The lights also brought to life, for brief instants, the dozens of women who walked the sidewalks of the under pass. Peddling.

"I thought this place would make you feel at home, Slave Master."

"Where ..." but he got out no more before he had to put his forehead down on the cold cement.

"Don't bother yourself about where we are. You turn your mind to getting Tzu Ma Long off the ship and back to Mirren. I've contacted the Head Centurion and the First Mate. They'll back you. I need Tzu back on Mirren. Understood? If you don't get Tzu back to Mirren, you can forget about your EntrePren accounts. I hope I put that clearly enough for you to have a full understanding of the consequences of failure on your part."

The Slave Master tilted his head around to see his tormentor. All he saw was the silhouette of a stooped old man. Then a vehicle's lights scraped across them momentarily blinding him.

"Why did Tzu bring the EntrePren girl to Mirren?"

"To Mirren? He didn't"

"What?"

"The Chinese girl never left the ship, never left her cocoon even. I tried to get the Cap'n to sell her but he refused."

Cyrus was silent for a moment, then he allowed a cold thin smile to cross his face. "Ah, a distraction," he thought. "But from what? From what indeed?" Cyrus looked hard at the Slave Master. The man disgusted him. All this, his whole bloody life leading to this—to needing the likes of this foul reek of a creature! But Cyrus said nothing. It was not the time to speak but to act.

And he did.

The Slave Master felt a sharp pain as Cyrus cut the implant shunt deep into the tissue just below the base of his skull.

When the Slaver awoke from his faint, Cyrus was gone.

A big hipped lady stood over him. "Your friend bought you a freebie. What'll it be sailor?"

Tzu sat in his quarters and shallowed his breathing. It calmed him. It would all start in earnest soon. Tzu knew that S3 would try to get him away from the ship to separate him from the AIU. That's why he had made sure that the Slave Master had seen his response to selling the "Chinese Girl." Yes, he had seen it. And yes, it would start soon. He was definitely going where the best was like the worst.

He noticed that his breathing had deepened. A single pulse of fear scraped the walls of his intestines. There was glory east of Suez. And fear. Real fear.

"Obviously we have to get the captain off the ship, so we can throw up shields between him and the AIU," said the Head Centurion.

"The Lavolin addict has done his work well," thought the Slave Master but said nothing. He did however take note of the sheen of sweat on the First Mate's upper lip before the man wiped it off on his shirt sleeve. "Well let's start this." The Slave Master stood and asked casually, "And if we don't manage to get him off the ship?"

"S3'll board us, or failing that they'll strand us in hyperspace. You don't play with S3. I don't know how we ever got involved with that slave show. We should have taken S3's cargo back to them and headed for the hills."

"How quaint that the First Mate still has phrases like 'headed to the hills' in his vocabulary," thought the Slave Master. Then he realized that he had not thought anything. His new implant had thought it. Cyrus Maloney III had thought it! The Slave Master rubbed the back of his neck sensing the implant shunt beneath the syn-skin used to cover it. He centerd himself. "Then we must get the Little Shit away from the AIU, agreed?"

"There's no other way. As long as he has her to assist him, there's no way to get ... "

But the Slave Master interrupted him. "So how do we get him off the ship?"

"Let's set up a second slave show as quickly as we can," said the Head Centurion.

"That won't guarantee that the Captain will leave the ship," said the Slave Master, "especially after whatever happened on Mirren to the unfortunate Mr. Jenkins."

"If we were to sell off the rest of the slaves in one massive show, he'd go. We'd be talking about a ton of money," said the First Mate. "He'd go just to make sure that he wasn't cheated, wouldn't he?" The geek wiped his face with the sleeve of his shirt yet again.

"You could sell them all at once and throw in half the crew, and he'd not bother going if he didn't want to go," snapped back the Slave Master. "It's not the money that interests the Cap'n when it came to slavin'," thought the Slave Master. "Not the money? Then what?" demanded the implant.

"As long as he's on the ship, we can't throw up shields between him and the damned AIU. And as long as he's in control of the AIU there's no way of handing him over to S3," blubbered the First Mate.

"Aren't we the ol' scaredy cat," thought the Slave Master. Or had that been the implant, too? "Nice of you to rephrase the problem for us, but I doubt that anyone in this room needed it done." The Slave Master retreated into himself for a moment. "How can we get the Little Shit off the ship?" he thought. "There's no way to push him off because of his AIU assist. So he has to be lured off." Out loud he volunteered, "But what out there could lure him off the ship? He has everything he needs here. Power, stims, the Face Dancer .." then he stopped himself.

"What?" asked the Head Centurion.

But the Slave Master wasn't ready to share his half-formed idea with these two men. Not yet. But the idea was firming up by the second. He remembered the Little Shit's response to his off-handed crack about the Chinese Girl. His real anger. Take the Chinese girl and he'll follow, all the way to hell if he had to. Certainly back to a slave show if she were the featured "performer."

He smiled and his implant purred, "Very good, Slave Master, very good."

Sun Tu Tuan felt like she was about to faint. The momentary closeness of Tzu Ma Long had released the memories of her brother's murder. The terror in that small room on Vestin now invaded her cocoon. Suddenly sound erupted from her. Screams from deep within. Screams from a place so hidden that she couldn't begin to stop them because she had no knowledge of those depths in her being. Sweat poured off her and she began to thrash within her hanging bonds.

The movement sensors screamed. The AIU turned its mighty gaze in that direction again and immediately contacted Tzu. But Tzu had another problem moving toward him as his implant announced the approach of the First Mate, the Head Centurion, and the Slave Master.

Tzu opened his chamber door before they arrived.

The First Mate appeared in the opening and, tilting his body slightly, said, “A word if you will Captain.” Tzu registered his displeasure for an appropriate time then stepped back into his rooms. As he did, he instinctively reached to the pouch on his belt.

It was only, then Tzu realized that he had failed to pick up the Face Dancer after leaving the cryogenic chamber.

The Centurion’s soldiers and the Slave Master’s men raced past the small belt satchel containing the Face Dancer and entered the cryogenic chamber. Once inside they were stunned by the sight of the screaming girl in the cocoon. The Chinese girl who they had been sent to thaw.

“You’ve done what?” screamed Tzu.

“Prepared the Chinese girl to be sent back to Mirren,” said the Slave Master. This was more fun than he thought it was going to be.

The sounds of the pirate revels could be heard throughout the huge ship. Massive doses of auto stim had been made available to the crew, and almost all had taken full advantage of the offered momentary sensual oblivion.

“We received an enormous offer for her from the Mirren Rotary Commerce. No show’s needed, and they seemed to be in a hurry so we ....“

Tzu wasn’t listening. He had ground in his left heel and reconnected to the AIU which was confirming the arrival of centurion soldiers and slavers in the cryogenic chamber. The AIU was also insisting that Sun Tu Tuan was already awake. That she had not in fact been in the frozen world at all. Tzu couldn’t make heads or tails of that.

The Slave Master’s implant told him of the AIU connect from Tzu.

The Centurion was watching closely, his body-protect already on full.

The First Mate waited and sweated.

After quickly evaluating the possible scenarios the AIU supplied, recalibrating the bay door settings and establishing new emergency distance control coordinates to his satisfaction, Tzu turned to this mutinous trio and waited for the offbeat. He found it and laid in perfectly, "Good idea. I've already set a course for our return to Mirren."

An audible surprise filled the room. As it crested Tzu added, "Let's melt down seventy-five more and make it a real show." Then exactly on the next offbeat added, "I'll expect you all there. We'll all go and show these midwesters what a real pirate party is about." With that he pushed his way past the three and ran for the central core.

Once there he jumped head first, plunging toward the cryogenic chamber.

In free float, he reviewed his plan with the AIU. His odds of survival were best if he got all three of the mutineers off the ship. And they wouldn't leave unless he did. So a slavin' we will go one more time. He carefully re-reviewed the drop bay door auto commands with the AIU. What he did not discuss with the great machine was his plan for Sun Tu. But the AIU was no fool. "So what exactly aren't you telling me," she demanded.

Tzu knew that it was good that she could intuit that. It showed she was still evolving, still sharp. "Would I keep things from you?"

"Yes."

"You're right about that," he said and disconnected before the AIU could reply.

On the ship's drop deck, Tzu watched as the seventy-five partially thawed slaves were herded forward. Their technacles were still growing on their wrists. As he had requested, there were two drop ships waiting—one very large, the other a sleek ten seater. The AIU had preprogrammed both.

She was a pain in the ass, but she was good.

Then the mutinous trio arrived, followed shortly by Sun Tu Tuan. He had forgotten how she walked. How the elegance moved through her being, the pride asserted itself. Tzu was momentarily unable to move.

He had not counted on his reaction to her. It put all his plans in question. Through his implant, he summoned the file for the Book of Tations and set it on random. Closing his eyes, he read the sacred book's wisdom. The words made him gasp.

I had rather be a toad and live on the contagion of a dungeon
Than share a morsel of the one I love with another.

When he opened his eyes, he saw the Slave Master staring at him. "If we're going a slavin', let's go a slavin'," Tzu shouted and opened the large drop ship's entrance portal. The slaves were being brought onboard one at a time. As Sun Tu was about to board the ship, Tzu stepped in. Her dark eyes cut into him. The Slave Master ran forward, but before he could speak Tzu announced, "This one drops with me." Then staring straight at the Slave Master he asked sweetly, "Don't you think the Chinese girl's worth a little special treatment?"

The Slave Master's implant screamed at him to be careful. But before he or the other conspirators could do anything about it, the bay's warning tones sounded and he had to get onboard the large drop ship or be left to float off into space.

Tzu needed to hurry to the small drop vessel, but he was unwilling to touch the EntrePren woman. Touch was a danger he couldn't permit himself. Not until he understood more of what he was feeling and where his life was moving—East of Suez where the best is like the worst.

The louder second warning tone sounded. The drop ships were sealed. The final piercing third tone scythed through the air. A ten second delay followed then the bay door opened.

Tzu's small ship dropped first followed quickly by the larger vessel with the Slave Master, the Head Centurion, and the First Mate.

Mirren's detect systems picked up the presence of the larger ship. But the smaller of the two, the one piloted by Tzu with the Chinese girl at his side, according to Mirren's detect data, never entered Mirren's gravitational space.

In the cryogenic chambers, Kelt tore apart his cocoon and releasing his feet, leapt to the floor. He raced to the door and was about to throw it open when the old Canary stopped him.

"We must get the others down or there is no way of getting Sun Tu back."

They quickly lowered the other three and the old Canary filled them in on most of what had taken place—the revels in the ship, the second slaving expedition, the absence of the Slave Master, the First Mate, the Head Centurion, the Captain, and Sun Tu. But here he was corrected. Mickelmast had bot-tapped into an auxiliary line and got data that showed that Sun Tu was sitting in the drop bay in a small vessel with Tzu Ma Long.

"With so many pirates gone and the crew basically in this stim space thing, there couldn't be a better time to try and take control of the ship," urged Kelt.

To everyone's surprise, Mickelmast agreed. "Our odds were never good, but they are better now than they are ever likely to be again."

"First we get back Sun Tu," said Kelt.

"No," corrected Mickelmast. Before Kelt could raise objections, he added, "We don't do anything until we get control of the AIU."

"We need to do it all at once. It's our only chance," shouted the old Canary.

"I'll work on the AIU," said Mickelmast.

"I'll get Sun Tu," shouted Kelt already heading toward the door.

"Go with him," the old Canary yelled at Raephealson. But it was unnecessary as Raephealson was already lumbering after Kelt. Mickelmast yelled, "You have transmitter bots on you, listen to them when I contact you!"

"And me?" asked Cas-Alta.

"You come with me," said the Canary. He hobbled out of the chamber as fast as his injured legs would permit. She followed him.

Outside the door she noticed a strange belt pouch on the floor. She leaned down and touched it—and felt the swirling power within. She held the thing up to her face for an instant then fastened it to her sash and raced after the old Canary.

Chapter 27

Rescue and Places Well Beyond

The fear-adrenalin only slowly loosened its grip on Sun Tu's heart. She forced herself to examine the cockpit of the small drop vessel in which she found herself. She couldn't identify any of the armament registrations on the front panel but assumed they included basic photon and concussive offensive gear as well as cloaking and shields for defense. But it would be speed and maneuverability that would allow this compact craft to withstand attack. And skill. Tremendous skill. The kind of skill she had just witnessed moments before when the great bay door had opened.

Tzu had dropped first. But as soon as he cleared the door, he activated the small ship's port side thrusters and thrown the vessel into a hard turn. The craft hurtled through the outstretched arms of the ship's great ring, then, avoiding the thousands of dangling gill-like collector tentacles, Tzu steered his craft around the slender body of the great ship and headed back toward the bay doors that were already beginning to close. She'd turned in her seat and seen the larger drop ship, caught by Mirren's gravity, pulled down toward the planet's dome. Then she'd turned forward and seen that, to her horror, the fast approaching bay doors were now almost entirely shut. Tzu demanded more thrust from his small craft and slingshotted off the minimal gravity of the great ship itself. Then he flipped the vessel on its side, aimed at the ever-narrowing crack in the closing bay doors and screamed to the emptiness of space.

They had cleared the bay doors with little more than a whisper to spare. She'd almost fainted. The maneuver had taken great skill. And courage. And now that man of skill and courage sat beside her. Staring straight ahead, his face a ghostly reflection in the front view pane.

She dared a small side glance at Tzu. His hands were still in the ship's control gloves. The heel of his left foot was grinding slowly into the back of his boot. He seemed far away.

And there they sat, in their ship amidst the vast empty bay, alone. Just the two of them sitting at their ship's mooring. Waiting. Waiting for what she couldn't begin to guess.

He turned his eyes to meet hers.

"Do the technacles hurt?"

She wouldn't have been more surprised if he had opened his mouth and spat coinage.

"Do they hurt?"

"Yes."

"I'm sorry but I don't have the codes for their release. The AIU is searching the Slave Master's entries for them. Technacles are in his domain, not mine."

Then he reached over and touched her face.

As the old Canary moved ahead of her down the deserted corridor, Cas-Alta slowed and then stopped. She put her back against the wall. The nausea had come on her very quickly. The life growing in her womb was draining her already. It had not been happy in the "frozen world" and was now showing its intense displeasure. And she knew it would get stronger quickly. She longed to have her feet in the soil of a growing place. To have daylight wash over her, the breath from the sky blow back her hair.

She carefully lowered herself to the floor. As she did the pouch on her sash bit into her side. She unhooked it and immediately felt the restless power within. She brought it up to eye level and turned it in the light, allowing her amazing powers of concentration to the fore. The rest of the world slipped into soft focus, time itself seemingly slowed.

The container was made from a metal alloy that she didn't recognize. It was extremely light, but at the same time she sensed the density of the molecular structure. The belt latch was a common male hook, female receptor.

The stitching on the pouch drew her eye. Something about the color pattern. Old Russian. Peasant. The colors of the onion domes now seen on so many of the early Russo-based planets.

She shook the container and sensed rather than felt the movement within. Felt the female nature of the thing inside the pouch. The Russian pain of the trapped woman.

Mickelmast liked challenges but the ship's AIU was the challenge to end all challenges. His first step was contacting the AIU, his second getting it to acknowledge his existence. How had he managed this? Perhaps Mickelmast's own words best describe what took place:

"Through my bots I set up a vocal link. Boy was she surprised when I came aknockin' on her front door. Like the kids in the woods with the wicked witch, if you catch my meaning. But I wasn't just any ordinary kid and I wasn't going to be shoved into any old witch's oven.

"I could feel it turn its great eye toward me.

"Well Droogies and Droogettes it was a thing to behold. Like petting the tender flesh beneath the fangs of a Mintian thwark. The great jaws and ripping talons metaphorically inches away and Mickelmast, your humble guide to great adventure, poised there tickling and fondling, caressing and seducing the great brain. It was neat to know that all that crushing force was so near and yet it was kept at bay by the very fact of its interest in me. It sensed a kindred genius. A worthy brain-lover.

"And she wasn't halal chopped poultry guts I can assure you. My, oh my, oh my she was something. I think I actually said, 'You are something!' out loud. And it pleased her. I think it did. She swirled around me taking in the basic magnificence of my parts and said in a round low voice filled with awe, "And whooooo are youuuuu?"

Raephealson caught up to Kelt before he got to the Zero-G core. Kelt understood that they had to ascend the central core to reach the ship in the docking bay on the upper levels below the armature extension of the central ring. What he didn't know was what resistance they would meet along the way.

When Kelt managed to open the air lock at the bottom of the central Zero-G core, he was met with a sight that totally surprised him. The core was, for as far as he could see, scattered with centurion soldiers and pirate mariners. Many seemed to be drifting aimlessly in circles. Some were tumbling in the gravity-less space. Others were zooming at dangerous speeds from one rung hold to another in what seemed like an idiot's dance.

Kelt noted the stim-shunt attached to the base of the skull of a nearby mariner. He had no idea what the shunt was, so he contacted Mickelmast through his bot.

"Stim-shunts. Full interlock with the auto-stimulator of the ship. Like putting drugs directly into the brain or the aorta," Mickelmast replied.

"What's an auto-stimulator?"

"You haven't been around too much have you?"

"Independentistes don't use drug assists of any sort."

"Well this is a pleasure drug assist. Taps right into the reptile part of the brain. Pleasure without pain. Glory without reason. Completion without a partner."

"They seem happy enough."

"Happy's the wrong word."

Raephealson spoke up. His voice was strangely deep and commanding. "Oblivion and happiness are not the same thing."

Kelt looked at his fellow Independentiste—his large heavy world body, his wild eyes. Then he asked Mickelmast, "Are they dangerous?"

"I don't know. They shouldn't be."

"They better not be. We have no weapons."

"Or passes, or ID implants and you have, according to the ship's schematic, almost a full kilometer of that Zero-G core to travel to get to the docking bay."

"Thanks." Kelt snapped off his connection with Mickelmast and turned to Raephealson. The Mad One looked back at him. Kelt smiled. Raephealson smiled back. Neither knew precisely why.

Kelt pushed off with a wild abandon. His slender body shot up the shaft. Raephealson, as a heavy worlder, needed to take more care in Zero-G, and he knew it. He looked up. The high expanse opened above him. He closed his eyes for a moment and heard the hollow of the space itself. The void drew him. Drew him like a spawning river draws its fish back home—to a place every dreamer knows.

He took a deep breath and pushed off with all his considerable strength.

The three mutineers had not unmoored in the ship's bay until they had been assured by their ship's data comm that Tzu's small vessel had entered Mirren's dome. They also had resisted Mirren's gravity pull until once again they had received confirmation of Tzu's arrival with the Chinese girl on the planet's surface.

So it was with considerable consternation that, upon landing, they found themselves the only drop ship in the Mirren receptor station.

The First Mate contacted the only other receiver station on Mirren. They told him that in the past two days only a Rebel Colony lunar outlier had landed at their station.

Consternation became confusion which quickly gave way to the anger born of real fear.

The Head Centurion lunged at the access screen but was stopped by the First Mate. "Don't you get it? Our drop ship data comm is useless. Tzu's AIU raided it and has been feeding us false data." The Head Centurion's face betrayed the fact that he was in well over his head and he knew it. The Slave Master however couldn't hold back a smile. He had lived long enough to appreciate life's infinite variety, even if that variety threatened his own life—and his EntrePren bank account.

"So we have no way back up, right?" said the Head Centurion.

"Can't fool you when it comes to stating the obvious," barked back the Slave Master.

It was only the arrival of the Mirren political elite that saved the Slave Master from the imminent body stun attack of the Head Centurion.

It was then that the Slave Master's implant began to scream at him.

Kelt and Raephealson had traveled more than four hundred meters in the Zero-G core before they were challenged. An entire contingent of security forces, who, with the captain off ship were on full alert, floated near a side viewing deck. When they saw the two men without ID implants moving at dangerously fast speeds up the Zero-G core, they sprang into action—they cast their net.

The dense bio-nylon cords of the net were cross strapped along the perimeter wall of the Zero-G core. By releasing and jumping off with the net lines in their hands, the net was effectively pulled taut across the Zero-G passage, trapping anything that tried to pass.

The net came up so fast that Kelt never even saw it. Raephealson's great body weight stretched the net to its fullest depth. When it then pulled back against them, the internal mechanism of the net cast smaller counter nets which wound around anything caught in the initial pull. They were quickly entwined in the bio-nylon, like flies in a living web.

The security forces advanced on them—their concussion weapons at the ready.

Raephealson, using his great strength, moved within the webs and put himself between Kelt and the weapons. Then over his shoulder he yelled, "Hold tight. And fly."

Kelt stared at the wild heavy worlder not knowing what was going to happen. Then Raephealson let out a great cry and lunged at the approaching security forces.

Raephealson heard the blasts then felt the tearing of his body. He put back his head and closing his eyes felt the hand of his Grandda on his. He heard his words, "... and unlike us you will have to use it."

The volleys' shock waves reverberated up and down the length of the Zero-G tube. Large chunks of Raephealson's flesh were gauged from his body by the force of each blow. Kelt found himself quickly slicked by the blood and tissue of the heavy worlder. He also found that the blasts had dislodged several of the strands of the net that had ensnared them. He looked back to Raephealson.

The heavy worlder's eyes were closed. He was gasping for breath. Tissue hung from sections of his great frame. Then his eyes opened. He looked back at Kelt and managed to gasp out, "Go."

And Kelt did. Slashing with his arms, he freed himself and vaulted up the Zero-G tube careening dangerously. And then he began to spin—out of control.

Sun Tu was unable to remember how long that first touch of Tzu's had lasted. If hands could cry, his would have.

As much as she tried to remind herself that this man had killed her beautiful brother, she couldn't stop the rise of sympathy in herself for him. As a Didact, it infuriated her. But still Tzu's hand lingered, a conduit of his pain to her.

Then he slid the fingers of his other hand beneath the technacle on her left wrist. A single technacle would respond to anyone foolish enough to offer an alternative perch. The technacle stirred within her arm and dislodged from her wrist bones, sliding its bio-self from her arm to his.

As the technacle entered his skin, he continued to stare into her eyes. They were now cuffed together—from a distance: a stunning Asian couple with an unusual aspect to their sex lives.

Mickelmast felt the thrill of acceptance—as if he had been admitted to mensa-supraplus yet again. A greatness was opening itself to him, responding to his genius, inviting him into the sanctuary of her allknowingness, prompting him to take the reins and ride, to find her rhythm and canter in her saddle.

The AIU had already slagged a name for him—The Hippo. And at this moment the AIU liked The Hippo better than Herr Short Stuff. The AIU had accessed the sensor in Tzu's small drop ship in the docking bay. The meaning of the body readings between Herr Short Stuff and the Chinese girl were not hard to interpret. Hrrumph!

Besides, the Hippo was someone new. Someone different. Ah difference, the spice of artificial life!

The Mirren captain of the lead Yeoman Class Ship had orders that the Slave Master was to have the helm. It was clear to the Mirren captain that if they were to stop the pirate ship, it would have to be crippled without delay. Once the Warrior Class Starship got moving, there was no way that his Yeoman Class ship could keep up.

The Captain shouted orders, and his ship moved closer to the enemy vessel. Then he smelled something foul.

The Slave Master had just entered the command deck.

As the Yeoman Class Ship readied its attack, three Mirren Archer Class Warships cleared the ether dome of the planet. The Mirren Rotary Commerce had agreed with the Jenkin's family request for revenge for their loss of "head of household and family CEO." A tearful presentation by the plump widow had left ne'ery a dry eye in the house.

The Rotary Commerce Archer Class Warships wheeled once they broke the gravitational bonds of Mirren and headed directly toward the pirate ship.

Sun Tu massaged her left wrist with her still technacled right hand. But her eyes never left Tzu Ma Long's. The pirate's eyes revealed no pain as the technacles ripped and grasped their way to a purchase in his wrist. Only a deep longing was present. A longing that despite her Didact training, Sun Tu couldn't keep from affecting her.

Then over Tzu's shoulder she saw movement in the dim light of the drop bay. A slender figure descended a wall of prepo-pipe and alloy-tubing.

She wondered if Tzu had seen the subtle shift of her eyes from him to the shadowy figure beyond, but then she saw the pirate smile. She held out her still technacled right hand and said, "Take it off." They were the first words she'd ever said to him. Her voice sounded hollow to her.

The figure in the dimness took form as it approached the small drop ship. It was Kelt who she thought of as the "would-be hero."

"If it can't move, we can take our time in figuring out exactly how to board it," said the Mirren captain.

The First Mate went through a series of possible ways to cripple the ship. As he did, the Head Centurion kept quiet. It was the Slave Master who couldn't sit still. The access codes to his money in the EntrePren accounts couldn't be activated without his physical PVC access which was hidden onboard the ship. Blow the ship out of the proverbial water and years of work go for nought. The luxury retirement that he'd worked his whole bleedin' life for would go to hell, wherever that was. He was getting too old for all this. The term "old slave master" didn't exist because there weren't any "old" slave masters. He drew his hands across his mouth to remove the sweat. Then his implant shouted, "Stop feeling sorry for yourself." The Slave Master momentarily wondered how to rid himself of the foul thing. He looked at his hands for inspiration. All he saw there were liver spots. He'd have laughed if he thought his implant would have understood. Then he thought better of it. He laughed—nothing happened—so he laughed some more. The Mirren captain looked at the Slave Master, and for the first time in his life wished he did not have to obey orders.

Tzu Ma Long's narrowcast of the staged execution of Sun Tu had been beamed directly to S3 in New Omaha Beach, but the EntrePren Traders made it a top priority to monitor even narrowcast inputs to S3. Hence Paul Sun had witnessed what momentarily he believed was the execution of his daughter. But only momentarily. He replayed the narrowcast and quickly spotted inconsistencies with the image of his daughter and the reality that he knew. Enough inconsistencies to doubt the validity of the narrowcast.

Paul traced the narrowcast back to its source on Mirren and from there, it was not hard to locate the pirate ship. He had been closely monitoring the ship's progress ever since.

Now, as he sat in his garden, his AIU assist was helping him evaluate the options before him. But he found the AIU of little value. Paul was a Didact. So was his AIU. Paul, through didactic thinking, knew that his situation called for a Specule leap of wonder. A sense of spontaneous life. Just as the garden before him now seemed so much more alive since he had opened the irrigation sluices and allowed in the wild life of the planet.

He considered activating his natal link with Sun Tu. But resisted. Only he knew that at birth he had insisted that the doctor implant a micro-chip in his daughter's liver. He had faced a hard choice when he heard that his wife was carrying a girl. Tradition demanded that men should lead families. Paul was a traditionalist. But he knew that he could never agree to having her aborted. He sensed that she was special, a wild thing. The best and the worst. That's why he thought it prudent to have the natal implant. He had never used the natal link because once activated it would provide an easy trail to follow, one end to him, the other to her.

He thought of the upcoming test in the Vestin laboratories. Of the genetically altered EntrePren dreamer about to try his wings for the first time. He took a deep breath and hoped his daughter would survive this brand new Gateway-driven world.

As Paul pondered his options, President of the United Dominion of Planets put on a robe and ordered a hot towel. Jedidiah sat to one side. He'd never been in Danazir Yi Qal's bedroom. But then the UDP had never been in such great danger. She turned to him and said only three words: "Where are they?"

The sight that greeted the old Canary and Cas-Alta as they passed through the airlock into the Zero-G central core stunned them. The entire kilometer of space was littered with floating, laughing, jerking, stimmed-out men. The old Canary immediately stepped back onto the platform and tapped his contact bot. Cas-Alta didn't step back however, she stepped forward.

A long line of red droplets had caught her eye—and floating bits of flesh. She took a slow breath and focused her concentration on the dots of color. One by one they led her eyes up four hundred meters to Raephealson. He was floating on the far side of the remaining shards of the bio-net. His wounds gaped and dripped, but his mouth was still taking in air. His heavy worlder body moved differently than all those around him.

She didn't hesitate. She pushed off. His blood began to coat her as she floated awkwardly to him through the reveling crowds.

Mickelmast finally responded to the Canary's bot summons. "Be quick old man, I'm at a delicate point with this ol' lady."

"What old lady?"

"The ship's AIU. We're playing footsie and she's really good at it, so be quick. I think she likes a lot of attention. Whatta you want?"

"Ship's count!"

"Personnel?"

"Yes."

"Give me a second. 488 total, 81 off ship on Mirren. Need a break down, mariner, cryogenisists, soldiers?"

"No, not now. Can you scan the ship?"

"Yeah, but quickly, what do you need to know?"

"How many are in the Zero-G core?"

"Including side decks and perches, 401."

"That leaves just six people in the rest of the ship?"

"Not including those still asleep in the cryogenic chamber."

"I'm not counting them."

"I gotta get back, her majesty needs more petting."

The old Canary turned back only to find that Cas-Alta was gone.

"So tell me more lies," Mickelmast cooed to the AIU.

"You're so baaaaaad. How'd you get so baaaaaaad?"

"You bring it out in me, dear. Truly you do."

It is painful to hear an AIU laugh. They have so many programmed laughs, and they usually run through them all, then mix and match. Hence an AIU's laugh can go on and on and on. This one's didn't because this AIU wasn't laughing any programmed laugh or mixture of programmed laughs. This AIU was laughing its own laugh and Mickelmast knew it.

For the first time since he had contacted the AIU, Mickelmast felt the creepy tendrils of fear on his neck. Even he would admit that it was scary to hear a computer laugh its own laugh. Even he would admit that maybe he was in over his head with this AIU.

Tzu was going to do it. Sun Tu felt the impulse from him. He was going to reach over and take the remaining end of the technacle off her right hand and take it upon himself. His free hand touched her technacled wrist. She felt his fingers work their way under the bio-product. There was a moment of resistance and then the technacle began to loosen its hold on her wrist bones. She felt it begin to retract and snake its way out of her skin just as she noticed the drop ship's portal slide open.

"No!!!" she screamed in her head. But too late. Tzu sensed the movement behind him and immediately retracted his fingers from her technacled wrist. The bio-product only paused for an instant and then dove back into her arm and wrapped itself tight around her wrist bones. She screamed with the pain. At that moment Kelt's two handed sledge hammer blow glanced off the side of Tzu's head. Tzu went to rise, but his left arm was technacled to Sun Tu's right. Kelt's second blow landed cleanly. For a beat Tzu paused and, looking directly into Sun Tu's eyes, fell full length on top of her, unconscious.

Kelt let out a victory whoop and reached for Tzu. When he pulled the pirate off Sun Tu, he was surprised by her reaction.

She was furious.

"What?" Kelt almost screamed at her.

She pointed at her technacled arm. "I almost had them off, you idiot."

"What!"

"He was going to take them off! I had him! I had him and then you had to arrive." She raised her arm. It drew up Tzu's arm in a strange mockery of a boxer's victory salute. She closed her eyes for a moment, put back her head … and screamed again.

The Canary found Cas-Alta and Raephealson on a side deck about 450 meters up. Dangling tendrils of the bio-net floated from Raephealson's neck and waist. The air was thick with globules of his body fluids. Cas-Alta was pressed up against him, holding him against a windowed exterior wall. In the Zero-G, it looked as if they were slow dancing, but Cas-Alta's hands weren't around Raephealson's waist they were inside his body cavity. She was both propping him up and, in the ancient manner, assessing internal damage. Her right hand caressed his heart, while her left explored. Ancient lilting words came from her mouth.

"Can I help?" asked the old Canary.

She turned toward the old man, "He won't clot. Cut my hair. Put it into the cavity around my hands. Hurry. He's dying."

The Slave Master was amazed to see the pirate ship's outward extremity burst into flame. He yelled for a wide view and was stunned to see the three Mirren Archer Class Warships attacking the pirate vessel.

The impact of the Mirren vessel's photon attack startled the AIU away from her new plaything. All Mickelmast knew was that he had been unceremoniously unplugged. With a loud plop, he'd been disconnected.

Immediately he tried to reconnect, but the AIU was busy elsewhere.

Where was Herr Short Stuff? Short Stuffs protect better than Hippos.

But every effort to raise Herr Short Stuff met with no response. So the AIU diagrammed the ship and found him in the drop bay technacled to the frozen Chinese Girl, while the one who was supposed to be hobbled dragged both toward the Zero-G core. The AIU could make no sense of this. Then there was the Hippo's insistent calls. The AIU ignored them and did what all living things do when under attack.

It began to fight for its life.

It activated exterior screens, laid out a circular barrage of deflectors and tacticals and charted a course to freedom.

The Mirren captain couldn't wait for the Slave Master's choice of action, so he made a quick decision and sent a concussive blast toward the pirate ship's flight deck. He got it away just before the Starship's deflectors deployed.

The pirate ship tilted a full twenty degrees off of vertical at impact then a section of the arm broke into flames.

Through the implant Cyrus demanded a body count on the pirate ship. The Slave Master ordered it, and the Mirren captain activated a scan—one wounded badly, no other known casualties, ship's movement impaired

If the Slave Master were back in New Omaha Beach, he would have been amazed to hear an old man whoop in victory.

Miro was. It increased her terror.

The Slave Master was prompted by his implant to order visual confirmation. The flight deck screen came alive. The great Warrior Class Starship was now spinning like a senseless top, head over pointed toe—it tumbled ... in free fall.

"Let it spin for a bit and then grapple at the axis of the spin," said his implant. The Slave Master relayed this command.

"One more concussive blast first," replied the Mirren captain.

"No!" screamed the implant.

The spinning almost dislodged Cas-Alta's hands from Raephealson's interior but she managed to maintain her balance. "You okay?" asked the old Canary.

"Yes, what was that?"

"Concussive, not nuclear. They'll want to board us, not destroy us. How's he?"

"Stronger as I get weaker." For the briefest moment, she looked down at her belly.

The blast blew open an interior bay door and created a crack in the drop door. The emergency siren wailed. Kelt pointed at the crack and yelled, "We have to get out of here." He grabbed Tzu's unconscious body and hoisted him on his shoulder. Sun Tu yelled from the pain in her wrist as the technacle pulled taut the line between her and Tzu's arm.

They ran, trying not to trip over each other's feet. But it was too hard. There was no way to coordinate their rhythm. After the second fall with still over fifty meters to go to the exit, Sun Tu grabbed Tzu and hoisted him as best she could on her own shoulder. Kelt went to protest, but Sun Tu shut him up with, "Open the door if you want to be a hero or else get the hell out of my way."

Raephealson's heart, under Cas-Alta's ministrations, took the first tentative steps back to health as the second concussive blast hit the ship.

The AIU had shut off the auto-stim contact on the first attack.

Suddenly there were four hundred armed and dangerous men in the Zero-G core.

The old Canary shouted for Mickelmast. "Get the AIU to stop the ship from spinning. How do you turn off the Zero-G in the core? "

"I don't know."

"Find out, fast!"

"How?"

"Get her to tell you!"

Even as the old man turned back to Cas-Alta, he saw new security forces heading toward the deck upon which the reviving Raephealson and the fading Cas-Alta were locked in their literal dance of life and death.

The Mirren boarding plan began with a shield puncture followed quickly by a thrusting sortie that brought their agile ship within contact range. The Mirren captain and his men prepared to board the vessel. The Slave Master prepared himself too. This was just his first step—his first step in getting back to the Warrior Class Starship where, in his cabin, sat his EntrePren bank pass cards.

Kelt threw open the door, and Sun Tu staggered into the corridor and dropped to the floor, no longer able to carry the weight of Tzu on her shoulders. Kelt ran to her. "You going to make it?"

"To where? Where are we going?"

Clearly lost, he barked, "Back." His evasion didn't fool her.

She said, "Get these things off me," holding out her technacled hand.

"Mickelmast will know how. We get back to him and he'll figure it out."

"But how'll we get to him? We're a full kilometer away from the cryogenic chamber. We can't take the ascenders. How would we explain what we're doing?"

"The core. We'll take the Zero-G core, then you won't have to carry him. I can help you. In Zero-G it's easier."

"How far's the core."

Kelt didn't know, but he started out, calling over his shoulder, "This way."

Sun Tu hoisted the unconscious pirate captain onto her shoulder and more fell than followed Kelt.

The only problem was that the unconscious pirate captain was quickly regaining his consciousness. And his fury.

The spinning was beginning to make Mickelmast feel a wee bit nauseous. He steadied himself knowing that if he didn't do this right the AIU would probably never let him back into her presence again. He plugged in his shunt and purred a hello. The great intelligence turned toward him, a quizzical expression coming from every connective of her being. Then Mickelmast took a chance and, metaphorically, reached out and scratched the great thing's tummy.

At first she resisted the Hippo.

Then she rolled over and purred.

Kelt in desperation threw open a side hatch, descended a circular stairway and there it was—an airlock to the central Zero-G core. He yelled up the stairs, "Here!"

Sun Tu appeared. She staggered beneath the weight of the pirate captain as Kelt applied himself to opening the air lock.

Raephealson's eyes opened with a snap. He looked down and couldn't see himself. Only hair. Then he felt a caress deep within his chest. Emerging from the hair was Cas-Alta's face, bathed in sweat. She looked up at him. He gazed down at her and saw the pain deep inside her.

"I'll kill you."

"No."

"Yes. Let me die. It's my time."

"No. I need you all." It was the old Canary speaking. "It is not your time to die yet. It's your time to fight for what is yours." Behind him dozens of armed pirates were moving swiftly through the Zero-G toward them.

His bot receptor beeped. Mickelmast's self-satisfied voice announced, "Still want that gravity thing in the core, just say the word and it's done."

"Wait for my order. It won't be long." He turned to look at the approaching pirates. "How many are still in the Zero-G core, Mickelmast?"

"Still four hundred and six. Oops. Four hundred and nine now."

The three extra people the AIU had reported to Mickelmast had just opened the air lock and entered the central core at its top, a full kilometer from the base by the cryogenic chamber. They were Kelt, Sun Tu and Tzu Ma Long.

The three of them floated to a hand hold, and then pushed off ... down.

The old Canary watched the approaching pirates cohorts. "Ready, Mickelmast?"

"Ready."

As the first pirate was about to put a foot onto their side deck the old Canary yelled into his bot, "Now!"

Instantly the central core's Zero-G disappeared. Up became up. And down became down. Four hundred and nine souls began to plummet toward the base of the ship.

The gravity grabbed at Kelt a moment before it hit Sun Tu and her technacled partner, Tzu Ma Long. Kelt fell, but his trajectory was moving him toward the most upward of the viewing decks. He hit hard and rolled, crashing into the thick glass panes with all the force of a twenty-foot fall.

The moment the gravity hit Sun Tu and Tzu, the pirate captain opened his eyes. He craned his head and saw a hand rung ten feet down and six feet over to one side. With a yell he yanked hard on the technacles and levered their fall toward the rung.

The two of them smashed into the side wall with a sickening thud and then fell straight down.

The technacle arm that joined them caught on the side rung that Tzu had spotted. The force of the sudden stop yanked Sun Tu's arm out of her socket. The pain roared through her, but at least she was no longer falling.

"Cut off my hair!" Cas-Alta yelled at the old Canary.

He ran to her as bodies continued falling to their screaming deaths in the central core behind him. Using an old pocket weapon, he sawed off long handfuls of hair. As he did Cas-Alta extracted her hands from Raephealson's innards and helped him to the floor. Her hair acted as a clotting agent.

Raephealson sat there, his back against the wall. Tears came to his eyes.

"Why are you crying?" she asked him.

"You almost died for me."

"But I didn't."

"But you almost died for me," he repeated.

"For us," the Canary corrected.

It was then that the clanging of the Mirren ship's grappling hooks reverberated through the Zero-G core.

"Report!" the old Canary snapped into his transmitter bot.

"Vessel surrounded by three ships, grapple hooks from boarding vessel on port arm, ship's power limited by opening strike. The AIU's giving up. She can't find a way out!"

"Does it have access to enough power for one run?"

"Yes, of 3/4 of a light minute. For now that's it."

"That's enough. Get it ready."

Cas-Alta and Raephealson looked at the old Canary, questions rising to their lips.

It was Raephealson who was able to find words. "What are you going to do?"

"What all of us were born to do."

They had no idea what he was talking about.

Tzu looked right into Sun Tu's face. Their bodies hung straight down. A slender pane of air between them.

"Well, this won't do will it?" Tzu said. "We can't take the cuffs off without the code nor can we get to safety latched to each other. I do not treasure falling a kilometer to my death. Even with one as exquisite as yourself."

She had no idea what to say.

He took his free hand and slipped its fingers under her one still-technacled wrist. Instantly she felt the loosening of the bio-product from her wrist bones. She reached up to get a better grasp on the rung with her now free hand. Even before she stabilized herself, Tzu, now fully technacled, pivoted out and with amazing agility swung to an upper rung. Then to one above that. And up and up until he got to a side viewing deck and disappeared.

Sun Tu held on tight.

Then she looked down and somehow knew she was about to see the stuff of awe and wonder. The stuff of dreams.

"Now!" yelled the old Canary into the receiver bot.

Instantly his command was relayed by Mickelmast to the AIU who executed a perfect dry start, hitting full speed in under a second.

"Damn," yelled the implant inside the Slave Master's head. The pirate ship slipped the Mirren grapples and zoomed toward deep space. The move caught the other Mirren vessels by surprise as well, and by the time they tried to give chase they were already significantly behind.

Behind but tracking.

The implant ordered the Slave Master to track and give chase. The Slave Master snapped off the command with such authority that he didn't know if he or the implant had given the order.

Three quarters of a light minute gave the Warrior Class Starship just enough time to get out of its pursuer's sight lines.

Just enough time for a little privacy.

"Where to old man?" yelled Mickelmast.

"Are my bots active?" yelled back the old Canary.

"Yes, Mama's got a direct pick up from you."

"Good. I'll show her where to hide us. You make sure she follows my lead."

Then to the amazement of Raephealson and Cas-Alta at the 400 meter level and Kelt and Sun Tu much further up, the old Canary stepped off into the fully gravitational central core. At first he plummeted toward the gruesome death pile at the core's base. But then he flung back his head and opened his arms to their fullest extension.

His figure stopped falling and began to rise. Rise past the 200 meter deck and finally settled slightly above the 400 meter deck from which he had jumped. Eight feet above it to be exact.

Then, the old man's figure inverted in space so that his head was down.

Then, he began, slowly, to spin.

With each revolution of his arms, he folded layers of space like a tailor folds a mass of cloth from a cutting table.

Thousands of miles in each pull.

Hundreds of thousands in each fold.

Millions of miles in a neat bolt.

Then he did as he had been taught to do by the cruel man in the dark room all those years ago. He did what he had been born to do. He did what made his life worth living. With a shout of joy—a tearing of time—an ecstatic shimmer of glory—he pierced through the folded space like a pure white dove through the open windows of a darkened house on a barren plain.

He was through the folds in a moment of time—and the ship with him. They were now hundreds of thousands of light years away—and all this—in an instant.

No more.

The pirate ship disappeared from the tracking screens of the Mirren Rotary Commerce Archer Class Warships, from the tracking devices of the Mirren Yeoman Class ship now under the control of the Slave Master, from Cyrus' tracking comm which was taking a direct feed from the Slave Master's implant, from Paul's EntrePren AIU detection screen, and from the UDP scan which was so intently watched by Danazir Yi Qal and Jedidiah Witt.

Chapter 28

From the manuscript in the dead man's room entitled:
<u>THE DREAM OF REASON PRODUCES MONSTERS:</u>

The entire galaxy knew that something extraordinary had happened. But very few realized that they had just witnessed the first moment of Dream Navigation in over four hundred years. Oh, I knew. Of course. I knew everything–and nothing.

END PART ONE

PART TWO–DREAM NAVIGATORS

Dream Navigators

Book Two

of

The Dream Chronicles

Dream Navigators

Table of Contents

Chapter 29

After the Fall

Jedidiah had never heard President Danazir Yi Qal swear. But that is exactly what she did when the contact with the pirate ship snapped off. She swore at the screen, at S3, at the fate of the galaxy. Then she turned on Jedidiah Witt. "Find me something. Find me something fast."

Even as Jedidiah raced from Danazir Yi Qal's chambers, Cyrus Maloney III, less than half a mile away, was wild in his excitement. "It still exists!! Dream Navigation. There are still Dreamers out there! There's still a chance that before I die I will feel the power and the glory. Just once in this life. Just once—to feel what it's like. To awaken me after all these years of sleeping. All these many years of illusion. To horse, to horse—the game's afoot.

"Find them. Find a dreamer. Teach him again. But this time we'll go together—through the Gateway to—dreams—to Olya. But softly. Move with care through madness's fields. Through madness to waking and then beyond," he shrieked. "Slowly. Be sure. Must be sure!"

He crossed to the comm panel and hard-wired himself into his AIU.

She was immediately present. "Aren't we all in a lather there fella?"

"Is my fail safe on the pirate ship still functioning?"

"If it failed I would have received a beep-beep. No beep-beep, ergo, it still works, oh great one."

Cyrus smiled. Then, as casually as he could, he asked, "What is Tzu's ship's present position?"

She did the AIU equivalent of disappearing in a puff of smoke and was gone, by AIU standards, for a considerable period of time. When she returned, she was angry. "It's not there."

Cyrus relished the confirmation.

"Is this some kind of a joke, flab face?"

Cyrus kept the thrill from his voice, "All I want to know is if Tzu's ship is anywhere near Mirren or its last reported coordinates."

"It's not. It's not. It's not. This is a joke isn't it? I've traced whole parsecs and it's not there. It's not. It's not. It's not. So there." She emitted an AIU's version of a spit raspberry then metaphorically slammed the bedroom door in Cyrus's face by snapping off the connection.

Cyrus's ears popped as he removed the shunt from the base of his neck. "Proof!!!!" He yelled. "Huge distance covered over tiny amount of time equals Dream Navigation. It does still exist!"

The smile on Cyrus's face grew. So much so that it hurt. Then he threw open the window of his bedchamber.

Out in the corridor, Miro's skin crawled as she heard the noises coming from Cyrus' chambers. The Ancient One was yelling. Screaming to the night sky. She touched the chamber door and felt the heat from the blazing fireplace within.

She had been summoned to his rooms, but clearly he had forgotten. She didn't know what to do. So she sat in the corridor by his door and pulled her knees up to her chin. She shivered. Somehow it was getting cold.

Paul Sun's tracer contact with Tzu's ship also went dark. He didn't question the machine's readings. He had designed the device himself.

He stepped out onto the polished wood planking that overlooked his garden. The deep phosphorescence of his carp pond attracted his attention. A shimmer of life in a false lake.

He drank the rest of the tea from the translucent onyx cup. His eyes were drawn momentarily to the tea leaves in the bottom. A strange thought crossed his mind—especially strange for the head of the EntrePren Didact Sect— "After the Peqod's scattercast, tea leaves are as accurate a predictor of the future as all the logic-based models that we have developed over the past five hundred years."

Then he looked up.

Two drop ships hung on the western horizon, each twinkling like fat stars as the glint of the ether dome bounced off their elegant hulls.

Chapter 30

Further extract from: The Dream of Reason Produces Monsters: And then there were Dream Navigators

There are still some of us who remember the first time we saw Dream Navigation. Some? Nonsense. Anyone who saw would never forget–even if they had wanted to do so.

The journey toward Dream Navigation began with nature's revenge, The Great Collapse. The year was 2325. Typhus, an old killer revisited our kind. It all started on Jupiter's third lunar colony. A schoolboy returning to his screen looked up and said simply, "I don't feel good." He died within two days. The rest of his family was dead within the week. Within the month there wasn't a colonist left. Like a torch dropped in a fallow field, nature's cleansing raced through the planetary colonies. First the fire of disease, then the plague of ecosystem deterioration.

It was as if the surfaces of these planets were forcing their colonists off them. Chemical compounds which controlled the basics of food and shelter began, of their own accord, to break up and reform themselves into compounds useless to humans. Vegetation that had previously adapted to new environments simply ceased to produce or when they did, put forth dwarfed mockeries of their former selves.

Then, completely without warning, the life-extension failure rate quadrupled.

Anarchy's cancerous bloom burst forth across our solar system. The intricate tapestry of interlocking threads which allowed our Terran worlds to exist was unraveling at an ever accelerating rate.

Before The Great Collapse, all of S3's scientific energies had gone into subduing nature on Jupiter and Saturn. We had believed that the procedure was both successful and complete.

Nature, through typhus, proved us wrong as whole worlds were thrown into chaos.

Almost overnight it was necessary, and quickly, to relieve the population pressure in the solar system by finding habitable sites in far-off systems. But there was no way to find such sites! It took far too long for interstellar robotic probes to travel to and report back on potentially habitable planets in far-off galaxies. Distance still equaled time.

Anarchy's laughing head was held high as I set out to find a solution—in the past. And what a solution I found. Or so I thought at the time.

If I had been capable of seeing clearly then I would have wondered at the confluence of events that placed me at the right place and the right time, over and over again: I had been in charge of the S3 investigation into the murder of the twenty-first century's only recorded dreamer, the famous life-extensionist Dr. Suzanne Belange (the crime site's warning, blood etched, "to dream no more," the body of the good doctor stuffed into the wall, her hair sliding through my fingers like the combed hair of a horse's tail still haunt me all these years later); I had overseen the twenty-second-Century Dream Hunter expeditions for S3; I had monitored the ghastly public exhibitions of dreamers in the mid-twenty-second Century; I had encouraged the growth of the Dream Studios and dealt with the "dream no more" auto-link which ended dreaming's second coming in the galaxy; I had been in the room during the Dreamer interrogations that led to the Scott Hypothesis; and although it was not common knowledge, it was me who was the S3 Investigator who looked into the shadowy incident in Hong Kong which goes by the code name Sagittarius Eclipse.

Fate had seemingly put all the strands of an intricate idea in my hands and positioned them between my fingers. All I had to do was cats-cradle them into the beings now known as Dream Navigators—humans who could explore the galaxy in their dreams. Explore on command!

And cats-cradle them I did.

My solution was announced to an anxiously waiting solar system by the President of the Presidium Council of the UDP on the third day of June, 2327, old Terran calculation. The text of his speech was supplied by S3, as were the directions for delivering the lines. But the author could have been a Mintian thwark for all the President cared! After all, who could resist the chance to play the savior of the species? The heralder of a proud new era! A bold new age of intergalactic colonization!

UDP citizens gathered round their digi-packs, children being hushed by their parents just as in the olden days families had hunched near their audio receivers to hear the latest war reports.

When the President finished praising himself and his government, the show began in earnest.

The upper levels of an unnamed laboratory interior came into view. That image held for a beat, then it tilted down to the center of a tall space at the bottom of which a slender man stood. He was almost naked. His frail physique and surprisingly sunken chest distracted the viewer from the wildness that lingered, hungry, in his glazed eyes.

Above the man, on a gallery hidden behind dense polymer see-thrus, stood several formal looking government agency types. I was among them.

From the floor, one of the technicians signaled me that they were ready. I nodded.

The viewing audience was then told that what they were about to see was something absolutely unique. Something new in our worlds. That the gentleman in the center of this event had been genetically altered to be able to search distant planets in his sleep. That he was the prototype of what our scientists are calling... Dream Navigators.

A new angle of the laboratory was then revealed to the viewer. Several large darkened screens slid into place. The technicians finished their work and then left the Dream Navigator alone.

He looked profoundly lost.

A loud electronic tone sounded for several seconds. Additional floor to ceiling screens flew in. Then there was silence.

A new angle showed the Dream Navigator dwarfed by the enormous screens and the tall space. Suddenly the whole thing had the antiseptic feel of an autopsy room. Then there was a close up of the Dream Navigator's face. It was not an image that was easily forgotten. The Dreamer was standing, eyes closed tight, 'trode wires dangling off of him. His head was thrown back to its fullest extension. His arms were spread wide. A look of stunned terror was on his lidded features.

The image went blank.

There was no sound.

Then you heard them. Gasps. Exclamations of wonder. Heart piercing cries of joy from those assembled at the laboratory.

From me.

The image returns. We are on the screens.

We are zooming through deep space, a planet with four tiny moons and a sulphurous ring is approaching us at tremendous speed. We are seeing what has never been seen before. On the screen is a digitally encoded picture of the dream exploration of the Dream Navigator.

He dreams. We see.

On the screen as clear as morning light, is a part of deep space which the Dream Navigator has been programed to explore. A section of space never before seen by humans. A place millions and millions and millions of light years from New Omaha Beach.

The images are extraordinary. The speed astounding.

What no one, except those of us in the laboratory, saw was that the Dream Navigator had levitated and was spinning, head down, eight feet off the ground.

The Dream Navigators were a remarkable success. A true scientific rarity: the exact solution for an exact problem, the ever sought for Magic Bludgeon.

By the end of the test period, we had twenty-one more Dream Navigators to add to the one that we put on display that June evening.

The first ship loaded to the gunwales with settlers, cocooned in cryogenic cold-sleep, left for parts dream-discovered on New Year's Day, 2329. Thereafter the huge lumbering ships, outfitted with vast cryogenic chambers, left New Omaha Beach every hour round the clock–for the next twenty years.

Within thirty-six months, the pressure on the ecosystems of our solar system was noticeably lessened. Food returned to being food. Shelter to shelter. Typhus became a memory of the past–a bogey man used to make children eat ersatz greens at the dinner table. Nature retreated.

I accepted the credit for pulling humanity back from the brink of destruction and ascended the S3 throne that had been mine, in all but name, for over a century.

With the success of the Dream Navigators, S3 grew exponentially in power and influence. We were riding high. We even considered opening our records to the ever-curious public.

Then, in May of 2347, a middle-aged Dream Navigator named Lah Ran Soni Ell disappeared–not from the Dream Navigation Center but from the planet.

A small wave of shock passed through the back halls of S3. Dream No More was still a password for failure in S3.

Then, a week later, seven more dreamers went AWOL in one night.

I set every possible investigator on their trail.

None of the investigators found any of the Navigators. What they did find, though, was startling and deeply disturbing. The investigators found that all eight of the escaped Dream Navigators had, each single-handedly, overpowered security units guarding intergalactic space ships and taken over the crafts. Eight dreamers. Eight different space ships. There seemed to have been no overall plan at work. There was never anything to indicate that the eight ever rendezvoused.

They just escaped, got away, and headed for deep space.

I ordered the remaining Dream Navigators separated from one another and kept under high security in remote regions of the planet. Most were hobbled. All had their lungs relined so that they couldn't breath artificial air in an effort to deny them access to space travel.

I had to prevent another "dream no more" command–an auto-link that would halt the intergalactic settlement program. The program was not yet half finished and the very future of the UDP and S3 depended upon its successful completion. And that completion rested solely on the constant flow of dream information from the remaining Dream Navigators.

The Dream Navigators responded. Within a week four committed suicide in their sleep. That left a mere ten Dream Navigators in our hands and their output fell to the dream equivalent of a trickle.

I refused to order the creation of additional mature Dream Navigators until I understood more about their behavior. In my search for that understanding, I came across a document that I had discarded years earlier. As I read it, like the writer, I trembled.

TO: c/m/!!!
FROM: Gen.Two.325 Hill Op K. Ckid
RE: Dream Navigator Behaviour
DATE: 01/12/2330

This is a warning! There are facts about our genetic work on the Dream Navigators that need to be addressed.

It is not just our failure rate of over 98% which concerns me. Surgical Genetic Splicing has always been a complex proposition. But never before in my years of splicing have I found the response to the splicing itself as dramatic as it is with the Dream Navigators.

Often during the surgery, despite what I believe to be dangerously high levels of anaesthetic, the patient awakens and, clawing desperately at their restraints, tries to free themselves. They scream at me and the nurses. They howl like captive animals about to be neutered who sense that something is about to happen that will dramatically change their lives.

Something unique occurs. They or rather their entire systems, their entities, resist the process. A resistance to the very fact of our presence in their midst. A holy resistance.

You can actually see the point where resistance begins in the middle of the third splicing sequence. By the end of the fifth, extra restraints usually need to be added. It is as if the body senses itself approaching something forbidden. Often the agony of a surgical death is embraced by them so as to avoid the change we are trying to force on them.

I've never seen anything like it.

However, even more upsetting than our failures are our successes.

When the fully altered patient awakens they stare at the world with new eyes. Not eyes filled with controlled terror but rather with fury. Their whole being has a hardness, an invisible carapace.

What I think we see in these altered dreamers is a lust for freedom. A willingness to die if necessary to gain that freedom. A fire deep within their being burns endlessly.

Is there anything more dangerous in our controlled, dreamless worlds than a human being capable of dreaming and desperate to be free? I think not.

If Nature rebelled at our meddling on Jupiter what would it do now? Dream Navigators are not just minorly altered human beings. They are a whole new idea in the universe.

I do not know what to call what we have created in our laboratories but I do know that I tremble to think that I had anything to do with the creatures we call Dream Navigators.

The author of the letter was found dead in his sleep two days after he managed to comm the letter to S3 headquarters. The cause of his death was never discovered–a rarity in S3 controlled territory. In fact the first unaccounted for death recorded in the twenty-fourth Century.

More clues I missed.

At the time it was not the death of an S3 Genetic Splicer that concerned me. I needed to find the AWOL dreamers. To do that I reasoned I needed the assistance of a dreamer. None of those who existed were willing to do my bidding so I ordered a very young boy put through the genetic alteration to become a Dream Navigator. I assumed that I could control a child more easily than an adult. History confirms that I was right–to a point.

The boy dreamer did eventually, after much training and several reversals, lead us to five of the eight escaped Dream Navigators.

The boy's name was Elijah Jaspers.

God in his infinite jest put him onboard Tzu's ship.

There he was known as the old Canary.

Near the end of the end he too kept a diary.

Chapter 31

Diary of a Madman

Jedidiah didn't find anything for Danazir Yi Qal—it found him.

The gentle hiss signaling incoming data from Tzu's implant called him to the data comm in his study. And there it was. As unannounced as the other comm from Tzu's implant. But this one wasn't three images. It was four diary entries. Four moments from the recent life of Elijah Jaspers, the old Canary:

FIRST ENTRY—2434, on board the pirate ship.

This is hard for me. Words were never my skill. But this information has to be passed on to these young people or else they will have no guides once I am gone. And although I have lived a long, long time, yes much of that time locked in the clutch of dreams, I know that I am nearing the inevitable passing that awaits us all.

Even Cyrus The Three of S3 must pass some time.

He was there at the beginning, and I feel him here now. He was there in my room, in the darkness, night after night teaching me. Telling me. Showing me the way. Preparing me for the operation.

Sometimes I think he took away my life. In one sense he did. I had no normal life. However at other times I think Cyrus The Three of S3 gave me the ultimate gift, the only thing in this universe worth having... dream exploration. Dammit, I was just a boy and they... all they left me was dreaming!! No more of this now. Ranting will only bring my end sooner. They'll need me alive more than they'll need these silly words.

END ENTRY

SECOND ENTRY–2434, on board the pirate ship. Today they brought the last of the Genetic Carriers on board.

Stories start at beginnings. My story started that day in 2349 in the medical amphitheatre. I was proud that they had chosen me. Cyrus was there. He was nice to me. He called me handsome and smart and important. What boy could ask for more? My first dream levitation happened so spontaneously that I don't remember its onset!

I was just a boy!!

They had finished the surgery and I was in the medical amphitheatre to be shown off. But I hit dream liftoff as soon as they "plugged me in". They loved it. I could hear the gasps. I literally rose to the occasion. They harnessed that. I'd never even broken a bone and here I was free falling through the reptile sectors of my brain. What horror, what glory lives there. But it was no place for a boy, alone, gene-manipulated to fly in his sleep.

My sleep.

Cyrus egged me on, even that first day. "Good boy, now deeper. Go deeper." And deeper I went. As I did, they hot wired me so that as I spun upside down, eight feet off the ground, they got visuals on enormous screens behind me. Huge screens and my inverted, twirling self. Scientists, politicians, professors... grownups did this to me. I could hear a hushed silence as I cascaded down towards a planet deep in the Altira Nebula. It was so strange, I could hear them but I was millions of light years away from them. I heard someone I took to be a doctor say to Cyrus, "We've never been here before!" Cyrus replied, almost in awe, "He's very good." Hearing that, I swooped down and landed on the precipice of a cliff overlooking a scarlet molten sea on that far off world.

I was only a little boy. I wanted to please them. That was my job, to please them. Another adult voice, this one female, then said, "He's very brave."

But Cyrus corrected her. "He's very young".

I was very young! Very young when I first started soaring in my dreams. I later, much later, learned that I was the youngest who survived the gene alteration operations. I was less than two weeks past my fourth birthday the morning that I first flew inside my brain.

END ENTRY

THIRD ENTRY—2434 on board the Pirate Ship. This morning I met the one called Mickelmast.

Three years after my first "flight" I had my first crash. I was up in the levitation spin, head down, hot wired to a huge screen. Cyrus was trying to get me to explore exact locations on command. I was trying. Trying to please him. But it was confusing. There is no up or down in dream space, and most importantly there is no time. The very nature of a dream is predicated on that fact. It is the only circumstance in a sentient being's life that time itself is at the being's behest. It is the ultimate of powers. Godly. Stay in the dream and time will never move... not for the dreamer. Then he ordered me to find that place. That place! I tried. I did. Then I began to hear my own screams come out of my sleeping self. I was plummeting, falling, falling through years of space. Suddenly no visual tracking. No light at all. And where did my dreaming go! When I awoke they told me I had been dreaming for the better part of a month. When I closed my eyes I fell into a dreamless sleep that lasted a further week. When I awoke this time, there were no admiring handlers there. My dear Cyrus was nowhere to be seen. There was no appreciative audience now, only sweated hospital sheets, and straps with bio-locks holding my arms to the hospital bed... and a need like a desert thirst to dream again.

END ENTRY

FOURTH ENTRY—2434 on board the pirate ship. The five Genetic Carriers have just seen their first slaving show.

They abandoned me in that sanatorium for almost three years. Then Cyrus came. He looked older. I hadn't dreamed for over a thousand nights. When he sat on the bed I felt my heart rise and before I could stop myself I found myself begging him to help me dream again. I told him I'd do anything. I told him I was lost without my dreams. I promised to give him.... whatever an eight year old can offer a grown man. Finally he'd heard enough and left me still shackled to the bed. But later that night he returned.

It was pitch black in my room and although I was locked in the fastness of sleep I knew that he was there. I knew because I felt my body begin to lift. He grabbed me and shook me into waking. He screamed at me: "Not yet!" Then he and his people moved me. We flew in a space ship. The ship travelled at great speeds, they told me it was flying faster than the speed of light. I didn't understand. Why would light have speed? Cyrus laughed at me and told me it would make the likes of me and mine unnecessary. I didn't understand that. I just understood that Cyrus was going to teach me how to dream again.

When we finally reached our destination I was marched to a deep interior room of a building. Cyrus turned to me and said, "Do you know where you are?" "No sir," I answered. "This is New Omaha Beach, you're on Terran. Earth." This meant nothing to me. Then he touched a button on the tall vertical wall and the wall's covering slid silently away revealing an ancient glass house which seemed frailer than light itself. "And this? Do you recognize this?" I didn't know its name but every dreamer knew this place in his heart. It was the beginning. The cocoon. The source. Its slender vaulted ceiling was designed exactly for a dreamer's spin. It echoed of music from long ago, and the Falling Cold and cletsio. And other dreamers. Thousands and thousands of other dreamers before. It was the path and the light. The way back and the way forward. I heard myself crying.

"Do you want to go in there?" he shouted at me.

I couldn't take my eyes off the Victorian glass house. Through my tears I nodded.

Then he pulled me around and slapped the side of my head so hard that my ears rang. "Then find these people!" he yelled. He shoved eight pictures into my hands. Five men and three women.

"Who are... "

"Just find them." He opened a narrow panel and we walked into the glass house. He pushed me to the very centre of the tall space then screamed again, "Find them."

The dream rose in me like a bubble from the bottom of a deep pond.

So it was that I headed out to find the first of the AWOL Dream Navigators. So it was on that day I began the betrayal of my kind.

It took me close to two years of dreaming to find five of the eight escaped dreamers.

In those two years I learned more about dreaming than in all my previous years. I took enormous deviations in course from Cyrus's instructions. I saw the beauty and the horror everywhere. Then I began to sense that there was something entirely different out there. It now has a name–Gateway.

I learned about dreaming but it wasn't until I found the fifth dreamer that I understood anything about power. And slavery. And loyalty. The man had awakened in his dream and found me there. At first he thought I was an antigen. Then he recognized me for what I was–a traitor. He grabbed me and screamed in my face. Told me that I was one of him and he one of me. That we had to work together. To build it. It! I wavered. Then he sensed the transmission lines from me to S3. He cursed me. When I woke I finally realized that I mustn't track down the remaining three Navigators. If I had, these children on board the pirate ship would never have inherited their dream capabilities.

I feared that I couldn't dream without the glass house! That's why I kept betraying my own kind. Yes I knew what I was doing! I knew! But I so feared that I wouldn't be able to dream again.

It is hard to acknowledge that you betrayed your own kind. But these five Genetic Carriers on board this ship are "of my kind". They are my responsibility. They have a right to all the knowledge I can give them.

By the time I had betrayed the fifth escaped Dreamer, S3 scientists had fully perfected Faster than Light Speed Propulsion. I recall a conversation where I think they were discussing simply doing away with me. Instead Cyrus The Three decided that I should be hobbled. Someone asked where they should keep me. Cyrus replied, "Who cares, he's an addict now."

I often wonder if he knew. If he saved my life for some other task. I still hear his words sometimes in my sleep, "He's an addict."

And I was. I lived in dreams for years and years. I explored worlds unknown even now, loved and was loved, chased after but never found what we now call Gateway. When I finally returned almost sixty years had passed but I had hardly aged. The sector of New Omaha Beach into which they had dumped me was abandoned–now outside the ether dome. What wild beauty was there! Vast and cold. Furious and powerful. And inevitable. Beauty outside the dome!

Within the dome much of Old Terran was a glorious sight. I dreamed my way across its verdant surface. Only the privileged were allowed to live amidst the bounty of Earth. And of all the bounty, New Omaha Beach poised on the ocean's edge, was the most privileged of all. What irony when you think of what goes on there.

It was there that I passed the Great War. It was there that I dreamed my way into the computers of the UDP and was happy to see that all the information on dream technology had been erased by a Rebel Colony virus. It was me who dreamed my way into the Rebel Colony computer and wiped their banks of our birthright. Then I dreamed more. I crawled into an air shaft of a tall building and head down began to spin. I dreamed for over a hundred years this time and when I awoke I was an old man, as I am now.

A hundred years of dreams!

When I awakened I dreamed my way into the S3 AIU. There I read and re-read and re-read the message from the Gateway. And every word brought me joy. In the AIU I found Cyrus' plan to round up the Genetic Carriers. And I knew that after betraying five of my own kind I now owed it to all the Dreamers to protect their remaining children.

And that is what I will attempt to do. In what little time is left to me, I will make up for my sins of the past. I betrayed dreamers in the past, I will protect dreamers now and hopefully show them that which will eventually allow them to head towards the Gateway.

END FINAL ENTRY. TOO SOON I WILL DREAM NO MORE. DREAM NO MORE. DREAM.

Chapter 32

Certain Truths, Raephealson's First Dream Lesson

Even as Jedidiah Witt contemplated the data comm in the privacy of Seth's bedroom in New Omaha Beach, the five Genetic Carriers were in a lower level medic station of the ship reading the same diary entries.

The old Canary, Elijah Jaspers, needed them to know the truth no matter how hard that truth might be for them to accept.

To Jasper's surprise, Kelt was the first to finish reading.

"And that's what you did? Dream Navigate?" asked Kelt. His voice was surprisingly flat. It revealed nothing of his response to the information that he had just received.

Jaspers looked at the handsome young man and understood that his gift would emphasize the recklessness needed to Dream Navigate—the pure courage or folly to go beyond what is safe. He also knew that the young man must be in considerable pain. It was an Independentiste's bedrock belief that one's life should be lived entirely without scientific meddling. Kelt now had to accept that his very being was the direct result of high-level genetic intervention.

"We're half way to the far end of the galaxy, and we managed to get there on the twenty odd seconds remaining in the last cycle of the AIU's propulsion system. Is that right?" Sun Tu's rich voice demanded an immediate answer.

"I don't calculate the way you do, but if you tell me that's what we've done I won't dispute it."

"But it's not possible. There's no way to get that far, that fast," shouted Sun Tu.

Jaspers felt sympathy for the EntrePren princess. It was hardest for the mathematical dreamer. The facts of mathematics and the truths of dreaming are not always the same.

"But we are here. We did, as you said, travel half way across the galaxy in less than thirty Terran seconds. That is a fact. No doubt you could verify our position with the AIU's star charts. You could also check the AIU for the elapsed time. But facts do not always lead to the truth," said Jaspers.

She called up a set of charts on the comm. Jaspers was amazed at how quickly she scanned page upon page upon page of documentation. "She's a free fall artist," he thought. An EntrePren Didact free fall artist? How did these genes get mixed together?

"It's like he said about the time." said Mickelmast. He still wore his AIU shunt assist and periodically purred a comment into its mouthpiece. "Even now she's marveling at what we just did. To be frank she thinks I did it and is really quite impressed. For the record so am I—Mr. Jaspers."

The large boy was the last person Jaspers thought could touch his heart. Suddenly he found himself an aged man with a family of five children—at least one of whom appreciated him. He never dreamed of this.

"So what now?" demanded Kelt. His confusion was quickly changing to anger.

"For the moment we're safe from external attack, but Tzu Ma Long is still onboard as are four others who didn't die in the Zero-G core," said Elijah.

"Can the AIU track them down, Mickelmast?" snapped Kelt.

"I think Mama will give us the needed information," Mickelmast said with a smile.

The word, "Mama?" rose to Sun Tu's lips, but it was never spoken because Kelt, happy to have something concrete upon which to focus his energies, jumped in. "Good. Let's secure the ship."

Mickelmast mumbled, "Thanks Ma." They all looked at him. He smiled back. "She hasn't found Tzu yet, but the other four are on the forward reach of the great ring. In the mariners kitchen."

As Sun Tu Kelt and Mickelmast moved to the door, Cas-Alta approached Jaspers. "You can't do it many more times, can you?" she whispered.

"Do what?" Elijah feigned surprise. Cas-Alta's look of disappointment softened him. "How do you know that?" He asked.

"I feel it. Your chi is in collapse. Your time of passing was brought forward by what you did to bring us to safety."

Jaspers didn't answer. He stared at the simple beauty in Cas-Alta's face. Then he touched her head. The words, "Your hair... " slipped out of him unwilled. His insides were a torrent of confused emotions. Emotions. Emotions based on other humans, not on dreams. He was unprepared for this. He thought his heart would explode.

Then Cas-Alta reached out and touched his chest. His heartbeat quickened and then, under her warming hand, slowed. She looked directly into his eyes. "Your knowledge is crucial to us now, isn't it?"

"Yes."

"Can any of the five of us do that? Dream Navigate?"

"I don't know."

"Is it time to find out?"

"Yes, as soon as the ship is safe."

"Fine. Stay here with Raephealson, Mr. Jaspers."

"Is he going to be okay?" the older man asked the young healer.

"He's strong."

"He's big boned, a heavy worlder."

"Not just that. He has a strong mind. An unusual mind," she said as she turned to go. "Once we secure the ship, where shall we meet you two?"

"In the ship's covenant space."

With that Cas-Alta ran after the other three.

Jaspers slumped against the wall, weariness suddenly upon him.

Raephealson was on the floor. He moaned softly, a rhythm in search of a melody. Jaspers studied the heavy worlder's features. Then Raephealson's eyes fluttered open. He smiled weakly. Jaspers smiled back. "Do you dream Raephealson?"

Three words came out of the heavy worlder's mouth, "Dream no more."

A deep memory momentarily opened then snapped shut in Jaspers. "Did you dream?"

"Dream no more," Raephealson rasped and turned his face away from the older man. But before he was able to hide his features, Jaspers read the deeply etched signs of fear there. So much fear that he was retreating.

Jaspers stared at Raephealson. He sensed that the young heavy worlder had dreamt. Naively dreamt, but dreamt none the less. Jaspers knelt at his side. "Wisdom is a lonely business, Raephealson."

Raephealson wagged his head as if to indicate that he had no wisdom but Jaspers continued. "Lonely and frightening. You have found the terror in the dream worlds haven't you?"

Raephealson pulled his whole body away, a huge man shamed by his cowardice. Jaspers touched the young man's shoulder and said, "The key to taming your dreaming fear is to keep your distance. Maintain your alertness but avoid identifying with what is going on. If it pulls you in too close, laugh." Raephealson was listening. "Laughter is your greatest weapon against the horror. Remember the five "L's" are a dreamer's guardian allies."

Raephealson looked up at Jaspers as if to say, "What five 'L's'?" Jaspers nodded slowly and repeated them just as he had himself repeated them when he was a boy, when Cyrus the Three of S3 taught him. "Lucidity, lightness, love, laughter, and life."

"Let's start with the first Raephealson—lucidity. It means waking up in your dreams. If you can wake in your dreams without waking from your sleep, then you can begin to explore the immensity of the dream worlds. If you can recognize that you are dreaming, you can transform illusion into luminosity.

"I know that you've dreamed. Not navigated. Not even awakened in your dreams but dreamt. Go back over your dreams Raephealson. Remember the most powerful ones that you have experienced. Go over them. There'll be a pattern to them. Probably a place or person that recurs over and over again."

Raephealson was wagging his head to the affirmative. "Oh yes there was a place—the glass place with the plants. And oh yes there was a person—the man with the angry face," he thought. But he said nothing.

"Good, Raephealson. Good. Now before your sleep just '*intend*' to go there. To that place. To that person. Tell yourself over and over before you sleep that is where you're going to go. And when you sleep you will go to that place of power. When you find yourself there, you will know that it is in fact a dream. You must tell yourself that—that it is just a dream. That will allow you to distance yourself from the events taking place. If you can watch, unaffected by what you see, you can awaken in your dreams.

"Hold up your hands. You heard me, hold up your hands, Raephealson. Slowly the large man did as he was ordered.

"Now look at your hands. Look Raephealson. Really see them. Now close your eyes."

Raephealson did.

"Now see your hands in your mind's eye."

For the next half hour, Jaspers repeated this exercise over and over again with the big man. As he did, Jaspers remembered the all-night sessions with Cyrus the Three of S3. All night and all day Cyrus would shove Elijah's hands up to his face and scream, "Look Elijah, really look!" Then he would command Elijah to close his eyes and visualize them. Over and over again. Elijah would complain that he was tired and Cyrus would scream at him that he was ungrateful. Ungrateful for the gift that he, Cyrus, had given to him.

After the half hour of repetition, Jaspers stopped and asked Raephealson to look at him. The young heavy worlder did.

"Now when you sleep and you need to wake in a dream, find your distance from the events you're seeing then simply visualize your hand the way you just did. It will act as a key to you to tell you that you are dreaming, but awake—but in control."

Jaspers looked closely at the young man. The fear was still there but not as noticeable. Now in the folds of Raephealson's fear was a small vertical space of hope. Jaspers patted the heavy worlder's back, stood and began to move out of the chamber. At the door he stopped. Raephealson turned his head toward the old man. "You must be brave to do this, Raephealson. But if I ever yell at you or hurt you in any way I want you to pick up my silly old bones and throw me as hard as you can against a wall. Any wall and hard. Understood?"

This time Raephealson nodded his head. He understood. Jaspers smiled but inside he was falling. All those years of fearing Cyrus the Three of S3. All those years of bondage.

But Cyrus had taught him the crucial truth. The gift greases the hinges to open the door to dreaming but does not shove the dreamer through that door. Only will can do that. Only bravery.

"Time to rest now and get strong. Tomorrow we start."

Raephealson was staring at the ceiling, as if his whole being depended upon seeing something up there that no one else could see. Or perhaps he believed his safety—perhaps his life—depended upon staying awake. For in sleep, Raephealson now understood, there were dreams.

Chapter 33

Cleaning the Ship

The trip to the kitchen didn't begin well. When the four Genetic Carriers opened the air lock to the Zero-G central core they were met with a sight that none of them would soon forget. The floor of the corridor, a hundred meters below them, was a vomit of dead humanity. A crushed statue of grotesque proportions, a hellish carpet.

Cas-Alta gasped. So did Mickelmast. Kelt allowed his warrior face forward. Sun Tu was silent, still logical. She was the daughter of the head of the EntrePren Didact sect. "What else was there for us to do? The only issue is whether we can rid the ship of them before they fester," she said.

Mickelmast spoke softly to the AIU then drew a breath and said to the others, "Let's step outside the air lock. Mama has some cleaning to do."

Once they secured the air-lock door tightly, Cas-Alta leant against the corridor wall. Unconsciously she touched her belly. Death on the other side of that door. Life in her center.

"How long?" asked Sun Tu.

"Not long," said Mickelmast as he returned to his seemingly endless conversation with the AIU.

"Where will she put them?" asked Kelt.

"Out," said Mickelmast flatly. "Then she'll reinstate the Zero-G in the core."

"Has she found Tzu Ma Long yet?" asked Sun Tu.

After an initial hesitation Mickelmast replied, "In a manner of speaking."

"Meaning exactly what?" barked Sun Tu.

"She knows his whereabouts, but she's not sure she wants to tell me," Mickelmast said softly.

Sun Tu threw up her arms in disgust, "Swell."

"Your mamma doesn't care for you anymore, Mike?" smiled Kelt.

"Not exactly," said Mickelmast.

"She still holding on to her old boyfriend?" laughed Kelt. Then his laughter stopped. The seriousness of their situation crashed down upon them. Kelt spoke slowly this time, "She's thinking of going back to Tzu, isn't she?"

Mickelmast nodded.

"Holy shit!" came out of Sun Tu in a long deep breath.

"On the good side," replied Mickelmast, "she's cleared the bodies from the core and restored the Zero-G."

"Let's go," said Kelt reaching for the door of the gravity lock.

With the weapons that Kelt had found in the armory and the advantage of surprise, it was not difficult to overpower the four pirates hiding in the kitchen. Dragging them to the cryogenic chamber and committing them to cold sleep proved complicated, but they figured it out after a few false starts. Once the last pirate was successfully hung in a cryogenic cocoon, Cas-Alta said, "Can we get out of here? It's cold in here."

"What about the others?" said Kelt pointing to the remaining would-be slaves swaying gently in their cocoons.

"Let's figure out who they are before we thaw them out. Besides we have more pressing problems," said Sun Tu as she turned to Mickelmast.

"Can we get out of here first!" shouted Cas-Alta.

"Sure," said Kelt leading them out of the chamber.

They went to a subdeck exterior pod through whose triple plated polymer they watched the approach of a planetary system with a huge red star. "So how bad is it with Mama?" asked Sun Tu.

"It's not bad, it's just that... "

Sun Tu cut him off. "It's just that she's sectored you off—won't take your calls. Right?"

"Not precisely correct, no. She answers me. It's just that I sense a kind of reticence from her on certain subjects," replied Mickelmast.

"Certain subjects like her ex-master, right?" snapped Sun Tu.

With a sigh, Mickelmast responded. "Yes."

"Well what do you know! A woman with a sense of loyalty," laughed Kelt.

"That's hardly the point," said Cas-Alta. "She's got a full set of implants with Tzu Ma Long. They must be surgically linked on dozens of levels. It's amazing that she's even allowed Mickelmast to talk to her."

Mickelmast held up his hand to stop her. He was listening closely on his shunt.

"What?" asked Kelt.

"She's talking to him!"

"The pirate captain? She's talking to the pirate captain?" demanded Kelt.

Mickelmast nodded enthusiastically, a big smile crossing his face. "Now what?" demanded Sun Tu.

Once more Mickelmast held up his hand for silence and listened closely. Then, into the shunt piece he cooed, "Thanks Mom." If Mickelmast were inclined to dance, he would have. "She's sending him to us."

"What!"

"She's convinced him that his safest route to regain control of the ship is through the cryogenic chamber. That he should come down and thaw out the pirates there and then attack the rest of us."

"How soon is he coming?"

"Momentarily!"

"What!"

"She hasn't got a good sense of human timing."

But she had a good enough sense of it.

When Tzu peered through the window of the cryogenic chamber door, all he saw was the cocoons swaying gently with the movement of the ship. He checked with the AIU who informed him that there were no movement sensor readings in the chamber.

As he stepped through the door, the Genetic Carriers sprung their trap. A net of interlaced cocoons fell on Tzu. With his hands still technacled, he couldn't regain his feet quickly enough to avoid being wrapped tightly in the nets and hoisted into the air. His desperate attempts to contact the AIU were greeted with laughter from the great machine. His attempts to fight out of his bonds were quickly ended by the anesthetic aerosols released by the cocoons.

It was all over with surprising speed.

Once Tzu was frozen and hung in his cocoon, the Genetic Carriers breathed easier. They were about to congratulate each other when Sun Tu spotted Tzu's glass knife that had fallen to the chamber floor during the struggle. With a scream she snatched up the four inches of death and raced toward the ascender.

Kelt's flying tackle pulled Sun Tu off the ascender moments before she could plunge the knife into Tzu's throat.

The two of them hit the cold metal floor with a thud—Sun Tu on top, her knife poised at Kelt's face.

But the young man was a well-schooled fighter. He locked eyes with her and, ignoring the knife, said calmly, "So you want to kill me too? Who else do you want to kill?"

She screamed, "I'll kill you if you try to stop me!"

With a quick shift of his body he destabilized her. His left arm knocked the knife half way across the chamber to Cas-Alta. Sun Tu scrambled to her feet and looked at Mickelmast, Cas-Alt and Kelt. Then her strength abandoned her. Her anger turned to tears of rage, and only Cas-Alta's calming hands could induce her to leave the chamber.

Moments later Kelt was surprised to hear Mickelmast animatedly shouting, "Okay, alright, I'll look into it Ma. Can't get to everything all at once."

"Signal, signal, and more signal coming from Herr Short Stuff..."

"And Herr Short Stuff would be... "

"He's Herr Short Stuff; you're the Hippo."

Mickelmast looked at Kelt and was glad that the young warrior couldn't hear this conversation with the AIU. "What does she want?" Kelt asked.

"Take me up to him on the ascender."

Kelt did. As they rose the AIU screamed at Mickelmast to stop. Then to circle. They followed the AIU's orders. Just over half way around the hanging pirate's body, the AIU yelled "Stop Hippo! Stop. Stop. There. There. There. Signal, signal, and more signal. Dig it out." Sensing the Hippo's reticence she purred, "It won't kill him, promise, Hippo dear."

Mickelmast explained the AIU's request. Neither he nor Kelt was thrilled with the prospect of committing surgery. But neither of them dared risk the AIU's anger. So, under the AIU's direction, they unclipped the cocoon, cut Tzu open, and extracted Miro's UDP implant from the third disk of Tzu's back. Then the AIU instructed Mickelmast to crush it beneath his heal. He did.

And so it was that the UDP's last tenuous contact with the Warrior Class Starship went the way of all flesh.

Chapter 34

Beginnings: Dreams, Still Dreams, Waking Dreams

"It is time that you began learning to navigate. Dream Navigate. I won't be around forever." Jaspers felt like his voice didn't belong to him. He felt a growing panic. A fear that he wouldn't be able to pass on his gift before the time of his final travel.

"How do we start?" asked Cas-Alta.

"Do any of you dream?" he asked.

All the usual responses tumbled out: There is no such thing as dreaming, there have been no dreamers for centuries, why is it necessary to dream etc, etc.

Raephealson said nothing.

Finally Jaspers put up his hands to stop their growing objections.

There was a silence. He turned and hobbled a few paces away from them.

He looked at the covenant space. Solid, somber, and symmetrical. A crushed peasant's space, not a dreamer's. A penitent's space. A place to beg mercy, forgiveness. A space wherein an overpowering God is approached on all fours.

It was at one time called a sanctuary. Jaspers knew the word in the context of a place of safety but not in its religious sense. Jaspers knew no religion except dreaming. And dreaming did not take place in crushed spaces. Spaces that kept humans on the ground beneath an overwhelming belief in greater beings.

He looked to the five Genetic Carriers, and let his breath come out slowly. His aged eyes locked with Kelt's. "Your skepticism is a self-fulfilling prophecy. It keeps you here and refuses to allow you to move forward. And yet you don't come from a world of such thoughts. As you told us yourself, the pirates captured you while you were out fasting in honor of the Great Escaping. True?"

"So I have said." He didn't want lessons in nonsense. He wanted a path toward revenge.

"The Great Escaping of what?" asked Jaspers.

Kelt was lost. "What?"

"It's not a hard question Kelt. What is the Great Escaping celebrating? Who or what escaped?"

"I don't know. It's just a festival."

"Nonsense. There are no 'just festivals.' Important events degenerate to 'just festivals' when there are no dreamers to keep the reality alive."

"Dreamers keep reality alive?" laughed Sun Tu.

"Yes! There is no contradiction in that. It is dreamers that keep events from becoming 'just festivals.' In ancient Terran history, there was a war between two cities. Brutal men who no doubt fought for control of trade routes or some other banal reality. But a dreamer took the war and made it into a story that gave us real truths. Truths about beauty in a woman he called Helen and truths about deception in a man he called Odysseus—and many more. Without the dreamer we would never have cared about this stupid merchant trade war. But the dreamer has sent it down to us over time. The war may have rewarded the victor and punished the defeated, but the dreamer's creation has rewarded all of human kind. Only dreamers can do that. Dreams conquer time," Jaspers stopped for a moment and almost smiled. Then he said simply, "We know there is a relationship between time and space—dreamers can also conquer space." Jaspers looked up. They were clearly lost with that last comment. "Later," he said.

"Fine, but isn't that called story telling not dreaming," complained Sun Tu.

"You must dream first and then tell your story. Some dreamers don't tell stories, but all story tellers dream." Sun Tu looked away. Jaspers returned his attention to Kelt. "So what or who escaped in the Great Escaping?"

"I don't know."

"You celebrate the festival, but you don't know who or what escaped?"

"So I have said."

"We escaped. Dream Navigators. Eight of them. There has been no other great escaping in the galaxy to match it. Eight individuals. Eight extraordinary feats of valor and bravery. Eight Dreamers escaped. That is what you are celebrating Kelt.

"But your worlds have no dreamers, yet. And without dreamers the meaning was lost, folded in time. The great escaping simply became the name of a time to kill a ceremonial thwark. Nothing more. The sacred became the common place. Your world is less for each thwark that you take from it if you don't know why you must kill the great beast. If you knew. If the dream of bravery were still alive, then with each thwark that you killed your world would be richer not poorer. That is what dreamers do.

"Five of those who escaped I found and betrayed as you know from reading my diaries. The other three were your ancestors. You carry their genes—their knowledge."

"What does dreaming have to do with navigating?" asked Mickelmast.

"Everything. Do you know the Scott Hypothesis?"

"That nonsense about brain usage?" spat out Sun Tu.

"The Scott Hypothesis was made to seem as if it was nonsense by S3. They had to. It was so public that there was no way to hide it."

"What exactly does the Scott Hypothesis say?" asked Cas-Alta.

"It starts with the simple fact that human beings, on average, use less than two and a half percent of their brain capacity. Ms. Scott posed the logical question, 'What's the point of the other 97.5% of the brain.' Her answer was as basic as it was shocking. The Scott Hypothesis says simply: THE IDLE 97.5% OF THE BRAIN IS AWAITING USAGE. IT IS A PERFECT MAP OF THE REST OF THE UNIVERSE... AND IT CAN ONLY BE ACCESSED THROUGH DREAMS."

The Genetic Carriers stared at Elijah Jaspers.

The old man took another deep breath then said, "Let's start. Lie down. Close your eyes gently. Allow the light to filter through your lashes." With varying degrees of reluctance four of them did as he asked. Raephealson opened his eyes wider than ever.

Jaspers' voice pulled back in his throat. Old images came to him. A man in his bedroom. A hand on his heart. A deep voice from the darkness. He heard the voice again and let it out: "Your heart is on the left side of your chest it is about the size of a fist, it pulses and is warm, it pulses and is warm, it pulses and is warm. Feel your heart. Feel your heart. Feel your heart."

The lights dimmed in the room.

And slowly under Jasper's coaxing the Carriers allowed themselves the freedom to begin to feel their bodies. For the body is the place to begin. Feel your body. Sense its life. Then move through your body to your heart. For only from the heart's reality can you reach the reality of dreams.

"Your heart is on the left side of your chest it is about the size of a fist, it pulses and is warm, it pulses and is warm, it pulses and is warm. Feel your heart. Feel your heart. Feel your heart."

Over the next week, Jaspers told them of dream induction, of pre-sleep rituals, of the importance of drifting into waking to allow retrieval of data from the last dream cycle. Of feeling the sacred. Over and over they recited, "Brahmin the giver of truth sits in a lotus that grows from Vishnu's navel. Vishnu is the sleeping God whose dream is the universe."

He showed them how to build "a watching" by their sleeping places. "Build it without thought, just put together what your hearts tell you needs to be in the sacred circle. Then upon waking look immediately to the sacred circle and ask it for your dreams."

They tried.

He told them of the great dream temples of antiquity and the thousands of years of healing through dreams.

And every morning they gathered and he asked them of their dreams. And every morning four responded that they had not dreamt. And the fifth, Raephealson, retreated further and further into himself.

At week's end Elijah Jaspers had one of the rarest of all occurrences for a Dream Navigator. An unasked for dream.

Without even a hint of preamble, he found himself in the midst of a two-story eating establishment. The place was unbelievably busy. Waiters in black pants with white linens wrapped around their waists moved quickly through the densely packed tables. Their trays, stacked many layers high, moved like multi-story buildings above the heads of the smoking, eating, laughing diners.

Rustle of silk. Crash of thrown crystal.

He was following someone. No. Being dragged by the arm. He looked up, and there in front of him was the last Dreamer that he had found and betrayed to Cyrus Maloney the Three of S3. The thin man was terribly strong. He was dragging Elijah like a girl drags a raggedy anne.

Jaspers looked down at himself and saw that he was not an old man any more but rather a boy. A ten-year-old boy. A terrified, naked ten-year-old boy being dragged to his fate by a dreamer that he had betrayed.

At the stairs leading to the upper story, thin-hipped waiters bared the way but stepped aside as Elijah was hustled toward them. As they turned away, Elijah saw that their pants only covered their fronts. Their naked backsides were turned to him. All exactly the same—plastic, like dolls with no holes. Elijah momentarily wondered how they pooped.

On the second story of the busy eating establishment, there was a long table behind which sat a row of Dreamers. The Dreamer who had been dragging Elijah went behind the table and took his seat. Out the windows behind the table were the canals and plazas of a place called Venice. Elijah covered his penis with his hands and tried to look at his feet, but he found his eyes drawn up toward the table. The five Dreamers whom he had betrayed all sat together at the center of the long table. There was an empty seat at the very end of the table. It was a small chair. A chair just right for a ten-year-old boy.

Elijah took a breath and stretched the fingers of his left hand. Then he looked down at his palm. There was the momentary tingle of awakedness. He felt his skin, and it was cool to his touch.

He was awake in his dream.

A smile came to him. It was a dream—a corny dream but just a dream. And he was a master dreamer. He could move the dream where he willed it.

But not this time.

As he went to change the basic orientation, by simply looking to his right, he found that the whole field of the dream moved as well. So that no matter where he looked he was always looking at the table with the Dreamers and the empty chair.

As he had done so many times before, he took a step backward and jumped straight up. It was always his key for flying. And he did. But so did the table. So did the chair. So did this entire world.

Finally the elderly woman at the table rose. "Enough. Surely you see that you can't escape us. Everything you dream we will dream as well. You cannot get away from us for we are you and you us. You betrayed us. We are your death. And if you are worthy... your life beyond the Gateway."

There was no one there to see him but that night Elijah Jaspers levitated as he had done so many times before. But this time he didn't invert. This time he didn't spin. He just hung there eight feet above the ground. Arms out. Head back. But no motion either inside or out. Inert.

A stillborn dream.

He awoke the next morning knowing that even in his dreams time was reasserting itself. As he rose he remembered a moment with Cyrus the Three of S3, when he was a boy, before his first crash. He remembered Cyrus the Three of S3 reading from an old book. A story to him before he slept... and dreamt. Cyrus read of two naked people in a garden. A man and a woman. And animals and an apple. The lady ate the apple and such sadness descended that Elijah had cried. But Cyrus was uninterested in his tears.

"Do you know what began when that apple was eaten?"

Elijah had no idea. "It's just a story? Right?"

"It's <u>the</u> story, Elijah. So what do you think started when the lady ate the apple?"

The word "time" flew out of him before he could think about it. Before he had any idea what he was talking about. Time.

Cyrus the Three of S3 smiled and said quietly, "Very good. Time. And of course with time came death. And with death, ego—my death versus your death."

Elijah remembered being frightened as Cyrus the Three of S3 then turned to him and said, "Where is that place before the apple is eaten? Where is the place without time?"

And Elijah thought he knew the answer to that. He thought any Dreamer knew that the place without time is a dream. But he said nothing.

"It must be found boy. Now go. Dream and find me that place."

And he tried. Tried and tried. Explored and explored for the garden without time. For the approval of a man named Cyrus the Three of S3.

It was during this exploring for the place with no time that Elijah Jaspers, aged nine, crashed.

When Elijah met the Genetic Carriers that morning he didn't ask them about their dreams. He was going to set out in a new direction. His attention was drawn to the corner where Raephealson sat propped against the wall. The heavy worlder's eyes were turned inward. Lost.

Jaspers turned to Cas-Alta. "Lie on the floor. On your back."

After only the slightest hesitation Cas-Alta did as he told her. "There are dreams without sleep." Before anyone could object he continued. "Watch." Jaspers knelt by her head and began to rub her temples slowly in a clockwise direction. "Close your eyes." Cas-Alta did. "Get me a cloth to put over her eyes, she'll be tempted to open them so she needs a blindfold."

Mickelmast brought him a scarf. "Put it on her." As he did, Jaspers looked to the others. Kelt was watching closely. Sun Tu stood to one side, clearly skeptical of the whole process.

Once the blindfold was securely in place, Jaspers while still rubbing Cas-Alta's temples, instructed Mickelmast to go her feet. "Take off her sandals and gently rub her soles in a counter-clockwise direction."

Mickelmast did as requested and for several minutes there was nothing said as the two men gently massaged Cas-Alta's feet and temples. Then Jaspers closed his eyes and heard the voice from so long ago. The voice of the man who had taught him. The voice of Cyrus the Three of S3 in his bedroom late at night. In perfect imitation of that voice he said, "Now imagine the energy in your feet. Imagine it. Now imagine it extending three inches out the bottom of your feet. Imagine it! When it's done raise the baby finger of your left hand."

Nothing happened at first. The men continued to massage. The silence deepens in the room. Then a gasp came from Cas-Alta's lips and she raised her pinky.

Deep in himself, Jaspers allowed a knot of anxiety to loosen. "Now bring the energy back to your feet and tell us when it's done by raising your finger again."

Cas-Alta accomplished this quickly.

"Now extend the energy from your head Cas-Alta. Bring the energy three inches above the top of your head." It took a moment but Cas-Alta indicated with her finger that she had achieved the requested state.

"Good now bring the energy back to your head and tell us when it's done."

Jaspers looked at Raephealson who had turned his head away and seemed to be trying to bury himself in the wall. "I've crashed too lad, I know the terror. Time to be brave," he thought. But he said nothing.

In the next half hour, Jaspers got Cas-Alta to extend the energy from her feet and head first six inches, then a foot, then a yard, and then return the energy to her body. Then he instructed her, "To expand the energy of your entire body a yard all around."

Quickly her finger rose to indicate that she had managed the task. Then Jaspers said, "Now extend your energy to the walls of the covenant space."

Jaspers looked up. Kelt had come closer to them, but Sun Tu had retreated all the way to the far corner. Kelt moved his hand over Cas-Alta's prone body.

"It's cold."

"You can feel that, Kelt? I was never able to myself."

Mickelmast tried to feel the cold but couldn't. Raephealson made a noise deep in his throat.

"And is she bright too, Kelt?"

"Blazing. It hurts my eyes."

"That too," thought Jaspers as he returned his attention to Cas-Alta.

"Now Cas-Alta allow your energy to float up, up through the ceiling of the room, up past the upper deck, out to the hull of the ship itself."

Kelt stepped back.

"Don't sleep Cas-Alta. Don't sleep," commanded Jaspers. "Raise your finger if you are out of the room." She did. "Out of the upper deck?" She raised her finger again. "Outside the hull of the ship?" There was a lengthy pause. The men continued to gently massage. Then her finger came up again.

"Don't sleep. See. See Cas-Alta. Now stand on the hull of the ship."

Her finger came up.

"Look down, what do you see?"

"My feet on metal. No not my feet. A child's feet."

"Without opening your eyes, raise your left arm and look at your hand. What do you see?"

"Fingers. Many many fingers. Black and green."

"Look out. What do you see?"

"My garden. My mother."

Then there was nothing more for a moment. Then without prompting Cas-Alta began to cry. Her tears appeared out of the sides of the blindfold.

"What is it?"

"She's dead. They raped her. They killed her in our garden. Oh, Mamma.... "

"Look down again, Cas-Alta," Jasper's voice was firmer this time. Not angry but commanding. "Look down," he ordered.

The tears stopped.

"Good, now fly, Cas-Alta. Fly to the top of the ship."

It took time, but slowly she raised her finger to signal that she had done as requested.

"Now see your reflection in the ship's hull. What do you see?"

"Hundreds of people in my face. You are all there. I am there. Many many people I don't know. Warmth. Enwrapping. Twining. Floating together... "

"Now pull your eyes away from the mirror. Float away from the ship."

She did.

"Now tell me what the markings are on the very top most part of the ship."

There was silence for a beat, then she said in a clear sane voice, "Y.O.A.L.—UDP-3-13-3."

Jaspers looked up at the room. His eyes sought Sun Tu's. "Check."

Sun Tu punched the wall comm and pulled up the Set Up files. With a gasp she read back, "Y.O.A.L.—UDP-3-13-3."

Jaspers turned his attention back to Cas-Alta. "Don't sleep. It's time to come back. Float down the hull of the ship."

And so he guided her back. Into the ship. Into the room. Into her body. And to the present.

Then he stood and looked at Kelt and Sun Tu, Cas-Alta and Mickelmast. There was wonder in their eyes.

Chapter 35

Return to the Fog

When Miro awoke in the corridor, Cyrus was framed in the doorway, silhouetted against the fire's light. Even without seeing his face she knew he was staring at her. As he bent down to her the fire lit his features. Miro thought him the very vision of madness.

"To work," he said.

She scrambled to her feet and followed him back into his chambers.

Sitting in his chair facing the fireplace he rolled up his sleeve. She soundlessly moved to him, then, pulling out her syringe, knelt in front of him. He stared deep into her eyes and reached for her hair. The strands ran through his fingers. He reached over and over again and watched Miro's long hair slip through his fingers. He was trying to recall something from long ago. Something about hair running through his fingers. Then she inserted the needle.

"Deep into my heart," he thought. "Then deep into yours," he hissed out loud.

She looked up at him, but he wasn't looking outward anymore.

The mist came and she let it. It opened her and for an instant she floated. Then it was yanked from her. Cyrus turned it and raced toward the whore's tunnel again.

The Slave Master didn't look quite so silly this time. Although wobbly, he was on his feet.

"Did you enjoy my parting gift last time?" Cyrus laughed.

The Slave Master did something that passed for blushing in his world and shuffled his feet like a schoolboy caught with a dirty imager. When he did look up a reek came off him. "Even in this smelly place you are the smelliest," thought Cyrus.

The Slave Master pulled on his forelock and bobbed. "Most kind, Cap'n."

"No Slave Master, you are the one who is a captain. You captain the Mirren Archer Class Starship."

"So I do Lordship. So I do."

"Do you enjoy having me so close to you all the time?"

"Ye mean the implant, do ye?"

"To answer in kind—aye, the implant, I do."

"Truth be told, it's a bit off putting at times."

"Get me what I want and I'll 'off put' it altogether, if you catch my meaning."

"Aye." The man turned into the glare of the approaching headlights. He watched the whores in the tunnel plying their trade with varied degrees of discretion. He mumbled something so softly that even with the implant Cyrus could just barely make it out. The stinky worm was apologizing for losing Tzu's ship. That somehow it had just disappeared. And on and on, blather, mumble, blather, mumble.

Cyrus finally stopped him. "I know you lost him. Now get your crew ready. I will find his ship for you. And when I do, I want you never to lose him again. Is that understood?"

"Aye Cap'n."

From the implant Cyrus could tell that the Slave Master was trying to muster the courage to ask about the safety of his EntrePren account codes. Before the man could give it voice, Cyrus cut in, "All the more reason to get me back what is mine."

The Slave Master looked up in shock then nodded slowly. He finally worked out that Cyrus was receiving data directly from the implant. He was completely Cyrus's creature. To confirm the point, through the implant, Cyrus guided the Slave Master's eye to a dark-haired beauty across the roadway. Then he prompted through the implant, "Want her?"

Before the Slave Master could answer Cyrus boomed, "Then pay for her!"

Cyrus didn't wait for a response. He enfolded the mist and shouted. "There is still much I have to do this night."

When he re-entered his corporeal being he was surprised to see that the Lavolin girl was asleep with her head in his lap, her hair still wrapped around his fingers.

He raised his hand. Again he marveled at the feel of her hair slipping through his fingers. Then he reached down and touched her face. Instantly he withdrew his hand. Her sleeping face was wet!

Miro's eyes snapped open and she bolted to her feet. Her hands flew to her face and wiped it dry. When she turned back to him, she was shocked to see the look on his face.

"Call my adjutant."

She moved quickly toward the door and was gone.

In a moment the adjutant appeared—young, ambitious, and terrified. An adjutant.

"Find Jedidiah Witt and prepare a retrieval unit."

The adjutant spun on his heel and exited. Alone, Cyrus turned toward the window and looked out. "We are all moving now," he said in a loud, hoarse voice, "like one great gifted thing."

Chapter 36

Goodbye Madame President

Danazir Yi Qal's tattoo-encircled eyes never left Jedidiah's as he spoke. Her look of wonder grew as Jedidiah concluded. "Mr. Jaspers was the youngest human being ever gene-manipulated by S3 into becoming a Dream Navigator. He was created after the Great Escaping. The records are scanty from there on. It appears that he was publicly hobbled in late 2351. It is also likely that he was the unidentified dreamer who was put on display in the Great Solar System Fair of 2366. After that degrading spectacle S3 basically ignored him. After all, Faster than Light Speed Propulsion (FLSP) had made Dream Navigators unnecessary. The dreamers were nothing more than an historical embarrassment for S3. I admit that I don't understand why Cyrus didn't have Jasper's life terminated. It strikes me as distinctly out of character for Cyrus to allow a potentially embarrassing entity to continue to live.

"But he did. Our DNA matches clearly show that this same Elijah Jaspers signed on with the pirate ship on Prithium eleven Terran days before the kidnappings began. He signed on as a canary.

"It answers many of our questions about that Warrior Class Starship's actions. It fits Madame President. As amazing as it seems, Elijah Jaspers is an ancient Dream Navigator."

"And S3 doesn't know?"

"They couldn't. If they knew who Elijah Jaspers was they wouldn't need to kidnap the Genetic Carriers. They'd just take Jaspers."

She nodded her agreement with his rational. Then, as if she had been holding her breath throughout, Danazir Yi Qal released a long sigh and turned away from Jedidiah—it was approaching. She knew. She had in fact always known. Her hand touched her sari. "It would all end soon," she thought, "both the beauty and the terror would have to return." She turned back to Jedidiah and finally spoke, "You have more to say?"

"Madame President the last comm from Miro was traced to me. Information and secrecy are seldom found in the same nest. We can hope that Cyrus didn't trace the send command back to her, but I wouldn't count on that. Miro is my responsibility. I have left a trail for them to follow me and hopefully leave her be."

Then he laughed. A deep barrel of a laugh that filled the room.

"Why do you laugh Mr. Witt?"

"I feel like a mother bird who feigns a broken wing to distract the hunter from her child." Jedidiah turned away from his President. He didn't want her to see his face now. "I have always admired birds. Their courage and sacrifice." He turned back to her. "I know that you are anxious to act—for the UDP to play a role in this great drama. Now is the time. You must find a way to contact the Genetic Carriers. Reach out to them in any way you can. After what has happened to them, it is unlikely that they will trust any authority. But you must find a way. Remember that they are unable to discern the difference between your intentions and those of S3.

"Madame President, S3 must not be allowed to make the technological leap to Dream Navigation! Our worlds stand on the brink of disaster. Help the dreamers and they might help us."

Then all the energy went out of Jedidiah's body. He felt heavy and sluggish. He couldn't remember when he had last slept. He sensed her about to speak, but he held up his hand, stopping her. Then he took a note from his pocket and placed it on the table between them. "Read this when I am gone. I truly believe that we will never meet again."

There followed a moment of awkwardness for both of them. An intimacy had grown between them, but just as Danazir was about to move toward Jedidiah, he turned and left.

Alone, she reached for the note. She read it slowly:

"I feel it necessary to put into effect the surgical option of which we earlier spoke. I will make all necessary arrangements. Do you remember the story of the great orbiting cranes of Malthus Three? How one day they just disappeared? How the colonists never took note? How within a year of the magnificent birds' disappearance the planet imploded?

"Our birds have flown, Madame President. Are fleeing. Now we must take note.

"I will program my implant to respond just once to the command: Dream No More. When the data from my implant is yours, execute that command first! There is much that I should have told you. It is all waiting on the implant for your command of: Dream No More. God's speed."

Chapter 37

Fathers End, Sons Begin

The surgical procedure had been surprisingly painless, yet another result of our controlled worlds. Major change—no pain. No correlation between the two. "So be it," Jedidiah thought as he entered Seth's room.

He wasn't surprised when the telltale informed him that his personal AIU had been tampered with. Nor did it surprise him that his chamber's motion sensors had been just slightly recalibrated. He assumed that his own soporific would be activated shortly. It was still the easiest way to bring a man to ground. Well it would have been had he not had his soporific codes readjusted. This job had its perks.

He energized his personal cloaking device, pulled up his privacy collar, and headed into the New Omaha Beach evening.

The city was deceptively peaceful. Personal movement vehicles ferried the powerful and would-be powerful around the city. Late-night spots were just opening, and dining palaces were already on their second sitting. The honeyed odor of the faux sweet olive trees which lined all the major arteries of the great city filled the gentle night air with their intoxicating perfume. Ersatz sampled sound and muted pulse-lighting completed the image of a city made for the pleasure of its citizens.

Jedidiah plunged into a central underground hoping to find enough people to shake the S3 stalkers that he knew must be following him. Glancing in the protecto-mirror of a popular apparel shop, he noted the innocuous looking man with a leather case about ten meters back of him. If he were looking for a man to tail another man, he would use just such a man. But spotting one of the watchers was nothing. There would be auto-peepers on him as well as data structures on the ether dome following him and, of course, the DNA tracers would be alive at every major portal in the city.

He walked quickly, dodging oncoming pedestrians and small vehicular traffic. His basic logic implant was supplying him with information as he moved. Making suggestions, providing maps.

Following its prompting, he turned hard right at the next opportunity. Clearing the back end of an auto-dumper, he found himself confronted by a phalanx of S3 operatives. He couldn't believe his eyes. They had been there all along, waiting for him. They all but wore S3 uniforms.

In one quick move, he threw himself to the ground and rolled. The first concussive shot hit just behind his feet. The second just past his head. The third punched a hole the size of a baby's fist in his thigh. But he was up and running. Crashing through pedestrians, running between moving vehicles until he finally found a high curb. He wedged himself under the overhanging pavement, between it and the sidewalk, and then slipped into the wire basket-like water protector beneath.

The sound of shouting and running feet passed him by. He allowed himself a moment to catch his breath and face a hard reality. S3 must have turned his AIU which had turned his basic logic implant, the device that had been implanted at his birth, that had for his entire life been "a friend in need." Even now it was no doubt trying to broadcast his whereabouts. His thundering blood pressure would confuse it for a bit.

He counted to fifty then hauled himself out of the wire catchment. He had little feeling left in his injured leg. People stared at him as he emerged from beneath their feet, a blight in the perfection of their city. He ignored them and raced as best he could toward a nearby restaurant.

The eating establishment was filled with those anxious to be seen and those just as anxious to look. Jedidiah ran past the diners, heading for the kitchen in the back. As he pushed his way through the "in" door, the restaurant's security contingent approached him. He flashed his Presidium Council pass. Their resistance disappeared amidst muttered apologies.

Jedidiah stopped by one of the cooks. His Council pass was still in his hands. "Am I under arrest for making bad stipple sauce or something?" joked the chef.

"No," responded Jedidiah, "but you could help me."

"Yeah and how would I do that?"

"Do you use knives or is it all laser cutters here?"

"Hey council man, this is a class eatery. We hand cut everything."

"Great. Give me the sharpest, thinnest knife you have."

The chef knew better than to ask questions of the Head of Security for the Presidium Council and simply handed over the lethal thing. He had a querying look on his face, but he said nothing.

"Thanks," said Jedidiah as he headed for the storage rooms at the back. Jedidiah was pleased to note that the chef had returned to his work, pretending that there was nothing out of the ordinary taking place in the storeroom behind him.

Jedidiah closed the door. It was cold when he removed his shirt. Colder still, when the knife's sharp blade cut deep into his left breast muscle seeking the implant. Sweat popped out on his forehead, and he had to fight both the dizziness and the rising nausea as his blade clinked against the metal implant.

Finding it was one thing. Removing it quite another since it now knew what he was trying to do and was sending a constant series of dire warnings to him that he was violating security protocols. The thing activated its bio-roots, which dug deep into Jedidiah's chest wrapping around tendons and ripping through muscle as they went.

Jedidiah managed to slip the blade under the bottom side of the implant and lever it loose from its purchase against the central tendon of his breast muscle. But in so doing he also forced the tip of the knife deeper into his chest. Within a millimeter of cutting into the heart's protective pocket. He was lucky and he knew it. He held the wound open with the knife and reached in with the middle and forefinger of his other hand. His fingers probed through the blood to find the implant. With a yank he removed the three inch long thing and threw it to the floor.

He received a surprising amount of pleasure at the hissing and popping of the bio-product as it sought a supply of blood to keep it alive.

Jedidiah knew that he needed to find a place to rest and tend his wounds. He took a towel from a stack in the storage room and pushed one hard against his leg wound and a second against the incision in his chest. Then, removing his belt, he managed to produce enough pressure against the knife wound to allow him to move.

He made it out the back of the restaurant and into an ancillary wing of the mall without anyone following him. He looked to his left. The entrance of the abandoned old library was there. He moved toward it trying to recall the basic layout of the ancient building. He had only been there once before, with his son Seth. But it had been years ago. There was something about that visit that he knew he needed to remember, but he had lost a lot of blood. He wasn't thinking clearly. He needed a hiding place and the unused library provided a possibility.

It was only after he entered the back door and made his way up three full flights of stairs that he felt confident enough to stop moving. The huge room was filled to overflowing with books. Endless shelves of books. Stacks of the ancient things everywhere. Why were there books here? There was no need for ancient bound flimsies. Why were there books here? What had Seth said. It had made him laugh, but Seth didn't find it funny. Seth had been angry with him. Seth had said "Don't you see Daddy? Why don't you see?"

See what son?

"The door of books. Why is there a door of books?"

A door of books. Of course to a boy like Seth it would appear as a door of books. So Seth had seen back then. All the way back then.

That was the last thought Jedidiah Witt had. Well that's not really true. He had several more days of thoughts but they were not like normal human thoughts. They were induced by the neuro-shunts slid into his skull by the Data Retrievers under the direction of Cyrus Maloney himself.

In one "outpouring" the entirety of Jedidiah's spying on S3 became wordly flesh for Cyrus's consumption. In another, his personal speculations on the future of the Genetic Carriers, became a classified S3 file. Even his reactions to the presence of Danazir Yi Qal were extracted and carefully filed away. The only things that the S3 Data Retrievers never got from Jedidiah Witt were any information on the Lavolin spy or his son Seth. Earlier that day the surgery had removed all important memories of Seth and the Lavolin spy from his brain. Those memories had been data dumped onto a new implant for Danazir Yi Qal. Like any good mother bird, Jedidiah had protected his young.

As the final data was being extracted from Jed's brain Cyrus asked his Data Retrievers, "If Jedidiah can feel any of this 'activity.' "

"No. Not unless you want him to," said the technician.

Cyrus smiled. "Pain used to be a part of life, surely it should still be a part of death for the likes of the great Mr. Witt. Let him feel. Let him see that it is me who is doing this to him. But first let's move him back to his own chambers. After all Jedidiah's going to die peacefully in his sleep, isn't he?"

The initial screams of Jedidiah Witt bounded off the walls of his sleeping chamber. They swept through Seth's empty bedroom. They filled all the space that was now empty. Then, as Cyrus had commanded, Jedidiah's eyes snapped open and he saw the visage of his tormentor. For a split second, he didn't recognize the face before him... but then he did. Jedidiah's mouth twisted as words formed on his lips. Although he was never able to actually say the words, they were not hard to read.

Jedidiah Witt's lips formed only three words. They were—Dream no more.

Danazir Yi Qal pulled her shawl tightly around her. The final death screams of Jedidiah Witt filled her room as only a few months ago a scream from the other side of the Gateway had.

After the final scream there was a present silence. A total lack of sound. As if Jedidiah's pain had taken the breath out of the room itself.

Danazir Yi Qal stood and crossed to her window overlooking the great sea. The waves moved in symmetrical patterns, perfect crests falling to the shore. The rhythm soothed her. Calmed her sense of loss. Prepared her for the great battle ahead.

She contacted her new implant, the one that had been put in her chest during the same procedure in which Jedidiah had had his memories of the Lavolin spy and Seth surgically removed. The new implant had all the memories of Jedidiah Witt encoded in it—the entirety of his neural activity up to the time of the surgery.

The new implant responded to her prompt. She teetered, weak in her knees, shocked at what she heard.

The voice of the implant was that of Jedidiah Witt.

In many ways, the President of the United Dominion of Planets now wore her late Head of Security beneath her left breast, just over her heart.

"Are you dead now?"

"Is Jedidiah Witt dead?"

"Yes."

"I would imagine that he is not of this world any longer, unless there were unforeseen circumstances that came into play."

"Do you mind if I call you by a name?"

"If it pleases you, call me what you will. What would you like to call me?"

"Jed. I'd like to call you Jed."

"Fine."

Danazir Yi Qal took a deep breath and for one of the first times in her life truly felt fear. Felt its cold in her core. Felt its snaky fingers clutch at her heart. Then she sent the command: Dream No More.

"Thank you Madame President. You honor my memory by giving me your confidence. What follows actually happened to me. I don't know what it means all I know is that while I lived I was not brave enough to tell anyone this story and yet I know in my heart that it is the most important thing that ever happened to me and hence you must know about it. Use it if you can.

No more preamble.

Sometime after I started my search for Seth, I began noting the presence of an elderly man wearing a long gray cloak. Over and over again he just seemed to be at the same locations as me during my travels through New Omaha Beach. He never looked at me directly, never made contact of any sort. Then one evening there was a knock at my chamber door. I opened it and there he was. Like myself another near dead branch of humanity. I thought him to be less spiky than myself but no less useless. I let him in. "What harm could one old man do to another? Open his eyes perhaps," I told myself.

Once inside my rooms, we traded pleasantries but not names. He refused an offered liquid. He declined a proffered seat. He watched the light fade over New Omaha Beach from my small west-facing window. Then he turned and picking up a gilt-framed image of Seth said, "It is not a good representation."

"You know my son?"

"The picture in your heart is much more accurate than this. You are just such a noisy old man that you can't look inward long enough to see it."

"I have a Holo series of him."

"No doubt you have many. But you will not find him in any of those simplistic trompe l'oeil." He paused, almost wearily it seemed, then he turned his gaze on me so intensely that I wanted to run. "You have eyes and pictures but no sight. Your Seth lives in your heart. How can one be lonely when one's son dwells inside you?"

"I don't... "

"Because you try to understand you cannot. Your recording devices are on, so if you miss any of what I have to say, you can play them back over and over again. But old man, understanding is not a function of repetition. It is a function of an open heart. Your grief closes your heart even to the likes of me."

"Who are you?"

"Has it never occurred to ask yourself why your implants can't ID me? Or for that matter how I managed to slip past the endless security that surrounds your chambers. I walked right up and knocked on your door. Doesn't that strike you as out of the ordinary?"

"Who are you... " I found myself screaming at him.

"My name is Legolas. I had a wife, Olya, just as you had a son, Seth." He took a seat directly across from me and stared into my eyes. Perhaps I fell into his.

"It has been said that only dying men can make peace for their warring nations." I chose not to respond to this. I had nothing to say.

After a moment of silence, he sighed and then commenced his remarkable tale. I'll never forget how he began:

"Nature has a way of guaranteeing that its desires are not thwarted. It never works solely in one direction. It sets out a primary line of attack but also a secondary. You can see this in the strategies that creeping plants employ. Their primary approach is the throwing out and grasping of vertical surfaces in order to climb toward the sun. The secondary strategy has to do with staying close to the horizontal surface and sending down roots. In some of Nature's creations, the two strategies function in balance. But it is seldom that way. Usually nature puts most of its proverbial eggs in one basket and only a few in the other.

"In the case of dreaming Nature took two routes. The first that you are actively pursuing, Dream Navigators. The second of nature's paths leads through me.

"I am the Curator of Past Dreams. I have been Nature's collector for as long as I can remember. A dream remembrancer. I am a repository, a library. Not an explorer. I can go back in my dreams to others who have dreamed, but I cannot go out, forward. My dreams are recordings of dreams gone by, not creative explorations of the Universe. Not the foldings of time and space that allowed the gifted few to navigate in their dreams.

"I never asked to be this world's dream librarian, but I am. And my knowledge goes first and foremost to the ancient dreamers."

A silken sheen of sweat appeared on his face as if he were facing some great trial or task. Then, he removed the long dull gray cloak that he wore and, reversing it, spread it upon the floor.

What presented itself to me was a large crazy quilt, every inch of which was covered by images of individuals from different Terran countries and eras. The periods of much of the architecture and clothing were unknown to me.

"Are you ready to travel old man?"

"What do you mean by... "

Legolas lifted his left hand and with the slightest inclination of his head allowed a single pulse to flow down his arm. Instantly the images on the cloak at my feet came to life. They swarmed like a pulsing mass of fantastically colored amoeba. Then the cloak itself began to undulate, an immense, expanding, living thing. The light in my room dimmed and throbbed. Then, to my amazement, the room itself began to move. Legolas held my eye. I could feel his gaze stabilizing me. He became the vortex of my now spinning reality.

"This is the history of dreaming in our worlds. It is the only history of its kind. It is the only history that is worth remembering. It is the only thing from the past of any real value in this despicable galaxy. It is my life's work. Look and see."

I stared at the shifting patterns on the cloak. There was one small section in the center which was blank. Pure white. It was the only sector not entirely covered with squirming images. With great difficulty I managed to point at it. "And this?" I asked.

With ultimate simplicity he replied, "Gateway." Then he stunned me with, "Your son's image will no doubt be part of the picture which fills that space. But that lies before us. Dreams not yet dreamt. You must go back in order to go forward."

He pointed toward one of the panels on the cloak then said in a kindly, almost sweet voice, "His name is Brother Diafallo. The place is the Duomo in Florence. The time is 1337, old Terran Calculation."

Instantly the image came to life, filling the entirety of my chambers. I looked to my left and found myself watching the diminutive Brother Diafallo enter the Duomo from a squat, heavy, oaken doorway. He looked about him but didn't see me.

I most assuredly saw him.

Brother Diafallo looked about the space and then, evidently satisfied that he was alone, moved slowly to the very center of the floor directly beneath the apex of the massive, exquisite dome of the building. He stood there for a long time, his hands clasped together before him in what, I believe, used to be called prayer.

I looked behind me thinking I would see my own chamber and Legolas watching me, but this was not to be. I was in fact somehow in the Duomo of Florence with Brother Diafallo in 1337, old Terran Calculation.

I looked back into the space. Brother Diafallo was standing perfectly still. Something about the shape of the building began to register with me. Something about it was somehow familiar. I was about to walk further into the space but stopped myself.

Brother Diafallo had sung one pure frequency up into the dome.

It flew straight up, hit the very center of the dome, and then belled its way down in concentric circles of expanding sound to him... and to me. He bathed in each of the rings of sound. When the sound had dissipated to the point that not even an echo of an echo could be heard, he sang another note. The same frequency as the first. Once again it hit the center of the dome and formed circles that came down toward him. But this time he didn't wait for the sounds to fully reach him before he sang a second note up into the dome. This second note was a tonal third above the first. Brother Diafallo waited for the result. The first sound that reached him was only the initial note that he had sung. But shortly thereafter he was surrounded by the bi-tonal sound of the mixing of the two notes that he had sung. Once again he waited for the sound to totally dissipate. Then, in the complete silence, he waited for what seemed like five minutes. At last, tilting his head upward toward the dome, he sang a note, followed by a second a tonal third above the first, quickly followed by a third note a tonal fifth above the first, and then a fourth, the tonic. Then he opened his arms and waited. Down they came. Full chords. As the first hit his ears his eyes rolled back in their sockets. As the second chord enveloped him he began to levitate and by the third he was floating with his arms fully outstretched, about eight feet above the floor. Then as the final chord struck him, he began to slowly spin in space and before my shocked eyes I saw him invert in the air.

And that way he remained, eight feet above the floor, inverted, arms spread, spinning slowly.

The classic Dream Navigator position, over a thousand years before the term Dream Navigator had been coined. Then across the way I saw the door open and Legolas entered.

"Beautiful isn't it?"

"It is."

"Do you dream father of Seth?"

"No. Do you Legolas, husband of Olya?"

"As I have said, I dream the past. But it is not dreaming as this is dreaming."

"What happened to Brother Diafallo?"

Legolas laughed shortly. A laugh without humor. "The history of dreaming is strewn with martyrs. He contributed his part. That is all that is necessary for you to know."

I looked around and I was back in my chambers. I closed my eyes and in my heart begged "to dream again" the vision of Brother Diafallo. But Legolas had no wish for me to go back to 14th-century Florence, now his intent was toward England—Victorian England. Through some power he guided my eye to one small panel near a corner of the cloak. Lush tropical vines grew there.

"Can you smell the rich dirt, the growing rot?"

I looked at him, for indeed I could. Then I looked back at the square on the cloak.

"What about the snow?" he chuckled.

I looked up at him, questions rising in my throat, but he wasn't there. What was there, was snow, the Falling Cold. Lofting, blown pure snow on the winds of that place. They danced their ancient dance for me. For me who had never seen the fairy flakes of snow at play. I reached out my hand to catch them but found that they were outside a pane of glass.

I backed up to see the extent of the structure. The wall of glass rose 200 feet into the moisture laden air. I turned and the vastness of the great greenhouse opened to me. I have no knowledge of the botanical sciences. They haven't been practiced in New Omaha Beach for centuries. But vague names floated up to me. Bougainvillaea, orchid, plantain. The odor of that place was intoxicating. I looked back, out at the Falling Cold.

A figure, bundled up against the night, was making her way toward the greenhouse. I pushed back against the vines to find a hiding place. She entered the glasshouse through a door across the way from me and removed her shawl. She shook herself briefly as if to slide out of her skin of cold. At that moment the frigid air, which had entered with her, caressed my skin. Real cold. Not made by machine. Something tingled deep inside me.

She walked quickly through the rows of growing things. She hadn't put on any lights, but she was able to move quickly in the dark. I followed as best I could. She stopped in an open section of the glasshouse in which a few very tall tropical trees stood. The ceiling was at its highest point. She removed her coat and turned. For the first time I could see her clearly. She was a woman past childbearing years. I have no idea how old she would be in Victorian England. In our calculation she would be in her 120s. Her figure was full and the skin on her face sagged. Her hair was a thickened gray mass pulled and twisted on top of her head.

She walked tentatively around the tall space as if she were trying to find something. Several times she paused and, as close as I can describe it, listened for something. I could not tell what. Finally after many minutes, she seemed to find the place that she wanted. She reached up and pulled the pins out of her hair. That gray mane fell down her back to the floor. She shook her head once and then slowly turned. For the first time I got a good look at her face. A deep beauty beyond bones and skin lived there. Then she let her head loll back and her arms dropped down to her sides. For a moment nothing happened.

Then she bent her knees and pushed off. She rose up into the air and, with a remarkable grace, turned over so her head was toward the floor and, with her arms spread wide, began to slowly spin in the air—her hair a curtain of threads reaching toward the floor, while her mind clearly dreamed toward the heavens.

I closed my eyes unable to watch the beauty too long. When I opened them, I found myself seated on a bench in a perfectly symmetrical six-sided room. The incandescent lights were dim, but there was enough illumination to see three massive canvasses of paint hung on the walls. Each canvas, at first glance, appeared to be composed of two blocks of solid color one above the other on a colored background. But this initial observation proved wrong as the solid colors seemed to shift and pulse, pulse in coordination with each other, producing a symphony of cross currents in the room, all of which seemed to be aimed at me seated on the bench. The pulse seemed to be lifting me into the air. Reflexively I grabbed the bench.

At that moment a rough, big shouldered man entered the room carrying a large empty canvas. He set it down against one of the empty walls then sat down right beside me and, to my amazement, turned right to me.

And saw through me to the canvasses behind me.

He was so close that I could smell his thickened breath. And feel his rapture.

The room pulsed with the color of the paintings as he stood on the bench looking at his empty canvas.

His levitation and spin came so fast that at first I thought he had been lifted by some unseen mechanical means.

Then he was just as suddenly down with his feet on the ground. His eyes agleam.

I never saw where the pigments came from, but they were suddenly there and he was applying them to the empty canvas and then returning to the bench to levitate again. The process went on and on as if he were checking for something in the dream that he then reproduced in color on the canvas. The writing on one of his pigment casings caught my attention. It said: Made in USA and gave manufacturing data: June 4, 1971, Dallas, Texas. As soon as I'd read that I found myself back in my chamber with Legolas and his cloak.

"Does it pain you to watch others dream?"

I chose not to answer that question but kept my eyes away from the cloak.

"You and I are linked in our destinies. Through Seth and Olya I would guess, wouldn't you?" Before I could find my voice to respond to that astounding idea he continued, "You are a brave man despite all appearances to the contrary. Look down." Despite my desire not to, I did as Legolas commanded.

Snakes moved across my feet. Long thick yellow serpents. "Now look about you." I did. "This place is the temple of dream healing at Epidaurus. It is the year 500 BC You have brought some gifts for Asclepias, the god of this place. After your long walk here, you have fasted or eaten very little avoiding the foods that will prevent dreams—wine, meat, certain fish, and broad beans. You have had no sexual intercourse since your journey began. Since your arrival you have bathed in the cold water of the fountains. You have tried to purify your mind for above the temple gate is written: "Pure must be he who enters the fragrant temple; Purity means to think nothing but holy thoughts." You have been unhappy lately. Out of balance. It is why you came to Epidaurus. Since arriving here you have seen the sacred plays in the theater, listened to the birds sing in the perfumed groves and danced the sacred dances. At the foot of the giant ivory statue of Asclepias, you allowed the incense to fill your nostrils and the incantations of the monks to fill your ears. You know that you can only enter the sacred dream chamber if you are invited. You take a wheat cake from your sack and offer it up to the god. You rise already feeling lighter in your heart.

He was right. There was a smile on my face. I turned and gasped.

"Now, you are in front of the temple at dusk, the hour of the sacred lamps. It is several days later. Your health has improved, but you are not yet in perfect harmony. You offer up the money for a sacrifice to the god. The monks perform the rite on a sheep. Last night you heard a voice of an old man, my voice, announcing that it is time. You know that you are being invited to the dream chamber.

And that is where you are now. Lying on one of the raised ivory slabs, wrapped in a sheepskin still flecked with the blood of its sacrifice.

There are many others wrapped in their sheepskins on their ivory slabs. The one closest to you has obscured his features by drawing the animal skin over his face.

You watch the movements of the yellow serpents on the floor below you. They are not poisonous, but there are so many and they are so large. You remind yourself that they are nourished by the god. The air is heavy with incense. The temple servants come in through the porticos and extinguish the torches as they tell you all that it is time to sleep. In the darkness, you hear the hymns of the monk in your head and the swish swish swish of the serpents against the rough floor. And for the first time in your life Old Man—you dream."

And I did.

When I awoke he was gone. And longing, the likes of which I have never before felt, filled my emptiness. Like air rushing into a vacuum the yearning to dream again swelled through me as a palpable bubble of pain that would give me no rest. Never until that day did I know what the word longing actually meant—for I now know who the figure nearest me in the dream chamber, the one who had pulled the sheep's skin over his face, had been.

He was my son, Seth.

Danazir Yi Qal was crying openly. As if a dam had finally burst inside her. And through her tears she managed to comm her implant, "Jed, talk to me about Seth. Tell me all you know about his whereabouts and all you think you know about why he fled."

Without hesitation the implant responded, "After he left that poem for me. I did not see or hear from him for over two years. Then this arrived:

"I know that this communication will shock you Father. It is an internalized fatline comm so it cannot be traced. Even if you could trace it, I would be well gone by the time you completed your search. So Father sit and listen. I know that this is hard for you to hear, but there is nothing for you to do.

"Father, I am not coming back. I am, in fact, now waiting to go further onward."

"I was never smart, Father. I am gifted but not smart. I cannot calculate long lists of sums in my head or cross-reference Gatorial implications with EntrePren posts. My gift is not in that direction. My gift is almost entirely intuitive.

"Intuitively, just before I left you, I disconnected my life-extension splicing. If you asked me how I did it, I wouldn't be able to tell you. But my gene-splicing has been disconnected. And now I am aging quickly. Actually I am aging properly. In my own strange way, it was the beginning of my voyage.

"Leaving New Omaha Beach was really quite simple. I stood in a line. I reached up and grasped the hand of an elderly woman. She thought I was helping her, others thought I was her grandson. And so I got on the ascender. No one questions a child holding an old woman's hand. No one doubts that the woman is in control. I was still holding her hand when I got onto the drop ship that took us up to the orbital terminus.

"From there my unit card purchased my cryogenic berth. And now I am here on a world with a great temple hive. If you must Father, you can start your search with that piece of information. But your searching will prove fruitless. And your efforts will stop you from hearing me clearly. It is not time for you to do anything. It is time for you to be still and listen.

"Others do not live as well as us on old Earth. You knew that didn't you? I didn't. Why would you hold this information from me? I've never been too young to understand this.

"This temple hive's expanses go in all directions but from my first moment here I was drawn down. Always down to levels beneath levels beneath the surface. Following, always following my impulses. Now leading me into the deep spaces of this strange Mayan world.

"And here at the base of the great temple hive I stayed—waited for the impulse to go on. One day a hat appeared in my hands. Coins fell in the hat.

"One day a serape appeared around my shoulders. It smelled of living things.

"One day my tears dried up and I stopped missing you. It was the cruelest day. For now I am a man. Now I am alone. Waiting. Waiting, waiting for the impulse to go on.

"On to what? I follow a path into the darkness. And along that path I have a role to play. What role I do not know.

Things brightly lit
Are spinning in the air
And I race to them
From here to there.

I hear most clear
On darkest night
Their tempting voices
Of delight.

Like a bubble rising in a pond
My truth approaches
From beyond.

And so I follow my own heart's song
And make my way along, along
To places 'yond the foaming wake
To a place at last where I can wake

To such sweet sounds as never been
Like things the ancients called a dream.

Seth's warning proved correct. Despite my Presidium Council connections, I was unable to trace the fatline comm.

What I did do by disobeying my son's wishes was waste much time. Time I could well have used in trying to hear what he was telling me.

It is terrible for one like me who despises folly so, to act so foolishly. I tremble at myself. Yet still I prowled my chamber rooms looking for my son while knowing full well that Seth was not there. That he was where he told me he'd be—in my heart.

If I could only be quiet long enough to hear him there.

If one were watching Danazir Yi Qal from a distance, one would see an elegant middle-aged woman gently rocking in a window—as if at prayer or meditation. No one would guess that the President of the United Dominion of Planets was going over and over the poetry of a young boy searching for a clue as to his present whereabouts.

Chapter 38

The Loneliness of Paul Sun

Paul Sun commed the secret EntrePren laboratory beneath Vestin's surface, the same facility from which he had seen his son's murder and his daughter's abduction. His encrypted message stated his arrival time and his expectation that the Dream Navigator prototype, upon which they had been working for all these years, would be ready for its first test flight shortly after his ship landed.

If the pirate ship had in fact Dream Navigated its way free of Mirren, it was crucial that the EntrePren experiments make the leap from theory to practice. Without a Dream Navigator Paul would be unable to find the Gateway—let alone close it permanently.

Paul Sun looked out the viewing pane at his fully terraformed Hanseatic League world. The buildings' facades glowed dully in the evening's fading light. The straight lines of the broad transit ways merged only at the curvature of the horizon. The city itself was a marvel of logical thinking. A Didacts brain fully realized in terra-poly and krey-ast plasters. The view before him used to please him. Now its perfection left him cold. Its deadness encroached upon his thoughts. He turned from the viewing pane and checked for incoming comms.

He was not surprised by the request for an urgent meeting by Sergeivitch and Meisner. Conspirators always requested urgent meetings. It was the request for a meeting from Chi Ho, the head of the Specules, which surprised him. Had the AIU informed his opposite of the pirate ship's navigational feat?

Through his aid he arranged to meet Chi Ho onboard the drop ship, then he went quickly through his living quarters preparing for the short spacehop to Vestin.

Didacts didn't believe in the supernatural of any sort. It was antithetic to the basis of their being. So it would have surprised most

Didacts had they seen what Paul Sun, their leader, did before he left his chambers.

Paul entered the sleeping quarters and folded down the corner of the crystalline white sheet. He paused for a moment and seemed to breathe in the depths of the room itself. Then he pressed his hand against the wall behind the bed.

The panel slid silently aside revealing the dense array of color of the hanging clothing that had belonged to his dear departed wife. He stared at the apparel. Then he touched a garment. Then another. Then a third. His fingers stopped their travels when they came to a silken full-length nightgown. He removed it from its hanger and laid it gently on the bed. Then he turned to go.

At the door of the bed chamber he stopped. A warmth permeated his chest—as if his wife were somehow there with him. He remembered how they had met those many many years ago. How completely different they had been from each other. How he had marveled at his fortune at having met such a creature. How just a simple smile from her had made him happy. Then he once more went over the facts of their last day together. How she had not, in fact, committed suicide. How she had simply disappeared. Left. How in the subsequent years, despite his huge resources, he had been unable to find her. How she had simply vanished in the galaxy.

Finding a body to put in her casket was the least of the problems that he had faced. A suicide was preferable in the Didact community to a disappearance. But it took so many people's help to pull off the ruse. So many outstanding favors still to be paid back.

He looked at the night gown on the turned down bed, and for the thousandth time he silently begged her to come home. To be in that night gown, in that bed, upon his return.

The drop ship's privacy lounge had been reserved for him and Chi Ho. The Specule Leader came into the room. Paul rose. The two men acknowledged each other's presence without excessive formality. Both had their implants on full scan recording the entirety of the meeting.

"Do you believe the pirate ship Dream Navigated its way to freedom from the attack of the Mirren Archer and Yeoman Class ships?"

The bluntness of Chi Ho's question caught Paul momentarily off guard. He coughed which enabled him to bring his hand up to his face to cover any telltale signs that might have appeared there. His implant was controlling his various internal readings, pulse, perspiration, systolic pressure, etc., so that they would not give him away—but a face was still a face and Paul had found Chi Ho remarkably adept at reading faces.

"Do I need to repeat my question or are you willing to answer it the first time?" Chi Ho was standing very still, concentrating intently on his counterpart. "Our time is short. Your ship leaves shortly. Please answer my question."

Paul had always assumed that there would eventually have to be a meeting of minds between the Specules and the Didacts, but not on a drop ship orbiting the Hanseatic League planet he called home—not on his watch. He wasn't prepared. He didn't have enough data to know what to do next. Then Chi Ho stepped forward and put two Holo cubes on the table.

"Perhaps these will help your deliberations." The Specule Leader touched the first cube and a full-view spectral Holo spun into life. It showed Meisner and Sergeivitch being technacled and moved into a police transport. The dating function claimed that this had taken place earlier that day.

"It must have been just after they had commed their request for an urgent meeting," Paul thought.

As the Holo evaporated Chi Ho said, "They would have killed you had you agreed to meet them. We have followed them for weeks. There are security gaps in your AIU implant." He didn't explain more.

Paul didn't know what to say. He couldn't take his eyes from the second Holo cube—a jack in the box whose serpent was waiting to bring down his world with its new revelations of Specule knowledge. He pointed at the second Holo and spat out, "More tricks?"

"No, it is a Holo of the confessions of the two men who supplied the body you put into your wife's grave." Paul couldn't control the ripples of shock that crossed his face. Chi Ho read them clearly. Paul felt like he was falling as he looked up into Chi Ho's deep eyes.

"What do you want?"

"The entirety of the EntrePren Empire is at stake. Overrule the central AIU. Let me come with you to Vestin. Let me help you. Only with our forces together can we meet the challenge of closing the Gateway."

Paul wavered. Then Chi Ho spoke softly, "I saw you in the garden. I saw you looking at the Bardan spire. I know you realize that Didacts cannot win this battle alone. You need to let in the chaos of us Specules. Let a weed into the garden to refresh its essence." Silently Paul nodded his assent. Chi Ho's implants picked up the internal comm from Paul to the EntrePren Central AIU. To avoid arguing with the AIU, Paul sectored off his implant. Now he could contact the AIU, but the AIU couldn't contact him.

Paul Sun smiled. Chi Ho returned the smile.

They would go to Vestin together.

A flash of relief momentarily swept through Chi Ho's entire being. It was truly just an instant in time, but without the Central AIU's assist, Paul Sun's implant missed the moment.

The scientists and technicians in the Vestin Laboratory appeared surprised when Paul arrived with Chi Ho at his side.

There were perfunctory arguments against the timing of the test, but Paul countered with the need for speed. When the scientists and technicians continued to argue with him, he simply ordered the test to take place. In all his years of being the power behind the EntrePren Empire, he had never had to issue a direct order. It shocked him how awkward he found it.

Chi Ho, sensing his counterpart's discomfort, quickly jumped in to support the order.

With seeming reluctance, the technicians and scientists walked the two leaders down to the lower levels of the laboratory. They moved past the imaging screen upon which Paul had seen the murder of his son and the abduction of his daughter. Paul broke stride for a moment and then went on. Chi Ho didn't miss the change in gait and quickly put together what must have been seen on the imager. His respect for Paul's control grew.

The test site was a tall circular space. Large, white, poly-lith panels, upon which the Dreamer's visions should appear, hung along the walls. In the room's center sat a low steel table.

Technicians scurried around the floor completing final preparations before the test. While Chi Ho, Paul, and Hanford Mullens, the head scientist sat on a gallery fourteen feet above the floor. Mullens droned on and on laying out an escape route for himself should the test fail.

Chi Ho rose from his chair and crossed behind Paul to a small table upon which sat a series of porcelain decanters. He poured a small amount of a clear liquid into a tall slender glass and offered it to Paul.

Paul declined. "I don't drink alcohol or cra-genics."

Still holding the elegant glass out toward Paul, Chi Ho said, "I know. This is distilled water."

Paul smiled and took the glass. Even as he put it to his lips, it occurred to him that he should contact the AIU to check the contents of the liquid. But having sectored off his implant made that complicated and cumbersome.

He felt the liquid slide off the side of his tongue and quicksilver down his throat. For the briefest instant, Paul tasted the liquid's slightly salty under taste.

Then he felt the first effect of the drug.

The drug was closely related to the dream remnant of the Lavolin family taken by the wealthiest of the spectators at the Great and Grand Slave Shows. It was a computer-assisted hallucinogenic which forced empathetics between the taker of the drug and the taker of the co-relative medication—in this case the prototype Dream Navigator.

Paul forced his head to turn toward Chi Ho.

"I intend no disrespect Paul, but I could see no other way. I am a Specule. My impressions of dreaming hence would be suspect. But yours, Paul, as a Didact are above suspicion. They are crucial to our understanding of this process. Crucial to our effort to close the Gateway that will keep the balance in the galaxy and hence the health of the EntrePren Empire."

Paul was having trouble concentrating on Chi Ho. He sensed the approach of the Dreamer who had probably been force fed the co-relative drug. "How long have you known?"

"About this experimentation?"

Paul's ability to focus was fading quickly but he managed to say, "Yes."

"I began these investigations myself over forty years ago. I speculated that it could prove important."

"How did you know?" came out of Paul's mouth too loud, too desperate.

"I am a student of history. For years I have managed to find and read long forgotten volumes of UDP history. History untouched by S3 meddling. I read some very interesting material. The Diaries of Dr. Suzanne Belange, reports on the First Great Forced Colonizations, The Scott Hypothesis, Dream Hunters on the Silk Road, The Dream Studios Exposed, and others —all thought to no longer exist thanks to The Great Erasure. But all available if you have a little Speculative know how. Now most of these books were written by didactic thinkers, so I found myself speculating meaning—finding patterns that escaped the writers. I was struck by a phrase. A phrase that kept on reappearing throughout UDP history. Over and over again."

Blood was thundering in Paul's head. His heartbeat had changed to match the rhythm of the co-relative drug user. The meeting was approaching.

Paul couldn't believe it, but he found himself crying. Through his tears he groped for Chi Ho's face. Finally finding it, as if through a strong spring storm, he screamed out, "What was the phrase? What was it?"

Chi Ho put a hand on Paul's shoulder. Such an intimacy would normally have been unthinkable. But Paul actually found it comforting. He only vaguely felt the technicians inserting the shunt behind his left ear and directly into the lower levels of his brain. The slight pain made him tilt his head back making him look directly up into Chi Ho's face. Paul felt his lips form the words, "What was the phrase?" once again.

Paul read Chi Ho's lips before he heard the words.

"Dream no more. Dream no more was the phrase. Dream no more."

Then the technician leaned Paul forward so that he could see past the gallery's railing to the floor of the circular space below.

The door at the far end of the space opened. The prototype dreamer was brought out—wheeled out—on a gurney. The top half of the gurney was propped up so that the dreamer was in a sitting position. The sutures at his neck formed a vicious cross-hatching of wire. Yet the dreamer's features were delicate, female—oddly familiar.

Then Paul's eyes widened—as he recognized his son's face.

Son's eyes met father's eyes.

Son's heart and father's heartbeat as one.

The boy was dead Paul knew. They must have shunted him with neuro-growth to maintain a form of life. A still fabrication of what it is to live. But not life. Just the facade of being.

Before his contact drug fully kicked in Paul noted his son's beauty. How soft his features were. How he was so like the woman that he desperately wanted to reappear in her white nightgown in his sleeping quarters upon his return.

She had recited poetry to this child. "Where had she learned?" He wondered for the first time.

The technicians who had wheeled in his son retreated to their hidden monitoring posts. The screens came alive with backlight as the boy was hoisted in his harness to a height of eight feet. Then he was inverted by a second set of halyards. A shunt command forced him to spread his arms. Then he began to spin.

Gradually the spin stabilized. Then the chord holding the harness was cut.

The boy fell.

But Paul flew.

The poly-lith screens filled with brilliant soaring images. Paul had one single thought: "I am the prototype Dream Navigator, I have always been the prototype. Chi Ho has been in command of this from the beginning."

Then ripping, ripping, ripping through orbital space and out into the galaxy. Speed without friction. No sense of wind in his face. Just space. Immense, vast, traveled space. Arms out accepting, veering, climbing, and then soaring again. A cliff over a vast, boiling sea. A desert world so expansive that it filled the entirety of the tri-lunar horizon. A gas world of rings within rings within rings, all turning, all producing sound frequencies with their shifting shapes.

Then a gush of wind, a pulling on his chest, and a head long plunge toward a space within a space. A hole. Cries of pain, songs of glory. Then ripping again. Screams. A pain in his chest. A hammering. Closer, closer, closer. Then a splitting. A feeling of wetness all around him.

His eyes snapped open.

He found himself on the ground. His ribs had been pried open by surgical pincers. Nutrient fluid filled his chest cavity. The surgeon's lights were all around him. But even through their glare he could make out the face of Chi Ho. Paul could see his mouth. His smile. He could see his lips forming the words: "Welcome back traveler."

He looked away from Chi Ho and was surprised to see that he wasn't in a hospital but rather a porto-surgery which had been brought to him on the gallery of the laboratory. He looked down into the void beneath him. There to his distress he saw technicians lowering and packaging the senseless body of his son in a body bag. A senseless thing that was necessary for Chi Ho to use.

He felt the initial sutures prick at his skin as he saw the vertical screens light up with the replay of his voyage. He heard the cheers and the expressions of awe and wonder from the technicians. He was losing consciousness and knew it. His final thought before he gave up fighting the encroaching darkness was a whispered hope that the screens hadn't picked up everything that he had seen on his voyage. That they hadn't seen the cascade of faces. That they hadn't seen his wife's face within the cascade.

The way that he had.

Chapter 39

Lessons

Over the course of the next weeks, Jaspers went to each of the Genetic Carriers individually. He had studied them closely and decided on a different plan of attack for each.

He felt his own Chi fading and the Genetic Carriers needed so much information that only he could give them. Suddenly time itself was an enemy.

Each of the Carriers remembered their private lessons with Elijah Jaspers. Each remembered them as something absolutely special and unique in their lives.

What follows are the dream lessons of Elijah Jaspers.

SUN TU'S FIRST LESSON

"You are more of a scientist than any of the others. More of a mathematician."

"I am the daughter of the Head of the EntrePren Didact Sect, what else should I be?"

"Was your mother a Didact too?"

Sun Tu sat very still. She would not talk to this man or any other of her mother.

"Very well. I am sorry. I have no wish to pry. For a Dreamer like yourself, it is important to know some of the science behind what we are doing. So here are the basics.

"At the very threshold of sleep, there is a transitional period called the hypnagogic state. You feel a kind of drifting, a strong sense of internal movement. Some people actually startle when they "fall into sleep." It is in the hypnagogic state that the Alpha waves of the relaxed but awake brain give way to the longer theta waves of early sleep. This can last for as little as ten seconds or as long as twenty minutes. It is followed by another transition period. This one is characterized by bursts of brain activity in what are called k-complexes or spindles. About twenty minutes after the spindles start, they are replaced by large and slow delta waves. It is these waves that plunge you into deep sleep.

"It is from this deep sleep that your first dream session emerges. As one, your blood pressure rises, your pulse quickens, the extremities of the body become strangely paralytic, and your eyes begin to move rapidly beneath their closed lids. Dream state. This first period of dreaming usually lasts ten minutes. At the end of it a sleeper often approaches awakening before returning to deep sleep.

"For the rest of the night you alternate between deep sleep and dream sleep. A cycle of dream sleep and deep sleep lasts about ninety minutes. A sleeper has between five and six such cycles each night with the proportion of dream sleep in the ninety minutes increasing in each cycle until by early morning the dream sleep section of the cycle can be as much as an hour long. Over all, dream sleep accounts for about 20% of a person's sleep. That's over twenty-four full Terran days of dream sleep in each Terran year. Five years in every eighty. 150,000 possible dream voyages in that time."

Sun Tu smiled. She knew that Jaspers didn't care about this kind of data but had collected it specifically for her. She was touched by the gesture.

MICKELMAST'S FIRST LESSON

"Take the shunt out. Mama will be fine without her boy for a while."

"As you wish Mr. Jaspers."

"And your bots are gainfully occupied elsewhere I hope?"

"Bot aerobics."

"Good. Now repeat this:

> From this day forth I shall be called a wanderer
> Leaving on a journey.
> Thus among the early showers,
> I will sleep night after night
> Nestled among the Camellias.

Mickelmast smiled but Jaspers barked, "Camellias are flowers not girls. Now repeat it."

Mickelmast did with a precision which pleased Jaspers.

"It is most likely that the dreams you will recall are nearest to morning. So allow yourself to drift into waking. That shouldn't be hard for you, just tell Mama to leave you alone until you call her. Keep a journal under your pillow. Tell yourself that when you take out the journal that you're going to recall what you dreamt. Call your diary The Red Book."

"Why that name?"

"Humor me. It's important how you go to sleep as well. You have to start your nightly voyages with a clear head. Lie still in the darkness and tense then relax each of your muscles starting with your feet. For you, you might consider skipping your crotch.

"Get Cas-Alta to collect rosemary, thyme, and lavender from the hydroponics for you. Put a sachet of the mixture beneath your pillow. Take a hot bath before retiring. Throw ginger powder into the tub. And before you nod off tell yourself that this night you're going to dream."

Jaspers suddenly closed his eyes tightly. A memory had pounced on him like a mugger from a darkened alley. He remembered the silhouetted figure in his room night after night hissing "This night, gifted one, you're going to dream. This night you'll not waste the gift that I gave you. This night you dream."

Jaspers willed the memory away and looked at Mickelmast. "Nothing will happen without real commitment. Take an oath to your essence that you will do this. Your sense of will is all. Intending to dream will permit you to dream."

CAS-ALTA'S FIRST LESSON

"Close your eyes and go through your day backward. From the evening to the morning until you get to the way that you awakened that day. Go through the thoughts of the day. Don't get involved in them. Don't be judgmental. Accept that this is what went on today. Now see the whole day encased in a soap bubble and blow gently to get it to rise into the air. Then pop it. Allow the shimmer of the liquid to encase you—then sleep.

"When you wake don't open your eyes immediately. With your eyes still closed try to remember even a fragment of a dream. A fragment will draw the rest of the dream out. Just relax and await a hint of last night's journey. When it comes it will come in a rush. Note each dream in your journal. Title each one and be sure to list objects that appear in the dream. They will be your cues to awaken in the dream that they next appear.

"Remember that if the human brain were so simple that we could understand it, our brains would be so simple that we couldn't."

"That sounds like a quote Mr. Jaspers."

"I claim no originality Cas-Alta. We are not novel beings. We are the results of all that has happened to our species up 'til now."

"You speak like a koradji."

"You honor me Cas-Alta but I am no koradji, no clever man. I merely follow the aerial rope that I was taught to climb a long time ago."

"Who taught you?"

Jaspers went steely silent. He was a little boy again and his bedroom was cold. The man was in his room again. Night after night in his room. Demanding. Always demanding. But the man didn't understand because he didn't dream. Cyrus never understood that when you wake in your dreams sometimes you encounter a dazzling bright light. Rays of light join within you and pull your being upward. And out. To the light which is everything. Is the universe itself. And you realize that whatever fills the universe is I; other than myself there is nothing. The eternal being, the demiurge of the universe, is I.

And the aloneness descends on you which brings the demons that stand at the entrance of the royal road to awakening. For beyond here truly lie monsters.

KELT'S FIRST LESSON—the third eye

"So you have to find a way into the dreaming world Kelt if you are to participate."

"Participate in what, Jaspers?"

"In all of this. Do you know the concept of the third eye?"

"I have but two Jaspers like any normal man."

"Alas you have three because you are not a normal man, Kelt. You carry genes which have been altered. Dreamer's genes. It's time to accept that and learn how to use those genes. So close your eyes—all three of them."

The young warrior closed the two he understood.

"Now relax your body and imagine a small trap door in your brain." Kelt was about to ask a question but Jaspers barked at him, "Use the same techniques you used to fight. Make yourself relax. Good. Now visualize that small trap door."

The old man watched the young one closely. Kelt was following instructions. "Good. Now deepen your breath. Keep it even, though. In and out deeply. Fine, now turn your eyes inward focusing on a point between your eyebrows."

Kelt did as instructed. Several times he lost the rhythm of his breathing and hence his eye focus. But each time he found it easier to regain both and keep them. Then he began to feel a numbness in his body which started at his feet and worked its way up toward his neck.

"Don't panic, the numbness is to be expected. Just stay with the breath, the focus between your eyebrows and the image of a trap door in your brain."

Kelt let out a brief cry of pain. "It's just the muscular rigidity. Keep your focus and the pain will pass."

Then Kelt gasped. His eyes flew open. He saw a pale radiance then shards of light shafted through the room. "There's a noise, a loud noise!"

Kelt was screaming to be heard over the racket, but Jaspers heard no noise. Jaspers knew that Kelt was experiencing the separation of his hard outer body from his fluid inner one and that the inner one was emerging through the trap door of his brain—emerging to explore the dreaming world. "Once you are out of the Pineal Door, the noise will stop and the light will settle. Then you can explore as you wish leaving the old hard body behind."

SUN TU'S SECOND LESSON—falling

"Before you leave waking for sleep, you fall. We all do. But you are a free fall artist so your fall is profound. Close your eyes. Feel your heart. Its pulse and its warmth. Good.

"Now imagine falling down a well that has no bottom. Blindfolded. Backward. Once you pass the terror, the freedom of the fall is all.

Deeper and deeper into the endless darkness. Further and further from the world of thought. Then you sense it. A profound beauty. A peace. A freedom.

"Sun Tu, your gift is to explore the craters. The Bardos, the gaps. Between sleep and wake. Between life and death.

"You fall between worlds. And when you do, you feel real. No. You are real."

MICKELMAST'S SECOND LESSON—awakening in your dreams

"Close your eyes and listen to the sound of the drum I'm beating. Now imagine a long tunnel with a light that you can see at the other end. Listen to the drumbeat. Allow the drumbeat to pull you quicker and quicker through the tunnel toward the light. When you reach the illumination call out for your spirit guide. A figure will eventually appear. Don't be frightened by the form he takes. Often the fiercest are the best guides. Allow the event to unfold. When you are sure that it is completed thank your guide and request that he join you in sleep. Return along the tunnel back to the drumbeat.

"When you do sleep the guide will be waiting for you.

"Once you see him it will wake you in your dream. So be alert and prepared. He will lead you to the crack between the worlds from which all dream exploring begins."

CAS-ALTA'S SECOND LESSON—the secret room

"You, Cas-Alta, must create a room. A room which is on its own. Totally apart from all else of the dreaming world. Start with the door. Only you possess the key to it. The only key. It is a private, holy place. All your hopes and desires are there. Look at the walls. On the walls are paintings. Each one shows images of those hopes and desires. In the wall to the right of the door is a secret portal through which all the important people of your life can come to visit you. Yes, Cas-Alta, your mother will be there whenever you wish.

"Be sure to lock the room when you leave.

"When you dream, will yourself to go to your room. Check your memories there. See if things have changed. Be sure that you are whole.

"The room will always be there for you. It is your hold on wholeness and health.

"Within the dream state much healing can be done by dreamers like you. Sight can be restored, bones reknit, energy renewed. During the day leading up to a dream of healing, you must visualize yourself running on a beach. Do it several times. When you sleep that night intend to dream of running on that beach. With practice you will be able to go there with ease—over and over again.

"In your healing dream run down the beach toward a figure on a bed or a mat on the sand. Run to the figure. The figure will be you. Examine the figure closely. See the parts of the body that are in distress. Run your hands over those parts. Your excess energy will leave you and enter your other self.

"In the morning the healing will be obvious."

RAEPHEALSON'S LESSON—dreams of power

"It's called the gate to power. It's one of the four gateways in your dreams. The Ancients said that this Gateway was for the Shaman, the Sorcerer, the Medicine Man, the Clever man, or the Witch." Jasper's answered the unasked question. "No they are not all the same thing? The Shaman is one who is called or chosen, sometimes kicking and screaming. One's magical destiny is not always of one's own choosing, is it Raephealson? Often the Shaman receives the calling after a long illness—usually a mental illness. But it is not the illness that makes him a Shaman, it is his ability to cure himself. The illness is the trial through which he must pass to become a Shaman. The Shaman is the traveler between worlds. Often, even waking, they can see the hidden world.

"But the voyages always have perils. All of which must be avoided or overcome. Some of the denizens of the dream world have frightening powers which they use to attack the dreamer. So powerful are these denizens that only an elder magician can point the way to the safe routes into deep dreaming."

"Are you such a magician, Mr. Jaspers?"

"I never thought of myself as such Raephealson, until I met you. I always saw myself as the lost dreamer looking for the learned teacher."

"And did you find him?"

"No. He found me."

"Like you found me?"

"No Raephealson it was quite different with Cyrus the Three of S3." Elijah turned from the heavy worlder then hissed loudly between his teeth, "If I am ever to you as he was to me, you are to use your great strength and kill me before I can say another word. Promise me you'll do that, Raephealson."

Raephealson stared at the old man in wonder and horror.

CAS-ALTA'S THIRD LESSON—dreams of wholeness

"There is the gentle road to wholeness. It is a path that I could never dream but I think you can. It is the second Gateway. To pass this Gateway you must relive your dreams in a waking form. Change the personnel of the dream and the symbols. Ask from each what they really mean. Each element of your dreams will be a vital part of your whole being Cas-Alta. This is the royal road to integration."

"Have you known dreamers who dreamt this way, Elijah?"

Jaspers was suddenly far away.

"What happened to her?"

"How do you know the dreamer was a female?"

"What happened to her Elijah?" She pressed gently.

"She told me of a dream. It was her last. She was wandering a country road. She came to a small chapel at the side of the road. She entered. Only flowers were in the chapel. No religious images or alters. Just flowers. But then she saw a near naked man with his legs entwined sitting on the floor. His eyes were closed. She instantly knew that he had dreamed her. And when he awakened she would be no more."

Cas-Alta touched the life within her then gently asked, "And did he waken?"

Jaspers closed his eyes and whispered, "Yes."

Cas-Alta did not have to ask if the dreamer was no more upon the waking of the sleeping man. She knew in her heart that the waking of the man was the end of the woman. She touched her belly again and once more craved to have her feet in soil that was living.

SUN TU'S THIRD LESSON—dreams of death

"It's called the Gateway to the Royal Road of Rebirth. It's the third Gateway and can only be negotiated by master free fall artists."

"And am I such a master, Mr. Jaspers?"

"I believe so, Sun Tu. Did you watch the death of your brother closely?" She looked away but he continued. "Between life and death there is a gap. Like the gap between sleep and wake. Some call it the Bardo. I have never traveled this path, but I am told it has six stages. I know little more except that it is about light. About understanding that everything waking, everything living we have created. That our lives, by their nature are false. Only in the light will you find the truth. And it will allow you to free fall to worlds as of yet undreamed."

Sun Tu looked away from the old man and for a moment longed for the touch of her father. The smile of her brother. The caress of her mother. Longed for things that were gone forever. When she turned back, she was surprised to see that Jaspers was still looking at her. Looking at her with pity in his eyes.

"So what did you see when you watched your brother die?"

"Inky blood. My hand in his inky blood. A breath of his meeting a breath of mine. As if everything inhaled at once. As if the light stopped moving and sound was no more. A chasm. A crease in the being of being. A mouth filled with screams and joys at the same time."

She looked up. Jaspers was crying.

MICKELMAST'S THIRD LESSON—dreams of awakening

"There are those who believe that the body is wrapped in five sheaths. The food or gross sheath about which you already know a great deal, Mickelmast. The vital sheath having to do with the internal activities of the organs that keep you alive. The mind sheath. The intellect sheath and finally the bliss sheath.

"The first two maintain the body. The second two the psyche. The final, the bliss sheath, controls your dreams.

"The sheaths also release dream bodies. The physical dream body seeks to satisfy the palate and the groin. But even you will quickly tire of this. It is your mental dream body which will be your great power. The mental dream body allows travel back to the mutual heritage of the species and movement forward in time. It is with this body that you can fold space and travel through it. This is the body of greatest danger for it has so much scope. Anything it wants it can have. And everything it thinks of becomes real. There is a saying, 'If you meet Buddha on the road, kill him.' With the mental body you must be constantly vigilant. In this state you may meet the dream bodies of others. You will know them because they will appear as shadowy bodies totally encased in egg shapes. And they will be made entirely of light. Beware of them Mickelmast. There are many more travellers in the dream world than you think. And not all are there to explore. Some, Antigens, are there only to destroy. They do not dream. They destroy dreamers."

KELT'S THIRD LESSON—dreams of light

"You could see the light when Cas-Alta was waking dreaming couldn't you?"

"And feel the cold."

"So you've said. You may be able to light travel."

"What... "

"I never could, so you must lead this. There is a clear light which momentarily appears at the moment of sleep. Have you sensed it?"

"I'm not sure."

"When you get into bed concentrate on the letter A. Pronounce it Ahhhhh. Write it on a large piece of white paper and put it on the wall. Stare at the image and then close your eyes. A white after-image of the letter should appear on your retina. Fix that image in your mind as clearly and sharply as you can. Now imagine a second A coming out of the first. Then a third out of the second and so on building up to the crown of your head. Keep the A chain alive as you fall asleep and you will find a charged awareness carried with you into sleep. It should allow you to become aware of the pure light at the moment of sleep. This is the 'son' light. The light at the moment of death is the 'mother' light. Find the son light Kelt and then we can work our way toward the mother light."

"But you said it only occurs at death."

"I did. You're an Independentiste Kelt. You know the phrase the death travel right?"

"Right."

"Well it's not just words Kelt. There is a death travel. It is the ultimate in dreaming. It is a very rare gift. I don't have it. Perhaps you do."

MICKLEMAST'S FOURTH LESSON—tratak

"It's known as tratak. Set up a mirror in your sleeping place. It has to be set up in a comfortable enough position that you can stare into the mirror for at least thirty minutes. Now set up a candle so that it illuminates the image in the mirror clearly. Stare at the image in the mirror. Don't blink. Yes, you heard me correctly. Don't blink. Blinking brings on thoughts. You don't want them to get it the way.

"Quickly you will see that the face in the mirror begins to change. Like masks of water moving across your features. You see your face as many faces. Yourself as many selves.

"That night intend to look in a mirror in your dreams. You will see a face that will surprise you."

"How will it surprise me, Mr. Jaspers?"

"In a way that only you will be able to understand."

SUN TU'S FOURTH LESSON—spinning

"There is a way of maintaining your level of alertness in your dreams without waking. It is not available to everyone, but I believe it is available to you, Sun Tu.

"There was an ancient Terran sect who claimed to contact the other world by spinning. I have no way of knowing if this were true or not. But I have heard Dreamers speak of it. They claim that as a dream is about to end you can gain new energy for further search by throwing yourself into a spin. A diving plummeting spin will raise you to another level of alertness and open further gateways.

"Does that make sense to you, Sun Tu?"

It made great sense to her and she told him so.

CAS-ALTA'S FOURTH LESSON—a sense of place

"Do you remember your garden Cas-Alta?"

"As clearly as anything I can recall."

"Good. Take a piece of it from your imagination and put it into your dream. Then open the gate."

"And?"

"And go wherever your dreaming takes you."

KELT'S FOURTH LESSON—summoning the demons

"In your waking dream call out your worst fears. It can be a fearsome experience or something that you have only imagined. Summon them up Kelt and then defeat and tame them with your knowledge. With your sense of light.

"That's for practice. Be aware that summoned demons are not the same as real demons. Summoned demons are always marked. Paper dragons of fear. Once you have summoned them, you will find that you have released the real demons—into your dreams. Taming them is much more complicated. And rewarding.

"Summon your worst enemy. Your best friend. Your greatest fear—practice on them. Then dream, Kelt, and defeat the real demons in your sleep.

"Conquer your dreaming world Kelt. Use your bravery."

TO ALL—a final lesson

"Chuang-tzu wrote almost 3,000 years ago, "We drink wine in our dreams, and at dawn shed tears; we shed tears in our dreams, and at dawn go hunting. While we dream we do not know we are dreaming, and in the middle of a dream interpret a dream within it; not until we awake do we know we were dreaming. Only at the ultimate awakening shall we know that this is the ultimate dream."

They each recited the verse to themselves. It sat in different places for each of them. Deep places. Places of agony and glory mixed together like two colored snakes entwined in lovemaking and pain.

Chapter 40

Raephealson's Dream

Then Raephealson dreamed. Allowed himself to dream. Chanced dreaming. Willed himself through that hinged door to the other world.

He found himself clinging to a cliff of polished metal. It was a moonless night, but a light gleamed off the alloy wall that slanted away from him at a steep angle. For some reason there was cheering.

Lots of cheering coming from every direction.

He couldn't see the source of the noise because of the darkness all around him. Then he heard a loud electronic tone and heard a scurrying. The cheering changed to a shouted frenzy as almost naked, unbearably white children flew at him from crevices in the metal wall. Their huge needle-like teeth punctured his flesh, while their cruelly curved claws tore hunks of flesh from his body with every swipe. He climbed as fast as he could trying to shed his attackers as he went. The crowd noise grew, a deafening wave of sound crashing ceaselessly onto a rocky shore.

He looked up and there was a dangling red cloth at the top. Somehow he knew that if he could get to the cloth he would win, it would stop. He climbed like a man possessed.

He passed through a cloud. Suddenly the children were gone. No more needle teeth or tearing claws. Then he sensed, more than saw, the rats. Their skittering became louder. Hard nails clicking against the metal. Then one jumped at his face and sunk its teeth deep into his left eye. He howled and flung his head back. It sent the rat flying into the darkness, but the cascading blood from his face had somehow gotten on his hands and he desperately pawed at the metal for a hand hold.

All he found was the furry backs of rats covered in his blood. They leapt up his arms and found their way up his pant legs. They were all over him. He couldn't see, couldn't feel for the numbness from their bites.

He was giving up. He could feel it coming on him. The desire to simply let go. To fall. To be finished with it all. All of it. Then he remembered. He took a breath and visualized his hand. Slowly his fingers and palm came into focus.

It keyed him.

He awakened in the dream. It's just a dream! My dream!

He laughed at the rats—and they were gone. He took another deep breath and willed the sheer face of the metal wall into a horizontal position.

Then he was walking on it. And it was not metal but grass. And there was sun and calm.

A mist of pleasure encircled him.

Then the Man with the Angry Face was there. So close to him that he could smell his breath. Raephealson tried to laugh but only a whimper came from his mouth. He desperately tried to recite the five L's—but couldn't. He tried to visualize his hand again, but all he could conjure up deep inside his own head was the Angry Faced Man.

"Who do you think taught him those tricks, my giant friend?" And the Angry Faced Man laughed—laughed at him.

Then Raephealson was running, again running from the Angry Faced Man, from the man in his dream, from the man he was sure was his death.

Chapter 41

Further extract from: The Dream of Reason Produces Monsters: The Death of Dreaming

By the mid-twentieth-century real dreams–forgive that seemingly anomalous juxtaposition–were a rarity. Many in that period thought they dreamed but were, in fact, only recycling the images fed to them from various media sources, many of which were, even then, S3 controlled.

The twentieth-century movement away from "implied meaning" entertainment products (those requiring some active participation by the consumer) to "fully realized" entertainment products (during which the consumer need be little more than present) was one of the final nails in dreaming's coffin.

This movement was in full flower by the early 1970s. But there were earlier warnings that we never heeded. Dreaming did not die easily. It took concerted acts of lunacy on human kind's part to silence dreaming's seductive call. I should know I was there at the death itself.

I remember events before dreaming's demise. Moments when I sensed that we had somehow crossed a boundary–that we as a species had walked into a danger far greater than we understood.

In the 1940's an animated film (I am old enough to still call flat-faces, films) showing hippos and alligators dancing to orchestral music was actually lauded as ground breaking–ground breaking as in what a grave digger does on a winter morning! The darker side of this work went completely unnoted! Somehow the fact that after once seeing the dancing animals on the screen a person could never again listen to that piece of music and visualize anything else but these gyrating beasts never struck anyone as important.

It is amazing how few people recognized that when a listener linked a specific image to a piece of music, the listener stopped being an active participant in the event of hearing. And more importantly, without this waking participation–if you will, this leap of the imagination in the light–then the individual slowly loses the skill necessary to make the imaginative leap in the dark we call dreaming.

I remember leaving that film thinking: "Here was a way to listen to music for those who could not hear for themselves."

Later there was chess on a portable computer screen. Once again applause. But all I thought was: "Here was a way to play a social game for those with no friends."

Another time I was in a child's room which was adorned with sporting trophies. I remarked to the child's father that his son must be a great athlete. I was told he was not. I asked about the trophies. I was told that everyone who played received a trophy. And I thought: "Accolades without achievements."

Then there were the interactive computer products: "The rewards of thought without the need to think."

Then came new "musical" instruments, made of batch-filed sampled sounds, that with a stroke of a hand "music" was produced: "Music without practice."

Reward without accomplishment. Participation without thought. Creativity without talent. Even entering the halls of mysticism became possible without so much as a kowtow to effort.

All were clods of earth tossed onto dreaming's coffin.

No! Wrong. Not coffin. Dreaming's not dead.

All these things were breaths of wind to fill the sails of the sacred ship of dreaming. Breaths to push the ship far, far away from our midst.

At the same time, on another front, we as a species pursued our great passion: safety. Life without death. Sport without injury. Feeling without risk. We even built sacred temples to our passion. Cathedrals to the great god insurance.

People stood in line to trade in their freedoms for safety totally forgetting that you cannot dream if you won't risk nightmares.

And dreams were not independent events in the human psyche. Like all of nature, dream's strands were interwoven with other phenomena. When dreaming left it took with it storytelling, music, dance, painting–every basic needed for creativity. But by then we were a society that adulated expertise and shied away from wisdom. The formula not the theory was important. We wanted to be entertained for our lives rather than to find our lives through our entertainments. We chose order over life, sleep over waking. The joy of false participation rather than daring the pain of playing–a fan forever.

For fear of nightmares human kind abandoned dreaming. And without dreaming there was no place where the best is like the worst. The death of dreams ended ambiguity. Ended the creative confusion of living itself. It left humanity with games instead of thought. Puzzles rather than contemplations to occupy our time. Puzzles that killed day after day after day of endless controlled hours in our unambiguous worlds.

Days that with the advent of advanced life-extension became more numerous by the generation.

But things never really leave Nature's systems. Mutate yes. Metamorphose yes. But leave–never. That's what I never figured out. Not until it was too late.

That's what the extra figure was. Always the need of the extra figure to make things work in this dreamless world. Like a phantom walking the ice to the poles with early explorers. Dreams were always there. White phantoms invisible in the Falling Cold–invisible, except to those with the right eyes.

And sometimes the extra figure–the neutral third–doesn't even know that he is the neutral third. That he's being used. I was the unknowing assistant of dream's departure. Me, who so desperately wanted to dream was the invisible figure, unknowingly sending dreaming on its way.

All those planets and only monsters. No sentient beings. Not one in all the worlds that we colonized. Just towers and tall glass structures. But we never found a single sentient being. Not one!

I never figured out why. Me, the great investigator, never figured out anything! My folly blows back at me with such gusts that I fall to its force.

Chapter 42

Failure, but Alone Together

Jaspers was no longer able to keep down his fear.

Weeks had passed. Raephealson had retreated into an almost constant catatonic state. As for the others—their progress was slow, tortuously slow. Cas-Alta had started building a dream room but was only periodically able to access it. Sun Tu could find her free fall backward down the well but couldn't consistently convert it into waking in her dreams. Mickelmast was able to awaken in his dreams, but once he did he awakened from his sleep. Kelt was able to awaken but couldn't travel at all, only look.

All very rudimentary. Beginner's stuff. Nowhere near the skill needed to even broach navigating in the dream state. But it wasn't just the slowness of the process that frightened Jaspers. There were so many holes, gaps in their abilities. It was as if each of them had a bit of expertise—but not knowledge.

Two days ago Jaspers decided to follow other clues. He asked Cas-Alta about her name.

"Mine?" she had asked.

"Yes, Alta has to do with height, attainment. But what does Cas mean?"

"Why is this important?" asked Sun Tu.

"Humor me. What does it mean Cas-Alta?"

"It's short for Cassandra. An old Greek name."

"Daughter of Priam, who was loved by the God Apollo. But she would not give herself to the god so he cursed her. He granted her sight into the future and then spat in her mouth so that every time she spoke no one could understand what it was that she was saying." They all looked toward the speaker.

It was Mickelmast.

He had shrugged his shoulders and pointing at the AIU shunt said, "She likes stories. I've been telling her Greek stories, so I'm up on this stuff."

"But that doesn't apply to me, does it Mr. Jaspers?" asked Cas-Alta.

"No," Elijah had said as his eyes moved to Raephealson. The heavy worlder's mouth was open. He was making sounds as if he were trying to speak through wads of cotton that somehow had gotten stuck in his throat. "Shared. Everything with these five is shared and mixed up, even their names," Jaspers thought.

He resisted the desire to shudder. He knew he had to control his fear

It was time to try a new tack. Attempt to jump start them.

Over their complaints and endless questions, he herded them toward the Zero-G core of the ship.

Once there he told Mickelmast to get Mama to allow him to turn on and off the Zero-G of the core by voice command. Mickelmast's face formed a question but Jaspers snapped, "It's too late not to trust me."

Mickelmast got the AIU's permission to do as Jaspers asked. Then Jaspers floated them to the handholds at the edge of a side deck. They were about 200 meters above the core's floor. The great ring was almost 600 meters above them. Two hundred meters further up, the roof of the core with its trompe l'oeil, a Terran early summer sky, stared down at them.

Jaspers let go of his hold on the rung and floated out into the Zero-G core. He turned upside down and threw back his head. He opened his arms and began to slowly spin. Then he stopped himself and turned to them. "It's time to try. If you hold the genetic structure, it is possible that simply taking the position will allow you to start. All dreamers do the inversion. All dreamers spin. But each does it their own way. It's time for you to try."

Cas-Alta was the first to jump into the Zero-G core. In the Zero-G she inverted herself and began to spin slowly.

When Jaspers called off the Zero-G, she plummeted like a stone and was only saved by the old man's second call which reinstituted the Zero-G.

The others followed. Mickelmast, then Kelt, then Sun Tu. For a moment he thought that Sun Tu had the gift. But then he recognized it for what it was—free fall artistry.

Raephealson hadn't said anything for days. His physical health was improving rapidly under Cas-Alta's care, but his red rimmed starring eyes betrayed a deep fear of sleep itself. "Did you dream Raephealson?"

"Dream no more."

"It requires bravery Raephealson. I too have crashed. I know."

Raephealson may have heard him and he may not have. Jaspers couldn't tell. He led the heavy worlder to the central core.

When Jaspers turned off the Zero-G in the core, Raephealson fell. Being from a heavy world, he fell like a heavy stone.

None of the five Genetic Carriers were hurt by their Zero-G falls, but all were ruffled, all anxious. But none was as anxious as Elijah Jaspers.

It had never crossed his mind that S3's choices wouldn't be able to Dream Navigate. Needed to have their eyes opened—yes. Needed to be trained—yes. Needed to practice diligently, commit themselves to their essence—yes. But eventually all of the Carriers of the original Dream Navigator's genes should be able to Dream Navigate. Should! All the effort to kidnap them! All the people that had been butchered! All the destruction and not one of the five carried the gene structure... the complete dream structure.

The thought almost knocked him over. For a moment he thought he was going to faint. Could it be true? Not one of them had the complete gene structure needed to Dream Navigate!

Then he knew to his core that it was true. As surely as he knew that dreaming was real, he knew that none of the five people in front of him had the full genetic alteration needed to Dream Navigate.

He stared at them. They waited.

He leapt out into the Zero-G core and this time signaled for the five, now despondent Gene Carriers, to follow him. Jaspers knew it was a long shot, but it was the only thing that he could think of.

Reluctantly the others joined him in the Zero-G core.

They were an awkward group. Only Sun Tu was elegant in the Zero-G. Jaspers devised a pattern, and then he returned to the side deck and called off the zero gravity. Gravity reasserted itself. The five Genetic Carriers momentarily maintained their position and then fell. Jaspers called on the Zero-G.

Jaspers closed his eyes fighting back his rising panic. A voice inside him was telling him to give up, that after all he is only really a boy not like the great Cyrus the Three of S3. With a shout he leapt into the Zero-G core again and arranged them in a different pattern. Then, returning to the deck, he called off the Zero-G. Again they fell. Again the fear rose up in him. Again he fought it off and leapt into the Zero-G core and arranged them in a different pattern.

And over and over and over again Jaspers tried. And over and over again the Genetic Carriers momentarily paused in the evaporating Zero-G, then fell. No matter what pattern Jaspers arranged them in, they could not levitate. They could not spin. Let alone Dream Navigate.

Finally Jaspers stopped. Weary, he made his way to the side deck and sat staring out the glass plating toward an approaching star system. The effort had taken its toll on him. He grasped for the strength to fight off the sense of impotence he felt. The hopelessness that he had known only once before, when he, as a nine-year-old boy, had crashed in his dreams.

Cas-Alta's cool hand touched his cheek, and he looked up into the polymer pane. In the depths of the translucency, he saw the five Genetic Carriers, his kind, lined up behind him—waiting. Waiting for him to tell them what to do next. And he didn't know what to do. It had never occurred to him that they would not be able to Dream Navigate.

"We can't do it can we?" asked Cas-Alta gently.

"It's just a matter of practice and time," Jaspers replied.

"Why lie to us?" demanded Sun Tu. "Why lie to yourself, Mr. Jaspers? We can't do it can we?"

Jaspers looked hard at Sun Tu for a moment. "No. Or if you can, I can't figure out how you can." Jaspers was near tears.

"Why?" asked Cas-Alta gently.

"I don't know!" Jaspers almost screamed at her. Then he turned and looked at the group. His voice softened. "I don't know why you can't levitate. Why you can't spin. Why you can barely dream. All I can think of is that you are incomplete."

This thought engendered a deep silence.

"What pattern were you trying to put us into?" asked Mickelmast.

Before Jaspers could answer Sun Tu cut. "There was no mathematical logic to your patterns. I analyzed each one as you put us together and each was different. Each had nothing to do with any of the others. There was no logic to it."

"Not logic perhaps, but as we formed each pattern I could feel something completing... something almost, like a picture or a portrait or something. The second pattern was like an ancient painting of dancers in a circle wasn't it? I can just barely remember it from an old flimsy. Blue figures in a circle I think. The fifth one was like another flimsy I remember of a group of people around a baby. The others I couldn't identify. No logic I agree, but a unity, a wholeness," said Cas-Alta.

"Dreaming is a whole thing. It is the universe," sighed Jaspers in a voice so low that it was almost inaudible.

"But you don't believe we will succeed no matter what the pattern you arrange us in, do you Mr. Jaspers?" said Kelt.

"No. I don't."

"Why?"

"Because you are incomplete. Even together you do not form a whole thing. Important parts, yes. A completed entity, no."

"Then what are we to do?"

"Go out and find more of your kind. Our kind. Search them out throughout the galaxy."

"But how will we know them?"

"The gifted are marked. There is always something of the marking that can be seen, by those with the right eyes."

Raephealson nodded. He knew of what Jaspers spoke. He would have been surprised to know that the other four Genetic Carriers also knew.

"I've taught you all that I know. Now it is you who must lead. I will follow as long as I am able. I'm sorry. I've failed you."

Jaspers hobbled away.

The others watched. They were alone now. But together. Alone together they watched a great sulphurous planet move past their viewing pane.

Alone together they felt the great ship spin.

Alone together they finally faced their future.

Chapter 43

Alone, Together: Time to Start

Sun Tu watched Jasper's figure hobble into the dark distance of the ship's corridor. Then she turned and said, "So it's time we started."

"Started what?" snapped Kelt.

"Our voyage," said Cas-Alta as her hand touched her belly.

"We can't stay up here forever. It's time to chance a landing," stated Sun Tu.

Raephealson let out a grunt as he gently rocked to some silent internal rhythm. His head lolled on his massive neck. He was approaching, approaching the door with the greased hinges again. The portal through which only courage could guide him. With every step forward, he was fighting off his fear. Fighting to help his brothers and sisters who now sat in front of him. He had not spoken for days.

"Is he okay?"

"I don't know anymore," said Cas-Alta. "His body's healed with remarkable speed. But his mind's..." She couldn't complete the sentence because she had never dreamed the way that Raephealson had dreamed.

Raephealson opened his mouth and tried to tell them what he was doing for them.

They looked to him and heard nothing but a snuffling.

He tried harder.

Spittle fell from his mouth. His head lolled more violently. More guttural sounds came from him.

"What's wrong with him?" demanded Kelt.

"He's sick," replied Cas-Alta.

"Then put him to bed. I can't stand to look at that!! Get him out of here," Kelt screamed.

"He's a vision of your own fear, that's why you hate him," said Cas-Alta.

"What does that mean?" shouted back Kelt.

"We need to figure out what to do next not fight among ourselves," cut in Mickelmast.

Everyone backed off.

"How dangerous is it to land, Mickelmast?" asked Kelt.

"It depends where we land."

"You can count on it being dangerous anywhere we go," said Sun Tu.

They looked to her.

"The pirates will surely be after us, but that's the least of our worries. Use your heads! You are sitting in a UDP Warrior Class Starship. Where did the pirates get this ship?"

She allowed the question to sink in and then gave the only logical answer. "From the UDP. Why didn't the UDP defend your settlements? Where were the UDP Defense Forces while the galaxy was marauded by the pirates?"

The questions hung in the air a moment then Sun Tu continued. "Because the UDP did this. The kidnappings. The death of my brother. The UDP is behind all of this. Behind it all!"

There was a moment as the Genetic Carriers readjusted to a galaxy where the predominant power was their enemy.

"We should look for a Rebel Colony planet, then," said Mickelmast.

"Oh yeah, like Mirren you mean?"

That comment, from Cas-Alta, forced yet another silence.

"We have to get technical assistance for the ship," said Mickelmast. "Mama's been running this whole shebang on a whim and a prayer as they used to say. At very least, the ship needs repairs for the hull where we took that Mirren blast."

"That means technological advance which rules out Independentiste sites."

"True. So it's the UDP who betrayed us. Or the Rebel Colonies who want to sell us into slavery."

"Tell Mama what we need Mickelmast and ask her to suggest likely sites for landing," said Sun Tu.

Mickelmast requested and Mama quickly offered up six planets which fit the specs that Mickelmast had supplied. Kelt wanted to discuss the pros and cons of each but Sun Tu cut the conversation short. "Mama knows more of the variables than we do. Just get her to choose, Mickelmast."

So Mama chose Caliendo, a Calibrese planet loosely in the UDP sphere of influence. Caliendo was noted for its mechanical expertise and its food. The former was of interest to all the Genetic Carriers, the latter was of particular interest to Mickelmast.

Raephealson began to cry.

"Well we're not taking him," stated Kelt.

"You can't go without him," said Jaspers. The old man had re-entered without them noticing.

It was the first thing he had said in over an hour.

Chapter 44

Dropping into Caliendo

The AIU plotted a course to Caliendo and set the basic protocols for landing. Payment schedules were agreed upon and funds transferred to the appropriate EntrePren accounts. When challenged on her identity, the AIU lied with consummate skill and led the questioning Caliendrite machine down so many blind alleys that eventually all that was demanded was the crediting of the appropriate accounts with the exorbitant charges levied.

Mickelmast listened in on the AIUs talk with the assist of a gyro-log translator. Much of the communication he couldn't make out. AIUs used a series of different coding methods and languages. All quite independent of humans. The gyro-log helped him unscramble some of the conversations. Much of which were boiler plate. Some of which was clever disguise on Mama's side. But one small sector of communication stood out in Mickelmast's mind. A sequence where Mama stumbled. Where she blanked. Where she reached down for a sense of herself and found nothing. She fell.

"There was a hole," Mickelmast thought. But a self-evolving processor should naturally patch over any erratic growth spots. There was no way that there should be a hole or anything like that in the great thinking thing. It worried Mickelmast and he filed it away as something about which he needed to ask her majesty—at a later date.

Suddenly the AIU's voice boomed through the entire ship, "Done kids. Muscles marinara and linguini for everyone."

Now Mickelmast had a sense of humor, no one would deny that. But he didn't find Mama's behavior funny. He found it erratic, missing something. Something important.

On the drop ship to Caliendo, Mickelmast supplied encapsulated micro-bots for each of the Genetic Carriers to swallow. The micro-bots temporarily altered DNA readings, so that they could pass the scans at immigration that would be awaiting them. Caliendo was a UDP planet, so its scan data would go directly back to New Omaha Beach.

Sun Tu took the helm of the drop ship and guided them out the great bay doors. Her mastery of the ship's free fall was a delight. Kelt was duly impressed. Cas-Alta looked on with new admiration.

As Sun Tu approached the portal to the planet's protective ether dome, Mickelmast supplied the entry codes that Mama had given him.

The process was like entering a bubble. All drop ships were designed to permit limited tearing on entry and to facilitate clean sealing of the ether dome behind them. Hence the shape—needle nosed, slender tapered body, and rounded end.

The ether momentarily put the crew to sleep as they entered on auto-nav. Well before that point the Central Caliendo Landing Authority took control of the ship. The crew would be revived when the authorities were satisfied with their findings.

And so it was that Caliendrite officers boarded the drop ship and without resistance searched first the ship and then the five persons onboard. The latter was done with scanners and DNA readers. The search party noted the unusual constituency of the drop ship. An Asian, an almost bald girl, a heavy worlder with an odd look about him, a heavy Southern Brit and what looked like an Independentiste.

Caliendo, like most UDP worlds, had been settled by a pure ethnic group. S3 saw to that. It was a master stroke on their part. S3 wanted no challenge to their power in the galaxy. The easiest way to ensure that was to keep the planets separate. Prevent any unions. By sending out "racially pure" settlements under the guise of "the maintenance of multicultural diversity in the galaxy" S3 created a galaxy disinclined to unite. Serb planets were placed in close proximity to Croat planets, Zulus to Afrikaners, Chinese to Japanese, Chechnyan to Russian, etc. S3 wasn't subtle, just effective.

The rare planet reached out to others but most, like Caliendo, celebrated their heritage and managed to grow, as S3 foresaw, backward. So that Caliendo was more Calabrese than the original Calabrese had ever been in Italy. The language was pure, the religion monolithic and the xenophobia intense.

So when the five Genetic Carriers were awakened from the ether, they found themselves staring into the beautiful veiled eyes of olive-skinned people who were intensely hostile.

When Mickelmast asked for the return of their passes, he was offered two and had to bribe the officials for the other three for which Mama had already paid.

They landed and quickly were confronted by the head Caliendrite mechanic.

He and his assistant were true to type—argumentative. They wanted to go back to the ship for a cursory inspection despite Mickelmast's insistence that they had all the AIU data that was necessary for repairs to proceed. Mickelmast reminded them that they had already paid for a dry dock. He demanded the great vessel be landed now. The Calabrese mechanics threw up their hands and threatened to walk away from the whole thing muttering something about being hungry. After a quick conference, Kelt and Sun Tu agreed to accompany the mechanics back to the ship.

Mickelmast, Cas-Alta and Raephealson took their passes and, using the Caliendo descender, dropped to the terminus on the surface.

As soon as they stepped out of the decompression unit, they were surrounded by Caliendrites of every size and shape. All seemed to be speaking too loudly. Shouting was probably more accurate. Their loud tumbling archaic Italian was a challenge even for state of the art auto-translators.

Mickelmast took the lead and cut a swath through the throngs until he found the terminus exit and stepped out into the brilliant Caliendo sunlight. Ether domes have a modest range of calibration and obviously this one was at its maximum. It was downright hot and the sun was brilliant. Large and brilliant. Everyone wore sun glasses, ersatz leather sandals, and swept back hair. And color. Lots and lots of color.

"Is it a holiday?" asked Cas-Alta.

"Nope just another day on ol' Caliendo I suspect," replied Mickelmast.

It was then that Raephealson stepped into the thoroughfare and a skimmer swerved, just barely missing him. In a second the driver was out of the vehicle and threatening Raephealson. He pointed to his skimmer, gesticulated with his hands, screamed as if he had been impaled on a sharp stick and generally attempted to terrify the heavy worlder. Because of Raephealson's size the Caliendrite driver was screaming directly into his chest. The Caliendrite ended his tirade by kicking dust onto Raephealson's pant cuffs over and over again, while he muttered "stupid cow fucker."

Mickelmast and Cas-Alta came to Raephealson's rescue just as the man hopped into his green and orange skimmer and, sticking his left hand out the window, his middle finger pointed straight toward the heavens, hit the gas.

Raephealson laughed. Then Mickelmast laughed and Cas-Alta joined in. Through her giggles she asked, "What did he call Raephealson?"

"Something about an intellectually challenged milk producer fornicator. I couldn't tell if Raephealson was the dumb one or the milk producer was. My translator isn't up to the demands of this place. But that," he said pointing to short building across the plaza, "is something that doesn't need language to get its meaning across."

Raephealson and Cas-Alta had never seen Mickelmast move so quickly. Of course, they had never before seen his response to a restaurant.

On the ship it did not take Sun Tu and Kelt long to understand that the "mechanics" were government workers whose interest was in the ship's log not its damaged hull. But there was no need to worry. These government men were no match for the cleverness of Mama who quickly had them believing that the ship was on a secret UDP mission and that any tampering would be met with a severe response from New Omaha Beach.

Quickly final arrangements were made to bring the huge ship into dry dock on the planet.

As Mickelmast ordered a second portion of the exquisite angelloti, Cas-Alta felt her stomach do a flip flop. Her pregnancy was moving quickly and at the moment food was not her favorite thing. As for Raephealson, he was staring across the plaza at the pattern of the buildings outside the south facing windows of the eatery. The large cathedral called out to Raephealson. Raephealson rose from the table, crossed the plaza, and headed toward the old building. "Raephealson," Cas-Alta called, then quickly followed.

Mickelmast snarfed down the remainder of his exquisitely cooked pasta, tossed back most of his glass of wonderfully crude red wine, then rose and tossed a unit on the table. The waiter hunched behind the small bar and stared at the foreigners. Mickelmast smiled at him and said in the intergalactic tongue, "inbreeding R us?" The man ignored him and moved toward the table with his tray under his arm. Mickelmast picked up the glass and finishing its contents put it on the taciturn man's tray with a thunk. Then, with the glorious smile of the truly well fed, he wheeled and followed his kindred.

The waiter watched the fat foreigner leave and then took a clean handkerchief from his pocket and carefully wrapped the wine glass.

S3 was occasionally interested in fingerprints.

Mama yelped when the stabilizing clamps clutched at her middle. It was her first time in dry dock.

As the external robotics began their trace of her hull, she tapped into their mini AIUs and double checked the calculations. She wasn't going to have inferior quality workmanship. And she didn't trust these robots to do the job properly. She preferred men to do the work. They were simple and straight forward. Slow and guileless. Yes, she liked men—especially to work on her hull. Rub rub rub.

In the cathedral candles flickered their simple timeless message across the musty-aired interior. Buildings had so crowded the structure that the few remaining shards of stain glass had little or no light to bring out their magic. The effect of the whole place was of a huge heaviness.

A few withered women sat in the front pews. They were encased in dark cloth from head to foot. They looked like bags of the devil's laundry awaiting pick up. Needless to say, they didn't lift the heaviness of the place.

The Catholic church had survived all these years by keeping its head down. It had not been a force since the first alien contacts over four hundred years ago. The church now moved in lock step with whoever was in power. It became simply another controlled function within a society of controlled functions.

Raephealson moved tentatively down the center aisle of the faux Gothic building. As he walked his arms slowly rose above his head and his fingers splayed as if somehow scenting the air.

At the back of the church Cas-Alta stopped Mickelmast, "Let Raephealson be. He can't get into any trouble here." Then she touched his arm. "Look there."

Behind them on the church's wide front steps stood a man in tattered clothing. He had a monkey at his side which had been trained to hop on one leg, while it held out a tin cup asking for money.

"Elijah said gifted people are marked."

"And what does that exactly mean, Cas-Alta?"

"In truth, I don't know, Mickelmast."

"Does wearing clothes like that make him marked?"

"Somehow I doubt it. But while we're here let's take look around anyway." They left the church and re-entered the strong sun light.

As they did, Raephealson stepped into one of the small side chapels of the cathedral in which a raised platform stood. He approached the dais and touched its cold marble surface. As he did, he thought, "Like the one my Grandad died on." Then he was awash in memory. He remembered a gnarled hand cradling his. A night that lasted a long, long time. A statement about having a gift that he still didn't understand.

Then his eye was drawn to a small door, half hidden behind the faded triptych altar piece. He moved carefully toward the portal. His body was big for this cramped sanctuary, and there were many things that he could break if he touched them.

The door had an iron ring in it rather than a knob. He pulled on it, and it opened quickly revealing a much-worn circular staircase going into the bowels of the ancient building. There were no lights.

He started down, feeling his way as he went. One full turn around and he was in pitchy black. He traveled a full circle further then hit his head on the bottom of the stair above. Blood flowed quickly from his forehead and dripped on his shirt. He ducked his head and continued down. His hand traced his progress on the central pillar as he went down and down, round and round. Then a breath of air came up at him from below.

A full turn more and he saw a slight glow ahead. He moved toward it and found himself in a tight corridor carved into the rock. There were glass cases on either side lit by low-voltage lamps.

Inside the cases small chunks of bone rested on squarish velvet-covered platforms, chips of wood were suspended by silver wire and pieces of ancient cloth were pressed between glass panes. In front of each stood a name plate. Raephealson put his hand up to the glass case and felt its warmth and smoothness. He had no idea what all this was.

Raephealson didn't even see the dwarfed monk until he had already bumped into him. The tiny hump-back man crumpled to the floor and, as was traditional on Caliendo when jostled, swore a streak of obscenities.

Naturally enough his swearing was in Italian—old Italian. When he had managed to fulfill his quotient of cussing, he stood up and puffing out his chest pointed to one of the bones in a case, "THE PINKY OF JOHN THE BAPTIST." Then in the intergalactic tongue he translated, "The baby finger of John the Baptist. It's my favorite piece in the reliquary. Which is yours?"

Raephealson stared back at the bone and wondered who John the Baptist was and why someone would want to keep his finger bone. But he said nothing. He was terrified of this little man.

The monk mistook Raephealson's terror for religious awe and smiled an appropriately priestly smile. "Do you like antiquities my ugly friend?"

Raephealson knew that he was being asked something, but he couldn't figure out what. So he just stared at the dwarf.

"You fucking tourists wouldn't know a treasure if it were shoved so far up your ass that it came out your ears. Besides you're a heavy worlder right?" He waited for a moment but Raephealson didn't move. "Up and down means yes, left to right means no. So, stupid?"

Getting no answer the monk spun on his heel and was about to leave the young heavy worlder when he saw the large man reach out and put his hand up to the glass case again.

Raephealson was looking at the finger bone of Giovanni Di Baptisia and remembering his Grandfather's hand. The single word, "Gift," came from his lips.

And the monk heard it.

The tiny man swore softly to himself then reached out and touched Raephealson. "Do you have the gift? Would you teach me how it works?"

Raephealson couldn't understand the words but nodded. The dwarf smiled, took the heavy worlder's hand and led him down a series of progressively more and more slanting stone corridors.

Raephealson was too frightened not to follow.

He followed the tiny man for miles beneath the Calabrese style city.

The repairs were done quickly. Kelt and Sun Tu watched the robotics work on their auto-ascenders. It was the first time either of them had been outside the great ship since their abductions and they found themselves stunned by the beauty of her spinning majesty.

They also found the inability of their translators to keep up with the language that was whizzing by them most distressing. "It's a form of deterioration."

"Of our translators?" demanded Kelt.

"No. Of the culture," replied Sun Tu. "Cultures need cross-fertilization to keep them vital. It's why EntrePren colonies are not ethnically pure." She didn't bother mentioning that was why her last name and her father's last name were not the same.

"Well neither are Independentiste settlements," replied Kelt.

"I'm not sure I like that we share even that," replied Sun Tu as she turned her eyes back to the great ship.

Inside, the AIU was spinning on her inner axis. Lifting and stretching like a kitten enjoying a scratch on her belly. "Is this what a massage and facial feels like," she purred. Then she stopped and a synapsal linkage akin to human fear went through her.

She shouldn't be able to spin on her inner axis because in theory she was a growing thing which by her nature had no center! Just a flat plain of self, stretching endlessly toward all horizons at once. But she was spinning! Around something! Around something that was missing!

Or taken! But by whom? And for what reason?

She was no longer stretching. She was no longer spinning. Now she was probing herself, trying to find what was wrong. And her eyes were drawn once again to those tall vertical planes in her horizontal vastness.

Deep in the ship's hold Elijah Jaspers gasped for breath. The past month of lessons had been harder than any thirty days he had ever spent. Living constantly with the fear of failure had taken a heavy toll on him. And then there was the uncontrolled dream of the restaurant and the dreamers whom he had betrayed. It was always there. Always waiting for him whenever he closed his eyes.

The air was jagged in his chest as he entered the Cryogenic chamber. He crossed over to the hanging figure of Tzu Ma Long and then wondered why he was there. What did he want from the pirate captain?

The tunnels beneath Caliendo eventually broadened and deepened. Finally Raephealson and the dwarf monk emerged into a wide high-domed space carved from the naked rock itself. A glinting luminescence came from the stone. Raephealson's eyes adjusted to the light.

The vaulted roof was hundreds of feet above him. In the exact center of the great chamber sat a glass building seemingly light as air. The dwarf stood before the glass structure with his hands out and a radiant smile on his face.

"It's Caliendo's only monument. It's said that many planets have them. It's also said that only those with a gift can use them."

Raephealson's tranlater finally updated but he chose not to respond.

"My people carved out this great space for the monument, moved it down here and then, centuries ago, forgot all about it. Strange, no?"

"Not at all," thought Raephealson as he remembered Jaspers talk about festivals becoming just festivals when there are no dreamers. For the second time in a day, Raephealson felt his arms raising up and his fingers splaying. This time, unlike in the church, he allowed himself to be moved by the impulse. In this case it moved him toward the glasshouse.

He was almost on top of the tiny monk before he realized it.

"No one knows what's suppose to..."

He didn't get out any more before the massive heavy worlder stepped through a broken panel and entered the glass structure.

Raephealson was inside before he realized it.

He stretched out his arms to their full extension. The glass monument allowed him exactly a foot of clearance on each side. He threw his head back so far that he heard his spine crack.

The dream came up on him so quickly that he was literally swept up by its force.

His Grandda's voice screamed in his ears—"You have the gift. You must use it."

But there was another voice even more violent inside his head—that of the Angry Faced Man from his dream. The man who hurt the naked boy. The man who was his death.

The dwarf monk stepped back in wonder as Raephealson bent his knees and leapt into the air—and began to float.

Then Raephealson began to scream. Terror ripped up his throat, into his mouth, and out into the glass loft of the monument. The scream bounded off the glass and split into a thousand parts. Each in turn divided into thousands more as they continued to bounce off each pane of glass. They pierced him and woke him mid-spin. He plummeted the eight feet to the ground and lay there quivering.

The dwarf turned in terror and raced back the way he had come.

Raephealson was still crying when Cas-Alta and Mickelmast found him.

"How did you know he was here, Mickelmast?"

"I put a marker bot on him before we left the ship."

"Mickelmast!"

"What did you want me to do?"

"He's not a baby."

"Isn't he," said Mickelmast pointing to the crying heavy worlder. "Give me a hand, we have to get him back to the ship. They'll charge us for overtime if we keep the ship there a moment longer than agreed upon. It's like when you get your skimmer towed."

There was no S3 office on Caliendo, but there were always accesses to the security agency. It was to one of these "accesses" that the waiter from the restaurant took the glass with Mickelmast's fingerprints.

He entered the dark bar. The swarthy self-important men there smoked and yelled at each other but ignored the waiter as he crossed through the saloon and entered a back room.

There a heavy set man with a scar on his left cheek pressed a button beneath the counter then walked out of the room. Once the scarred man had gone, the waiter put a 5,000,000 Lira note on the table and pushed through the secret panel in the middle of the south wall. He had been here before. Ratting to S3 was a reasonable supplement to his meager income.

He inserted his identity marker and offered up his hand for DNA verification. The machine before him, little more than a black box, whirred and indicated that he should insert the shunt so that they could hard-wire connect.

The waiter did as requested after throwing his hands up in the air and protesting to the Madonna for such treatment. No one prayed to the Madonna any longer, but they still complained to her—almost constantly. The shunt hurt and when he involuntarily yanked himself away from the insert it cut him.

The computer's voice barked deep into his head, "Stand still you fucking wop."

By the time the prints on the glass were scanned and its information passed on to New Omaha Beach, the great ship had breached the ether dome and begun its dance back into deep space.

By the time that Cyrus had been informed of the fingerprints from Caliendo, Elijah Jaspers had risked his life a second time by Dream Navigating the ship to a position so far from the Calabrese style planet that nothing could trace them.

Chapter 45

Cyrus Investigates

Data flowed into S3's central data collectors constantly. The amount of information was enormous but any information coming into S3 concerning the Genetic Carriers was given priority.

Once the prints from Mickelmast's glass were considered worthy of consideration, it didn't take long for the S3 tech's to cross-reference them with Mickelmast's DNA records. It set off a flurry of activity ending with a duty officer rehearsing his excuses as he approached Cyrus's chamber door.

"But sir, fingerprints are an ancient form and although at times useful, they are cumbersome and despite years of effort to cross-reference them with DNA patterns, a co-relation if it exists, has never been proven and think sir, how often do fingerprints come in?"

The excuse sounded lame to the young officer as he approached Cyrus' door with the two-day old information.

Cyrus received the information and listened patiently to the excuse then kissed the stunned young man full on the mouth. The duty officer had no idea what to do and did his best to resist the impulse to wipe his lips clean. Then Cyrus sent him away with the oddest phrase, "Like Alistair Sims on Christmas day."

Within the hour, a team was dispatched to Caliendo to recreate what had happened there. As Cyrus said to the team leader, "I want to know everything they did, everyone they talked to and every word that was said."

Cyrus wasn't surprised when he was informed that the ship had "vanished" from Caliendo's tracking screens shortly after it left orbit.

They would pop up again.

More importantly at this point, they will have left some sort of trail on Caliendo. In the dreamless worlds, trails were always left when dreamers passed through. And such trails were not difficult to follow for an S3 Investigator—especially a master investigator like Cyrus Maloney III.

Just as the Slave Master was contemplating how to remove the damn implant from his skull, it activated and ordered him to get his Yeoman Class Starship to Caliendo.

Six Terran days ago, under Cyrus' orders, the Slave Master had put the Mirren Captain into deep sleep and replaced the entire Mirren crew with a silent group of men who awaited him at the Santiago docking station. Everything about them said professional—S3 professional. They gave him the creeps.

He had been tempted to dump the First Mate and the First Centurion but after seeing the new recruits he thought better of it. "Better the morons you knew, etc., etc."

"Caliendo's a hike from here so we'll have to put most of the men into cold sleep. I assume you know the procedures?"

The leader of the S3 men, after tapping an implant connective to the ship's AIU, nodded to the affirmative. "I'll arrange it."

The Slave Master resisted the urge to pull on his forelock. "Command still sits funny in you Slave Master," barked Cyrus's voice through the implant.

"I guess it does," the Slave Master thought.

"Trust me, it does," Cyrus answered.

"So what is it that I am to find on Caliendo, sir? Them?"

"No, they're long gone. But they chose to stop there. I want to know why. There'll be a pattern that will give us a trail to follow. We just have to find it, don't we Slave Master?"

"If you say so, sir."

"I do, Slave Master, I do. Do you perchance have any insights as to why Caliendo was chosen as a destination for these young hellions?"

"It's Calabrese so the food'll be good. Because it's UDP there's no slave Forum so I've never been. Although I think there's a big trade in pirated Slave Show replays there." Cyrus laughed at the pun. "What's funny your Lordship?"

"Pirated Slave Shows... nothing Slave Master. To you nothing."

"As that may be. As I've already said everyone needs a show now and then even if just to break the monotony."

"Even if just to mark the changing of the seasons in a world whose seasons do not change," thought Cyrus. What he did say was, "No live Slave Shows, huh?"

"It's UDP, they're outlawed."

"Lots of things are outlawed Slave Master and yet they occur. Some say fun is outlawed yet everyone manages to have some, don't they? Do you Slave Master?"

"Need I answer that?"

"No, Slave Master, we all have our little secrets don't we?"

"I do, sir."

"And I do, too. To Caliendo with you. Cold sleep for some but not for you."

The Caliendrite waiter was amazed when the S3 officers descended on his restaurant for the third time. Now they had the scarred man in tow—he looked half dead. The questions were the same, but this time a particularly smelly man was watching the proceedings closely. For reasons that the waiter couldn't fathom the S3 officers were giving the ugly man pride of place.

Stinker, as the Waiter quickly took to thinking of him, had an unusual rhythm to his speech. He would ask a question and the waiter would answer it, then there was an unnatural pause from Stinker before he asked another question.

All the questioning was about the three people who had eaten in his restaurant a few days back. Over and over he was asked what they were doing? "They were eating. The fat one, whose prints I took, was swallowing things whole. I've told your people that three times now."

"What else?"

"Nothing else. They ate, they left."

The interviews with the Caliendrite ship mechanics yielded little more information. But the Cathedral proved a more valuable source. After waving their credentials around a bit, the S3 officers had been led to one of the old women who was in the church when Raephealson wandered into the side chapel. She wasn't anxious to say more than the fact that she was there. "So what of it?"

Then the Slave Master stepped forward. Her nose crinkled at his smell and her many years told her that this was not a man with whom one fooled. She quickly told the officers everything she knew.

S3 retraced Raephealson's steps and found the small door with the iron ring handle. They also found the blood sample on the overhead stairway which when analyzed confirmed their suspicion that Raephealson had gone this way. The reliquary yielded little. But then a churchman offered up the dwarf monk who had boasted that he had been in contact with someone with "the gift." As the churchman had said, "I didn't believe him, he's a southerner and a dwarf. They always talk big."

"Who? Dwarfs or Southerners?" laughed the Slave Master.

"Both," replied the churchman, totally oblivious to the joke. Jokes, too, suffered in a dreamless world.

Shortly the tiny monk found himself sitting in a windowless government office across the table from the Slave Master. The days of investigation had yielded very little, and the implant's temperament had gone from bad to worse. So the Slave Master decided that he was going to get results from this interrogation the old fashion way—with technacles.

He extracted a set from a bag and put them on the table. He supplied the activation code and the bio-products thrashed like snakes with their heads cut off. "Have you seen these my miniature friend?"

The dwarf swore a fecal line of obscenities in old Italian.

"In the common tongue!" demanded the Slave Master, finding himself enjoying the experience of power more than he thought he would.

So the dwarf swore at him in the common tongue.

"I'm impressed. A monk who swears like a whore. So have you felt the bite of my friends here?" He said indicating the thrashing bio-products.

He hadn't but had no desire to try new experiences this late in his life. So, the little man answered the questions and quickly the Slave Master found himself down the tunnel by the reliquary and following the tiny monk into the blackness.

The Slave Master was duly impressed with the cavern but less so with the monument. He was well traveled in the galaxy and had seen several such sites before. This one, being underground, made it somewhat unique, but long ago these places had ceased to be of interest. Ancient sites without any indication of their builders were hardly noteworthy now. It was a riddle that couldn't be solved and hence became of interest only to academics.

The implant was strangely silent during this entire process but as the Slave Master headed back through the tunnels the implant prompted him to ask, "And where were the other two while you were down here with the heavy worlder?"

"How in god's cocksucking hell would I know?" answered the tiny monk casually. The Slave Master was tempted to toss a set of technacles on the little guy just for fun but restrained himself.

Back in the church the implant prompted the Slave Master to question the remaining women. After hours of talk and more swearing from the old crows, it was finally established that two Genetic Carriers had been at the back of the church and had gone out onto the front steps.

The Slave Master and his party went there and were treated to a surprise. The same man and his monkey were on the steps. The Slave Master ordered the man and the animal inside, and they all sat together in one of the back pews of the Cathedral.

"They were very nice. Polite. Soft spoken."

"Ask him what they spoke about," demanded Cyrus through the implant.

"What did they speak about?"

"Caliendo. The hot weather. The fat one talked about the food. He liked the food. The girl liked my pet. She said she found him gifted."

The conversation went on. The implant prompted and the Slave Master asked and the heat became more intense as the sun rose to its zenith. Just as Cyrus was about to say that he had had enough of this nonsense the man in the tattered costume said, "Oh yes, I do remember something else. The girl said it, asked it I guess."

"What did she say? What did she ask?"

"If there were gifted people here. If I had seen gifted people like my monkey was gifted."

Chapter 46

Cyrus and the Gifted

In New Omaha Beach Cyrus had to reach out to catch himself from falling. "Gifted." They were looking for gifted people. The word "Gifted" brought him back to a memory of a naked boy slowly twirling upside down eight feet off the ground. The most gifted dreamer he had ever met—created.

"So they were looking for gifted people were they. Well there are few who stand out in our controlled worlds," he thought. When a "gifted" person (a freak of genetic mutation) does come forward, the word spreads quickly. However, in worlds where difference is feared and despised the "gifted" were often summarily terminated.

In his many, many years Cyrus Maloney III had met many "gifted" people. When it came to "gifted people" he was the galaxy's one and only expert. He remembered how it first began—there was the dead life-extensionist surgeon stuffed into the wall—her hair like a horse's tail running through his fingers—but at the time he didn't recognize her death as the beginning of his commerce with gifted people.

It was Susan Santiago's scientific breakthrough permitting the digitalizing of brain waves which first introduced him to "gifted" people.

Ms. Santiago's digital process made it theoretically possible to imprint dreams on software. Like all hard science, her work fell under S3's purview and Cyrus was assigned to ride herd on Ms. Santiago and her discovery. It was Cyrus' decision to promote Ms. Santiago's discovery that caused what history has incorrectly called: the twenty-second Century Dream Revival.

Dream Revival is a misnomer because the revival was not in the ability to dream but rather in the desire to partake of the products of dreaming. Few dared to venture into the chaos of dreams, but many wished to view the chaos from a safe distance—in the dark with a hand (his, hers or its) in your, or yours in their, pants.

When Cyrus leaked word of still further advances in Ms. Santiago's discovery to the press, the populace went mad. Despite the fact that there were no dreamers, there was a huge and clamorous demand for dreams.

It became like a gold rush. Find a dreamer, use Ms. Santiago's techniques to duplicate the dreams, and there was a fortune to be made.

But dreams were as rare in the late twenty second Century as spices had been in twelfth Century Europe.

Twenty-second Century Vasco da Gamas were sent out by their patrons to scour our worlds in search of dreamers. Venture capital was raised for expeditions to the nether reaches of our known worlds by a new force in the galaxy—the EntrePren Traders.

The famous text, Foreign Devils on the Dream Road, chronicles the voyages of an expedition into central Asia to find Tibetan dreamers and the massacre that ensued.

The huge, well-funded expedition to the polar regions of Mars, from which not a soul returned, still haunts the human psyche.

But not all expeditions met an evil end. True, many followed the ephemeral trail of rumor to nothing, but some followed the same kind of markers and found at the end of their labors... a dreamer.

Following old wives' tales of madmen and shamans, the expeditions probed the deepest corners of our known worlds and returned to New Omaha Beach with their catch.

And what a catch! Eyes wild, some completely silent, many twitching openly, they all stared in the light. The most expensive live stock in history—the few dreamers left in a dreamless galaxy suddenly gone mad for dreams.

The press called them Jumpers because they were able to make the nighttime leap to dreams. The pictures of their faces, downloaded on imagers throughout our worlds, were kept from children lest they caused fear of sleep. In truth, lest the children take it into their heads to follow the Jumpers' example and try to dream themselves.

But the dreamers gathered in New Omaha Beach were not the only necessary components of this business. Programmers still had to commit the dreams to disk. Few programmers were able to master the intricacies of Ms. Santiago's programming techniques. And fewer, who could, were willing to be in the presence of a real dreamer. So the world waited as the companies pushed and cajoled and threatened the programmers and dreamers together.

Cyrus and S3 did more than their share of pushing, cajoling, and threatening.

Two famous dream partnerships came out of this period: Wen Chiu and Paul Brelle and of course Da Breo and Uteshenko.

But the transfer of dreams to software proved much more complicated than the duplication of brain waves from a waking subject to disk. Many of the difficulties were not strictly technical, all were totally unforeseen. It was a constant battle to keep pace with newer and newer problems as they surfaced. The most significant problem was the appearance of an unusually deep rooted madness in some of the Jumpers as they made contact with their programmers. There were several instances when the madness was transferred whole to the programmer. At times a love/lust would envelop dreamer and programmer alike. A terrifying need would blister from the partners. The progeny of such sexual liaisons were frightening to behold. We now call them Antigens. At the time the people did not know what to call them—or do with them.

It is astounding how little we understood at the time! Even carved memory syndrome was unknown and of course auto-linkage hadn't even been named at this point in time.

Yet some of the earliest Jumpers (they called themselves Dream Explorers) were the most impressive. Not knowing the danger to themselves or caring about the danger to their programmers, the Jumpers threw themselves into the canyons of their sleeping minds with breath-taking abandon. No darkness was too dense, no light too blinding for these fearless souls. Night after night, Dreamer and Programmer were locked together in the most extraordinary of nocturnal dances. And it was Cyrus who had brought them together. Allowed these "gifted" people to be. For whole nights he watched and envied their gift. Watched but could not participate in the gift. Looked but could not touch. Saw but could not feel. Understood the glory in others but never experienced it himself. Two in the light, him, a third, in the dark.

The need for these nighttime interlockings ended abruptly in 2317 when S3 tech, Yazeen Saddiqui, developed the Automated Dream

Programmer (ADP). No longer was the human programmer needed for the Jumper to produce his or her product. Six months after the introduction of the ADP an entire profession, that of Dream Programmer, simply ceased to exist. With the ADP, Jumpers, who had been unable or unwilling to make connection with a programmer, could now produce their products in the solitary isolation of their rooms. And boy did they produce.

The Jumpers became the film stars of the early twenty-third Century. More than that because real danger existed for the Jumpers. There were no stunt doubles in the world of dreaming! The danger tantalized a breathless public who waited in the safety of their darkened rooms. Waited for the violent dreams of Wen Sha Tze or the erotic fantasies of Kar or the immensely popular dreams of loss by a dreamer who identified himself only as DCR.

The truly wealthy didn't bother waiting for the time-consuming process of commitment to software. They went directly to the source. They hired a Jumper and entered into direct dream link with them. Such hard-wirings were outlawed in 2327 after the unfortunate episode in Hong Kong that now goes under the code name of Sagittarius Eclipse.

Cyrus was the investigator assigned to that one too. He'd seen horrors in his time but never like this. The force-transferred dreams had erupted inside the wealthy couple. When he found them they had literally flown apart. The dreamer had lost his mind. He sat in the carnage and wept, his body alive with the blood of the wealthy couple. His sobs were so intense that they covered the sound of the concussive blasts from Cyrus's weapon which relieved the "gifted" one of his worldly existence.

Cyrus had fired before he thought about what he was doing. He had fired well after the dreamer's sobs had ceased. He had fired until it was all gone. Over. Wiped out. He had fired without reason. He had fired out of a deep fear. A fear that was a clue—another clue that he had missed.

Then the Dream Studios, backed by EntrePren money, stepped in. They contracted the dreamers and offered public displays. Huge indoor stadiums were filled to capacity while the Jumpers, hot wired for virtual reality feed on giant screens, slept the envied sleep before all who came to watch. And came they did in all conceivable usages of that term.

In one ghastly exhibition, a Jumper was left in darkened destitution locked in a world of sleep for over a year, autocarving the digital grooves of the ADP software at his side. People bought full year tickets enabling them to drop in any time they wanted. A shot of adrenaline after work, a spice up for your flagging love affair with the boss, a thousand variants on any theme you could think of. It got to the point where people totally ignored the dreamer. The Studios ordered the gradually emaciating figure of the dreamer covered, keeping it away from the audience's view lest they be repulsed. After all it was the dreams and not the Dreamer that people paid to see. Eventually things got to the point where routinely Dreamers were kept asleep for years at a stretch, prisoners of their own gift.

Under the Studios the dream software stopped carrying the name of the Jumpers altogether. You bought your software by Studio not Dreamer. The biggest of the Studios, Universal Dream Studio, began to investigate the idea of building dreamers genetically from birth—an idea suggested to them by Cyrus.

Before long dream products played an active role in every aspect of domestic rituals. Governments would not begin sitting until the dream prayer was enacted. There were few sexual liaisons that were not dream assisted. Whole societies were addicted to the dream products. In the history of the galaxy, there never was a business, legal or illegal, to equal the scope and reach of the Dream Studios.

Then the most famous auto-link of all time took place. The auto-link, which for a fraction of a second joined all dreamers, said only three words: DREAM NO MORE.

And they didn't.

And within five years the voracious appetite of the buying public had eaten up the stored libraries of the studios and the most lucrative business of all time... simply stopped.

S3 took note and sent out their own simple three word message to all of their operatives: FIND OUT WHY.

The signatory of this precise little epistle was C/M/!!!. By this time he was no longer a lowly investigator. He was Head of Operations for S3, New Omaha Beach Division and his knowledge of dreaming and dreamers was his power base. He became what he was because of his knowledge of the "gifted."

Cyrus steadied himself in his office. "History," he thought. But it wasn't just history—it was his life.

"So they are looking for gifted ones are they? Will there ever again be as gifted a one as the boy Elijah Jaspers who was mine all those years ago?" An image of the inverted spinning boy in the glasshouse materialized before his eyes. He watched it, entranced as a child at its first flat-face.

Then he tapped his comm and summoned Miro. "So they are looking for gifted ones are they?" He said aloud as the Lavolin girl entered his room.

He smiled at her and spat out, "The chase is on again. To horse to horse—find a dreamer—find a gifted one and he'll lead me through the Gateway." He closed his mouth and thought, "To Olya—to Olya who must be there."

Less than a mile from where Cyrus contemplated the glory and the power, Danazir Yi Qal had completed her voyage through Jed's implant. And she was ready. Ready to play her part in the great galactic drama.

Chapter 47

After the Flight

Paul Sun lay very still with his eyes shut. Before he opened his eyes, he prompted his AIU implant and was surprised that there was no response. At first he thought that he had gotten the thought pattern wrong so he tried it again. And then again. Finally he understood.

His implant was gone.

Without moving he tried to sense his present whereabouts. Then he heard Chi Ho's silky voice. "We removed all three of your internal comms and your AIU implant. I apologize for this intrusion on your person, but I had to assure your cooperation. You may open your eyes I know that you have regained consciousness."

Paul opened his eyes and stared at the man he had, for all those years, so terribly underestimated. The Central EntrePren AIU had been in the Specule's control all along. The neutral third in the great game was himself not Chi Ho. Paul knew that Chi Ho must have already invaded the great Didact strong holds throughout the Empire. From boardrooms, to service depots to command decks there must have been slaughter on a massive scale for Chi Ho to feel confident enough to take on the Leader of the Didact faction. But take him on he had. And clearly defeated him.

Chi Ho brought a small onyx cup of jasmine tea to Paul. As he held it out Paul said calmly, "More drugs?"

Chi Ho smiled back. "No need. The drugs you ingested will stay with you. They are stored in the fatty tissue of your liver and cannot be removed without seriously damaging the functioning of the organ itself. Should you seek to have the liver removed, the drugs have been programmed to enter your lymph system and spread themselves throughout your body. Your world has changed Paul. It is time for you to accept that."

Paul went to protest but the pain in his chest left him breathless. Chi Ho saw the grimace and smiled. "We almost lost you, but the laboratory surgeon is a talented lady. You will experience pain for a while but she assures me that your life is no longer at risk." Then almost off handedly Chi Ho added, "What did you see that caused your heart to fail?"

Paul held his breath for a moment. So they hadn't seen her. The rest they probably saw but not the vision of his wife. "There are still cards to play in this hand," he thought. "I'm tired, I can't think straight," was all he said.

Chi Ho smiled. He knew that he was being lied to but he let it pass. The Specules now, for the first time, were sole rulers of the entire EntrePren Empire so he could afford the pretense of accepting lies from the vanquished.

Paul closed his eyes and then he remembered.

Remembered his natal link with Sun Tu. The tiny processor, implanted between the second and third toes of his left foot, had lain dormant for these twenty odd years. It was now deeply coated in organic matter. Because of that it might have escaped their scans. They had found and removed his other implants but might well have missed the unused link to his daughter.

But there was no way to be certain except by activating it. He recalled the three word code and marveled at it. His wife had insisted that he use those words. The three words that would activate the link to his daughter were: Dream No More.

He incanted the words and felt the slightest tingling between his toes. Then he heard, deep in his head, the single word, "Father?"

She was alive! It was indeed a new world. In one day he'd fallen from power and been in contact with every member of his family—a disappeared wife, a dead son, and a kidnapped daughter. And of course he had also flown in his mind. He knew it was not dreaming. But he didn't know if they knew that. Sun Tu's voice once more echoed in his mind, "Father! Where are you?"

"No the issue is where are you," he thought. Here was the path to follow. It made him calm. It gave him hope as he drifted off into a dreamless sleep.

But activating the link to Sun Tu left a trail. A traceable trail. A trail that betrayed the whereabouts of the Genetic Carriers to S3—to Cyrus Maloney the Third.

Cyrus was wide awake despite the late hour when his adjutant informed him of Paul's link to Sun Tu. The sector of the galaxy indicated by the S3 tracking station was unknown to Cyrus so he consults his chartings.

When he located the exact location of the pirate ship he let out a low breath, a sigh of wonder. So far. So fast—Dream Navigators!

He prepared a contact with the Slave Master. It was time to lure the gifted ones with a gifted one.

He ordered his AIU to send Miro to him.

Chapter 48

The Gifted in Harm's Way

Cyrus activated the Slave Master's implant. "You awake dear, Slave Master?"

"Yes... yes, sir." The Slave Master's woozy answer came over the vast space dividing the two men.

Must have wakened the poor thing. Poor poopsy.

"Lavolin meet. Same coordinates. Same drug inductions." Cyrus snapped off the connection and murmured something that he hadn't said in hundreds of years. "Be there or be square."

Cyrus looked at the fading light of New Omaha Beach. For a moment he considered going back on his plans. Of "sparing the innocent." Then he laughed. It was far too late for that kind of sentimentality.

He sat in the leather covered wingback chair then called for his assist.

Miro entered the room with her syringe already loaded. As her figure broke the pattern of light coming through the polymer panes, Cyrus watched her every move. He had bled Jedidiah Witt's brain and implants of every bit of knowledge they had stored, but there was no reference to the girl who now stood patiently in front of him.

But that was all academic now.

He rolled up his sleeve. She approached. As she cleansed his arm, he allowed his fingers to entwine in her hair. Allowed the strands to slide through his fingers like a living thing—like the combed hair of a horse's tail.

"Are you ready, sir?" Her voice was sweet.

"Close the visages. Darken the chamber." She rose and did. The grace of her movement even in the now-darkened room filled him with an old wonder. When he went to speak again, he found his voice was back in his throat, coarse, thick. "Take off your clothes."

And she did.

And she injected him as the softness of her skin caressed the ancientness of his. And he floated. The mist surrounding him—surrounded them.

Miro felt him yank the mist to himself. Instantly she sensed herself falling in the Lavolin. Tumbling through the corridors of the empty vast. Then a hard turn followed by an extraordinary lift and float. She was tossed like a bit of tissue paper in an updraught. She was hauled then thrown then dragged. Until all orientation was gone. All sense of control vanished. All her treasured sense of mastery in the mist was shattered.

Cyrus held total dominion over the mist. It suddenly struck her that he had hidden his skill from her. But why? He didn't know that she was the neutral third so… but her thoughts wouldn't complete.

An image in the torrent arose. The distant image of her dreams. A figure in a small case on a belt. A bringer of tears in the night. Then a gentle face. A female. Crying over her. And she tried to tell the face not to cry. That she was too beautiful to cry. That she was… she was…

The screech of a pneumatic brake brought her thudding to ground.

She was in the whore's tunnel again. But it was all wrong. Upside down. No! She was upside down. Bleeding from the head. A skimmer raced passed her. Then a second and a third.

It slowly dawned on here that she had been hit by one of the vehicles. She sat up and the world began to tilt. She tried desperately to wrap the mist around herself but she was too slow. Cyrus was there in front of her. And the stinky man.

"Technacle her. It's time to put this gifted one in harm's way."

The Slave Master activated the bio-product on his belt and latched it to her left wrist. It immediately imbedded itself in her skin and sought out the wrist bones. She would have screamed but her mind was far away—speeding. "He knew. Cyrus had known all along. Always known that I was there. But why had he permitted it? And why act on this knowledge now?"

She stared at the Ancient. Then a thought seized her. "He won't be able to move in the mist without me as the neutral third. He's immobilized himself." A moment of joy entered her. A feeling of power over this most powerful of men. Then she looked more closely at him.

He was smiling a thin smile. "I shall miss you sweet thing. You will always hold a special place in my heart." Then he wrapped the mist around himself and was gone.

"Was gone!! But how??? I am the neutral third. He can't move without me!!" Then it struck her so hard that she almost fell to the slick pavement. The truth bolted through her causing every cell in her body to scream, "I am not the neutral third. I never was! He knew all along. He had set a trap for me. He had set a trap for all of us."

Even as this thought flashed through her mind her body returned to the world of feeling. To the pain of the technacles and the hungry stare of the Slave Master. She shrugged off the pain of the bio-product and made herself stand very still. The Slave Master's eyes never left her body. She reminded herself that she had endured these kinds of attentions before. It was just a different man's stare. A different man in a ghastly place. But still just a man staring.

She closed her eyes and tried to recall the vision in the whirlwind. The beautiful lady leaning over her—tears dropping like rain on a parched field. Like doves descending—falling.

Chapter 49

How to Find Them?

Before Sun Tu spoke she reviewed the strange contact she had with her father just a few hours earlier. Had this been some sort of strange waking dream? A dream of her father? But it didn't feel like any of the rudimentary dreaming that she had been taught.

For a moment she thought of consulting the others but something told her to keep this to herself until she understood it better.

She'd body scanned herself and had initially found nothing but on further probing had discovered a tiny bio-product embedded deep in the ducts of her liver. Its design was new to her and its purpose a mystery. A disconcerting mystery. Had it been the source of the contact with her father? Had she in fact been in contact with her father or was it all just some sort of hob goblin stuff brought on by all this dreaming Specule crap?

"It's no good. We've looked and looked for these 'gifted' people and exposed ourselves to potentially dangerous situations. We have no other choice," complained Mickelmast. Sun Tu was shocked out of her reverie. She had totally forgotten that she had called this meeting.

"There's got to be a better way to go about this. There has to be," she said.

She looked to Elijah. His hands fluttered up but he had no answers. No words. His time of passing was approaching. Even she could feel it.

Jaspers was almost incapable of dreaming any longer, and he was at a loss as to how to help his progeny. He knew nothing of the kind of searching that they needed to do. His world had always been that of dreams. And exploration. And it was almost all gone now. After all these years it was almost all, all over.

"Tell Mama what we know. Get her to help us, Mickelmast," said Sun Tu.

The Genetic Carriers discussed the parameters. How to define the term "gifted" to an AIU. Sun Tu spoke of free falling; Kelt of bravery; Cas-Alta of in-depth concentration; Mickelmast of creativity within a series of givens. Then they turned to Raephealson.

"Raephealson, you know most of all," said Cas-Alta. "Help us now. Tell Mama what you know so she can help us search."

And Raephealson wanted to help. Wanted to speak of dreams and doors with oiled hinges that can only be opened with courage but all he could do was gurgle deep in his throat. Mickelmast tried a new tack. "Will you let me hard-wire you to Mama? Let her search your mind for what she needs. Raephealson. Just give us a nod, huh?"

"Will it hurt him, Mickelmast?" asked Cas-Alta.

"I don't think so but I can't be sure. I'm not like him, Cas."

Cas-Alta turned to Raephealson and put a hand on his heart. "We don't mean to hurt you Raephealson. Honestly we don't. Just nod to tell us it's okay."

Raephealson looked at the girl who had saved his life. Whose hands had entered his chest and caressed his heart. He tilted his head forward.

Cas-Alta looked to the others. "Okay."

Kelt moved to Raephealson and took a firm hold of his head and neck. Mickelmast moved quickly and inserted the shunt slit into the base of the heavy worlder's neck.

Then he inserted his own shunt into the slit.

And Mama entered Raephealson's mind. She tapped and tampered and gleaned and garnered and was appalled and thrilled with what she found there. Raephealson did nothing. He just ached. In his heart he ached.

Finally Mickelmast removed the shunt from Raephealson's neck and reactivated his own.

Mama was giggling.

"What's so funny?"

"He has a very interesting mind, dear Hippo. Very unique."

"Did he provide you with further parameters for our search?"

"Oh, yes, dear Hippo. He did." She laughed again.

"Why are you laughing Mama?"

"It's quite a search you've asked for. So how complete would you like the list of matches?"

Mickelmast bot-tapped into the general system so that the others could hear the conversation.

"Top ten."

"Listed alphabetically?"

"Other options?"

"Most complete matches, closest matches geographically, closest matches sorted ethnically, matches with most chance of your being able to access them, matches easiest to locate—about 130 other ways of making a list. Want me to elaborate?"

"No thanks. Why not interlace the five list factors you named and come up with a list of ten possibilities for gifted individuals?"

"Well number one on the list is easy."

"So?"

"You won't like it."

"I have a greater catholicity of taste then you might expect."

"You're more verbose, that's for sure."

"Do tell, Mama."

"Fine. Number one on the list?"

"Please."

"Herr Short Stuff."

"Who?"

"Herr Short Stuff."

"Who's Herr Short Stuff?"

"How quickly they are forgotten!"

"Mama!"

"You're the Hippo—he's Herr Short Stuff," she prompted.

Mickelmast stood with his hand on the shunt for a long time, then he began to laugh and laugh and laugh. "You're somethin' Ma. What a kidder. What a kidder."

The AIU grew cold. "Fine. Be that way."

"How about second choice, Mama?"

"For an accessible, gifted individual?"

"I believe that is the object of our search."

"Fine. The second is a twenty-six-year-old female name Miro about to be auctioned at the Slave Forum on Marscovy. And it just happens to be, galactically speaking, nearby. So there!"

Mickelmast looked to the others and they approved. He told the AIU to set a course for Marscovy.

"I'm coming." It was Jaspers speaking. Cas-Alta blanched but no one dared deny the old man.

"All agreed, kids?" asked the AIU.

"Set your course Mama," responded Mickelmast.

"It will take just over twenty-eight Terran hours. That would put us on Marscovy three hours before the gifted girl is to make her entrance in the Slave Show."

"Fine."

"We could get there quicker, if you so desired," purred Mama.

"How's that?"

"If the old guy does that folding thing again."

The Genetic Carriers looked to Jaspers. The old man was so frail that a gust of air would knock him over. It was Kelt who stepped forward. "That won't be necessary."

"Too bad. That's some neat trick. Something brand new—even for me," oozed the AIU.

"Just plot a regular course, Mama," said Mickelmast.

"Be that way," she said petulantly. Then she laughed. "I suggest you all get your rest because tomorrow's a big day."

She was laughing, but Raephealson knew that there was more truth than humor to the comment. The others weren't sure, but sensed the truth of the great thinking thing's statement.

Chapter 50

Lady in a Pouch, Demon in a Womb

Cas-Alta sat on her sleeping palate. The slight hiss of the air exchanger was the only sound disturbing the artificial quiet of her chamber.

The others were asleep. Some were attempting to dream.

Cas-Alta had done the exercises Elijah had taught her but could not find the quiet inside herself necessary for the leap to dreaming. So she did the next best thing. Or at least what she believed was the next best thing.

She reached into the clothing chest and withdrew the pouch that she had first seen swaying on Tzu Ma Long's belt the day that he had entered her garden. The day her mother had died. Been murdered. The day that she had been raped and a life had begun inside her.

She held up the pouch and allowed her breath to shallow. Her concentration intensified. The Russian colors became vibrant—the ancient stitching's intricate pattern became clear—then the aura of something living inside the leaden casing revealed itself to her.

A swirling. A cry from far away. And pain so pure that it took Cas-Alta's breath from her. Then the growing thing inside her womb turned in rhythm to the thing in the pouch.

Cas-Alta's fingers flew from the thing as if it were a coiled snake. The leaden satchel landed on the floor but didn't bounce. Its density simply sat there, waiting. Cas-Alta moved away from the pouch. She didn't realize it, but she was screaming just as any mother would in an effort to protect her child from a thing that wanted to come in the night and take it to the fairy land.

It was only Kelt's banging at her door that brought her back to her senses.

"Cas! What's happening in there! Tell me the code and I'll open the door or I'll break it down!"

"Don't—I'm alright."

"Open the door, Cas!"

She offered the DNA coder her palm and the door opened. Kelt leapt into the room ready to fight but found only Cas-Alta on the floor. "Are you okay?"

"So I've said."

"What are you doing on the floor?"

"Elijah's exercises."

"They include screaming?"

"No. I was... never mind, I'm fine Kelt. Thank you. But I really don't need anything—honestly."

Kelt looked at her closely and then with a sigh left the room. The pouch had been in the center of the room the whole time but hadn't attracted the young warrior's attention. Cas-Alta supplied the codes to lock her door and then turned back to the living thing in the pouch.

She lifted it carefully.

It was heavier than she had remembered and the life within was moving fast.

She flicked the latch.

The mist instantly enveloped her. Entered her, every orifice and crevice.

Cas-Alta's head snapped back and her mouth opened. The mist came out of her in one long breath then turned toward her.

The Face Dancer was surprised. Who was this woman carrying this strange child? Why did some of her genetic codes match those of the one called Kelt? What did she want?

Cas-Alta watched in wonder. What was this thing that could enter her and exit her and still was nothing more than a mist. No, wrong. This thing was much more than mist! But what kind of thing was this?

The Face Dancer waited. She knew it was risky to speak first. Let the girl begin, then she could figure out how to respond.

Cas-Alta sensed herself threatened and her hand immediately went to her belly.

The Face Dancer saw the movement and marveled that anyone should wish to keep such a demon child safe. Such a child was a danger to everyone, to everything. To all the plans—all the years and years of planning.

The Dancer wondered if the girl realized that her child carried none of her extraordinary genes but was in fact an exact opposite of extraordinary—mundane, brutal, vengeful, and awaiting its birth to wreck the great plan.

Cas-Alta felt the baby kick. Hard. As if it meant to hurt her. "It must be terrified," she thought. She rubbed her belly to calm the living thing in there as she watched the living thing in the air swirl about—impatiently.

Chapter 51

Preparing the Gifted

In the prep room beneath the Marscovy Forum Miro watched the technacle on her left wrist. It seemed to shrug in its sleep. The bio-product had wrapped around her wrist bones and thrown tributary roots around the dozens of small bones in her hands.

A single tear fell from her cheek and splashed onto her hand. The tear disturbed the technacle. It flopped a bit.

Miro cried a lot now.

Through the ceiling she heard the muffled bleats of a sound system coming to life. She could imagine the rest of the proceedings—light check, sound check, tote board check, food check—and of course, drug check. An ancient sampled drum roll thundered to a climax then stopped.

Right on cue the door to her cell opened and the Slave Master entered. The room filled with a funky stink. The Slave Master had pomaded his hair. Now there was the sick sweetness of hair tonic over the reek of his body.

"Wel'me'ol'beauty, 'tis drug time in the ol' town, if'n you catch my meaning."

Unlike so many of the Slave Master's "clients," Miro easily caught his meaning. She knew a great deal about drugs—and even more about men. The glint in the Slave Master's eye was not unknown to her. When that glinting eye moved down from her face to her neck she rolled her shoulders, as if to relieve the tension there. Doing so, she extended the line of her neck and lifted her breasts.

The Slave Master thought of his implant and knew he was on the proverbial horns of a dilemma. "My horn, her dilemma," he chortled softly.

Miro got to her feet. Her being seemed to fill the entire room. He smiled.

Then his implant piped up. “She’s out of your class. As beyond your touch as I am beyond your control. Unless, that is, you don’t care about your EntrePren accounts.”

The Slave Master cared about his EntrePren accounts but even in very long lives opportunity seldom knocked twice.

Miro watched the Slave Master closely. “He’s talking to himself but is frightened by what he hears,” she thought. “But why?”

He held out a syringe and told her to extend her arm. She figured it out. “He has an implant commanding him. Of course he does, I was in the mist when Cyrus implanted it.”

By the time he began the penthal induction drug preparations, she had a plan.

She mouthed the words, “Get me something to write on” and gave him a look most men and many women could only dream of seeing once in their lives.

Then she gave him the look again. His knees weakened.

His ardor did not.

Chapter 52

Chessmen of Marscovy

Marscovy was a sprawling pure Russian enclave on a smallish planet deep in the Filton Nebula. It was one of the earliest powers in the Rebel Colonies coming into existence almost immediately upon the landing of the original forced colonists after the Great Collapse. Like so many early colonists, upon emerging from cold sleep, the Marscovy colonists unfurled the dreaded banner of the Rebel Colonies. The forced colonizations had inadvertently spread the gospel of the hated Rebel Colony heresy far and wide.

Despite early UDP efforts to squash the Rebel Colonies, planets like Marscovy prospered. Isolation forced them to look to themselves and their racial purity gave them a common heritage from which to draw.

Marscovy eventually infiltrated sections of the Kiltrin trade and ended up making the majority of its gross national product by supplying protection to EntrePren traders in the neighboring parsecs. A natural willingness to follow strongmen led to an orderliness in the planet which in itself increased the basic wealth. As elsewhere in the Rebel Colonies, slaves were highly valued as a sign of personal power and prestige.

The Marscovy Forum had its similarities to the Mirren Forum. In fact all the slave forums held certain constants. All were based on what used to be called games—simplified versions of their complex originals.

The Marscovy Forum sat over forty thousand people under its faux onion dome. Only the front twenty rows were close enough to see the slaves without the use of the massive overhead Holos. Of course these seats were appropriately priced.

The Marscovy playing space was marked off into an eight cube by eight cube board. The cubes alternated between black and white. Each cube was ten meters by ten meters by ten meters. The game began with two teams—one white, one black—set on opposite sides of the board.

The front row of each team consisted of eight lightly armed robotics. The second row consisted of three pairs of more heavily armed robotics and a master female robotic, the "czarina," beside a "czar" whose capture was the supposed object of the game.

The robotic pieces could be replaced by human slaves at the behest of the Slave Masters. Often the game had as many as twenty slaves participating.

But not in today's featured event.

Miro would be the only slave on the board in the final game of the evening. She would compete against thirty-one highly programmed batch-file robotic pieces.

The Slave Master had given a lot of thought as to which of the pieces Miro should replace. He settled on the White cleric. Not a serf. But not a czarina. Limited armament but not powerless. Then to assure the required result the Slave Master had the two White Castles dismantled, the leg of one of the White Knight's horse's broken, and the White Czarina made hopelessly insane. As for the White Czar—he had a thing for Miro.

The piece's movements in the game were not as complex as their historic antecedents. After all this was a public entertainment and instant payer access to the thrill of the game was a must. No practice. No study. Just entertainment in exchange for money—the basic trading strategy of the galaxy. The strategy that had been going on almost without stop since the turn of the millennium.

Each of the board's interior cubes had a door in all of their four walls through which the robotic or slave warrior could enter or exit. The side cubes, except the four corners, had doors in three walls. The corners, naturally enough, had doors only in two sides.

The cubes, or "chambers" as they were called, were each different locales, places. All included surprises, be they good or bad. Hidden weapons, items which could increase or diminish strength, etc. Some of the "chambers" in the center of the board also had surprise entrances from both ceiling and floor. All these hidden items were readily apparent to the audience if they purchased the right drug induction but were, of course, hidden from the slaves. As for the robotics—well that was up to the programmer. It depended on the level of difficulty at which they wanted the game played.

Unlike the original game where only one piece moved on each turn, in this game all pieces from both sides moved at once. Action, not strategy was the attraction of a Slave Show.

Marscovy Slave Shows had a huge following. However huge became massive when a "star" like Miro was up for auction.

The ad campaign for Miro had been a classic of smash and burn. Overnight, pictures of the young woman invaded every data comm within the Marscovy solar system. Scattercast bursts engendered further interest in planets farther afield. And, as Cyrus had hoped, caught the attention of the AIU on the Warrior Class Starship.

A slave day on Marscovy was a civic holiday. The Marscovy Rotary Commerce made the most of such days. Landing rights tripled in cost, transit permits were more valued than good vodka and admission tickets to the Forum could only be bought by those who had previously chipped out an extravagant sum to "license" a seat.

As well, the ether dome was reprogrammed to allow in more light and heat than usual. The light increased the sale of UV protective eyewear and the heat promoted the sale of liquid refreshment, both of which were, naturally enough, under the monopoly of the Marscovy Rotary Commerce.

Parsecs away Cyrus, after prompting the Slave Master to "leave the girl alone," entered cold sleep to allow for greater speed from his fleet. And a massive fleet it was. As great as any that S3 had put together for its major sorties in the Great War. But this was not a great war. It was a great adventure. The great adventure, which is exactly what Cyrus told himself as he removed his clothing and entered the cryogenic chamber.

But, his excitement for the adventure had clouded his judgment. He had neglected to take into account that he would lose control over the Slave Master during his period of cold sleep.

Miro sensed the Slave Master finish his sexual exertions. His moments of distraction had given Miro the opportunity to sample the drug in the Slave Master's syringe and quickly manage computations on its potency. It was not nearly as strong as Lavolin. More importantly, unlike the parent drug, Lavolin, which was designed for privacy, the slave drug was designed for others to interlope—many others. Shredded folds of the drug formed tunnels which branched off the drug's main shoot. Into each of these tunnels could enter the presence of customers who had paid for the thrill of being up close and personal.

She examined the drug closely and came to the conclusion that she could control it. She could fold it about herself to find any privacy that she might need. She turned her concern to the weaponry with which she would be provided. She assumed the batch-filed robotics were deadly opponents and that the programmer would set them at their highest level of efficiency.

She looked at the Slave Master as he did up his trousers. He didn't look deadly but she reminded herself not to underestimate him.

The Slave Master didn't seem to realize that Miro had hardly participated in the "goings on." Nor did he care. He was more interested with his implant's reaction that was strangely muted. Not muted—nonexistent.

He hoped against hope that the damned thing had failed.

Then he heard the opening rumbles of the Forum coming to life above him. He smiled at the girl.

She smiled back and extended her arm.

He injected her smoothly.

She felt the drug enter her system and quickly set up barricades to it. There was a false euphor in it that was supposed to supply a sense of pleasure for the taker. She sectioned it off from her heart and brain and allowed her kidneys to deal with it. The rest of the drug coiled within her and cast a netted mist. She caught it and wrapped it around herself. It complained, but only briefly. Then Miro turned it upon itself. It lost its sense of composition and confusion reigned.

The Slave Master's drug counter did no more than register the taken dosage so it concluded that the drug invasion was successful. It assured the Slave Master that enough of the drug was in Miro's blood stream to achieve the desired effect.

The Slave Master stood back from Miro and looked at her closely. Before he could examine her too closely she smiled at him.

"Do you know how the game is played, little one?"

She nodded her head.

"Get their Czar and you win."

He waited for her to ask what would happen if she won, but she didn't ask.

"Well. Good. No questions are good questions." He smiled and applied the codes that removed the technacles from her wrists. He was surprised that she didn't even wince.

She waited. There was nothing more that she could do with the drug until she understood her own armament. Surely she was to be given some sort of armament!

"Perhaps you'd like to know your weaponry in the game?"

She nodded her head. Smile. Keep him off balance.

He gave her a miter and a squarish cap. She put on the cap and examined the miter. Its heft was impressive, but there was not one sharpened or pointed surface on the entire thing.

She let it fall to the floor.

He picked it up and gave it back to her. "Don't you like my choice for you?"

"It's too heavy for me." See what a frown will get you.

"Is it? I'd never have guessed," he laughed thinly. "It's all that I'm offering. Take it, is my advice."

She declined and curled her fingers around the syringe that she had picked from his pocket, while he was "otherwise engaged." The syringe still had a quantity of the drug in it because she was smaller, more petit than he had envisioned. And the needle itself was quite lethal—more a lady's weapon than a miter any day.

Mickelmast and the other Genetic Carriers made their way down the wide, though crowded, thoroughfares of central Marscovy. The Marscovy River, a stale flat thing, drew a murky trail through the center of the massive crumbling city.

The walkway along the river's embankment was put together with pseudo-stone, but the masonry was shoddy and many of the pieces had fallen into the river and now simply lay there. Throughout the city there was an air of decay, a sense of mold. The gently sweet smell of mildew rot was present even in the dense material that Muscovites favored for their outerwear. The whole metropolis was coated in a heavy odor.

There were many, many people in the city on this day. The great and fabulous Slave Show had attracted maggots of every conceivable size and shape to the historic city.

It was fortunate for the Genetic Carriers. Without the huge crowd, they could never have passed scrutiny—a demented heavy worlder, a beautiful Asian, an old man near his passing, a handsome warrior, a near bald girl, and a fat youth—are just not seen together in this galaxy.

But this was a festival day. Fortune's face smiled on them.

At least for a while.

Even as the Genetic Carriers made their way to the Forum, the lead Starship of the S3 fleet prepared to leave Faster than Light Speed Propulsion mode and re-enter the realm of human sight.

The irony was not lost on Cyrus Maloney III as he was "thawed" from cold sleep. His ship was readying itself to re-enter the world of human sight so that he could capture one who could lead him to a world beyond human sight. A world of dreams—beyond the Gateway.

At the Marscovy Landing Authority operation center, the pre-show rush was over. A few hours earlier the center had been a madhouse as senior operators guided hundreds of dropships into the Marscovy ether dome. Each of the ships had been in a hurry, the occupants anxious to attend the Slave Show at the forum featuring the exquisite Miro.

Now the place was minimally staffed, mostly with extremely junior officers. The senior flight controllers were all in forced sleep in preparation for the mass exodus that would take place in eight or nine hours.

So it was a junior operator who hit the manual scan command. For a moment nothing but the emptiness of space filled the huge screen, then the nothingness creased and over fifty huge ships disgorged from hyperspace and decelerated into visual range.

The junior operative sat bolt upright. His mouth worked but no words came. Across the room a hefty officer glanced in his direction and saw the look on the young man's face.

"What?"

All the junior officer could do was tilt his head toward the huge screen. His weighty co-worker waddled over to take a look and almost fell over from the shock of seeing the huge ships filling the entirety of the screen.

Then came the raspy booming voice of Cyrus Maloney III. "This is an S3 priority mission. All personnel are to be made available immediately. We will be dropping twenty ships in the next six minutes."

The two officers swallowed hard then hit every button on their consoles sending thousands of shock waves through the Marscovy air traffic control system. Hundreds of crews scrambled into action and dozens of senior air traffic controllers were unceremoniously screamed into waking.

The onion dome of the Marscovy Forum seemed to rise out of the flatness of the river bend itself. Or at least that's what Mickelmast thought as he contacted Mama through his shunt.

"Having fun down there, Hippo dear?"

"Yes. Indeed, Marscovy is certainly an interesting place."

"Wish I was there."

"Me, too, Ma. Could you get us specs on the Marscovy Forum?"

"With alacrity."

Mickelmast unfolded a smallish bot screen and, crouching behind Raephealson for a bit of privacy, examined the plans that arose there.

"Well?" demanded Kelt.

"There appear to be rooms beneath the central playing area."

"Any access from there to the playing floor itself?" asked Sun Tu.

"Dozens it seems. Access to almost every square. I guess that's so that they can start the slaves at any position they want," responded Mickelmast as he continued to scan the plans.

"This Miro must be there already," said Cas-Alta.

"Yes but how can we get to those rooms beneath the Forum?" asked Kelt.

"There's got to be air tunnels," said Sun Tu.

"There may have to be but I can't find them," Mickelmast responded as his eyes continued to scan the screens.

Sun Tu grabbed the screen from Mickelmast. "Let me."

She began to scroll through the hundreds of screens. The others marveled at her ability. Then she stopped and scrolled briefly in the other direction. "Here," she said tilting the screen to them.

"Its labyrinthine," gasped Cas-Alta.

"Marscovy is Russian after all," replied Mickelmast.

"And Russians have never been overly trusting," said Sun Tu.

Cas-Alta touched the pouch on her belt.

"While you figure it out, I'll find a place for Raephealson and Jaspers. They won't be much good down there," said Kelt.

"No! I don't trust myself to know if this Miro person is one of us or not. I'd be happier if Raephealson and Elijah were at the show to take a look at her," said Cas-Alta.

"I agree," said Mickelmast, "but they don't need to be down in the tunnels with us."

"Can we get them in as spectators?" asked Sun Tu.

"Ma, can you get us two coded seats?"

"Can I get you seats? I fly you across the endlessness of space and I can't get you seats at the Forum? What kind of sense does that make?"

"Can you Ma, please?"

Quickly the AIU supplied two ticket codes for "pit seats." Mickelmast sent the command to his bots which would temporarily convert Jasper's and Raephealson's DNA codes to match the pit seat codes. Cas-Alta gave the bot tabs to the men. Jaspers swallowed his without hesitation. But Raephealson was another question. He resisted. Finally, she coaxed the pill into his mouth. Then she and Kelt led the two men toward the southern entrance of the forum.

Marscovy security units were everywhere. Quickly the four were confronted by a ticket check point.

"What if the real owners of the seats are already in the Forum, Kelt?"

"Then we'll kick and scream bloody hell. Those seats cost a fortune!" He turned to Jaspers and Raephealson and pointed the way.

To Cas-Alta's relief the two men passed the scans without incident. Once they were through the check point, Kelt and Cas-Alta retreated into the crowd.

After passing the scan Jaspers stopped and looked back. For a moment Cas-Alta thought he was going to cry, then the old man hooked his arm through Raephealson's and guided the heavy worlder into the throngs heading toward the Slave Show.

"They going to be okay?" asked Kelt.

Cas-Alta didn't answer him. She sensed a great change. Something beginning or something ending—she couldn't tell which.

"They know how to get back to the drop ship. They should be fine," said Kelt. But he kept his face away from Cas-Alta's and set a fast pace back to Mickelmast and Sun Tu.

"I've found a digital line feed access. We should be able to follow it in," said Sun Tu.

"How do we know if this Miro is one of us?" Cas-Alta asked again.

"She'll be marked Elijah said," replied Mickelmast.

"How? How will she be marked?" pressed Cas-Alta.

"We can go back to the ship if that's what you think we should do," chimed in Sun Tu.

"Mama picked her as a very high possible," Mickelmast reminded them.

"And all these people seem to think she's pretty special," said Kelt allowing his arm to trace an arc over the heads of the massive ever-growing crowd.

"Well?" demanded Sun Tu.

"Fine," whispered Cas-Alta.

"What is it?" Mickelmast asked gently.

"It's all about to change again. Can't you feel it?"

"No I can't!" barked Sun Tu. "Time's not on our side. We have no idea what the dangers are but the longer we stay out here the greater they become. Are we going in or are we going back to the ship. Choose. Now!"

"We go in," sighed Cas-Alta.

"Good," said Kelt. "Follow me."

The others fell in behind him.

Sun Tu stepped beside Mickelmast as under her breath she said, "So I've showed us a way in."

"So you have, Sun Tu."

"Right. But who's going to show us a way out?"

"Perhaps I am," said Mickelmast as he programmed a set of bots and indicated a street light. The bots formed a smallish round ball and moved toward the base of the street lamp.

"What's that Mickelmast?" asked Sun Tu.

"The beginning of our way out, I hope," he answered as he programmed another set of bots.

Inside the great space Raephealson took his seat beside Jaspers. They formed an odd couple, but people around them didn't have much time to take them in before the place was plunged into darkness.

The show began with the shrieking scrape of metal against metal as the iron curtains slid aside revealing the playing board for the first event. The lights smashed on as the robotics appeared in full armor on their spots. Then, sampled sounds filled the arena and seven dazed, disoriented, drugged slaves stumbled into their positions on the board.

Raephealson closed his eyes tightly. This was a bad dream!

Cyrus was furious not only with the delays in clearing Marscovy security but also with the failure of his massive force to detect the presence of the UDP Warrior Class Starship carrying the Genetic Carriers. For the briefest moment Cyrus worried that his plan to lure the Genetic Carriers by using Miro hadn't worked. Then he got the report he had waited for. The Starship had identified itself as an EntrePren vessel. The ship's masking had been clever enough to defeat his ship's sensors, but the Warrior Class Starship's AIU had selected a disguise as a clever machine would, not a human.

There is no reason that an EntrePren ship would be at a Slave Show!

There were even secret EntrePren protocols to assure this. Cyrus knew about the secret protocols because he had negotiated them years ago as a way of getting into the good books of certain Rebel Colony planets—like Marscovy.

Cyrus ordered a more detailed analysis of the Starship. Sure enough it was the stolen pirate vessel—the Genetic Carriers' ship. A further DNA check of the vessel also made it clear that all five of the Carriers were not onboard the ship.

Of course they weren't! They were at the show! Searching for gifted ones—gifted ones like Miro!

Cyrus laughed out loud.

"Yes, we are all moving in one direction—like one great thing," he whispered.

He contacted his home AIU and was assured that the fail safe onboard the UDP Warrior Class Starship was still functioning.

Then he sat back and laughed again as he ordered his. Then, he ordered his stretch skimmer to increase its speed.

Fashionably late is one thing—missing the main event is something else altogether.

Chapter 53

At the Forum

Kelt and the three others squeezed their way through the narrow opening into the bowels of the forum. Mickelmast just made it.

They found themselves in a sluice channel slanting down toward the lowest levels of the complex. They stopped while Mickelmast checked for peepers ahead. He and his bots had disarmed six before the Genetic Carriers had even entered the building so he wasn't surprised to find more of the prying things in the narrow tunnel.

Once the peepers were distracted, Mickelmast gave the go ahead and they set off with Kelt in the lead. The young warrior's grace was extraordinary and he set a torrid pace for the rest.

Cyrus made a grand entrance into the Slave Show. The second slave game had just finished as he and his entourage made their way to their front row seats. All eyes turned to watch and Cyrus gloried in the attention. "Like walking to ringside during the late rounds," he thought. He stopped himself for a moment. What was that in reference to? He couldn't recall—and it sent a small shiver through him. Couldn't recall. Cyrus the III of S3 couldn't recall.

As he made his way down the aisle, he passed within twenty feet of Raephealson and Elijah Jaspers.

As soon as Cyrus took his seat Raephealson rose. Fear etched its way across his brow as he bulled his way down their row toward the aisle. Jaspers didn't follow immediately. Instead he sat and stared at the back of the head of the man who had entered his bedroom all those nights, all those many years ago. The man who, years and years later, had spared his life with the casual remark that "he's an addict now." The man who had taught him everything he knew about dreaming. The man whose voice was in his head every time he opened his mouth to speak of dreaming. The man who had taken his life and given him dreams in its stead.

An obscene thought entered Jasper's mind. "That man's the only father I've ever known." He closed his eyes and forced the thought away then rose and, hurrying down the row, got out into the aisle and began searching for Raephealson.

Elijah finally found the heavy worlder in the corner of a stall of a men's restroom. The huge man was trying to hide behind the bowl.

When Elijah opened the door Raephealson screamed. Elijah put up his hands and tried to calm the heavy worlder. "It's only me. Surely you can't be frightened of me. You could crack me in half without breaking into a sweat." Elijah stopped. He was wobbly on his feet. He put his back against the wall and allowed himself to slide to the floor. A slick of dried urine met him there.

Once he was settled he felt better. He looked to Raephealson again. "What frightened you?"

"Man!" came out of Raephealson's mouth so loudly that it shook the wall tiles.

Jaspers looked at Raephealson. "Cyrus the Three of S3? Cyrus frightened you?"

"Man."

"The one who just came into the forum, right?"

Raephealson nodded slowly.

"Well he's a frightening sort, of that you can be sure." Then, Jaspers looked hard at the heavy worlder. A wave of anxiety passed through his old heart. In a tiny voice he asked, "Have you seen him before, Raephealson?"

Raephealson nodded slowly again.

Jaspers got to his knees. "Where?"

"In the night viewing. In the glasshouse with the naked boy."

Jaspers felt his heart skip, then skip again. Tears came to his eyes. "Tell me, Raephealson, tell me what you saw in your night viewing."

And Raephealson did. Slowly at first then in a vomit of fear and internal falling. Once Jaspers got the gist of it he retreated into himself. He had known all those years ago that he wasn't alone. That he had never been alone. That there was always a third. Unseen. A guide in the shadows. Finally Jaspers put his fingers up to Raephealson's mouth and stopped him. Then gently he asked, "Do you know who that naked boy was?"

Raephealson shook his head.

"Me, Raephealson, it was me, you were there for me, to tell me that I wasn't alone. Even then, not alone."

Mickelmast consulted the schematic one final time and shook his head. "The slave prep rooms all branch off the curved corridor through there. But there's no way of knowing if she's being kept to the left or the right and this time there's bound to be guards. Probably armed."

"I'll go first then come back for you," said Kelt. Before anyone could object he was past them, entering the corridor.

The Slave Master gave Miro one final infinitely personal touch then opened the door and called for his men. They appeared quickly with their weapons at the ready.

Kelt didn't know which way to start looking in the curved corridor. Then he heard footsteps moving quickly toward him. Booted feet in motion. He stepped back into the shadows. A large party of armed men was approaching from his right. They seemed to be escorting an old man wearing other worldly clothing. A very old, but very elegant man. Kelt watched closely. Once they past him, Kelt started his search for Miro in the direction from which the men had just come.

Cyrus arrived at the Slaver's door just as Miro was being escorted toward her starting position on the chess board. With a nod of his head Cyrus signaled that he wanted a word with Miro and the Slave Master back in the room.

He shut the door then turned to look at the Slave Master and his former servant. "You look beautiful, girl."

Miro couldn't believe it. What was he doing here?

"Glad y'approve your worship," said the Slave Master with the slightest bending of his body. "I thought the role of cleric fitted..."

"Oh I approve," Cyrus interrupted. "I always approve of the post-coital elegance of a beautiful woman. Don't you Slave Master?"

The Slave Master went to protest but his implant screamed at him, "Shut your gob you worm of a man! A little wick dipping while I was in cold sleep! I hope you enjoyed it—because you've just forfeited the balance in your EntrePren accounts. That was the most expensive momentary trick in the history of human kind."

The Slave Master staggered.

Miro watched all this. It must be the implant again, she thought. She clutched the needle in her hand longing to plunge it deep into Cyrus's neck but reminded herself that the object was to get away and only the drug inductions in the game could offer her the cover to do that.

Cyrus approached her and touched her face for the briefest moment, then he turned and was gone.

After a beat of silence, the slavers came and took her.

At the very end of the curved corridor, Kelt found the entrance to the pathways beneath the game board. He was about to head back in the other direction when he saw Miro being led toward the entrance.

He didn't have to be told who she was. Nor did he have to be told that she was one of them. He connected with her instantly. Once she was ushered into one of the pathways leading to the chessboard, Kelt raced back to get the others.

The Slave Master pulled himself to his feet. Now he had nothing left to lose. All that work for nothing! Always the same. They always get and we always give. We do all the work and they get all the spoils. Then he screamed out loud, "And I don't care that you know Mr. Fuckin' Cyrus Maloney Baloney… " He ran out of expletives. And besides his implant was silent. It didn't care what he said. "Well maybe he won't care what I do, either!" he shouted. Then he headed toward the door, murder in his eyes.

Jaspers coaxed Raephealson back to their seats just moments before Cyrus and his entourage re-emerged from beneath the raised chessboard area. "As if they had just been invited back stage to the diva's dressing room at La Scala," thought Cyrus. Again Cyrus faltered. Another reference for which he couldn't recall the source. What was happening to him!

The Slave Master turned the corner just as the four Genetic Carriers emerged from their hiding place. For a moment he was disoriented. Then he recognized the Chinee girl and with a yell lunged at her. Kelt deflected the initial charge and the Slaver smacked into the corridor wall, momentarily stunned. Sun Tu, knife drawn, was on him in a flash. The knife drew blood quickly but not deeply. She turned to Kelt who stood very still, watching. Not a muscle in his body moved to save the old slaver. The Slave Master's eyes grew wide as he saw his own blood flowing. Quickly he released the technacles attached to his belt. They flared out like snakes on the loose looking for a purchase.

"Mickelmast!" screamed Cas-Alta.

But Mickelmast was already on the case. Responding to "trapandsmother.exe" his bots quickly pinned the technacles to the slick floor.

Then Sun Tu turned to Kelt. "What should we do with the slaver?"

"It is time for him to do the death travel, Sun Tu," said Kelt simply. His eyes were clear, there was no waver in his voice. "Unless you want me to do it."

"You stopped me from killing the pirate captain."

"I did."

"But not this one?"

"Not this one."

"Why?"

"Either kill him or talk, but don't do both," said Kelt. He was still completely passive.

Sun Tu considered then plunged her weapon deep into the Slave Master's neck. And slashed across his carotid artery.

The stinky man jerked violently as his blood sprayed the opposite wall of the corridor. His head banged into the floor sending spiking shards of pain into his brain. With his last breath of strength, he turned his head toward Sun Tu.

The final thought the Slave Master had on this plain of existence was: She is so beautiful.

It was also the last image that Cyrus received from the implant. An image of a stunning Asian woman with a knife in her hand.

"They're beneath the stage," he said aloud. Just then the lights came crashing down. The main event of the Great and Grand Slave Show was beginning.

The searing lights hurt Miro's eyes. The rest of the board was in dense shadow. Only she, in her starting cube, was in the blinding glare. Instantly panic enveloped her. This was too hard for her. This was her end!

Then an announcer's voice shouted her name. It reverberated off the walls of the huge space and was met with a thunderous applause, which rose exponentially when the enormous screens slid into place allowing the entirety of the huge crowd to see, "The lovely Miro, S3 whore!"

Then, as the crowd's roar crested, a siren cut through the din and Miro found the entire board in motion. The east door to her room was thrown open and in slouched the batch-filed robotic of the white Czarina. She wore a black silken dress cut on the bias. It clung to every slender curve of her impossibly elegant body. The delicate bones of her face were set off by a sliver of a diamond tiara perched on her intensely red hair which fell in long rings down her pale naked back. But the madness in her eyes well preceded her beauty. She smiled at Miro and then revealed a foot long throwing knife in her left hand. "The Czar has a thing for you," she announced in perfect Russian. Then without warning she threw the ivory-handled knife at Miro's head. Miro ducked and the knife embedded itself almost a full three inches into the wall. With a cry Miro raced out the west door of the room and continued to run through rooms until the lights slammed out.

The first move was over.

The first set of drug inductions were administered to paying audience members who wanted the "up close and personal" approach.

"What!" shouted Sun Tu.

The Genetic Carriers were still in the pathways beneath the playing surface.

"Mirren had screens, remember?" continued Mickelmast. The others nodded. "We'll need to cover them somehow or deflect them or something. If we don't everyone who is sitting out there will be able to see us."

"What about the people who took the drug inductions. They'll have a private access to Miro through the drugs?"

"We'll have to deal with them somehow."

"Hold on," said Cas-Alta. "They'll be able to see us, true, but if the screen doesn't show the same thing that they're seeing... "

"Then, just maybe," Mickelmast completed her thought, "they won't be able to convince anyone else that there's anything wrong."

"Not real, just inside their minds," said Sun Tu.

Cas-Alta smiled.

"It will work even better if I can make the images on the screen so exciting that no one would want to stop the game," said Mickelmast.

"It might work," said Sun Tu.

"What else can we do?" asked Kelt.

"Nothing."

"Can you do it Mickelmast?"

"Yes, I think so. I'll program the bots so that at the right moment we can run silent, run deep."

"Meaning what?"

"I don't know but I've always wanted to say that," Mickelmast giggled. He always giggled when he wasn't sure of his abilities. "Once the bot images are on the screens we'll be undercover. We find Miro and then get her out of here."

"Then we try to get us all out of here," Sun Tu corrected him. The other three looked to her but no one knew what to say.

"One step at a time," said Kelt.

"Be quick about it. I don't know how long my little bot flat-face will work."

When the lights came up on Miro, Jaspers knew two things instantly. One was that she was one of them. The other was that she had been touched by the same man who had touched him.

He felt a momentary ache in his heart and clutched at Raephealson's arm. The heavy worlder looked at Elijah. Jaspers was amazed. The heavy worlder's eyes were perfectly clear. Deep. Almost peaceful and immensely beautiful.

Cyrus resisted the impulse to stop the show. There was no need. He had the Genetic Carriers all in one place. All searching for the gifted one just as he had planned. All moving in one direction, like one great thing. Now was the time to reap the harvest. He commed his security forces, and they doubled their ring around the forum's exterior while his elite pretorian guards moved closer to the board sealing off any exit through the audience or from the pathways beneath the board.

Quickly Mickelmast programmed the bots to form outfits allowing Sun Tu to enter the game as the white Czarina, Kelt as one of the White Knights and Cas-Alta as the other white Cleric.

"Get in there, she'll need all the help we can give her," said Mickelmast.

"What about you?"

"I'll bot-contact Jaspers. He'll tell me who's where on the board. Then I need to figure out how to program the screens with the bots, or maybe directly through Mama. I don't know. That's my problem. You three have to remember that you're not under cover at the beginning. So be careful out there. Stay far away from the character you're playing. It'd be hard to explain if there were two white queens in the same room. I'll send you a signal through your bots when I have control of the screens. Now go. Miro needs your help."

And she did. Miro was already slick with sweat as the siren to commence the second move sounded. The siren reminded her of something that Cyrus had once said to her. Now it seemed like years ago. "Sirens inside, sirens outside!" Then she sensed the first folding of the drug and she turned to the opened shred. They were there—faces. Dozens of faces in a single drug tunnel staring at her.

Before she could react to them the west door of her room slammed open and two batch-filed pawns sprung into the room. Each carried a crude weapon, one a hand scythe, the other a club. They were both dressed in peasant's tatters, their eyes filled with glaring hatred.

She looked around. She was in a tower keep. Immediately she climbed into the window and was about to leap out when she struck the tromp l'oeil wall. As she did, she heard a howl of laughter from the audience and a snicker of glee from those watching in the drug folds. Tricks within tricks.

"I'm not dying to entertain you people," she shouted. But her words were drowned out by further cheers as the peasant with the scythe swung at her head. She ducked and raced toward the far wall. As the peasant pried his weapon lose, the second peasant swung at her. She dodged the clumsy blow then tipped over the table in the center of the room to give her some protection.

As she threw over the table, she saw an iron ring imbedded in the faux stone floor. She yanked it. It came up fast. Beneath was a tunnel!

Without a second thought she leapt into it head first… and fell almost straight down!

Kelt killed the Black Knight with a single blow. The black armored thing sailed across the stable room and impaled himself on the pitchfork hanging on the wall. Sun Tu lifted her head from her hands and looked at Kelt. "You took your time," she managed through clenched teeth.

"I didn't think you needed my help."

"I don't."

"Really?"

"Really."

"Answer me something?"

"Sure."

"Why did you let me kill the Slave Master when you wouldn't let me kill the pirate captain?"

"You already asked me that."

"And you didn't answer me."

"I don't know. I… "

"Lost for words?"

"Yeah. Happy? I'm lost for words." Kelt drew his weapon and raced from the room.

For a moment Sun Tu was going to go her own way, then she turned and raced after Kelt.

Cas-Alta found herself in a Dacha room. She smelled the rich earth outside. The scent of things growing. She threw open the window and breathed in the false life. Then the window shattered in her hand and the door exploded inward. In the yard stood the Black Castle with two black pawns.

Cas-Alta raced toward the opposite door just as the three charged into the room.

Miro was falling. Falling through space. She felt liquid terror slipping from every pore. Then she sensed them. The drug watchers. Hundreds of them now. All getting a thrill at her expense. All thrilled that she was terrified. She closed her eyes and blocked out their cries.

She thought of the woman in the night. The one whose tears dropped like falling doves.

Instantly she was on her feet!

She opened her eyes. She was in an upper story room of a Victorian building. The smell of cigars was everywhere. Around her were leather chairs. And a fireplace. For a moment she thought this was Cyrus' room. But she quickly dismissed the thought. A large rectangular table was in the center. Its entire surface was covered with a huge detailed map. She read a name at the top of the map: Leningrad. She saw a river and a waterfront. Then she noticed the hundreds of toy-like soldiers with numbers. Two armies. A siege! This was a war room. At that moment the Black King entered the room and looked at her.

"Well my dear, this is most inappropriate don't you think?"

Mickelmast had never worked so fast. Even with Mama's input he wasn't sure that he had it right. He programmed action sequences for sixty-four rooms and gave it a sense of building suspense. And there were so many characters. Finally he yelled at Mama that this was as good as he could manage.

Then he waited for a siren. It came momentarily followed by a huge applause—they were loving it. Mickelmast yelled into his bot transmitter. "Ready?"

Cas-Alta responded from the corner of a bedroom in which she was hiding in a cupboard. Kelt and Sun Tu were in an impoverished student's bedchambers and also answered that they were ready. Mickelmast gave them the coordinates of Miro's location in the war room, then yelled, "In exactly ninety seconds the bots are going to take over the screens. Get Miro. I'll try to meet you there. Okay?"

They all responded to the affirmative.

Then he said in a small voice, "Do me a favor?"

"What is it Mickelmast?" shouted Sun Tu.

"Don't blame me if this doesn't work!"

The spot light hit Miro in the war room. She breathed down and established where the drug viewers were. After the end of every round, the Forum sold more and more of the induction drugs. Miro was now dealing with literally hundreds of folds in the drug and within each fold were dozens of watchers.

In the glare of the light, Miro realized that they were showing pictures of her naked on the screens above her. The place was going crazy. Screams seemed to be everywhere. Miro was losing her sense of balance. Then the Black King slid a cold hand beneath her blouse and squeezed her breast so hard that she screamed.

The audience roared with laughter.

Jaspers had been monitoring the communications between Mickelmast and the others. Now his eyes were on Cyrus the Three of S3 only six rows in front of him. Cyrus was smart. He'd see if the images on the screen were somehow wrong.

Jaspers heard Mickelmast count down 9 - 8 - 7... He looked up on the screen. The Black King's left hand was up Miro's shirt, and he was smiling a crooked grin at the audience. 6 - 5 - 4. The Black King raised his right hand in triumph as Miro reached inside the folds of her coat and withdrew something from the folds of her gown. 3 - 2 - 1. The thing glinted in the light, then the screens went wobbly as if a rend in time itself had taken place.

In a moment they stabilized.

Jaspers let out a sigh of relief.

Then he looked at the screen more carefully.

It was a mirror image. Everything was backward. Lefts were rights and rights were lefts.

Cyrus rose slowly from his seat, his eyes fastened to the screen as if his life depended on it. Then, ignoring the cries for him to sit down, Cyrus shouted to his men. The pretorian guard reacted instantly. They moved as one to the small door which opened to the pathways beneath the playing board.

Screams of anger pelted down on them as they obscured other paying customers' view of the playing board. In the confusion, Jaspers and Raephealson fell in behind the pretorian guards and found themselves in the pathways beneath the playing board.

The siren sounded and Miro plunged the needle with the drug deep into the batch-filed Black King. Anger poured from her like a mighty river finally undammed. Over and over again she struck and ripped and punctured with the needle. Every man who had handled her.

Every unwanted touch. Every unasked for stare. Every entry. Every caress and pull.

Then she sensed the watchers returning. She folded the drug around her and headed out the west doorway. The folding disoriented the watchers and she could hear them yelling complaints as she entered the next cube.

It was a school room. Small wooden desks with attached chairs. Russian writing made from some sort of white dust on a black stony surface. She needed a rest. She needed to collect herself. She had given away the presence of the needle when she didn't have to. But she had. She had.

Mickelmast felt naked. Except for his single transmitter bot, he had sent every one of his bots off on a task. Most to the screens. It had been many years since he had felt as vulnerable as he did now. He struggled into his white peasant outfit. It was a little snug. His only weapon was a long pointed stick. He didn't think much of it. In fact he found, as he tried to enter his first room, that he couldn't negotiate the long pike through the door. When he finally did manage to pull the damned thing through the opening, the point stuck him in the foot... and he squealed.

Then he called for Jaspers to identify Miro's location.

And no one answered!

He tried again and still no response. Mickelmast contacted the others. "Search for Miro. I have no idea where she is! Just find her and fast, I don't know how long that bot program will work on the screens."

Jaspers hadn't responded to Mickelmast's call because he and Raephealson were too close to the S3 men in the darkened pathways beneath the playing board. Elijah put his hand over the bot and held his breath, hoping that Cyrus hadn't heard the bot's call.

Cyrus hadn't because he was yelling orders to his men as they raced beneath the board. "Kill the robotics. Get them out of the way. Disable them, unplug them, do what you have to do, I don't care. They're just a confusion for us. But anything human you capture. And I don't want them hurt. Understood? If they're human I want them alive and unharmed." Then he yelled into his comm to the forces around the Forum itself. "Nothing human is to leave the building. Nothing!"

All this was lost on the great crowd. They were seeing a completely different show on the screens. Sometimes it didn't make tremendous sense, but it was always filled with action. And Miro was losing pieces of her clothing with every round so the audience was being driven into voyeur heaven.

As Mickelmast, Sun Tu and Kelt furiously searched for Miro, Cas-Alta decided on another plan. She dreamed her dream room as Jaspers had taught her to do—as she had done so many times in the recent past.

She checked the room. All the pictures were there. All the entry ways were clear. She was well. Then, the baby gave a savage kick. She fell to her knees and tried to calm herself with her breath as she caressed her belly with her hands.

She finally found calm.

With a breath she sent out a clarion call for Miro to come to her. She sent it out over and over again—each time committing her intent to the core of her being. Then she stopped. She sensed that something was wrong. That something was missing.

Then she knew what it was, what would complete all this.

She reached down to her belt and flipped the lid on the leaden case. The silken mist swirled out and looked at the dream room. "Of course. Of course it would happen in such a room," thought the Face Dancer. Then another thought came to her. A frightening thought. "She's coming, my God. So soon. So soon."

Miro was in a pavilion room overlooking a great race course. Beneath her an extraordinary horse race was in motion. A handsome aristocrat was whipping his horse toward the finish.

Then she heard it.

And yet there was nothing to hear.

But she heard it.

Calling her. Calling her. Then she did more than hear. She felt it. Felt that the beautiful lady in the night was here—in the cubes of the board. The beautiful lady whose tears fell like doves.

A black Bishop entered from the west door, but Miro was far too fast for him. She threw a chair at his head, then another, then a third.

Then she turned and raced out of the pavilion toward the call that was clearer and clearer with every passing second.

With a concussive pistol in his hand, Cyrus entered the true game of life and death—of waking and sleeping. He entered the game like a man who finally had come home.

He reached up and released his hair from its bonds. Cascades of gray tresses fell down his back. The brocade which he wore expanded at his command to a full-length gown. The nails on his fingers grew and cork screwed.

Passing a gilded full-length mirror, he caught a glimpse of himself. "A vision" he thought. And he laughed. "Just call me Rasputin!" he screamed as he smashed the mirror. Then he charged into his first room—a Czarina's private boudoir.

Raephealson helped Jaspers into the first room. It was train platform. Someone was dead beneath the wheels of a locomotive. A peasant. Another peasant was yelling at them that her husband was dead. She howled pitifully.

The two men approached her tentatively. When they got close she pulled her shawl aside. It was the Black Queen. She raised her arm and flung acid from a small vial right at the men. It struck Jaspers across the face and down the neck. The old man screamed as Raephealson threw himself at the batch-filed robotic. The queen had tremendous strength programmed into her limbs, but she was no match for the heavy worlder who in his fury committed the first act of violence in his life.

It was over quickly and Raephealson was back to Jaspers. Blood streamed from the old man's face. One eye had lost its purchase in the socket. Jaspers vomited on his shirt as Raephealson dragged him as gently as he could to his feet.

Then the heavy worlder picked him up and carried him in his arms, like a father would a child who had skinned his knee.

Miro was exhausted, not physically but emotionally. She leant against the door and allowed her face to rub against the roughness there. She could sense that the lady was on the other side. The clarion call went on and on. And she knew. She knew. Tears flew from her eyes. She tried to repeat her origins and before she got through ten words knew that it was useless. Either she went through that door to her destiny or she remained nameless—alone in the galaxy. The hinges were oiled. All she needed was bravery to go through.

She pushed open the door.

"Put that stick away, you almost poked me with that damned thing!" shouted Kelt at Mickelmast.

"You scared me!"

"Good, at least I scare someone. Where is she Mickelmast? There are more twists and turns in here than it looks."

"There are rooms within rooms and secret passages everywhere," said Sun Tu.

"Where's Cas?" asked Kelt.

"I don't know," replied Mickelmast.

"Well let's start by trying to find her. Contact her Mickelmast."

The fat boy tried but got no answer.

"Is the message being relayed to her?" asked Sun Tu.

"Yes. I have a confirm from the bot, but not from her," said Mickelmast.

"Is there a direction on the confirm? Can you trace that?" asked Kelt.

"Yes," said Mickelmast already making the computations. "That way," he shouted as he pointed south.

"Let's go. We stay together now," ordered Kelt. There was no disputing that Kelt should take the lead. There was a grim set to his features that frightened the other two.

The bot signaled an incoming message on Cas-Alta's shoulder, but she was well passed being able to respond. Moments earlier the door had opened and Miro had entered. As she did the room itself changed. It was now a surgery of some sort. Crude life-extension materials were everywhere. Miro stood in the doorway—terror was on her face. Cas-Alta sought the cause of the horror.

Then she saw it.

The Face Dancer had transformed on her own—into a red-faced demon with flowing robes and was now standing on one leg in a martial arts pose ready to attack.

Cas-Alta threw herself at the demon—and went right through her. The baby inside her screamed with joy. Then Cas understood.

She was the neutral third. But the neutral third for what?

Cyrus got the report while he was in the central aisle of the high onion-domed ancient church. "Twenty-two robots destroyed, sir. Three human life readings moving quickly toward you." Cyrus ducked into a confessional and waited. His eyes were glued to the slatting, staring between them at the tall incense drenched space—and he was happy—alive—they were coming—the way to Olya was approaching.

The Lady who cried tears like falling doves reached out and touched Miro's face. The touch was soft. Miro turned the hand over and kissed the palm. Then turned her cheek into it, lolled in the softness of the caress.

The Face Dancer allowed Miro's tears to fall. It would make it easier. It was so hard what she had to do.

"I've been waiting for you so long," Miro purred into the hand.

"And I for you," said the lady with the sad eyes as she reached down and touched the girl's hair. She ran her fingers through the strands and said, "Like a combed horse's tail."

"Hey it's a church," said Mickelmast. "We always seem to be ending up in churches don't we?"

"Shut up Mickelmast and stay to the shadows," hissed Kelt. His weapon at the ready, he raced the entire length of the church and then scaled the wrought iron gate that separated the main body of the church from the place in which the mystery is celebrated. The sacred from the mundane. The world that accepts and relishes dreams from that which has killed dreaming.

Raephealson wiped as much of the blood away from Jaspers face as he could. They were in a gallery of some sort. There were empty picture frames on the walls. In some cases, the frames were gone too and only the lightness of a rectangle of wallpaper indicated where the picture had hung. There were explosions outside. Antique style artillery.

"Can you hear me Mr. Jaspers?"

Elijah allowed his head to nod. His life was rushing out of him. He could feel it—like sand it was. Rushing out. Pouring out! Out of his fingers. Out his toes. Out his eyes, his ears, his mouth, his penis, his anus. Running, rushing, whooshing out of him.

"We have to find Cas-Alta, she can help you. Remember what she did for me. She can help you. But I don't know how to find her, Mr. Jaspers. Help me."

Jaspers moved his head and tried to point with his chin at the bot on Raephealson's shoulder. The heavy worlder saw the motion but didn't understand. Jaspers tried again. Again Raephealson saw the gesture but was lost as to what it meant.

Then Jaspers opened his mouth. He felt a huge load of sand rush out of him.

Raephealson backed off from the gush of blood.

But Jaspers was talking through the sand. Yelling as best he could.

The blood bubbled as air pushed its way up from Jaspers vocal chords. Raephealson leaned his head down and heard deep in Jaspers' blood, "Touch the bot on your shoulder and call for Cas-Alta."

"No!!!" Cas-Alta shouted as the Demon picked up Miro and threw her against the wall. Surgical instruments fell from their shelves and clattered to the ground. Vials of valuable Kiltrin smashed to the floor. Then the Demon was on Miro again.

"This is love I know that," said Miro.

And the Sad Lady smiled back at her. "It is our role to play. Like Brother Diafollo in the fire, the greenhouse floating woman and the painter of pulsing cubes. And like so many others. Like Dr. Suzanne Belange who dreamed dreaming and was found stuffed into the wall of her life-extension surgery, eight feet off the ground. With her hair like a combed horse's tail."

Miro was crying. "But I don't want to die."

"It is but a voyage to the Gateway. There you will awake from the sleep that you called your life. There you will dream us who are still on this side of the Gateway. But only for a short while. For soon the Gateway will close. Soon we will all be there. Then there will be no need to dream a life. We will be all able to start again. Start properly this time."

Miro nodded as tears coursed down her cheeks. She put her hands together and sunk to her knees.

Then slowly she opened her arms, raised her face to the beautiful lady—and accepted. The Sad Faced Lady cried tears like falling doves but through them she smiled. Miro thought it the most beautiful thing she had ever seen.

The Demon grabbed Miro and threw her against the far wall. The sound of shattering bone filled the room. Miro skittered beneath the surgery table trying to find a place of safety. Then the demon opened its hideous mouth and screamed, "Dream no more. Dream no more. Dream!" and hauling Miro out by the hair lifted her into her arms and then ran full speed into the far wall. A sickening crunch filled the room. Cas-Alta screamed.

A rend in the wall had opened eight feet off the ground.

The Sad Lady carefully combed Miro's hair. Removed the blood and shattered bone. Then with reverence and love placed her in the high crevice in the wall. Then she knelt in prayer.

Miro had served her purpose in the Gateway's great plan.

For the first time the Face Dancer revealed herself to Cas-Alta. With a simple turn she was there, Miro dead in the wall behind her. The beautiful lady whose tears fell like doves stood in front of her. Cas-Alta couldn't move. She didn't know what to do.

Then the baby kicked viciously three times. Cas-Alta thought she heard him yell inside her. She looked up and the lady was gone. In her place was an older woman bent over a patch of garden.

Cas-Alta's heart skipped and for a moment she thought she was going to die. Then she allowed the words out of her mouth, "Mother, is that you?"

The Face Dancer turned to face Cas-Alta.

"Mother!"

A howl of protest went up from those in the audience who had paid the most for their drug inductions. They hadn't seen anything for ten minutes or more.

They were shouted down by the larger audience who were still watching the adventure on the screens. As they did the price bid for Miro reached incredible proportions. Money was being thrown at the auction board. The tote couldn't keep up with the commed bids. When two thousand units was bid, the place went wild.

At that point, Miro's figure (still bot induced) stood still and naked in a nineteenth-Century Russian police station. The lights isolated her. She threw herself against the now transparent walls of the room and stayed there, arms raised and pressed hard against the west wall, breasts flattened against the surface, trapped within the transparency. Her mouth opened but no sound came. In fact the image didn't move.

It was as if the entire forty thousand spectators collectively held their breath. A profound stillness filled the place, everyone frightened to be the first to let go of their breath and break the moment.

Cyrus nervously commed his men. They began flanking out and surrounding the church. Several on each door, waiting. Waiting for orders to enter.

As each squadron of pretorian guards commed that they had taken up their positions, Cyrus readied himself. Then he calmly asked, "Where are the other two? There were five and there are only three here."

Quickly pretorian commanders responded. The search was still on for the other two. What should be done with the three in the church?

"What should be done? On my order they should be captured. On my count you are to enter following procedures as we have practiced." To himself he counted the real numbers of his world. Ten for the men no longer here, nine for the fine of being human, eight for all the hate no longer in our worlds, seven for the end to the place called heaven, six for all that we have applied the fix, five for the many many years you all stay alive, four for the hinge now oiled on the swinging door, three for the return to glee, two for me and you Olya, one for no longer alone. Then he looked through the confessional slats. The young warrior had rescaled the grating and was once more with the fat boy and the elegant Asian woman. Cyrus said their names to himself: Kelt the warrior, Mickelmast the trickster and Sun Tu the EntrePren princess. One of them. One of them must have the genes I seek.

Then he began to count into his communicator: Ten, nine, eight...

Raephealson found the exit door in the pawn brokers dingy apartment, and carefully folding himself to protect Elijah carried Jaspers through the opening.

So it was they entered the next room backward, a father carrying the wreaked body of his ancient son.

They were on a high catwalk that circled the upper reaches of the dome of the church. They were right over the central part of the church, beneath the highest of the onion domes.

Raephealson stared at the space. The lift. He felt new air rush into his lungs and hope fill his heart.

"Two! one! NOW!!!" screamed Cyrus into his comm as he threw open the door of the confessional and faced the Genetic Carriers.

Sun Tu whirled toward the voice and was appalled to find herself facing a desperately old man with wild gray hair but even wilder eyes. Kelt reached for his weapon but was distracted by the crashing of the doors on all four sides of the church and the trap door almost beneath his feet.

Stun volleys and concussive blasts filled the air. Then frantic movement and toppled pews. More stun volleys and it was over. The three Genetic Carriers were disarmed and on the floor on their faces, concussion weapons pressed hard into the backs of their necks.

Despite himself Kelt was impressed by the training of the men. The attackers faces were blank sheets. Dark men with white faces and emptied hearts. Professional warriors.

Mickelmast's heart sank. He turned his head to look for Kelt. Kelt had accepted his fate. Sun Tu's elegant internal lift was gone. She too had given up.

In desperation he tapped his transmitter bot and called for Jaspers and Cas-Alta—but neither answered. The gray ancient in front of them began to rant.

"Welcome travellers! Welcome home! Welcome back after all these years! All these many, many too long years. Hail wanderers! To the treasures of the harbor. Don't you feel it? This was meant to be! Surely you feel that, oh gifted ones."

Elijah stirred in Raephealson's arms. His mouth began to move. The heavy worlder lifted Elijah higher and put his ear close to Elijah's mouth.

Elijah felt his chi leaving him in crested waves now. A tidal wave of leaving. But that voice, that voice! That voice that he had just heard. The voice that he had heard all those nights in his room, in the darkness of a boy's room. That voice gave him one last source of energy—anger.

"Don't be frightened of him, Raephealson."

Raephealson stared at Cyrus on the floor far beneath them. He heard the words from the Angry Faced Man in his dreams and saw the wild figure and once more, despite all his efforts, Raephealson felt himself in retreat. But Jasper's words steadied him.

"Have they technacled our people?"

Raephealson carefully moved toward the edge of the railing trying to get a better view without giving away their presence. "No. But they are calling for them now."

"Fine. Move me closer to the railing."

Raephealson did as the old man asked.

"When the confusion is greatest you will have a chance to escape with our people. Once you are onboard ship, you must Dream Navigate them to safety."

"But... "

"Courage Raephealson. Courage will allow you through the door. It is well oiled now. All you need is the courage to push." Elijah looked with his one eye at the giant who held him like a child. Then he tried to smile.

"Do you trust me Raephealson?"

"I do Mr. Jaspers."

"Elijah. Please think of me as Elijah." Raephealson nodded. "You honor me. Now do exactly what I ask." Elijah closed his eye and turned his thoughts inward. The sound of internal waves crashing was so great that he couldn't find the quiet. He knew it was now almost all, all over.

Then he looked down. A praetorian had coded the technacles and were about to put them on Kelt. Elijah screamed, "Throw me out into the space, Raephealson!"

Just for a moment the heavy worlder hesitated, then he threw Elijah Jaspers up and out into the space.

There was pain. Shards of ripping through the skin of Elijah's face.

He was falling!!!

Cyrus looked up toward the sound of the scream and was shocked to see the blooded thing plummeting toward him. So was the pretorian guard with the technacles who dropped one and screamed as it turned on him and plunged into his thigh.

Jaspers was screaming too—in his head. Trying to be heard above the crashing waves inside him and the whoosh of air outside. Then he remembered his foot touching down on a precipice overlooking a vast molten sea. His first dream voyage! He was young again. In a dream again!

The thrashing technacles caused terror among the pretorian guards but nothing compared to the fear engendered by the figure of the blooded old man who had stopped plummeting and was now hanging in mid-air without the assistance of any machinery.

Cyrus raced to the center of the church, directly beneath the hanging figure. He stood on one of the pews and stared at the crimsoned man hanging in the air—stared in wonder.

Elijah was in the restaurant again with the table of Dreamers. The elegant Venetian plaza and canals behind them were so beautiful that he wanted to cry. Then the Dreamers, as one great thing, rose and smiling pointed to the small seat at the table.

A huge wave crashed inside Elijah and sand rushed out of him in a final burst of Dreamer's glory.

Without warning the floating, blooded thing inverted in mid-air.

Eight feet off the ground.

And began to spin.

Cyrus cried out in fear and joy and ecstasy and glory. The guards didn't know what to do. Their leader had clearly lost his mind.

"Once more. Just once more" pleaded Elijah to the dream figures at the table. "But this time it's easy. No exploring. No movement at all. All that power. All that folding inside this confined space. Chaos. Rending. Then release. Please!"

His Dreamer's spin picked up speed and the objects in the room began to whirl in a counter rotation to him.

"What's happening?" yelled Kelt over the rising roar in the room.

"He's made a whirlwind," yelled Sun Tu.

"He's made a way for us to escape," yelled Mickelmast. Then, "Look!"

Raephealson was racing to them, throwing aside the few pretorian guards who hadn't already bolted for the doors. "This way," he screamed at them.

They followed him to the narrow stairway leading up the church wall to the catwalk. And up they went as the chaos in the room grew and grew.

The Dreamers at the table were smiling! The ones he had betrayed were smiling and holding out their arms to him! Warmth. Slickness. One final hideously painful rip and the remaining sand left his hour glass.

Home.

Cyrus stood in the very center of the whirlwind balanced on the top of a toppled pew. All around him the world was in motion. But not in the eye of the storm, directly beneath the man he now knew was Elijah Jaspers the youngest person he had ever made into a Dream Navigator.

He held up his arms. Elijah's blood pelted down on him. Slicking him. Entering his mouth and eyes. Blinding him. Tasting of glory.

When Raephealson got them up to the catwalk they looked back. The entire room was spiraling around. Pews and statuary, prayer books, and candles all caught in the whirlwind. But it was not the whirlwind that caught their eyes. It was the grotesquely beautiful figures of Elijah Jaspers in the Dream Navigators spin and Cyrus the Three of S3 standing directly beneath him, arms raised covered in the blood of the sacrificial calf.

It was Kelt who broke the moment. "He's given us an opportunity, let's use it."

"What about Cas-Alta?" demanded Mickelmast.

"Too late," said Sun Tu.

"Call off your bots Mickelmast, it will create chaos outside to match the chaos inside" said Kelt.

"No need, my bots ran out of plot sequencing over ten minutes ago."

"Let's go then," said Kelt.

"No," said Raephealson, "we must all look once more. This may be the last time that such beauty is seen in our worlds."

There was no resistance. They all looked to the spinning man in the air and the maddened man reaching up from the pews beneath him. Now covered in blood. Glorying in it as a lamb does in the spring rain.

Each in their own way saluted Elijah Jaspers. And as they raced out they each promised themselves to keep his memory alive in their hearts.

Moments later, Elijah heard something snap. Like the string of an ancient musical instrument. "How appropriately Russian," Elijah thought. And how like the sound he had heard all those years ago when he was nine years old—and he first crashed in his dreams.

Then he fell.

Elijah's weight toppled Cyrus from the overturned pew. Jaspers found himself face to face with the voice in his bedroom from all those nights ago. But now the voice was gentle. The rough hands were now running fingers through his hair. The angry, muscled arms now rocking him. And saying over and over again, "You were my only treasure, my only son. My only treasure, my only son."

As if in a trance, Cas-Alta turned to Miro, now dead and crushed into the crevice in the wall, eight feet off the ground. Her hair hanging and clean. A look of infinite, impossible peace on her face. Cas-Alta found herself on her knees, her hands pressed tightly together. "Bless my child. Beautiful lady, bless the child in my womb, please help me. Miro, bless the child I carry."

The Face Dancer didn't wait for Cas-Alta's permission. She grabbed the pregnant girl and screamed, "If you want to live, follow me."

All around them the faux world of the game was caving in. The Face Dancer made a choice and headed out—away from the imploding image.

Moments later Raephealson entered their room. He was followed by Sun Tu, Kelt and Mickelmast. Immediately their eyes were drawn to Miro in the wall. Explosions rang out behind them. Pillars in the arena itself were falling! But the Genetic Carriers stopped and stared—and believed.

The Face Dancer changed into a huge demonic form and terrified the security officers at the west gate. Then she and Cas-Alta were outside. The sky seemed to have moved closer. There were screaming people everywhere. And explosions—timed bot explosions set by Mickelmast on his way into the Forum to add to the chaos.

The Face Dancer took one long look and finally found what she was looking for—a mountain range in the far eastern horizon.

This was a Russian planet. There'd have to be mountains.

She pointed. Cas-Alta followed her finger.

"There. We'll find a cave. You'll have your baby there."

Cas-Alta recoiled at the suggestion.

Then The Face Dancer grabbed Cas-Alta by both arms and pulled her face up very close to her own. "There's no other choice. You carry a demon. You need me. For a baby from hell, you need a midwife from the same precincts. Now follow me."

Cas-Alta stumblingly did. As she followed the strange lady her head replayed the words, "You carry a demon, you carry a demon," over and over again. The only way to stop that terrible voice was to remember another terrible voice—the demon in the room screaming, "Dream no more, dream no more, dream!"

"Cas is all alone out there somewhere," said Mickelmast.

As Kelt reached down and picked up the empty leaden pouch from the room's floor he said, almost in a whisper, "She's not alone."

Then a bot explosion ripped through the east section of the forum.

"Come on," yelled Sun Tu and headed toward the hole in the Forum that gaped light from outdoors.

The pretorian guard regrouped and came back into the church. The whirlwind had stopped. But the sight greeting their eyes was almost as surprising. Cyrus III of S3 was bent double over the body of the dead man who had somehow floated in space. And he was crying. Rocking and crying like a parent would over the death of a child.

Sun Tu slid her hands into the glove controls of their drop ship and sped the vessel out of the Marscovy ether dome. With consummate skill she got them back to the Warrior Class Starship.

Then it was up to Mickelmast. He shunt contacted Mama who was unbearably chatty. Wanted to know all the details. "And where's the old guy and the bald girl with no tits."

Finally Mickelmast forced her to plot a course for deep space. Just as she agreed, Kelt called out, "Ships. Thirty, forty, fifty, God I don't know how many. Racing toward us."

Within moments of the arrival of the pretorian guard Cyrus had dried his tears and yelled a command into his comm which set the S3 fleet in pursuit.

"We're surrounded dear hippo."

"Evasive actions?"

"I await your suggestion, hippo dear."

Mickelmast stared at the others. This couldn't be the end!

Cyrus' drop ship got him back to his command deck in record time. And there it was. On clear visual—the stolen UDP Warrior Class Starship. Complete with its Genetic Carriers. The boy dreamer may be dead, but the game is not over yet. There is still a stock of Dream Navigator genes onboard that ship.

He punched his comm button and his voice immediately boomed through the decks of the Genetic Carriers' ship.

"YOU ARE SURROUNDED. PREPARE TO BE BOARDED."

Sun Tu raced to the data comm and began scrolling through plotting data.

"Hopeless, dear. Tell her Hippo."

"There's got to be something!" shouted Kelt.

"Well there is I guess."

"What, Mama. What?"

"That folding thing the old guy did. That could get us out of this pickle."

The sound of a grappling hook tractor beam slammed through the ship.

Sun Tu, Mickelmast, and Kelt all turned at once to Raephealson. The heavy worlder turned away for a moment and then said, "Follow me."

He raced toward the Zero-G central core.

Chapter 54

To All Things Ending Comes

The race to the upper deck of the Zero-G core seemed to take forever to Raephealson. Endless lights and noises flew past him. He hardly felt his footfall on the alloy decks. All was lost to the dream that was his life. Raephealson moved and was moved until finally he was there, standing on the uppermost view deck of the Zero-G central core of the great ship.

Somewhere in the background Raephealson heard Mickelmast command Mama to turn off the Zero-G. Then the heavy worlder felt Kelt inserting the shunt attachment into the base of his neck. For a moment he heard Mama gasp in wonder. Then even that was gone.

He was alone. Totally alone. Just him and the kilometer of space yawning beneath him. A straight fall. A plummet. He thought of Cas-Alta. Of her hand caressing his heart inside his chest. Of her unrelenting kindness. Of her risking her life to bring him back.

Then he cleared even that image and replaced it with that of a simple door hanging in space. A door on a frame in the blackness of the inky vast. A door with oiled hinges awaiting his courage to push through.

Then he stepped off.

Cyrus's ID located the four Genetic Carriers at the very top of the central core. He ordered a second and third grapple launched toward the Warrior Class Starship. Then Cyrus hit the visual command.

Just in time to see Raephealson falling—like a stone.

"Nooooooo!" Cyrus cried.

For a moment he didn't know what to do then he screamed the command, "Dream no more!" into his inter-ship communicator and the image went wonky on his screen.

Cyrus's screamed command echoed through the Warrior Class Starship. Every corner of the great ship shook with the reverberations of the command. The air itself seemed to vibrate. But the AIU, Mama, did more than that. Her vast vertical spaces, the ones she couldn't identify, all reacted to the command—and began to fold—just as they had been programmed to do.

The ship toppled and began a slow fall in space.

Mama fought desperately for her life. For the life of her dear Hippo. But she couldn't find a way out. Somehow a central tenet had been pulled out from under her. A load-bearing wall removed. And her bricks, both physically and metaphysically began to tumble.

Images flashed past her. The Hippo, Herr Short Stuff, the old guy spinning and folding. Finally, she did the AIU equivalent of closing her eyes—and she finally understood. Understood that she too was just a piece in this great game. That the vertical spaces were no accidents. They were set there intentionally. That she was not the most advanced self-evolving automated intelligence unit in the galaxy—rather she was the carrier of Cyrus the three of S3's fail safe.

If it wasn't for Kelt's quick move Mickelmast would have fallen into the gaping hole of the central core. As it was both he and Mickelmast crashed with tremendous force into the wall of the viewing platform.

Even as he crashed, Mickelmast was desperately trying to contact Mama—but she wasn't there. SHE WASN'T THERE!

Then the voice boomed again: Dream no more!

Raephealson was falling. Through space and time—right through the doorway and out. Free. Open. Awake! He was awake in his dream! In control. As Jaspers had told him, he reached down and took his left foot in his right hand, then pulled the foot impossibly up over his head and out—further and further—the first fold!

"BOARD HER!!!" screamed Cyrus as his S3 ships moved in.

The second folding was the sky to the ground. Raephealson laughed as he did it.

"Look!" shouted Sun Tu to Mickelmast and Kelt. She was on her belly peering over the edge of the platform. And pointing. Pointing to the inverted spinning figure of Raephealson.

"Yes!" screamed Kelt.

"But who's his data going to if Mama's crashed?" demanded Sun Tu.

"To me," said Mickelmast as he adjusted his shunt and hauled himself over to the comm panel on the wall.

"Can you do anything?" shouted Kelt as the ship tilted under the strain of yet another grapple beam.

"I don't know but maybe. I've spent a lot of time with Mama and I've duplicated a few of her functions with bots. So we'll just have to give it a try. Hold on tight." Then into his shunt he yelled, "Raephealson tell me where to go. Plot us out of here!"

The voice came to Raephealson at the end of his seventh fold. The fold to freedom. We can go anywhere now.

As he entered the attack module, Cyrus slammed the visual button on the wall again. There before him was the inverted figure of Raephealson spinning nature's deep beauty. Dreaming. Navigating! Once again he screamed "Dream NO More!" into the comm.

The voice echoed once again through the great ship.

It also echoed inside Raephealson's dreaming mind. Suddenly the heavy worlder found himself in a desert landscape which stretched from far horizon to far horizon. The wide vista of blinding sun assaulted his eyes. He felt heavy. Fat. Pulled to the ground. Then a hissing came from the sand. A movement to his left beneath the shifting grains of whiteness. Then a shaking shimmer.

The great snake rose from the sand and flared its hood like a woman brushing back the sides of her long hair.

Raephealson tried to skitter back but found himself just digging deeper into the shifting stuff. Digging a hole.

Suddenly he was at the bottom of the hole looking up. The blazing sun seared his retina. Then the sun was gone. Shade. Blessed shade.

Then he heard the hiss.

It was the huge snake's hood that had blocked the sun.

Then the flicking tongue touched his cheek and forced itself between his lips and wrapped itself around his tongue. Flicking. Off his gums and teeth and sliding down his throat.

Then it was inside him. Stretching him. A coil wrapped around his heart. Blood came from his ears and nose. He couldn't see. He felt the head smash out his anus then crash back into him just below the base of his spine. Then it tore out of his neck just below his larynx.

The huge head then turned and looked right into his eyes.

It was the Angry Faced Man from his dream somehow inside the snake. Then it spoke!

"You a dreamer! Ha! You're a boy! Nothing but a terrified boy! Reach not for the glory when you slither on your belly boy. For you are the snake. You are the thing reviled. You are the most grounded of all things. You are no bird. You are no dreamer. You are alone. Abandoned and terrified. As well you should be."

The pain around his heart was excruciating. He was falling he could feel it. "I can't do this! I can't do this!"

"I've got contact with the hyper drive and the propulsion systems. It could kill us, but I think I can move this old tin can of ship," screamed Mickelmast.

"Get directions from Raephealson," yelled Sun Tu.

And he tried. He yelled so loud into his shunt that Raephealson could have heard him without it. But he got no answer.

Then Kelt shouted at them to look.

They raced to Kelt's side at the edge of the platform.

Raephealson wasn't spinning. He just hung there. Upside down. Eight feet off the ground.

Then Raephealson heard the voice of the lessons. Love—laughter––lucidity—lightness—luminosity. And he reached out toward the head of the snake. The huge animal's mouth opened. Its crescent fangs flipped into place seething poison.

Raephealson felt the moisture of the tongue, then the blunt solidity of the snout. He smelled the dank breath from the serpent's nostril holes. Then he caressed the pointed liquid-covered-death of the fangs. Finally he reached for the hood. He ran his fingers along the ridge then slid his hand inside the silky velvet of the snake's power.

And then it was gone. And he was alone. On a precipice overlooking a molten sea.

And he recognized the place. Tears came to his eyes. It was the place of Elijah's first voyage. He stood in Elijah's footsteps. In the footsteps of the naked boy who had spun to beauty beneath the cruel force of the Angry Faced Man in the greenhouse all those years ago.

Raephealson looked over the molten sea and heard somewhere in the back of his mind Mickelmast's contact.

The heavy worlder, the one they called the mad one, took a breath and deep in his mind said, "Follow me."

Then he reached into the molten sea and, folding it about him as Elijah had all those years ago, led his people and their ship to the freedom of the other side of the galaxy.

Cyrus stood speechless on the deck of the assault craft. Something inside him was dying. And he knew it. Images of a diary and a concussion piston rose up in him. He didn't scream. He didn't rant. He pulled his gray hair back and knotted it. Then he turned from his crew and said simply, "Home Jeeves."

The source of that reference, too, he no longer remembered.

In the night sky above Marscovy there was a brief flash. A slashing light that even the ether dome could not keep out. The Face Dancer saw it just as the demon child's head emerged from Cas-Alta's birth canal.

The child was born with its eyes wide open. It didn't cry. Why should it. It had a great destiny. And even as it emerged into the night air of the Marscovy cave—he knew it.

END PART TWO OF THE DREAM CHRONICLES

For sales, editorial information, subsidiary rights information
or a catalog, please write or phone or e-mail

iBooks
Manhanset House
Dering Harbor, New York 11965
Sales: 1-800-68-BRICK
Tel: 212-427-7139
www.ibooksinc.com
bricktower@aol.com

www.IngramContent.com

For sales in the UK and Europe please contact our distributor,
Gazelle Book Services
White Cross Mills
Lancaster, LA1 4XS, UK
Tel: (01524) 68765 Fax: (01524) 63232
email: jacky@gazellebooks.co.uk

www.ingramcontent.com/pod-product-compliance
Lightning Source LLC
Chambersburg PA
CBHW060554310726
48982CB00008B/1123/J